Austen at Sea

Also by Natalie Jenner

The Jane Austen Society

Bloomsbury Girls

Every Time We Say Goodbye

Austen at Sea

NATALIE JENNER

ST. MARTIN'S PRESS
NEW YORK

First published in the United States by St. Martin's Press, an imprint of St. Martin's Publishing Group

AUSTEN AT SEA. Copyright © 2025 by Natalie Jenner. All rights reserved. Printed in the United States of America. For information, address St. Martin's Publishing Group, 120 Broadway, New York, NY 10271.

www.stmartins.com

Designed by Gabriel Guma

Map designed by Andrea Nairn

The Library of Congress Cataloging-in-Publication Data is available upon request.

ISBN 978-1-250-34959-0 (hardcover)
ISBN 978-1-250-40905-8 (international, sold outside the U.S., subject to rights availability)
ISBN 978-1-250-34960-6 (ebook)

Our books may be purchased in bulk for promotional, educational, or business use. Please contact your local bookseller or the Macmillan Corporate and Premium Sales Department at 1-800-221-7945, extension 5442, or by email at MacmillanSpecialMarkets@macmillan.com.

First U. S. Edition: 2025
First International Edition: 2025

10 9 8 7 6 5 4 3 2 1

For Jane
who saved my life

— and —

for Lindsay Shirreff, M.D.
who saved it again

Women have served all these centuries as looking-glasses, possessing the magic and delicious power of reflecting the figure of man at twice its natural size. Without that power probably the earth would still be swamp and jungle. . . . That is why Napoleon and Mussolini both insist so emphatically upon the inferiority of women, for if they were not inferior, they would cease to enlarge.
—Virginia Woolf

A clear horizon—nothing to worry about on your plate, only things that are creative and not destructive. . . . I think that's as happy as I'll ever want to be.
—Alfred Hitchcock

A man always has two reasons for doing anything: a good reason and the real reason.
—J. P. Morgan

Life is nothing without enthusiasms.
—Dr. Richard Pankhurst

CHARACTERS

<hr>

The Bostonians

WILLIAM STEVENSON, *widower and Massachusetts Supreme Judicial Court justice*

THOMAS NASH, *bachelor and Massachusetts Supreme Judicial Court justice*

CHARLOTTE STEVENSON, *disaffected youngest daughter of Justice Stevenson*

HENRIETTA STEVENSON, *disaffected eldest daughter of Justice Stevenson*

ANNA DICKINSON, *known onstage as the Girl Orator*

CONSTANCE DAVENISH, *Boston bluestocking*

FRANCIS CHILD, Ph.D., *Harvard professor of rhetoric and oratory*

SAMUEL CARTER, *coachman to the Stevenson household*

LOUISA MAY ALCOTT, *writer and travel companion*

PHILIP MACKENZIE, EZEKIEL PEABODY, ADAM FULBRIGHT, RODERICK NORTON and CONOR LANGSTAFF, *justices of the Massachusetts Supreme Judicial Court*

GRAYDON SAUNDERS, *Southerner and Boston barrister*

LITTLE BOBBIE ACHESON, *street waif and newspaper boy*

The Philadelphians

NICHOLAS NELSON, *rare book dealer and Civil War soldier*

HASLETT NELSON, *rare book dealer and Civil War soldier*

SARA-BETH GLEASON, *state senator's daughter and occasional gambler*

The British

DENHAM SCOTT, *foreign correspondent for* Reynolds's Newspaper

SIR FRANCIS AUSTEN, *Admiral of the Fleet and brother to Jane Austen*

GEORGE FLINT, *manservant at Portsdown Lodge*

FANNY-SOPHIA AUSTEN, *daughter and caretaker of Admiral Austen*

RICHARD FAWCETT ROBINSON, *London theater impresario*

VALENTINE NORRIS, *captain of the SS* China

MRS. BERWICK, *housekeeper at Chawton Great House*

PETER WRIGHT, *tenant of the former steward's cottage in Chawton*

SIR CRESSWELL CRESSWELL, *London judge and amateur physiognomist*

DR. RICHARD PANKHURST, *barrister at Lincoln's Inn*

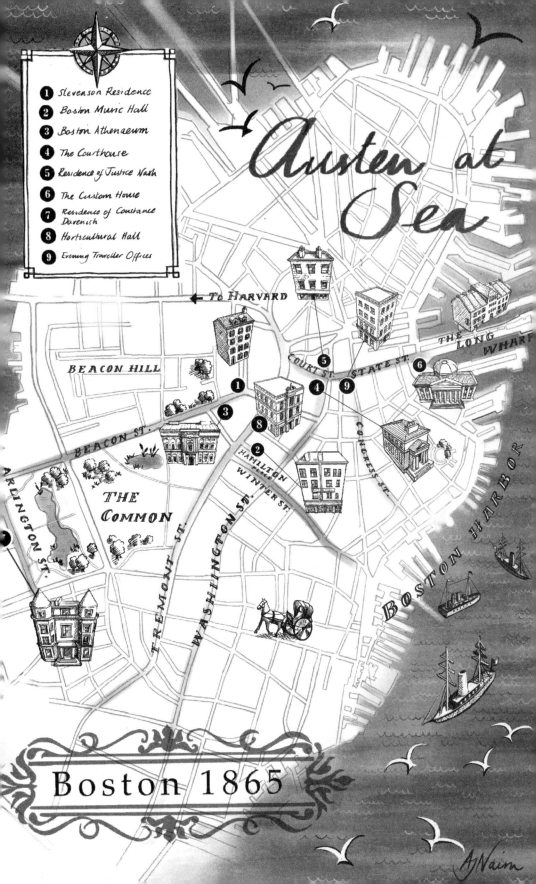

1. Stevenson Residence
2. Boston Music Hall
3. Boston Athenaeum
4. The Courthouse
5. Residence of Justice Nash
6. The Custom House
7. Residence of Constance Darvenish
8. Horticultural Hall
9. Evening Traveller Offices

Austen at Sea

← TO HARVARD

BEACON HILL

COURT ST. STATE ST. THE LONG WHARF

BEACON ST.

ARLINGTON ST.

THE COMMON

HAMILTON ST. WINTER ST.

CONGRESS ST.

TREMONT ST. WASHINGTON ST.

BOSTON HARBOR

Boston 1865

AJNaim

AUSTEN AT SEA

⚓

BOOK ONE

—∞—

Boston

ONE

The Revere Bell Strikes One

The Massachusetts Supreme Judicial Court
April 5, 1865

Six justices were assembled in chambers to consider the case before them. A seventh judge had recused himself due to a conflict, leaving the dreaded possibility of a tie. Certainly, based on precedent and the contentiousness of the matter, these men were unlikely to agree.

It was long past the evening hour, the oral dissertations having proceeded at great length. Food and refreshment had been replenished several times during the closed-door session: plates of cold veal and green salad, a decanter of Madeira, and chestnut-colored coffee from a large silver pot.

Justice Philip Mackenzie was leading the discussion. He impatiently tapped one finger on the leatherbound book before him as Justice Ezekiel Peabody, making his usual plea for restraint, droned on. Finally, there was a lull. Justice Peabody refilled the goblet before him; Justice Mackenzie stopped tapping.

"Well?" He stared pointedly at the other five faces about the room. "Are we at last ready to vote?"

Chief Justice Adam Fulbright rubbed his speckle-bearded chin; with one notable exception, the judges were all grey-haired and portly after decades spent listening from the bench. "My preliminary vote is in favor."

Half the room sighed. The chief justice was, for all his leadership, the softest member of the court.

"You can't be serious." Justice Roderick Norton turned to the occupant of the wingback chair on his left. "Tell me *you*, William, will join the dissent. You, who always consider ideas more salient than surface charms. The Mansfield Judgment alone gives our position undeniable weight."

Justice William Stevenson raised his right index finger in the air. "My daughters—"

Now all the men groaned.

"—gentlemen, gentlemen, steady on. Both young ladies are experts in this matter, which you would do well to remember. They heartily agree with the chief justice, as do I. So, that leaves Nash."

Justice Thomas Nash was the one notable exception, the youngest member of the court. He lounged in the armchair closest to the fire, long legs outstretched and crossed at the ankles, hands clasped behind his full head of blond hair complete with fashionably long sideburns. "I'm afraid I must concur with the Misses Stevenson—for once."

"Then we have a majority—Fulbright, Stevenson, Nash, and myself—in agreement that this text"—Justice Mackenzie waved the bound volume before the group—"is the supreme example of its author's genius."

Mackenzie stood up, placed the volume on top of five others on a nearby side table, then gingerly—even reverentially—righted the pile with both hands. The other men also stood, removing the robes they had donned since daybreak and hanging them by the door for the morning washerwomen. Norton patted Peabody on the back in commiseration as they exited the dark-paneled room, dimly lit by the smoldering fire.

"Time will prove them wrong, Zeke," he practically hissed. "It always does."

As the Revere bell struck one from nearby King's Chapel, the six justices headed down the hallway and out into the spring-scented night. The servants discreetly entered after them, knowing from experience how late the monthly discussion, given its rancor, could run. One of them glanced curiously at the volume—simply titled *Emma*—resting on top of the others, before carrying the pile of books away in his white-gloved hands.

At the other end of the courthouse, the library clerk sat dozing at his station. He jerked awake as the servant put the books down with a cough, then checked his watch in a panic. The mail steamship SS *China* was due to arrive soon from Portsmouth, bringing a dozen different British newspapers for the clerk to place in each judicial chamber by dawn. Before heading to the Custom House to collect the news, however, he had one last task to complete.

Placing the books in an empty mahogany trolley, the library clerk wheeled the cart to the first row of standing shelves. One by one, he carefully slid each volume back in its well-worn spot under an ivory plaque the size of a postage stamp, finely marked AU, and in strict order of composition:

Northanger Abbey
Sense and Sensibility
Pride and Prejudice
Mansfield Park
Emma
Persuasion

TWO

In Which the Girl Orator Comes to Town

THE NEXT MORNING
Beacon Hill, April 6, 1865

W ell, Father, who won the majority? *Emma* or *Mansfield Park?*"
William Stevenson answered from behind his newspaper
at the head of the breakfast table. "*Emma*, of course."

Charlotte, starved for victory no matter the hour, gave a little cheer. For
the past two years, following her graduation from Miss Pride's Peacock Academy, Charlotte had asked older sister, Henrietta, more reserved but no less
radical, to tote her to every suffragette gathering within carriage distance.
The academy had turned both of William's daughters into ladies but failed
to qualify them for college, making them disaffected as well as dutiful. Lucy
Stone, Julia Ward Howe, Angela Grimké—New England was in no shortage
of angry women. As the century wore on, they seemed to grow only angrier.

Charlotte pecked her father on his left cheek before heading for the sideboard to pile her plate high with johnnycakes, sausage, and eggs. William
always marveled at his youngest daughter's ravenous diet, being strictly veg-
etarian himself. He was a strict man in many ways, even more so following
his wife's untimely death. Something happened with premature loss—a realization that the ancient cartographers had been right. One sailed too hastily, too happily, until the darkest depths of ocean yielded their unknown

threat: *here be dragons*. As a widower, William Stevenson's way of coping with two little girls had been to batten down everything in sight.

His sole indulgence was books—there could never be too many of those. In fact, he had been the one to suggest a reading circle at the state supreme court. The seven justices regularly met to discuss fictional characters as a refreshing change from the rigors of the bench. In contrast, local women's reading circles were becoming increasingly vocal on social issues at large. Barred from most universities, women like his daughters were intent on finding intellectual spaces of their own.

William's favorite such space was his library at home, to which his daughters had always enjoyed full access. Henrietta in particular spent hours at the large partners desk, poring over old law texts and political pamphlets. Now when his girls quoted Thoreau or Milton or Carlyle back at him, William knew he had only himself to blame. Still, he loved their youthful curiosity—very much like their mother, who had kept him young, too, for a time.

"Is Henrietta on her way down?"

Seating herself to his left, Charlotte nodded back between bites of sausage, little streaks of oil dribbling down between her long, bare fingers. Neither of his daughters wore jewelry—all of his late wife's remained in the opaline glass casket on her dressing table, next to the untouched hairbrush and half-empty bottle of Otto of Roses. From childhood, both girls had kept their hands free for climbing, digging, and secretive writing. William could only hope they were composing inoffensive novels up in that shared attic room of theirs.

"How did Nash—"

"*Justice* Nash," he corrected Charlotte.

"—how did *Justice* Nash vote?" She licked her fingers free of the sausage fat, then drenched the cakes in maple syrup from the jug she had decoratively painted while at Miss Pride's. Those simpler days of music, art, and deportment, her father wistfully recalled: French lessons for Charlotte, German for Henrietta, Latin at home for them both.

"He is as susceptible as anyone to Emma's charms."

"I bet." Charlotte grinned. "Was it another close decision?"

William took a sip of coffee. "The usual minority—although Justice Norton did make some strong points on the Mansfield Judgment."

"Lord Mansfield?" Henrietta asked from the doorway, bowing slightly beneath the head jamb. She was the tall one in the family; it didn't help matters that she wore heeled boots and used the fashion for elaborate hair styling to pile hers high upon her head. This made her taller than most men she met and risked eliminating them as suitors, which worried her father. Could height alone be keeping Henrietta, teetering on the cusp of spinsterhood at age twenty-five, from marrying? Who could tell? Whereas twenty-year-old Charlotte was his wife's daughter, energetic and fearless, Henrietta was his cipher and impossible to read—which was especially odd, since she was most like him.

"Yes, the justice who ushered in abolition for England—long before these United States." William Stevenson put down his weekly copy of *The Liberator*. "But now the two countries are at one on this issue. Parity among nations *and* people is a wondrous thing. After all, our ancestors left England due to religious persecution—it is only right we put our own house in order."

Henrietta came over to peck her father on his right cheek (*"Right will be for Harry—left for me,"* Charlie had early on declared) before heading to the sideboard. Returning with a plate of fruit, toast, and jelly, she seated herself to his right and nodded at the newspaper on the table between them. "Garrison says he'll wind down *The Liberator* to focus on women's rights now that slavery's being abolished."

"The war's not over yet." William Stevenson had noticed this with everyone lately: the eagerness, after four long years, to just get on with things. But the law took time—and justice even more so. As for the vote that his daughters were after, something William did not necessarily begrudge them, he feared suffrage would take far longer than the angry women of New England were willing to accept.

Henrietta and Charlotte each placed a hand over one of his. "Yes, dear Father," Henrietta tenderly began, "but with the fall of Richmond, surely the worst is behind us. They say Lee is to surrender any day."

"On a happier note," said Charlotte as she peeled a hard-boiled egg, "what does the bench read next?"

"Justice Peabody was angling to start *Moby-Dick* given the influence of Carlyle, but the chief justice lobbied for *Persuasion* and won. In fact, we voted—four to two—to examine all of Austen's works over summer recess."

"*Persuasion* is her masterpiece," Henrietta firmly declared.

"You say that of each one," William replied with a smile.

The grandfather clock in the hall struck nine and Charlotte jumped up. "We better dash, Harry!" Both girls folded their dining napkins and kissed their father goodbye. They did everything together, a united, petticoated front.

"We'll be missing tea," Henrietta called to him from the doorway. "Garrison has brought the Girl Orator—Anna Dickinson—back to the Music Hall."

"Imagine being our age," Charlotte pined with envy, "traveling all over and lecturing, the first woman *ever* invited to speak before Congress."

"Imagine," William said as they raced out. But deep in his heart, he did no such thing. He wanted the world for his daughters but a known one, already discovered and mapped out. No unforeseen surprises, no lions or dragons in wait. He was immensely proud of both his girls' intellects but knew for a fact—he saw it in operation every day—that the world was not yet ready for anything more than the mere possession of that.

The Boston Music Hall on Winter Street had been built in 1852 with Harvard money. Along with its massive coffered ceiling and tiered galleries, the venue housed the first and largest pipe organ in the nation. Most famously, abolitionists including Frederick Douglass, Harriet Beecher Stowe, Harriet Tubman, and William Lloyd Garrison had assembled here to celebrate the Emancipation Proclamation taking effect as church bells rang in 1863.

Newspaper editor Garrison loved bringing the Girl Orator to town. When she was only thirteen, Anna Dickinson, the daughter of devout Quakers and abolitionists, had written to *The Liberator* in outrage over the reported treatment of an anti-slavery schoolmaster in Kentucky. Now in her early twenties, Dickinson spoke with an electrifying and poetic style to standing-room-only crowds on the issue of equal rights for all. She had consumed literary classics as a girl—an example not lost on the bookish Stevenson sisters—and possessed a natural gift for rhetoric.

Daylight streamed through the arched windows at the top of the Music Hall's four stories, casting Dickinson in a cone of radiance as she stood alone on the podium, an unremarkable slip of a girl—until she spoke. Henrietta and Charlotte watched her from the nearest gallery above the stage, rapt. Charlotte paid close attention to how Miss Dickinson used her blazing eyes and animated hands to win over the audience. Charlotte wanted to be an actress, something many in their society considered even closer to prostitution than nursing.

Henrietta, on the other hand, was most intrigued by Dickinson's use of language—especially her homespun ask-and-answer style—to support her plea for women's rights. There were dozens of rhetorical devices one could use for persuasion, and the Girl Orator appeared to be master of them all. Henrietta particularly noted the pleasing rhythm and cadence to the examples and hypotheses Dickinson shared:

The widows who see the homes they have helped to earn, the lands they have helped to buy, the very house with which they have been served their household work—swept away from them by an unjust decision of a dying husband, and a wicked law . . .

Are these duly represented and have they all the rights they want already?

The toiling wives who, struggling hard to save a home, to educate their children properly and clothe them decently, see their wages week after week, year after year, paid to their husbands or taken afterwards by them to be squandered in folly and vice, yet living on, staying on, enduring all things rather than part from their children whom the law would give to the degrading control of the husband . . .

Are these duly represented and have they all the rights they want already?

Both sisters enthusiastically nodded at every argument that Dickinson made. Gazing about the audience to witness the impact of the speech, Charlotte inadvertently caught the eye of Denham Scott watching from the gallery opposite theirs. Scott was a foreign correspondent for *Reynolds's Newspaper,* twice a month mailing dispatches back to London on the Civil War and other American political and legal events. Recently he had begun sniffing about the lyceums and lecture halls, trying to capture the pulse of the struggling nation when it came to women's rights. Although American women were a smidgen ahead of their British counterparts in that arena, agitation was springing up in tea salons and reading circles on both sides of the Atlantic.

Denham nodded at Charlotte, then hurriedly scribbled something down in his reporter's notepad. She did not acknowledge him back, and gently elbowed Henrietta instead. "I'm awfully sorry, Harry," Charlotte whispered. "I must have engaged his eye."

The minute the Girl Orator finished her speech, Henrietta rushed her younger sister out of the Music Hall.

"Miss Stevenson! Charlotte!" Denham Scott called to them from the rush of the exiting crowd. When he wasn't writing, Scott was running. Tall and lanky, with auburn locks falling across high cheekbones, he never appeared worried—just fast. Always in pursuit of a story, always seeking entrance to the very world of privilege he disparaged in print.

"Ladies, please, some words on Miss Dickinson?"

"Harry's the writer," Charlotte called back as she and Henrietta whirled around together to face him. "Your paper would do well to employ someone as eloquent as her."

"I have no doubt Miss Stevenson would excel at anything she put her mind to." Denham cocked his head at her. "And the performance just now, by your Girl Orator? How would you sum up that?"

"You call it a *performance*, do you?" replied Henrietta.

Denham smiled as if a secret ploy had worked. "I call it theatrically effective, yes."

"But not eloquent?" Henrietta smiled back. "Because surely it can be both. Or is that only the case with male speakers?"

"Do you not think there is something of the mesmerist in her?"

"Why, Mr. Scott, you don't need words from me—it appears you have already written your article." Henrietta turned around to triumphantly shoulder a giggling Charlotte forward through the crowd.

"Harry, Harry!" Charlotte urged her once they were out of Scott's earshot. "I am certain he likes you! He wants your opinion on everything!"

"Some things are meant to stay quiet," Henrietta said with a sigh, while Charlotte grinned.

"Just imagine if he knew of the letter."

But Henrietta motioned to Charlotte to hush. For they were not composing inoffensive novels in that shared attic room of theirs after all. They were writing something entirely different.

THREE

Of Some Satisfaction to Know

———•———

THAT SAME DAY
Portsmouth, April 6, 1865

Admiral of the Fleet, Sir Francis Austen, G.C.B.
Portsdown Lodge, Hampshire, England

March 26, 1865

Dear Sir,

We write with esteem for your stature and gratitude for the writings of your late sister, to whose works we were at an early age introduced, as devoted sisters ourselves, by our father, Mr. Justice William Stevenson of the Massachusetts Supreme Judicial Court. He, in turn, first learned of the genius of Miss Austen from our beloved late mother, Alice Gibbons Stevenson.

We write with esteem and gratitude, but also in supplication, for we are eager to learn more of Miss Austen. Her books are very popular amongst our set, and we would be honored and most grateful to receive any such thoughts of her as you may deem appropriate to share, should you have time and inclination.

We realize the impertinence of such supplication, but trust in your charity and tolerance. In the spirit of our request, we offer our abiding hospitality should you ever cross the sea in our humble direction.

Lastly, you may find it of some satisfaction to know that the honorable justices of our state's great and supreme court equal us in their devotion to the writings of Miss Austen.

A letter addressed to

"Miss Stevenson,
care of Mr. Justice William Stevenson,
Boston,
Massachusetts,
U.S.A."
would reach its destination.

Sir Francis "Frank" Austen sat by the bow window in his study, his trusty wood-and-brass telescope on a nearby stand, the cream-colored letter from Boston resting on the Davenport desk behind him.

Admiral Austen was a widower twice over, which might explain why—now in his nineties—he thought more and more of love and how to inch it along. Looking out at Portsmouth Harbour miles below, he recalled escorting Princess Caroline of Brunswick and her entourage from Cuxhaven to England many moons ago. Then-lieutenant Austen and the other lonely men at sea had admired the princess's mellifluous skirts and honey-colored curls—even more her composure under cannon fire from France. She was on her way to marry a stranger, the prince and future King George. The voyage had been rife with the momentousness of the occasion, even though the union later proved doomed from the start.

Frank—called "Fly" as a mischievous boy—was a hopeless romantic, just as his father and brothers before him. The women in the Austen family had always been much more hardheaded when it came to love—and possibly much less satisfied as a result. Fly had entered the naval academy at the tender age of twelve, and this early separation from home had carved an empty space inside his heart that he quickly sought to fill. God—a complete and evangelical dedication to Him—had been Frank's initial foray into love. His first wife, Mary, had come next, bearing him ten children until dying with the arrival of the eleventh. Martha—dear Martha, whom his sister Jane had always decried was perfectly matched for him—had been the last, and most lasting, love of his life.

Frank's devotion to God, which had sustained him through decades of war against Napoleon and the slaveholders of Santo Domingo, was finally beginning to wane along with his own time on Earth. Few had seen more of it: Egypt, India, Turkey, Greece, Italy, Belgium, Spain, America, Mexico. Yet what had it all come to in the end? A few military honors and decorations, a new title every few years starting with midshipman to lieutenant and ending in that finest of gradations: Vice Admiral to Admiral to Senior Admiral of the Fleet. Meanwhile, his beloved sister's books were accruing immortality with each new reader and every passing year.

It was a cool night for spring and the fire waned like Frank's spirits. His manservant George entered to stir the embers with an ornate iron poker, a souvenir from long-ago travels along the Flemish coast.

"Sir Francis, shall I bring you anything more?" George was almost as old as him—no wonder Frank felt starved for youthful energy and companions. His spinster daughter, Fanny-Sophia, was no substitution for that.

"Just today's post, George, thank you."

George brought the letter over and closed the study door behind him; the moon in the window shone clear as saltwater pearl; the bedroom above soon rocked with snoring. Admiral Austen put on his eyeglasses and unfolded the thick paper, which had been delicately fragranced by a far-off feminine hand. He breathed in the heady exotic scent of jasmine and mimosa before reading it again.

FOUR

✳

O Captain! My Captain!

•——•——•

Beacon Hill, April 18, 1865

Aletter marked to Miss Stevenson's attention slid through the door in the floor. Henrietta and her sister lay in bed at opposite ends of the attic, weeping, while the body of President Abraham Lincoln lay in state. The letter, composed just eleven days earlier, was now less an intended talisman than a relic of a more innocent time. Dressed in mourning black, bereft of hope, the sisters wondered if they would ever feel happy again in a world whose citizens seemed bent on destroying each other. With General Lee having just surrendered to the Union Army, one war was effectively ending. What did the murder of their beloved president foretell in its place?

The cream-colored envelope coaxed Henrietta Stevenson out of bed. The minute she saw the name of the sender, she called Charlotte over. Charlotte, who rarely looked tired or worn, whose beauty seemed to only grow with each new day, showed a sudden new frown line between her eyes; Henrietta had woken that morning to the shock of her first grey hair. The world outside their home was literally making them age.

They sat together on the edge of Charlotte's bed as Henrietta read the letter aloud.

Miss Stevenson, care of Mr. Justice William Stevenson,
Boston, Massachusetts, U.S.A.

April 7, 1865

Dear Miss Stevenson,

First allow me to assure you that your letter was received with most sincere gratitude for its contents and amenability to its request—or, as my Sister once wrote much more elegantly on behalf of Fitzwilliam Darcy, "Be not alarmed, Madam [sic], on receiving this letter . . ."

Secondly, I am a great admirer of your society, having previously commanded the North American and West Indies Station of the British navy in the years 1845 to 1848. I am not unique among my family for my time across the Atlantic, but I lay claim to being the most inclined in its favor.

Finally, you ask if I might share some thoughts regarding the example of my Sister. It would be a privilege to do so. Of the liveliness of her imagination and playfulness of her fancy, as also the truthfulness of her description of character and deep knowledge of the human mind, there are sufficient evidence in her works.—Less in evidence, but no less impressive, she was cheerful in temper and not easily irritated, and tho' rather reserved to strangers so as to have been by some accused of haughtiness of manner, yet in the company of those she loved the native benevolence of her heart and kindliness of her disposition were forcibly displayed. On such occasions she was a most agreeable companion and by the lively sallies of her Wit and good-humoured drollery seldom failed of exciting the mirth and hilarity of the party. She was fond of children and a favorite with them. Her Nephews and Nieces, of whom there were many, could not have a greater treat than crowding round and listening to Aunt Jane's stories.

I trust the contents of this letter shall meet with your satisfaction and approval, and that our correspondence shall serve as an example of the goodwill that can—and surely does—exist between our two nations.

> *Most respectfully and sincerely yours,*
> *Francis Wm Austen*

"Imagine," Henrietta finally spoke in amazement. "Austen's own brother, closest to her in age. The two of them as close as we are!"

"Oh no, Harry—no one can be that," Charlotte answered, and Henrietta affectionately patted her hand. "But he *is* the only sibling left, they say—whatever will we write back?"

Sitting down at their shared desk, Henrietta tapped her fashionable steel pen against the blotter several times in thought. "We asked Mr. Dickens for his autograph, although he has not yet obliged."

"Sir Francis seems most obliging, though," Charlotte was quick to point out. "Unusually so."

Henrietta stopped tapping and began to write. Charlotte watched over her shoulder, caring just as much about the reply. Charlotte worshipped Miss Austen second only to Mr. Dickens, despite their lack of successful correspondence there. But the two young women remained undaunted in their pursuit of literary nuggets, their own personal Gold Rush, their only way of striking out.

When Henrietta finished writing, Charlotte spritzed the page with the fragrance she had chosen to evoke the sensuality of far-off climes. She could not resist this girlish ploy, determined as both sisters were to win the admiral's favor and attention.

"I hope we've not been too forward with this new request."

"There's no harm in asking." Charlotte flopped back down onto her bed. "I wish we could ask for even more. Oh Harry, to visit England one day—all those museums and churches—the *theater*. But Father will never take us. He's not been so far as Manhattan since Mother died."

The bell rang for dinner, and Henrietta carefully placed both letters inside their mother's copy of *Pride and Prejudice.* This was the 1833 edition from Philadelphia printers Carey & Lea, published when Alice Gibbons had been stuck in her own childhood bedroom. At that time in Philadelphia, Jane Austen was already a star, a literary constellation discovered and brought to light by Mathew Carey of the City of Brotherly Love in

1816. *What had Carey seen back then*, Henrietta wondered, *that so many even in England had not?*

As a political refugee, Carey had fled Ireland in 1781 for Paris, where Benjamin Franklin, a son of Boston and America's first ambassador, had taken him under his wing. When Carey emigrated to America a few years later, Franklin favored him again by helping secure money to start a publishing firm and bookshop. This was now known as the Ben Franklin effect: *"He that has once done you a kindness will be more ready to do you another, than he whom you yourself have obliged."*

Henrietta was fascinated by this contrary notion. She never asked for much—that was Charlotte's way. Charlotte was the lucky one, with the rabbit's foot in her reticule (a graduation gift from coachman Samuel and Mrs. Pearson, the cook), lead casting in every Peacock Academy theatrical production, and general irresistibility to men. But what if Charlie's luck was simply a matter of being willing to gamble? After all, one might win as much as one lost in life, for all the asking of kindness, but at least one occasionally did win.

In fact, it was Charlotte's prodding that had emboldened Henrietta to write to Admiral Austen in the first place, just as Franklin's dictum emboldened her now to write again. Henrietta took inspiration wherever she could: although dedicated to the advancement of women, she lacked a singular or daring ambition for herself. Meanwhile, male suitors came and went against the shield of her silence and restraint. She alone remembered the happy house of their childhood and how it had shattered. She was afraid to shatter even more.

With each new lecture, each new attempt at correspondence, however, Henrietta could feel her naturally cautious self give way before the prospect of success. The admiral's kind response—who could have foreseen it? Perhaps her own quiet surveillance of others had fostered an understanding of like-minded souls—perhaps there were far more of like mind in the world after all. As for any unforeseen effects of the sisters' correspondence with Sir Francis, the world about them was already crumbling. How could anything two young women might do possibly upset things more?

FIVE

The Pride of Peacock Academy

Harvard College, April 28, 1865

J ustice Thomas Nash stood behind the classroom lectern at the invitation of Francis Child, Harvard's Boylston Professor of Rhetoric and Oratory. During the winter term, Professor Child's sophomore class met every Friday at four o'clock for his vaunted course, Rhetoric: Themes—Readings in English Literature. Harvard did not yet have a professor of English, something that Child hoped to rectify by providing lectures on the relevance of literature to politics, society, and the law.

For this term's guest lecture, Professor Child had asked his friend Justice Thomas Nash to speak to the second-year class. Small of stature but large of heart, Frank "Stubby" Child had graduated from Harvard a few years ahead of Thomas Nash, but the two men shared an interest in rhetoric— the art of effective writing and speech—as well as markedly humble origins. A proud sailmaker's son, Professor Child particularly appreciated the democratic nature of oral speech. Everyone could understand a folk ballad— everyone loved a fireside tale.

For his lecture today, Justice Nash—the son of a poor widow—wanted to discuss rhetoric in the context of a much more surprising source: the novels of Jane Austen. No one was teaching Austen at Harvard; no one was writing academic dissertations on any of her works. Thomas Nash firmly believed that more men needed to read and study Austen, who so brilliantly used the rhetorical device of irony to satirize society and show up the natural weaknesses shared by everyone, regardless of class.

Nash surveyed the lecture hall full of boys—for there really was no other word for them, with their beardless faces and cheeks made ruddy by Boston's coastal winds. Only once they were settled did Nash spot two young women huddled together in the middle row, their little hats askew as they flipped through a shared copy of *Pride and Prejudice*, tumbles of wavy hair and yellow and purple ribbons everywhere.

Charlotte and Henrietta Stevenson.

Nash looked down at his notes. His colleague William Stevenson had not warned of his daughters' attendance today—perhaps he didn't even know. *That would be just like the two of them.* The practice of allowing women to audit lectures at Harvard was a fairly recent phenomenon and at the sole discretion of the professor. Looking back up to see Stubby mischievously grinning from the side of the podium, Nash reluctantly began his lecture.

"Austen's use of alliteration is particularly impressive. Such repetition of sounds is, in fact, one of the most effective of all rhetorical devices. You were asked to read chapter twenty of *Pride and Prejudice* in preparation for today." With a lawyer's sense of audience, Nash had tailored his talk on a lady author to the disinterested male youth before him. "Who can provide an example of how Austen uses alliteration in this scene to convey character and theme?"

Charlotte immediately threw up her hand, and Nash glanced over again at the grinning Professor Child. "I am afraid, Justice Nash, that our rules for auditing do permit participation."

"Yes, Miss Stevenson?"

Charlotte stood up and began to recite. "'*Could* you expect me to rejoice in the inferiority of your *connections?*'" she quoted Mr. Darcy from the book. "'To *congratulate* myself on relations whose *condition* in life is so decidedly beneath my own?'"

Charlotte seemed to transform into Darcy before everyone's eyes. Her erect carriage, her haughty expression, the deep, resonant tone to her voice: all became strangely masculine in an instant. Discomfited by the sudden display, Nash recalled William's frequently voiced worry over his younger daughter's interest in the stage.

"And how does Austen utilize the device of alliteration here to advance theme?" Nash felt almost desperate as he looked about the room.

The eldest Stevenson daughter slowly put her hand up next. The rest of the class remained silent, and Nash motioned for Henrietta to stand.

"That harsh *c* consonant repetitively used here acts twofold. It *sounds* as angry as Darcy is, and it *shows* his lack of composure. His hurt pride has caused such ungentlemanly behavior in that moment—the very behavior that will further put Lizzy off." Henrietta paused as if for effect. "This illustrates the book's theme of the follies and dangers of pride."

"It is certainly no way to treat a lady," one of the male students called out.

"It's no way to treat anyone," Charlotte fired back.

William had taught his girls well, thought Nash. Aloud, he said, "Very apt—yes, very apt indeed. Thank you, ladies, both."

A fter each guest lecture, Professor Child held a small reception in his residence at Miss Upham's rooming house. Despite the lady proprietress, however, female visitors were not allowed. Flushed with scholarly victory, Henrietta and Charlotte, the pride of Peacock Academy, gave dismissive waves of their hands at the news and left for Gore Hall instead. Only two decades earlier, Margaret Fuller had become the first woman allowed to use its library, said to be the largest academic and private one in the world.

The Stevenson sisters spent a pleasant hour separately wandering the stacks inside the Gothic, cathedral-like building—Henrietta drawn to anything classical or historical in nature, Charlotte always on the lookout for high drama. Charles Dickens, with his reams of eccentric characters as familiar as friends, was her great favorite. No one made Charlotte laugh out loud like Dickens did. She loved to entertain their father after supper by reading from the latest monthly serial of his work. They had recently started book three of *Our Mutual Friend*, which William Stevenson was importing from London. Charlotte enjoyed amusing her father by acting out all the characters, especially that Bella Wilfer, so lively and ambitious, so unafraid to *ask*.

With a new stack of novels under her arm, Charlotte searched in vain for Henrietta, always the last to leave any library, before heading out to Harvard Yard. Spying reporter Denham Scott on a nearby bench, Charlotte spun around in another direction to find Henrietta and Justice Nash in conversation up ahead. Nash gave a gentlemanly wave upon seeing Charlotte; she narrowed her eyes back at him.

"Professor Child's little shindig is over?" she called out, still smarting from not being allowed at the reception due to her sex.

Nash raised both his hands as if in surrender. "I don't make the rules."

"Ha!" Charlotte laughed as she caught up to him and Henrietta. "I'd say that's *exactly* what you judges do." He smiled back, and there it was again—that little spark between them that lately flickered in his eyes and ran like a current along her skin. Charlotte wondered if Henrietta could tell—Henrietta, who could verbally counter any argument but was strangely obtuse about men. Charlotte suspected her older sister would require great and persistent pursuit when it came to the matter of love—or a knock on the head.

But Henrietta was not observing Charlotte and Nash's interaction. Instead, she was watching with increasing consternation as Denham Scott crossed the grassy square in their direction.

"The *Reynolds's?*" Nash repeated when Henrietta introduced the British reporter. "I'm afraid that's not one of my subscriptions."

"Father says the courthouse brings in a dozen different papers at least," Charlotte piped up.

"There is never enough news for us."

"Well, there is for me!" she protested. "Father reads aloud all the disasters at breakfast."

"Followed by the inevitable proclamations for our safety," Henrietta added.

"There is still much social unrest out here." Denham gave her an intimating nod. "At least among the ladies."

"Mr. Scott is not a friend of the suffragists," Henrietta turned to Nash to explain. "He attends our lectures with a somewhat dubious eye."

"I am no foe," Denham corrected her. "Just endeavoring to understand you."

"But you are happy with things as they are," Henrietta replied.

"I'd say all happy people are." He raised an eyebrow inquisitively at her. "You are not so happy then, I take it, for all your efforts at reform?"

To Charlotte's amazement Henrietta failed to refute him—if anything, she looked caught out by the question. *Was Harry happy?* Charlotte wondered to herself. Ever since their president's assassination, her sister's reserve had only intensified. At least Charlotte had her dream of the stage to occupy her thoughts—poor Henrietta didn't seem to have any dreams at all. She was simply there for her family, as reliable and stalwart as the many Greek sculpture replicas that watched over their house in the absence of the mother who had collected them.

"Where is your carriage?" asked Nash. Both sisters, grateful for the change in subject, nodded in the direction of Quincy Street. "Are you ladies dining at home tonight?"

"Are you angling for an invitation?"

"Justice Nash, pay Charlie no mind," Henrietta, looking somewhat red-faced, apologized for her sister. "I'm sure Father would love for you to join us."

"I do get a little spiky when hungry," Charlotte had to admit.

"Talking about Jane Austen always works up one's appetite," Nash agreed. "I'd be honored."

An awkward silence followed as everyone's eyes went to Scott's battered leather satchel, where a crumpled plain brown wrapper from the butcher poked out.

"Should we—" Charlotte widened her own eyes inquiringly at Henrietta, who gave the slightest shake of her head in response. Scott watched them both with amusement until breaking the silence himself.

"No need to stand on ceremony with me—besides, tomorrow's headline awaits. Ladies, Justice Nash—enjoy your evening."

D inner at Eleven Beacon Street was at seven P.M. sharp every night and a carefully orchestrated affair, given William Stevenson's dislike of meat, Charlotte's hearty appetite, and Henrietta's surprising weakness for sweets. For this evening's meal, Mrs. Pearson had prepared parsnip soup, roast lamb, green salad with pickled beets, scalloped Irish potatoes, and stewed rhubarb for dessert.

Justice Thomas Nash looked quite at home whenever he visited. Having the previous year joined the state supreme court at the tender age of thirty-four, Nash had become a trusted friend and colleague of Justice Stevenson over the course of the past judicial term. Nash had been first to leap at William Stevenson's suggestion of a discussion group dedicated to novels, while Stevenson had been first on the bench to welcome the young justice into his home.

This was an unusual invitation because the justices rarely socialized outside the courthouse. In fact, such congregation was frowned upon—something not difficult to heed, since one half of the court fundamentally opposed the politics of the other. Three of the seven men believed in treating the constitution like the Ten Commandments, set in stone—three men believed in its Darwinian evolution—and one of them changed his mind depending on the issue of the day.

After dinner, the party of four moved into the Stevenson front parlor. William and Nash sat amiably together by the fire, smoking their pipes with one hand, a cut-crystal glass of whisky in the other. Charlotte rested on the floor near her father's feet, playing with the family spaniel, Coco; Henrietta silently worked by the light of a kerosene lamp on some half-finished needlepoint in her lap. The two men were discussing Nash's plans for the summer, which included a trip to London.

"I'm hoping to see Mr. Dickens speak at St. James's Hall."

Charlotte widened her eyes again at Henrietta, who looked up from her work at Nash. "Which steamer, may I ask?"

"Cunard's the *China*—a British ship recently built in Maine. It sails twice monthly to Portsmouth. I'm booked for July."

The sisters exchanged another silent look. "How much is first class on the *China*?" Henrietta asked again.

Nash shrugged. "A hundred and thirty dollars or so."

"*Or so*," teased Charlotte.

"That's three months' wages for a schoolmaster." Henrietta had on her *maths* face, as her sister liked to call it. "Twice that for a schoolmarm." She kept the household accounts with her logical, mathematical mind, which was how both sisters knew their father's salary of four thousand dollars a year.

"That's one reason why we don't teach," added Charlotte.

"Only one?" Nash put down his pipe and nodded at her with a smile. "Tell me the others."

"We would be taking jobs away from hardworking women who need them."

"It's a matter of principle, then?"

Charlotte let him think this even though it was only partly the truth. The other part was that the idea of teaching—the only acceptable profession for women like Henrietta and Charlotte—bored each of them stiff.

Henrietta put her needlepoint to the side. "How many days will you be on the water?"

"Eleven each way—ten, if we're lucky with the winds."

"You're lucky the court is in recess until the fall," William now spoke.

"Very lucky all around, I'd say," added Charlotte.

"Charlotte, really!" her father exclaimed. "Your *mood* tonight!"

"It's all right, William. I'm afraid Stubby's reception earlier was men-only," Nash explained.

"Ahh." Justice Stevenson gave a smile of fatherly comprehension.

Meanwhile, Charlotte gave her sister a meaningful stare, then returned to stroking Coco as if there was not a thought in her head. Henrietta half-heartedly resumed the labor of her needlepoint, by candlelight such a strain on the eyes. All the while the men smoked and drank and talked, happily oblivious to any insurrection in their midst.

SIX

A Brace of Bluestockings

Boston, May 9, 1865

Henrietta and Charlotte sat in the newly built Horticultural Hall on Tremont Street, listening to an afternoon of speeches while avoiding eye contact with Denham Scott across the aisle.

The mostly female speakers were celebrating two upcoming anniversaries: Boston's first annual Woman's Rights Convention on June 2, 1854, and an impromptu march that same day to protest the abduction of escaped slave Anthony Burns by federal authorities under the Fugitive Slave Law of 1850. The convention members had flooded onto the city streets to join fifty thousand others in the march, which had ended up one of the largest anti-slavery protests in American history. Boston's bluestockings continued to take inspiration from that historic day, when their city had come together regardless of sex or race.

At the conclusion of the final speech, Henrietta hurried Charlotte onto the pavement outside the humid hall. "It's the heat of summer already," she said, wiping her brow with a lace handkerchief.

"Oh, look, there's Connie!" Charlotte cried out.

On the cobble street lined with hansom cabs for hire, Constance Davenish was being helped into a stately brougham by her driver. One of Boston's most famous advocates for women's rights, she was a formidable presence in any crowd with her swoop of silver-streaked black hair and penetrating ice-blue eyes. Charlotte stood on tiptoe and waved to catch Constance's attention, hoping for a quick ride home along the park.

"Harry—Charlie—do let me give you girls a lift!" Constance motioned to her driver, who came forward to help the sisters into the carriage.

Henrietta settled back on the foldaway seat next to Charlotte's. "You rescued us from the heat."

"And that awful reporter from England, Denham Scott," Charlotte added. "He's always chasing us for comment."

"He should come to my weekly salon if he wants an earful so badly." Constance tapped the window and the horses started up. "What did you think of the speeches today on our famous march? It was a very galvanizing time back then, although I suppose you were too little to remember much."

Henrietta nodded. "I do remember how upset Father was."

"They imprisoned Mr. Burns in the federal courthouse for days. That valiant attempt by abolitionists to rescue him . . ." Constance shook her head. "City authorities should have ignored Congress's Fugitive Slave Act. Such is the Cornelian dilemma that has long faced our country: how to behave morally in the face of an amoral law." She sat back and waved out the carriage window at the pink and purple lilacs lining the Common. "But now we have spring, a proposed thirteenth amendment to guide us—thanks to our late president—and, finally, a path to freedom ahead."

"Connie," said Charlotte, "are you really so confident we will see equality in our time?"

"The prospect is indeed daunting. But our only option is to keep fighting. I've fully pledged my life to that."

"You don't miss having a family?" asked Henrietta. Most of the women advocating at lectures and salons for the upheaval of their patriarchal society were nonetheless married to men who reaped its benefits. But Constance had grown up wealthy and improved her lot through shrewd investments (*not that lack of money alone should be the reason to marry*, Henrietta reminded herself).

"Your question implies I lost something—in point of fact, I never went looking."

"I would like to be a wife and mother one day," Henrietta confessed.

"I haven't scared you off the notion?" Charlotte turned to Constance to explain. "When Mother died, Harry was seven to my two and demanded to run the nursery. I am told I was quite the handful."

"I have no doubt." Constance smiled. "But what about you now, Charlie—do you want motherhood?"

"What I want right now is to be a great actress."

"Is one of us more correct than the others? How can anyone—any society, any court, any *man*—be an arbiter of what women want, when we three alone are so different?"

"Our father doesn't question his authority in that regard," replied Henrietta.

"That is because he believes his heart to be in the right place." Constance leaned forward as if in confidence. "He is afraid, like all fathers—surely the result of not properly preparing their daughters for the world. Now that you are grown, he needs greater occupation. Find a way to give it to him—*without* more worry."

"There's always the judicial reading circle. They're discussing all of Austen this summer at Father's suggestion."

"Oh, I do like the sound of that for *him*—Austen has always left me cold. Well, and what do you two young ladies have planned for the season?"

Henrietta wasn't quite ready to share their secret letter-writing scheme, not even with someone as trustworthy and enthusiastic as Constance, so she mentioned their more public undertaking instead. "We petitioned Harvard to let us sit in on some classes before winter term ends."

"I remember when they finally let Margaret Fuller use their library." Constance snorted. "*My*, but how far they've come."

The brougham pulled up before the massive steps to the Stevenson family's five-story Federal-style brownstone, and the three women entered the front vestibule just as William Stevenson appeared, hat on, heading out. "Oh, Miss Davenish, hello. How nice. I didn't know we were expecting you."

As polite as he sounded, Henrietta could see the worry in her father's eyes. He had always been suspicious of his daughters' older female friends, as if they were the personification of the very dragons that those ancient mapmakers had warned about. "Father, Miss Davenish is joining us for tea."

William gave a little bow. "I am sorry to miss it then."

"Can't we tempt you to stay?" Constance tried to catch his eye with a smile.

"I'm afraid I'm due at chambers. A big Exchequer decision just came out that could alter liability law in England forever."

Charlotte gave a little yawn, while Constance looked intrigued. "I'd love to hear more."

William stared at her in surprise. "You would?"

She nodded. "I wanted to be a lawyer when I was a girl, just like *my* father. But of course, only men are allowed to sit the bar."

"Ah, yes, well, if my girls are anything to judge by, there is good reason for that. There'd be no getting a word in edgewise. You women would surely outtalk us all."

"Now, Justice Stevenson, I am quite certain that is *not* the real reason," Constance lightly intoned, at which William, apparently sensing he was beat, tipped his hat and gave his regrets one last time.

The three women moved into the parlor where a low center table had been set for tea, complete with candle warmer, porcelain cups and saucers, and Mrs. Pearson's famous custard cake. While Henrietta poured out the black tea imported to Boston by Chase & Sanborn, Constance appraised the well-furnished room.

"So many pleasing feminine touches in your home. The seven nymphs in the hallway mural—I see the theme continues there"—she nodded at the fireplace's painted tile surround—"in the depiction of Artemis. Goddess of the hunt."

"Mother was fascinated by women in mythology," Henrietta explained.

"We're not sure why," added Charlotte.

"Perhaps because they could do far more than us, imaginary or not?" Constance offered.

Charlotte shrugged. "I respond most to what is real."

Henrietta laughed at her statement. "Charlie, all you do is pretend!"

"Yes, but what I pretend is rooted in what can happen—why act it out otherwise?"

Constance lifted her porcelain cup to examine its underside. "This is lovely, too—Tucker?"

Harry nodded. "From Mother's bridal trousseau. They make the porcelain from clay beds south of Philadelphia, where she grew up."

"I should have liked to have known your mother—how proud she would be of you both. I myself was abroad then."

"Studying?"

"Mostly being chased over the Alps"—Connie laughed at the memory—"by a rather wily and determined Southern suitor."

There was a soft knock on the parlor door and a maid entered carrying an oval-shaped silver tray. On its gleaming surface rested a single, cream-colored envelope. Henrietta glanced at Charlotte before reaching for it.

"A suitor of your own?" Constance asked as Henrietta silently read. "I thought I spied an extra bloom on someone's cheek of late."

Henrietta looked up from the letter in surprise while Charlotte burst out with a laugh. "Harry better hurry then—he just turned ninety-one."

"Ninety-one! How amazing. Whoever could it be?"

Henrietta made a face at Charlotte before answering. "Admiral Francis Austen—Jane Austen's brother."

"Fascinating—but why the correspondence?"

It all came out. The mutual boredom once Charlotte had finished with school, a certificate from the Peacock Academy still failing to qualify either sister for college. The seeking of Austen's signature and information of any kind. The letters back and forth across the Atlantic. And now the old naval officer's latest, most cryptic, reply.

Miss Stevenson, care of Mr. Justice William Stevenson, Boston, Massachusetts, U.S.A.

April 29, 1865

Dear Miss Stevenson,

Your letter of April 18th was received with utmost sympathy for the loss you and your nation have so recently suffered. Please allow me to extend my most sincere condolences and heartfelt prayers for the continuation of peace that so many have toiled and sacrificed to ensure, your great president foremost among them.

I sincerely hope that my last letter may have ameliorated your spirits—one often feels there is little to be done at such times.

You mentioned in your most recent letter how honoured you would be to receive a memento of my Sister, such as I may be able and willing to part with. It would be my honour to bestow on such devoted readers of hers a lasting tribute of some kind, with the hope that it may act as further balm.

Accordingly, I enclose a letter written by my Sister to my second wife, may she rest in peace, who was a dear friend, first to Jane as Martha Lloyd, then to myself as Mrs. Francis Austen, later Lady Austen. Such words by my Sister were always intended for only the most personal of use, and I would ask that you keep this letter entirely for the same.

It feels serendipitous that our correspondence began of late. I myself have experienced a recent bout of illness, which, along with my advanced age, has put me in mind to settle some affairs. Your letters have cheered and alerted me to my prevailing duty in that regard. In sending you this letter of my Sister's, I hope to begin the process of safely distributing certain objects, so that Jane's personal reputation can grow, as her writing so amply did, from strength to strength.

I remain, most respectfully and sincerely yours,

Francis Wm Austen

The letter tucked inside the admiral's was a single, fragile page, folded several times and crossed to its edges with heavily slanted writing that concluded in the signature of his famous sister. These words Henrietta did not read aloud to the other two women, who were passed the letter instead; these words were sacred.

These words were also about laundry, and baking apples, and the latch on the tea caddy breaking. It amazed the sisters that a writer like Austen had apparently led as domestic a life as them. Not for her were the lecture tours of Dickens or Emerson, the European castle-hopping of Byron or Shelley. If this letter proved anything, it was that Austen conjured her worlds from within a most mundane one. A world of women, at that.

"But you don't know of *what* certain objects the admiral writes? How intriguing." Constance returned the letter to Henrietta. "Ninety-one, though, you say? Well, you know what men of contracts law would stipulate." She gave a wink. "Time is of the essence."

SEVEN

City of Brotherly Love

Nelson Brothers and Co., May 11, 1865

Nearly three hundred miles south of Boston, just north of the kaolin clay beds that had forged Alice Stevenson's tea set, lived two brothers two years apart in age. Nicholas and Haslett Nelson were bachelors and proprietors of Nelson Brothers and Co., the antiquarian bookshop they ran together on Chestnut Street. They lived above the store on two separate floors, where over time thousands of books for sale had invaded their private rooms like seaweed. The brothers were raised by another bachelor, their uncle, following the tragic loss of their parents in a theater fire. Called Nick and Haz by each other—for there were few others to do so—they could live and work wherever they pleased now that the fighting was over. Instead, they stayed in the very house where they were born, the war having forestalled their adulthood in more ways than one.

"Haz, listen." Nick sat with his brother after supper, a well-worn copy of *Emma* open on his lap; he read it every spring like clockwork. "Listen to Miss Bates."

"Looking for more clues?" Haz was an enthusiastic but much less diligent reader than his older brother.

"'*The chaise having been sent to Randalls to take Mr. Frank Churchill to Richmond. That was what happened before tea. It was after tea that Jane spoke to Mrs. Elton.*' There, right there—Miss Bates gives it up. All that babbling is telegraphing the plot—Jane's accepting the governess position has been precipitated by the departure of Frank, her secret love."

Haz put down his snifter of whisky. "But who would bother listening to Miss Bates, that ninny?"

"Nobody—not even the reader." Nick shook his head in wonder. "How does Miss Austen do it? Keep clues like this hidden in plain sight?"

"Perhaps her brother the admiral will shed some light—should he write back."

While the Stevenson sisters of Boston were spritzing their correspondence in jasmine and mimosa, the Nelson brothers of Philadelphia had recently written Sir Francis of the first American edition of *Emma* in their possession. Mathew Carey, a turn-of-the-century tradesman on Chestnut Street, had published the novel in 1816 within months of John Murray doing so in London—the only known foreign edition during Jane Austen's lifetime. Since then, London publishers continued to print books by authors not resident in England without their permission, and American publishers —in the spirit of the freedoms afforded by the First Amendment—returned the disfavor.

"The Austen family may have no idea of our early edition," Nick reminded his brother, "for all Mr. Charles Dickens's efforts in decrying such piracy abroad. He writes even more outrage on the matter in today's *Tribune*, alongside mention of the Anti-Slavery Society meeting in Boston—did you see Mr. Frederick Douglass's words of warning to that audience?"

This was a question solely out of brotherly politeness. Haz never kept up with reading the news; they both knew his older brother would always do it for him.

"Douglass says the Anti-Slavery Society should not disband after the war," Nick continued, "without their knowing 'in what new skin this old snake will come forth next.'"

After the war had been the brothers' shared refrain during its course—but what if the war never really ended? After all, there was a Confederate bullet lodged in Nick's leg to remind them, and Lincoln's assassination last month had thrown a whole new wrench in the works. Black cloth still covered the windows of the bookshop, the spring air hung heavy with waste and regret.

So many years spent fighting and killing, so many dead, in service to a time that the Nelsons were beginning to fear might never come.

Seen in this light, the letter to Sir Francis Austen was more than transatlantic literary diplomacy, aimed at keeping authors apprised of unauthorized editions of their works: it was also a last-ditch effort by the brothers to stir up enthusiasm of any kind. Nick now read his beloved Austen at night with the hope of one day hearing back from the admiral, while Haz genially indulged all his talk. The brothers would love to have been part of a discussion group far less exclusive than two battered young men living above a shop. They would be as surprised as anyone to know that in another state, a group of argumentative supreme court justices was doing that very thing. For now, the Nelson brothers only had each other.

And one lonely old sea captain, sitting in Portsdown Lodge, staring out his bow window through a handcrafted telescope, watching for any ships from oceans away.

EIGHT

The Benjamin Franklin Effect

Portsdown Lodge, May 20, 1865

Admiral of the Fleet, Sir Francis Austen, G.C.B.
Portsdown Lodge, Hampshire, England

May 9, 1865

Dear Sir,

Your second missive was gratefully received by us, both for its kind sympathies and bestowal of such a gift as we could only dream of. We will forever count the enclosed letter and signature of your sister amongst our most treasured possessions.

We read your final sentiments, however, with increasing concern and sorrow, and hope this reaches you in an improved state of health. We would also assure you that we are "ad idem," as our father the judge would say, when it comes to all matters concerning your late sister. What weight of responsibility you must feel with respect to her immortal legacy and its preservation.

We write this reply in the hope that we might be of some assistance to you in that regard. Forgive our boldness, but perhaps our objectivity as relative strangers from abroad—and our mutual devotion to Miss Austen's genius—can assist in your decision-making.

We concluded our initial letter of March 26th with an abiding invitation of hospitality on our far shores, yet are mindful that you have seen much of our world and your health remains our paramount concern.

May we come to you instead?

We would travel as sisterly companions, but our father's worry for us is constant and unyielding. Assurances of your attention once we arrive would do much to appease him, should you graciously agree to our proposal. In the meantime, we have begun inquiries into passage and believe we can join the SS China from Boston Harbor on the sixteenth of June.

We fervently hope that this letter will reach you in time to reply in the affirmative to our unusual, but no less sincere, request.

> *Gratefully and respectfully yours,*
> *Henrietta and Charlotte Stevenson*

Admiral Francis Austen read the cream-colored letter three times in his astonishment. Then he breathed in its delightful fragrance again, placed it on the desk next to another letter, and gave both an affectionate little pat.

Settling himself by the window, Frank lifted the four-pull naval telescope from its nearby stand and aimed it at the harbor miles below. The Stevenson sisters' words filled his head as he looked out for any transatlantic steamers. Frank often wished for visitors from these modern vessels, a change in company. Even with the blessings of his children and grandchildren, there was too much family agony going on. The Austen descendants were many, and Jane's legacy most significant—and no one could agree on what to do about it.

Their sister Cassandra had once been stewardess of it all: every letter she chose not to destroy, every piece of Jane's juvenile writing, every manuscript rife with redaction. Now Frank was last to have the most say—this despite all the cousins, the aging nieces and nephews, the many relatives long since scattered to Ireland and the Americas.

The sun began to set; the tide loomed high. The massive steamships docked and disembarked their first-class passengers on grand tours of Europe. The former occupants in steerage heading west—each allotted only two feet of underwater space—had been roundly deposited two weeks ago in Philadelphia or Boston or New York. For these immigrants to the New World, travel was not luxury but escape.

Frank put down the telescope and surveyed the much more comfortable two hundred square feet of space surrounding him. The study's walnut shelves were full of objects from his voyages proudly open to examination— the Davenport captain's desk, bought years ago for his retirement, was securely locked against any of that. Biding his time, Frank ran his fingers along various artifacts on display: the sacred Egyptian scarab beetle under glass; a carved coconut shell from the southern Goa coast; several small terra-cotta heads believed to be Aztec.

Travel had also furnished Frank with something less tangible but even more valuable: a firsthand understanding of how differently others lived yet how similar we all were. He wondered whether such sympathy would be travel's great reward in a future world where nothing was impossible— where every corner of the earth could be walked and mapped—where even the planets might one day be reached. If we ended up able to visit it all, would we finally understand each other better?

Like his famous sister, Admiral Austen was curious about other people while steadfast in his opinions of them. He must now be equally resolute on behalf of Jane. She had not suffered fools—she would not want just anyone dissecting her work. His sister had destroyed the drafts of her finished books for a reason, having worked impressively hard—sometimes over years—to make her meaning so brilliantly clear in the printer's copy. How could there be need for anything more than that?

From the bedroom above, Frank heard his daughter finish her meager toilette and climb into bed. He waited until her floorboards rattled with snoring—Fanny was loud even in sleep—before returning to his desk.

The other letter on the blotter had arrived a few days earlier from the city called Philadelphia—coincidentally the name of Frank and Jane's own paternal aunt. But Frank didn't believe in coincidence: he believed in God. Meanwhile, the sisters' words in the second letter—*May we come to you? May we come to you?*—resounded in his head. Frank had so little opportunity to make anything anymore, his arthritic hands no longer able to fiddle with woodworking. He thought of Emma Woodhouse, her desire to make a match—if nothing else—amid the monotony and boredom of life, and would write *two* letters back to America instead.

NINE

✵

Recalled to Life

◆────◆────◆

Nelson Brothers and Co., June 1, 1865

Messrs. Nelson Brothers & Co.
Philadelphia, Pennsylvania, U.S.A.

May 21, 1865

Gentlemen,

    I was most grateful to learn of your possession of a first American edition of our dear "Emma." The family was unaware of this foreign publication—certainly we have not received any compensation of note from your American publisher Mr. Carey. Mr. Dickens himself has brought attention here to the prevalence of such piracy abroad—a word I hesitate to use, having been involved in an altogether different kind! But such is the world of commerce, at which you surely excel, and I myself have avoided in favour of the sea.

    It might interest you to know that Emma is my favorite of all the books, as well as that of my late younger brother Charles, who read our Sister's own presentation copy threefold while on the high seas. Emma has long been considered by the family as an antidote to self-indulgent thoughts and a reminder of all that is great in English country life.

As I understand, your trade includes that of rare books and, as such, it feels serendipitous that you should have chosen to correspond with me at present. I have experienced a recent bout of illness, and this has put me in mind to settle some affairs. I wonder if your skills for appraisal might be available? I have certain objects in my possession which I am hesitant to introduce to the London market just yet, and which I seek to keep in the greatest of secrecy for the time being.

I would encourage you both to consider a visit this summer when passage will be most uneventful and secure. I understand the SS China, a remarkably competent American-made vessel, departs from Boston this coming June sixteenth. I would be happy to undertake payment in advance of your tickets and to arrange pleasant accommodation for your stay. Do consider what I know to be a rather odd, even impertinent, request. I can only promise, it will be worth your while.

Most respectfully and sincerely yours,
Francis Wᵐ Austen

The shop bell rang out, and Haslett Nelson instinctively tucked the letter inside the account ledger on the desk. Poking his head out the office doorway, he caught sight of Sara-Beth Gleason sweeping through the front vestibule to the shop. The young man prevaricated over what to do next: Sara-Beth was the most frequent customer of the Nelson brothers, although they doubted she read anything she bought. Haz sat back down at the desk, deciding to wait to be called. He knew he would be.

The rustle of expensive silk and cotton along the floorboards could be heard coming nearer, *swish, swish, swish.* Sara-Beth's father was a powerful state senator and her mother socially ambitious, leaving nothing beyond their eldest daughter's reach. The four younger Gleason daughters displayed nowhere near the nerve of Sara-Beth, who appeared to have used up everyone's allocation like so much extra salt.

Every season, she received trunks of the latest clothing designs by Charles Worth, Royal Couturier to French Empress Eugenie. There were tailored outfits for morning, afternoon, tea, evening, the opera, balls, riding, travel, and even sleep: Sara-Beth lived a jam-packed life and needed the clothes for it. From his brief glance, Haz knew she was donned today in her special shopping outfit: an overcoat fashioned from tightly woven herringbone tweed, which gave her an interestingly masculine air, and a little feathered cap at the back of her head to suit her huntress spirit.

"Oh Mr. Nelson!"

Stepping into the corridor, Haz discovered Sara-Beth high up on the rolling ladder, perusing the shop's small collection of books on equestrianism.

"Miss Gleason, please—do be careful!" he cried.

"You'll catch me!" she happily called out. "Your eye is unerring!"

A slender volume from the top shelf now hurtled straight for the floor, and Haz dashed forward to grab it just in time.

"See?" Sara-Beth triumphantly said. She had been taunting him like this since their Sunday School days, when she had first set her cap at the older Nicholas, shy to a fault. Then one day Haz shot up in height to join his brother, and her acquisitive gaze turned on him.

Haz tucked the book under his arm. "Our insurance won't cover you if you fall." The Philadelphia Contributionship company, founded by Benjamin Franklin, extended coverage to the city's property owners for damages caused by fire—*not* by the likes of Miss Sara-Beth. She beamed down at Haz from the ladder as if his words were an invitation to play. She was always willing to test her luck that way. He never responded to any of Miss Gleason's advances, yet still she circled him like a shark.

Sara-Beth descended the rolling ladder and extended her hand well before his was within reach. Helping her down the last few steps, Haz caught the scent of vanilla in her French perfume and realized he was late for his lunch. He held the book out to her with his other hand, grateful to put something concrete between them.

"Thank you, Mr. Nelson. I shall take it."

"Then I shall add it to your account." Haz headed for the counter, which had been situated in the middle of the shop floor so that customers could easily be watched.

"You're still not ready to leave Nicky to all this?" She waved one gloved hand about the book-lined walls as he wrapped her selection in brown paper. "Father thinks you the perfect specimen for political life." Haz didn't answer, but that was no hindrance to Sara-Beth. "You should discuss with him at Mary-Beth's coming out in July—you did receive the invitation?" She tilted her head admiringly as he concentrated on tying an indigo-blue ribbon about the package. "Addressed to you and your brother as one, of course."

"I'm afraid we must decline." He was out with it before he could stop himself. "We're to sail soon to London."

Miss Gleason's face fell, a rare sign of real emotion, but she quickly recovered. "I should love to return to Europe. But *you* are always here! I rely on it."

"We're hoping to make some needed acquisitions for the store abroad, and establish valuable connections."

Sara-Beth brightened at the unusual note of ambition in his voice. "You are looking to the future, then? I like that. It's as it should be."

Except, of course, it wasn't. It was a way to put an ocean between them, and Haz inwardly grimaced over how he would explain any of it to Nick once he had read the letter for himself.

H az, we will *not* go all the way to England just to escape Miss Gleason."

Nicholas Nelson sat with his brother in the parlor above the shop, reviewing the letter from Admiral Austen with its surprise invitation. Neither brother had ever traveled farther than the South, where Haz had skirted death near Sharpsburg and Nick took the bullet to his leg. Somewhere along the way, travel had lost much of its appeal.

Haz and Nick were part of the first generation of American men to be conscripted for war. The brothers could have hired a substitute in their place or paid three hundred dollars for an exemption to the draft. Their postwar existence felt equally conscripted: a daily life of carrying on the family business (their uncle and late father having founded Nelson Brothers and Co. in 1836), a life at night above the shop. The two men received their fair share of invitations from the Sara-Beths of the world, their guardian uncle having made sure to introduce them to society and enroll them in the best schools. Yet both men's spirits remained stuck in the war—in fact, the war was actually still being fought on sea with one last gasp, as Confederate ships resorted to hiding out in British ports.

"But we *will* go?" As he said the words aloud, Haz felt something stir inside him—*recalled*, even, to life, like that famous line from *A Tale of Two Cities*. Ever since seeing muddy rivers full of floating dead during Sherman's march, Haz had been content with regular buying trips to New York City. Manhattan was his Box Hill—now, like Austen's Emma Woodhouse, he suddenly yearned for the sea. Perhaps a wider horizon was exactly what he and his brother needed.

Nick gave one of his slow, methodical nods.

"Your leg—you believe yourself up for it?"

Nick nodded again. "Thank you, Brother."

"'*I promise it will be worth your while.*'" Haz beamed with excitement. "What do you suppose the admiral *means* by that?"

They ticked off all the possibilities together: letters, manuscripts, first editions, unknown works, a piece of jewelry or clothing that Jane once wore, a lock of hair. Whatever was physically left of her, Francis—the sole surviving sibling—might today be in possession of it all.

Neither brother could guess that Admiral Sir Francis Austen was in possession of an entirely different notion altogether.

TEN

Persuasion

•———•———•

The Massachusetts Supreme Judicial Court
June 9, 1865

This is a tale of the sea," pronounced Chief Justice Adam Fulbright at the start of that month's discussion group. "Its dangers, its beckoning, its caliber of men. Austen had two sailor brothers, after all."

The associate justices nodded in surprisingly ready agreement. They each held a different copy of *Persuasion* in their laps: imported British editions which included *Northanger Abbey*; Richard Bentley's more affordable Standard Novel series from 1833; the pirated Philadelphia edition of that same year from Carey & Lea.

"What I find fascinating is the note from her brother Henry, inserted at the start." Justice Ezekiel Peabody always focused in court on the one thing that no one else was. "We know so little about her methods, yet surely we can all agree that there is such fineness—a precise selection of word—a delineation as razor-sharp as we ourselves aspire to in rendering judicial opinion."

Peabody opened his volume to read from Henry Austen's preface to his sister's final, posthumous work. "'Though in composition she was equally rapid and correct, yet an invincible distrust of her own judgement induced her to withhold her works from the public, till time and many perusals had satisfied her that the charm of recent composition was dissolved.'"

"'That the charm of recent composition was dissolved,'" repeated Justice Thomas Nash. "How true. We each here have our own conceit when it comes to that."

"Which is why there are seven of us, to flog it out," Justice Philip Mackenzie reminded the group. "As a genius, Miss Austen had only herself."

"What I find interesting is the depiction of family in *Persuasion*," observed the chief justice. "The vilest of natural relations for heroine Anne Elliot at home, while the sailors have created such voluntary, steadfast bonds at sea. That is the world Anne chooses to marry into at the end—the very world she was years earlier persuaded by Lady Russell to reject."

"Who is not as blameless or benign as Anne wants us to believe," added Nash.

"The narrator distinctly calls Lady Russell 'good-hearted,'" countered Justice Roderick Norton who, along with Justice Peabody, was the most literal member of the court.

"But isn't the narrator part of that same world? A gentry voice, susceptible to—and reflecting—its own environment?" suggested Nash. "I would argue that there is a third, *supra*, voice in the book. Present through its very absence. One that looks down in judgment on it *all*."

The other men fell silent, thoughtfully smoking their pipes as they took in the intriguing notion of *two* invisible narrators, one even more omniscient than the other. The chief justice turned to Justice Stevenson. "William, you are quiet tonight. Are you forming our dissent?"

"Quite the contrary." Stevenson sat back in his chair. "The dangers at sea are indeed manifold. Look at that last paragraph in the book—*'the dread of a future war . . . the tax of quick alarm.'"* Just one week ago, Henrietta and Charlotte had come to him with a letter from an esteemed man of the sea and a most troubling request. It was all the beleaguered father could think of since. "My daughters—"

The other men groaned in recognition, except for Justice Nash.

"William, my friend, what is it?" he asked. It was clear from the poor man's face that Stevenson was not fretting over a novel.

"Henrietta and Charlotte have asked to sail to England."

Nash downed his wine with a frown. "I hope I didn't put the idea in their head at dinner."

"It's entirely their own. A pilgrimage of sorts, *on* their own, to visit their favorite authors."

There was a murmur of both disbelief and envy from the group of men on summer recess. Justice Norton, the most cynical and disbelieving of them all, spoke first. "When you say *visit*—"

"I mean exactly that, yes." Stevenson turned back to Nash, who always sat closest to him. "Not just Dickens, of course, although they plan to capitalize on your information there. Oh no, they also wish to pay their respects to Jane Austen's brother, Admiral Austen, who is to greet them in their first port of call, should they go."

"How on earth?" exclaimed Justice Mackenzie.

"They've apparently been corresponding with the admiral for months. The three appear quite taken with each other." William rubbed his deeply lined brow in anguish. "My only consolation is that the admiral is ninety-one and a father ten times over himself."

"William, you can't let them go without a chaperone." Justice Peabody looked positively stricken by the possibility.

"I am not sure I can stop them. Henrietta is twenty-six soon, and claims the right to chaperone Charlotte herself."

"In total disregard of their marital situation?" pressed Norton. "It's simply not done."

Nash gently placed a hand on Stevenson's drooping shoulder. "William, no one's in a hurry to see your daughters set loose abroad. But such travel is not unheard of, and Henrietta is a most capable older sister." He hesitated. "Shall I move up my own trip to accompany them? I have the cabin at the lake first, but if you truly felt it necessary . . ."

William shook his head. "I'm afraid they are insistent on no chaperone as integral to the entire endeavor. They cannot be dissuaded."

He sighed again while the chief justice passed around the decanter of Madeira. All fathers themselves except for Nash, the justices of the Massachusetts Supreme Judicial Court had rarely been more in need of it.

ELEVEN

De la Terre à la Lune

The Boston Athenaeum, June 12, 1865

As the *China*'s date of departure fast approached, Henrietta and Charlotte asked Constance Davenish to meet them at the Athenaeum across from the Stevenson home.

The private library, one of the oldest in the country, had been founded by a literary society once led by Ralph Waldo Emerson's father. Fronted by a unique neo-Palladian sandstone façade, the Athenaeum comprised three separate floors of books, sculptures, and paintings. George Washington's Mount Vernon library was largely housed there, and famous learned members over the decades had included Emerson himself, Nathaniel Hawthorne, Henry Wadsworth Longfellow, John Quincy Adams, and Margaret Fuller.

The library interior was as delicate and dreamy as a wedding cake, with ornate wrought-iron spiral staircases, trellis Juliet balconies, and dark leather volumes set against creamy alabaster walls. Entering the second-floor reading room, Henrietta and Charlotte immediately spotted Constance's head of voluminous black hair above that of the other patrons. She was seated at a long table divided lengthwise by a tripod shelf displaying the most current newspapers and periodicals.

"Don't tell us Papa has you tallying up shipwrecks, too," Charlotte only half joked as she and Henrietta sat down on either side of her.

"That poor man."

"He requisitioned two junior clerks to pull this month's listings of maritime disasters." Henrietta shook her head. "It doesn't bode well."

"He'll come around. He cares most for your happiness, after all."

"Even if we define the notion differently from him?" asked Charlotte.

Constance shrugged. "We all do. I myself am happy with a battle well fought, if not won. What is it Pericles says about bravery? Going out undeterred to meet what is come?"

"Father wants a clear horizon," Charlotte explained. "Never a worry in sight. He would banish all worry if he could."

"But he has not said no for certain? *C'est bon*—there is still time then. And what is first on your itinerary?"

The sisters began enumerating the many sights in London that they hoped to see.

"When at Fortnum and Mason, you must remember to stop in at Hatchards, the Royal bookshop next door."

Henrietta removed a small journal and Faber pencil from her reticule; Constance was always full of suggestions worth copying down.

"John Hatchard used his shop for anti-slavery protests," she continued. "Many great men and women of their time gathered in the back parlor, quite like Beacon Hill. And the selection in England far exceeds our own."

"You must give us your reading list," offered Henrietta.

"Dumas's newest, *La San Felice*, for one. And any Jules Verne—the translations here are so poorly done." Constance was proficient in several languages, having spent her formative years on the Continent. "*De la Terre à la Lune* is all the rage over there."

"'From the Earth to the Moon,'" translated Charlotte. "What's it about?"

"A Baltimore gun club full of Civil War veterans and weapons enthusiasts—can you imagine?—try to launch three men onto the moon using a giant space gun in Tampa Town. But Verne has been quoted in the press as saying it's really about us—about *our* war."

Henrietta's face lit up. She had a keen interest in anything strategic or military. "How so?"

"Verne wonders how we might pull together again. Now that we're done trying to kill each other, that is. Oh, and do look out for Sir Burton's account of Dahomey—*A Mission to Gelele*—from last year."

"The Amazons of West Africa." Charlotte nodded in recognition. "You told us about them—women who fight even better than the men. Imagine being allowed *that!*"

The Stevenson sisters had to wonder: If they had been born in another time and place, what would have been their lot? Warriors, concubines, slaves? Would they have suffered more—experienced even less freedom? William Stevenson dared his girls to find examples of a better life than theirs, but lack of travel made that difficult to do—perhaps that was even the point. Meanwhile, all the men of their society continued to praise the necessity of women's protection, and the safety and sanctity of home.

B efore leaving for another engagement, Constance made the sisters promise to attend her upcoming weekly salon. Henrietta stayed behind in the reading room to research more naval history, hoping to converse with Admiral Austen about his exploits at sea, while Charlotte headed to the top-floor paintings gallery.

The Stevenson sisters had practically grown up inside the Athenaeum, whose red-leather brass-studded front door was across the street from their own. Harry had been seven years old, and Charlotte only two, when the cornerstone of the present building had been laid in 1847—the same year they lost their mother. Charlotte had no memories of Alice at all, but Henrietta occasionally shared hers, tiptoeing around those final, dark-bedroom, must-be-a-good-girl days.

Charlotte ascended the green wrought-iron spiral staircase to the third floor and headed straight for the unfinished portrait of George Washington that dominated the gallery. The fragment of the president's face, surrounded on two sides by white canvas, gave him a ghostly "half there" appearance as if he continued to paternally watch over them all.

Charlotte loved the painting of Washington for its very state of incompletion, whatever had been artist Gilbert Stuart's reasons for that. In his lifetime, the great portraitist had done likenesses of presidents, kings, first ladies, Mohawk chiefs, chief justices, and over a thousand others, including Charlotte's own father upon his call to the state bar. William Stevenson later recounted for his daughters how Stuart had painted him straight from life without any sketches, wittily conversing the entire time. William con-

ducted his own profession solely from the facts presented before him. With
a note of envy, he had praised the intuitiveness of Stuart's artistry: his complete immersion in the moment and comfort with uncertainty, his meeting
undeterred whatever is to come.

Charlotte loved to act for these same reasons. Loved to feel her own
self slip away—the thrilling unsteadiness of it all—and something new
and unknown rise in its place. Not because she didn't care for herself:
quite the contrary. With her robust ego, Charlotte wanted to bring a little
bit of *her* self to everyone else—to become all people—to experience both
that strange birth and dominion. Perhaps that was why Sir Richard Burton and other explorers traversed the globe. It was intoxicating, the pull
of the distant horizon, the chance to leave behind everything you know
and impress your mark on something—or someone—else, be it for love
or exploration.

In the meantime, girls like her and Harry were barely allowed out of
state. *What,* Charlotte wondered, *was the real reason for that?* Why were so many
solitary pursuits only suspect when pursued by women? Doctors had recently asserted that even writing—the mere *penning* of one's thoughts or
actions—was harmful to female health. Anything exciting or challenging
was presented to women as a risk, a danger, a shame, when for men it was
the very adventure and glory of life. How could something be so vastly different for one half of the world?

Charlotte wagged her finger at the painting—with her lively imagination, she could make anything feel real. Before her now stood George
Washington, the father of their country, with his firmly set jaw and declaration of independence. It had been almost twenty years since women
and anti-slavery activists had signed a declaration of their own at Seneca
Falls:

> *We hold these truths to be self-evident: that all men and women are created equal. . . .*
> *in view of this entire disenfranchisement of one-half the people of this country . . . we*
> *insist that [women] have immediate admission to all the rights and privileges which*
> *belong to them as citizens of these United States.*

Turning her back on the portrait, Charlotte returned to the twisting
staircase and her sister in the reading stacks below. Lost to the resentments

of her mind as well as her imagination, she took a step forward in her fashionable new boots and felt her own self slip out from under her.

Thomas Nash was leisurely strolling through the Common, enjoying the randomness of his summer recess days. He was soon to leave the city for a one-room cabin in the Adirondacks, where he looked forward to a spartan, Thoreau-like existence. He would fish and boat during the day and read by campfire at night. Currently he was knee-deep in Austen's *Mansfield Park*, although struggling once again.

Fanny Price's charms as a heroine always proved elusive. Lucie Manette and Hester Prynne, Elizabeth Bennet and Shakespeare's Beatrice—all felt more real to Nash than the litany of potential brides made ever-present to him in Boston, whether at the opera or theater, the lyceum or even church, but the character of Fanny Price felt the least real of them all. Interestingly, Austen had followed *Mansfield Park* with *Emma*, whose title heroine was in many ways the ultimate Victorian woman: vitally attractive while still deeply attached to hearth and home.

Nash turned onto Beacon Street and saw the very real specter of Charlotte Stevenson leaning against the Athenaeum front door, a black lace-up boot in one hand.

"Are you in need of assistance?" he called out.

Charlotte looked up and down Beacon Street as if hoping to see someone else. "I broke a heel," she finally called back.

"I shouldn't wonder." Nash missed the delicate satin slippers of the past. Many Boston women had lately taken to wearing heeled walking boots in the style of their British counterparts, as if intent on traipsing about the moors themselves. "Let me help you home."

"I can manage."

"It's too far in your condition."

"It's eighty-nine paces," Charlotte replied. "I've counted—with all my idle time."

The chill in her demeanor was unmistakable. For the past year, Nash had enjoyed their moments together, Charlotte's quick humor and teasing manner, the fresh beauty she so boldly displayed. But lately she seemed to regard Nash as an enemy to the sisters' plans, from lectures and all-male receptions to transatlantic voyages. He suddenly felt less like a man around her and more like someone with the ear of her father—someone not to be trusted.

"This is foolishness." Nash bounded up the Athenaeum steps to take her arm, and Charlotte made a low growl of irritation in response.

"If you mention this to Father . . ."

"Oh, I see." He smiled in understanding. "I wouldn't dream of interfering with your travel, I promise."

"Charlie!"

Nash and Charlotte both turned to see Henrietta rushing toward them from the direction of the Common. "I went to get some air," she explained upon reaching the steps, her face deeply flushed. "Whatever happened?"

"I tripped on the staircase heading down. This weak ankle of mine."

"The only part that's weak." Henrietta smoothed Charlotte's tousled hair and took the broken boot from her as Nash helped her to the street. "I'm so sorry I wasn't here."

"I know such boots are the fashion now," conceded Nash as they walked together, "but what would you do if this happened on board ship?"

"What would *you* do?" was Charlotte's quick retort.

"Fair enough." Reaching the Stevenson townhome, he gazed up admiringly, even enviously, at the impressive brownstone before them. Nash had no real home of his own, only fashionable but rented rooms near the courthouse. "What if I were to move up my own travels and chaperone—would that fix things for you?"

"It begs the very question," Charlotte curtly answered him.

"Justice Nash, consider, do all gentlemen disappear when women travel?" Henrietta stated her question as if in formal debate. "Is everyone we encounter a threat? If so, then isn't forcing us to rely on the protection of others foolhardy at best?"

Thomas Nash didn't know what to say to that. Henrietta could clearly hold her own with any of the law clerks at the courthouse, and he recalled the similar rhetorical skill of the Girl Orator. He had attended Anna Dickinson's recent Music Hall lecture out of curiosity, in the manner of visiting a new exotic animal at the zoo, only to walk away with a dismal view of current relations between women and men. Was this why he loved the world of Austen's novels, where everyone knew their place and happily stuck to it? Or did he simply work with too many old men, full of too many old ideas?

All Nash knew was that his professional life had been a success: what he didn't have was a wife and family with whom to share it. In the wake of change wrought by war, women seemed as transformed as the men. Boston's female populace was dividing into battle camps of their own: the simpering ones, sinking under the weight of society's expectations, and those like the Stevenson sisters, champing at the bit to be free—which Nash feared meant free of men. What on earth was going on, and what might such discord mean for him?

✦

TWELVE

The Sinking of the Admiral DuPont

Back Bay, June 13, 1865

Constance Davenish was the proud owner of a well-appointed home in the Back Bay, a neighboring district to Beacon Hill. Here she held weekly salons at which the city's dissatisfied women could congregate. Constance was dissatisfied but also very social, and enjoyed bantering with men. This was how Henrietta and Charlotte Stevenson found themselves in Connie's rococo drawing room of white and gold, sitting across from reporter Denham Scott, an exquisite tea tray on the silk damask ottoman between them.

"We dine en famille after all," he announced, alluding to their recent encounter in Harvard Yard and Charlotte's invitation to dine that Henrietta had quashed.

"I shall pour." Henrietta busied herself with the tea service.

"We call that 'being mother' back home."

"I thought we *were* home." Henrietta added a slice of lemon before passing the cup and saucer to him.

"If one wants to be so specific with words—which, of course, *you* always do." Denham sipped the tea and grinned approvingly. "Just like England, *my* home, then. Thank you."

"You must miss it." Charlotte accepted her own cup of tea from Henrietta while not-so-discreetly rolling her eyes.

"I miss my brothers and sisters. There are eight of us." Failing to catch Henrietta's eye as she passed him a plate of French delicacies, Denham turned back to Charlotte. "They rather depend on me, being the eldest by many years—as your sister here is to you. This assignment was too remunerative to turn down."

"Harry and I have always dreamed of visiting England."

"I hear the two of you plan to do that very thing on the *China*."

"Now, where did you hear something like that?" Charlotte asked in surprise, the madeleine created by Constance's French chef suspended halfway to her mouth.

"It's the talk of the town," replied Denham. "Actually, I'm off as well."

"You are?" Henrietta finally looked up from her cup to regard him.

He nodded at her. "With the war done, the paper just this morning recalled me."

"You're not sailing soon, though?" Charlotte burst out as if panicked by the very thought, and Denham turned back to her with a charmingly boyish laugh. "Not on the *China*, if that's what worries you! My stipend is insufficient for the cabins it has left—I send most of my wages home. So, you and your own travels are safe from me." He met Henrietta's eyes again over the porcelain cups and saucers and she quickly looked away, choosing to examine the series of mountain landscapes by local artist Sarah Freeman Clarke on the drawing room walls. "I'm just back from Nantucket myself. I'm filing for the *Herald* on the sinking of the *Admiral DuPont*—have you ladies heard? It'll be in the morning edition."

Henrietta stifled a gulp as she glanced over at an equally nervous Charlotte. They could only hope that their father would somehow miss this particular item of news.

"An awful business, that. So many lives lost—enough to make any protective parent change course." As Denham spoke, Henrietta returned her gaze to the paintings while Charlotte busily finished the last madeleine on her plate. He was forced to break the silence again. "What's the real reason for the trip?"

"Hmm?" Henrietta absentmindedly asked.

"Miss Stevenson, you won't find your answers on the walls." He raised both his eyebrows at her in amusement. "My sources mention a certain Admiral Austen of Portsmouth and your recent correspondence there."

"It's hardly worth a mention," countered Charlotte. "We only wrote to the admiral out of devotion to his sister's books."

Denham sat back admiringly. "I call that cheeky—and the timing awfully coincidental."

"We call it an ultima ratio," Charlotte insisted while Henrietta refilled her plate of delicacies as if to feed her into silence. "No one's eager to let women like us do much of anything—not even to write about it."

"I know several women working in Fleet Street" was Denham's quick retort. "Most of them married, of course."

"Why does it matter whether a woman is married?" Charlotte angrily demanded to know.

"Perhaps England is simply more advanced," Henrietta suggested.

"I highly doubt that," declared a new voice.

All three of them turned around as Constance came and perched on the arm of Henrietta's chair. "Women in England still lose all property to their husbands upon marriage, whereas Massachusetts women can now keep any earnings and bequests, make a will, and much more easily *divorce*." She gave Denham a pointed look at this last word.

"Someone has to be the head of the family," he matter-of-factly stated. "Shouldn't it stay the man, who engages the most with outside commerce and trade?"

"Which begs another question altogether," Connie quickly countered again, while Denham pulled out the ever-present notebook and pencil from his jacket pocket.

"You don't mind?" he asked his hostess.

"Not at all. I encourage such transcription of our views—*and* their dissemination."

"Men must succeed outside their home, for their family to do so within," he continued to argue. "There is only so much employment available in the world—surely we fare best when a wife is a friend to our interests, rather than a rival."

"They should each be a friend to the other." Constance nodded at the pencil now moving with such haste in Denham's hand. "But until women have the vote, we are at the mercy of men and their decisions."

"Men have the better experience and education to protect women's interests. It would take years—decades—to alter that. Do you not think you are putting the cart before the horse with such matters?"

"Not when men won't even let us ride!" exclaimed Charlotte, and all three women looked at each other and laughed.

"Yet you say Massachusetts law is being reformed in your desired direction," Denham pointed out. "Does that not give you hope for future suffrage?"

Constance waved a dismissive hand. "Politicians can be quite crafty with their hidden motives. Indiana may soon allow women to attend law school—even to divorce without grounds. And yet still—no vote."

"Why do you think that is?"

"We have a shortage of women when it comes to the western expansion," Henrietta readily answered.

"Something your little island doesn't suffer from," added Charlotte.

He looked taken aback by their shared cynicism. "Perhaps lawmakers here are simply having a change of heart, rather than trying to rustle up more settlers?"

The three women laughed in unison again.

"Oh, Mr. Scott." Constance stood up and clasped her hands together. "As our great abolitionist and friend to women, Mr. Frederick Douglass, has said—'power concedes nothing without a demand.'"

"Or as *your* poet Byron once wrote," Henrietta chimed in, as she and Charlotte also stood to join her, "'who would be free themselves must strike the blow.'"

The next morning started like any other for William Stevenson. Henrietta sat on his right, sparsely buttering her toast, which she then slathered with jelly; Charlotte slouched on his left, her nose in the latest instalment of *Our Mutual Friend* after devouring Mrs. Pearson's cider cake with a helping of bacon.

William's own meatless plate of eggs and hashed potatoes sat untouched. How could one eat? His daughters were trying to leave him—and by transatlantic steamship, no less! With a pang in his heart, William realized that if they were successful, he and Charlotte would no longer be finishing Dickens's latest masterpiece together by the fire at night; the serial would run its course that fall, long before she was likely to sail back.

Even more distressing was the discovery by his junior law clerks of two dozen British and American shipwrecks in the first week of June alone. Some of this was the cost of doing war: the ferrying of troops, the shallow seasonal waters, the poor communication now that telegraphy with the Southern states had stopped. At least, this was how William tried to console himself as he wavered back and forth. The decision of whether to stop his girls from sailing must soon be made, with the SS *China* due to depart in two days. Meanwhile his physician had detected a new irregularity to William's heart, which the doctor chalked up to a state of worry that must be overcome. The prescription: *confront the very thing that terrified him.*

William turned the page of his newspaper and felt anew that strange, butterfly-like sensation in the vicinity of his heart.

SINKING OF THE ADMIRAL DUPONT
By Denham Scott on guest assignment for the Boston Herald
June 14, 1865

The steamship Admiral DuPont, *from New-York for Fortress Monroe, was run into and sunk on the night of June 10th by the British ship* Stadacona, *from Philadelphia for St. John, New Brunswick. The steamer sunk in three minutes of the collision. The* Admiral DuPont *was a 473 gross ton iron side-wheel steamship built in West Ham, England, in 1847, and formerly a blockade runner for the Confederacy until her capture in 1862. The ship had left the port of New-York on June 9th with a small detachment of United States troops amongst the passengers on board, and encountered dense fog on the morning of the 10th. Capt. Simon Pepper and all the officers of the steamer are safe and have landed at Nantucket, together with other survivors. There were 17 persons drowned: 15 soldiers, one fireman, and a colored woman. The names of the lost are as yet unknown.*

This is the latest in a series of steamship disasters which are giving rise to great concern and alarm among the public at large. The Boston Herald *contacted for comment Sir Edward Cunard, 2nd Baronet, of the Cunard Company of Britain, who promptly invited any* Herald *correspondent to voyage on one of its fleet, in attestation of the particular safety of its vessels and of sea travel in general.*

"Father, what is it?"

William did not look up. Instead, he answered Henrietta by reading aloud the entire account in the slow, stentorian voice he normally reserved for court.

"Father," began Charlotte the very second that he finished, "this is really nothing to—"

"Charlotte, *no*." William heard his youngest daughter push her chair back hard, intending to come over and embrace him or take his hand—to somehow soothe him out of his worry. But he alone knew how impossible that was. The worry was as much a part of him as anything else. His love for his daughters, his admiration for their spirit, his confidence in their intellect: the worry was at least equal to all of that.

Head still down, William put out his left hand at Charlotte's approach, then heard Henrietta also get up. She joined Charlotte to stand before their father as if facing a tribunal—as if there was anything they could do or say to move him. But he had the world on his side. A world that would always give him the final verdict, and would always let him say no.

His daughters kept to the attic, paining him with their silence at his refusal to let them go. Mrs. Pearson's meals were passed on trays through the door in the floor; there would be no more reading *Our Mutual Friend* aloud by the fire.

On the second night of this estrangement, William lay in bed, dreaming. Alice was back, neatly tucked in his arms. Soft crying could be heard coming from the fifth-floor attic bedroom above. Someone had fallen from the old oak tree on the Common . . . developed an abscess in a newly missing tooth . . . left behind a rag doll in a hansom cab. Alice stirred and William pulled her closer. For once, she didn't try to leave. Instead, they reminisced over other past injuries, the small relief when the hard, physical earth itself was at fault. Most terrifying, like everything in life, were the dangers one could not see.

Alice sat bolt upright in bed. "What was that?"

"Darling, it's nothing."

"No, listen—there—a scraping noise, along the floor."

"Shh, my love. Please. Go back to sleep." He kissed the top of her head.

It was not like Alice to worry so much. He didn't wonder why tonight was different—why he was the one being carried along for once, not resisting, not fretting. *Things aren't falling apart, they're only changing,* he heard a voice inside him proclaim. Suddenly he could hold all the possible dangers of the world within his imagination and not mind one whit. For the moment at least, the horizon ahead looked free and clear.

This must be the key to happiness, he heard the voice say next. He was stunned by the ease and simplicity of it all: you could clear your own horizon. Just keep hoping for the best, stop worrying about the worst, stop fighting so hard. The fighting pushed away the very thing you were trying to hold on to—the thing you were most terrified of losing. *Shh* he told Alice again, while also telling himself *it will all work out.*

He opened his eyes at a sound. From the street below, a carriage door could be heard slamming shut, followed by the gentle thumping of horses' hooves. The sweet chorus of American robins in the summer lilac tree put the hour at just past four. The night men with their "rude carts" had come and gone. All of Boston slept. William took a deep breath, turned over onto his side, and wondered how real any of it was, before going back to bed.

BOOK TWO

The Sea

ONE

The Owl and the Vortex

FIVE O'CLOCK IN THE MORNING
Boston Harbor, June 16, 1865

The figure stood alone at the prow, lit by a last-quarter moon. Black woolen coat trailing along the deck, short-rimmed cap over choppy waves of hair, corncob pipe set firmly in one corner of her mouth. Staring toward the open sea, only ten miles out.

Below were the lengths of piers where several other ships had berthed. The steamers could be heading anywhere: Liverpool, Luxembourg, Liberia. Boston Harbor was situated closer to Europe than most North Atlantic ports and connected with every major rail line at home, making the city feel like the center of the world—or at least the pounding heart of a nation. Here tea chests had once tumbled into the sea, plunging British America along with it. Here word had arrived by ship of the newly signed Declaration of Independence. And here *Old Ironsides*—the USS *Constitution*—had fortified itself for action in the War of 1812.

Today the SS *China* was due to depart with the tide in a few short hours. Meanwhile the solitary figure continued to stare out at the night sea, liquid-silver like mercury—the very poison that had saved her two winters ago. She had been enviably well until then, the picture of health; she feared she would never be well again. For her to make this trip and hopefully heal, the rest of the family had borrowed against her earnings. Yet even with her own debts clear, she still felt as if she owed something to the rest. Painting lessons for May, clothes for Anna's new baby, servitude to the crabby old woman she had accompanied on board.

What if she could be someone new on this trip? She often tried on different names for size: Flora Fairfield, A. M. Barnard, Nurse Tribulation Periwinkle. Louisa—Louy—Lu. There were also the occasional amateur theatrics to help her forget who she was—the one not quite pretty, not quite good enough at writing, not quite good. Even nursing at the Union Hospital in Georgetown, a city as divided as the country, had been a kind of performance. During those short six weeks, until typhoid and pneumonia almost did her in, she had attracted the injured and suffering to her like a celestial queen. This had never happened with any of her students. God, she hated teaching. Perhaps her father, Bronson Alcott—acknowledged to be the greatest educator of his generation—had ruined it for his "golden band of sisters." Instead, May had her art, Anna her family, and Lizzie—well, Lizzie had got what they all feared she most wanted in the end.

Chewing on the pipe, she tucked behind her ear a stray patch of the hair that once nearly brushed the floor. Her one indisputable beauty, until the doctors had shaved it off to lance the typhoid out. Like everything after the war, the hair had grown back slowly, sideways. God appeared intent on teaching that lesson to them all. There was no rising phoenix from the ashes, no lasting accolades. War, like mercury, was as much poison as cure.

Her thoughts always ended up here, at the very point of distress, until she could trot or write them out. She began to saunter about the deck as if without a care in the world—as if she really were someone else. Rounding onto the ship's port side, she noticed a carriage stationed at the end of State Street. The stooped coachman was carrying a large steamer trunk along the length of the pier as two cloaked female figures shuffled behind him. It was barely five o'clock in the morning, far too early to arrive for eleven days at sea—ten, if the weather brought good fortune.

She swiveled about on one foot to finish her circuit of the top deck. Then, as the sun began its ascent, she flopped down onto a steamer chair and took out paper and pencil to write.

She was still writing two hours later, grateful for the mug of bitter coffee that one of the stewards had brought, when another carriage pulled up. This time two male figures descended, carrying their own shared trunk between them. These passengers were not in a hurry. One even walked with a slight limp—both looked the exact right age for war. Chewing on the pencil end just like the pipe, she carefully observed everything else about the two men: The still-boyish looks. The nicely cut clothes. The prevailing mood, which was a little lost, like her own.

Two more hours of writing passed. This was the divine afflatus she always invoked in the early morning, the vortex that descended when the idea-box was finally full. With only minutes to spare before the ship set sail, she looked up to see a man running onto the pier from the direction of the Custom House. Tall and lanky, long auburn locks, *very* fast. As fast as she had been as a girl, able to outrun anyone in the fields of Concord or along the shores of Walden Pond. This late arrival carried the tools of a reporter's trade: handy notebook, pencil tucked in hat brim, well-traveled carpetbag. He bounded up the gangplank and the chief steward greeted him as if expected.

The ship horns blasted. She was about to resume her writing, certain there could be no one else left to board, when a large, well-appointed carriage pulled up. Despite the loud warning noise, its principal occupant took her time descending. She had not fled home under the cloak of darkness but wore an outfit precisely calibrated to the journey ahead: a straw hat ribboned in deep indigo and a matching blue-and-white dress with nautical flourishes. A lady's maid and an older female companion walked in procession behind her; two coachmen struggled with several trunks at the rear. The young woman imperiously glided along the pier, her perfectly pointed chin tilted upward, and ascended the gangplank to be warmly greeted by the chief steward.

The ship horns continued; the pencil end was chewed in time; the writing stayed stopped. She watched with all the scrutiny of an owl—her sister May had painted one on the mantel back home to inspire her—as the chief steward examined the passenger list before handing it back to one of his men. With everyone on board, the gangplank would soon draw up. It was exactly nine o'clock in the morning and high tide: the perfect time to depart. From the deck chair, she spotted movement on the dock, put the pencil down in surprise, and picked the little corncob pipe back up.

She was not done watching yet.

TWO

✳

Here Be Dragons

◄ — • — ►

HALF AN HOUR EARLIER
Beacon Hill, June 16, 1865

William Stevenson woke from the dream with a start. Something was amiss in his house.

He dashed into the hallway and pulled down the attic door latch, jumping back as the ladder tumbled toward him like a drawbridge. This had always made the room above feel even more separate and fortified from the rest of the house, more conducive to secret letter-writing to lonely old sea captains.

William scrambled up the rickety steps and poked his head through the door in the floor. Henrietta's bed was awash in tousled sheets and Alice's dowry chest sat at its foot, shut and secure. Swiveling his head, William peered across the floorboards at the opposite end of the room. Charlotte's bed also looked slept in, but the dark patent-leather cabin trunk, the one stamped in gold leaf with her initials and bereft of travel tags, was gone.

William skipped the last two ladder steps in his hurry to get down, hitting the landing painfully hard in his moccasin slippers. He grabbed the banister with one hand to push off for extra speed—never in his fifty-five years had he descended so quickly the upper four floors of his house.

When he reached the back kitchen, William skidded to a stop. The smell of ham and popovers—his sweet Charlotte's favorite—filled the air;

his heart fluttered wildly. The cook and coachman stood in the center of the warm room, their heads close together in congress. For a second William wondered if there was something of an intimate nature between them, until he spotted the paper gripped in Samuel's hand. The two servants broke apart guiltily but said nothing; Mrs. Pearson sank down at the kitchen table, head in both hands.

"What is it? Where are my girls? Oh, for God's sake, will someone not tell me what is going on?"

Taking a tentative step forward, Samuel held out the note. "I was under strict orders, sir, not to give you this till after breakfast." He coughed. "I took the misses to Long Wharf at dawn. They came to the back and asked me—swore me to secrecy they did—and I carried Miss Charlotte's trunk to the ship—the *China*—and . . . well, I'm afraid, sir, I left them there."

William collapsed into a chair at the other end of the table as he read the note, then stared up at both servants in despair. "What time does the boat depart?"

"Nine, sir, by all accounts."

William jumped up. "Get the phaeton ready out front while I dress. Five minutes—you understand?" He stopped to pat the coachman's shoulder reassuringly—since Alice's death, both servants would carry out any of his daughters' bidding. "And don't worry, Samuel—I know you were only doing your duty."

William drove the phaeton himself the short distance to State Street, then turned east in the direction of the old courthouse. A massive steamship could be seen half a mile ahead, berthed where State Street ended and Long Wharf began. William's hands shook on the reins, his heart pounded all out of rhythm. Stopping the carriage before an attractive red-brick house, he scrambled down and rushed up the steps to bang repeatedly on the black front door. He didn't stop banging until it finally swung open to reveal Thomas Nash still in his housecoat and slippers, one cheek lathered in soap.

"My God, William, what on earth? Is it the chief justice?"

"My girls are on the *China*—they made poor Samuel swear not to show me this until good and gone."

Nash scanned the scrunched-up note taken from William's trembling hand, then checked the grandfather clock in the foyer behind him. "That's barely ten minutes from now." He rubbed the soap off his face with the towel over his left arm. "Wait outside for me—I won't be a minute."

Returning to the carriage, William sat down on its dimpled leather seat for two, out of breath and exhausted. When Nash joined him just a few minutes later, only his hat was in his hands.

As William raced the horse down State Street at breakneck speed, he shouted to Nash all that had been happening in the Stevenson household of late. The more he cried out, the more Nash found himself reluctantly pulled into his friend's orbit of fatherly worry: *Someone must accompany them—someone must protect my girls.* It had always been impossible to resist widower William Stevenson in court and in life, so utterly decent and without guile as he was. Nash had never met a more honorable man and knew, in that moment, that there was only one decent and honorable thing to do.

At the end of State Street was Long Wharf, the bustling center of Boston Harbor. William swerved the phaeton onto the pier, barely missing the water splashing below with the curve. He pulled the carriage to a sharp stop in front of the SS *China* and Nash jumped down to bound up the gangplank just as it began to rise. He presented himself, breathless, to one of the stewards, and pressed some coins in his hand. The young man looked to be no older than seventeen, and Nash felt his own age more than ever.

Grabbing on to the railing, he waved down at William as the ship horns and celebratory cheers of the passengers drowned out all other noise. "It'll be all right!" Nash called to him as the gangplank pulled up. "I promise!" He waved his hat, having done all that he could to reassure the poor father, sitting alone in the carriage, one hand over his chest. Only then did Nash realize how he had failed to contemplate what any of this might mean for his own beating heart.

The ship began to move—the city of Boston receded—the horizon cleared ahead.

Henrietta and Charlotte Stevenson sat on the bottom bunk bed in their cabin, feeling sick to their stomachs even before the ship set sail. They had never, not once, disobeyed their father before.

"The first time we do, and we go and do *this.*"

"We were desperate." Charlotte stood up and sighed. "You said yourself there was no other way. Imagine being stuck with one of our great-aunts or a complete stranger. I want to trot about and smell the sea air and do and see whatever I choose."

"I still feel awful for Father. *You* he'll forgive anything—but he'll say that I should've known better."

Charlotte gave her older sister a curious look. "Is that why you behave, truly?"

Henrietta smiled warily. "No. But it's my excuse."

"Well, I'm mightily glad to be of service to you, Harry!" At the sound of the ship horn, Charlotte rushed to the porthole of their first-class cabin. "We're not moving yet."

"You'll know when we do. They say the trick is to stay in bed the first day."

"I will do no such thing, seasick or not." Charlotte stumbled. "Harry— it's happening!" She steadied herself against the washstand as she spoke. "Let's go up now, on deck! We haven't seen a single soul yet—and we can wave goodbye to all of Boston!"

The main deck was full of first-class passengers celebrating their departure. Despite the morning hour, a small bar had been set up in the prow, and champagne poured freely while rivulets of tobacco juice ran across the deck. Henrietta and Charlotte purchased coffee instead from the dining saloon on their way to join the merry crowd.

"Oh Harry—no! It can't be! Tell me that is *not* our father . . ."

Both women looked down over the railing at the sight of a very sad old man, alone on top of a black phaeton, waving his hat.

"Does he see us, do you think?" asked Henrietta, leaning over the railing. She and Charlotte tried calling down—*Father! Father!*—but there was no way he could hear them over all the noise. "No, we're just one of many to him. Oh, poor Father."

The slouched figure began to slowly recede as if time and space were moving backward, until disappearing from view altogether. Charlotte bit her lip to stop the tears as the SS *China* carried Harry and her away. Eventually they both stepped back from the railing, too conflicted to join in the merriment, and wandered along the port side of the deck.

"Oh no, not *him* now." Charlotte pointed toward the man leaning with his back against the wheelhouse stairs, intently watching everyone who passed. For a second, she considered turning in the opposite direction, until realizing there would be no escaping Denham Scott while on ship.

"Ladies." He tucked his notepad into his front jacket pocket and tipped his cap.

"Mr. Scott." Henrietta crossed her arms.

"Fancy meeting you here after all," Charlotte added in bitter reference to his assurances at Connie's salon.

"I sail at the invitation of Sir Edward Cunard—a state cabin."

"How luxurious, despite your meager stipend," Charlotte replied. "At least *steerage* will be spared."

Henrietta hushed Charlotte like a child, then pulled her along as Denham laughed after them.

"What bad luck running into him!" Charlotte exclaimed when they were far enough away, motioning about the crowded deck. "And with nowhere to hide."

"There's the ladies' saloon—I hear men are excluded."

"How ironic," Charlotte replied with a relieved smile, thinking back on life in Boston, where it almost always worked the other way around.

THREE

The Reluctant Chaperone

FIRST DAY AT SEA
June 16, 1865

Thomas Nash felt the stubble along his jawline and debated what to do next. He was ravenously hungry, only half shaven, and completely unprepared for the day ahead.

Keeping an eye out for a familiar pair of bonnets, he circled the celebratory crowd gathered on the main deck where the dining and lounging saloons were located. The passenger cabins were on the first deck below, ranging in size from narrow single rooms with double cots to state cabins with two rooms and windows to the sea. Nash's own room was small but functional, all of the state cabins being fully occupied. One more deck below was steerage, where families slept and cooked together, bathroom amenities were crude, and access to the outside was permitted in turns for only a few minutes a day.

The ladies' saloon on the main deck was closed to men, and Nash did not feel it proper to barge in on the Stevenson sisters' cabin to announce himself. He could either send them a message or wait until they ran into each other in person, although the element of surprise was unlikely to work in his favor. In the meantime, Nash purchased some hard soap, linen, and undergarments from the goods store. He returned to his cabin and, despite the ship's rocky start, attempted to shave with the bowl and pitcher of water.

Once he felt more presentable, Nash ventured back up to the main deck. Determined to get his morning exercise, he counted one hundred and twenty paces after completing his first circuit of the ship. He calculated that if he walked the entire deck seven times a day, he would finish a mile: that would have to suffice on board for both exercise and fortification for the encounter ahead.

During his second circuit of the ship, Nash noticed a woman writing while furtively watching the other passengers and chewing on a little corncob pipe. She was dressed in a long woolen coat to protect against sea spray as well as rain—the kind made by boiling the wool, something his own mother had done to economize. Nash was a self-made man, although he did not mention this as much as his dear friend Stubby—Professor Child—did. Nash wasn't sure why. It wasn't due to shame, but it wasn't due to so much pride, either. He simply liked the life he had built for himself, despite the odds, far more than the life he had happily left behind. He was always a man to stay focused on the future—*ambition*, his widowed mother would have called it.

The woman in the deck chair stopped writing and stared up at Nash with dark-circled, deep-set eyes. Suddenly, she lifted the pipe and gave him a little salute. She looked to be his age or older and rather beaten down by life. Immediately he felt a pang of pity for her, alone on deck, watching everyone else.

"Ahoy," the woman called out. Her voice, low but energetic, startled Nash out of his thoughts.

"Ahoy there," he replied with a smile, tipping his hat. "Thomas Nash. And whom do I have the pleasure of meeting?"

Her sallow face softened at his introduction, and she tucked the notebook under a pile of newspapers by her feet. "Louisa May Alcott—but my friends call me Lu."

"And how are you enduring this first day at sea, Miss Alcott?" Nash asked, coming closer.

"Oh, splendid—and you?"

He smiled. "Yes, splendid. Are you traveling alone?"

She shook her head and gave the side of her nose a little scratch. "No, sir, I'm accompanying a family friend as a nurse of sorts. I've not much training, mind you—just some time at the Union Hospital. Though the ol' gal below really doesn't need much tending to. She's sleeping even now." Louisa leaned forward and tapped her right temple hintingly with the bowl of her pipe. "A change in scenery might do her wonders."

"It might do for us all." Nash was charmed. He thought of Austen's Emma and Elizabeth, Dickens's Bella Wilfer, Shakespeare's Beatrice and Viola. The lively ones. It was a shame that the marriage market too often offered up the opposite—not that he would contemplate marrying someone like Lu, and he winced again on her behalf.

"Are you off to London, too?"

With her many questions, Nash wondered if Lu was a lady journalist; he had heard that someone from the London papers was on board snooping around. "May I join you?" He nodded at the empty deck chair next to hers before sitting down. "I am indeed visiting the great city on holiday." He had no intention of volunteering his more pressing, private mission to anyone.

"I can't wait. I plan on seeing all the places Dickens writes about."

"How intrepid of you."

She vigorously nodded. "Yes indeed, starting with the home of Sairey Gamp. Another nurse of sorts—like me!" Nash smiled at the reference to the tippling, irascible character from *Martin Chuzzlewit*. "Then Mr. Dombey, Tiny Tim, Artful Dodger . . ." Lu continued to happily recite the names of characters from Dickens as if they were as real as any of the thousand people on ship.

Noticing the empty mug on the deck next to her scuffed boots, Nash waved over a steward. "Allow me," he said to Lu before ordering them both tea with milk.

"There are two cows in the pen below, did you know? Bessie and Sugar. I've already said my hellos. That's a few hundred cups of milk a day for those of us in first class." She pointed at the copies of *Lloyd's List* and *The Times* resting on deck near her booted feet. "We even get the London news up here—days before home."

This was one advantage of traveling on a mail steamship, although the postal sorting rooms came at the expense of certain first-class luxuries (*No barber shop, for one*, thought Nash with a grimace as he felt the burn along his chin). He had recently read about plans for the SS *Great Eastern* to begin laying undersea telegraph cable across the Atlantic from Ireland to Newfoundland, which would change news delivery forever. For now, everything reached America in exactly the time it took a mail packet to sail from Liverpool or Portsmouth to Boston or New York and beyond.

At Louisa's nod of invitation, Nash lifted up the newspapers and caught a glimpse of the notebook underneath. "Forgive me." He hurriedly dropped the papers back down, but she waved off his compunction with quiet pride. "You are a writer, then, as I surmised? I envy such talent."

"There's not much to envy. It's hard grubbing, getting paid by the word."

"I myself would surely starve, then." Nash gave her an encouraging smile. "I cannot write words to excite—only to explain."

"Oh—are *you* the reporter they talk of?" Her face lit up.

"I'm afraid not. I sit on the Massachusetts state bench."

"But *we* should be the ones afraid—what power! Did you study the law at Harvard? My friend Henry James just finished his year there. Just a year, mind you—nose always in a novel, that one."

The Jameses were a socially prominent Boston tribe, and Nash was intrigued. Perhaps he had been passing too much judgment on her clothes and demeanor. "How do you know Mr. James?"

"Our families." She cleared her throat. "My father is Bronson Alcott, the educator."

"And famous reformer! Yes, I know of him well." There was much *to* know: good and bad. Alcott had innovated teaching through conversation and the importance of play, and admitted a Black child to his last school over parents' objections, resulting in its closure—but he also held scattered, self-indulgent lectures on the lyceum circuit and once founded an ill-conceived Utopian community on a Harvard farm. Then there were the disturbing whispers in Boston society of which even Nash, who always did his best to avoid gossip, was aware.

The steward returned with two mugs of milky tea. As they drank and chatted together, Nash noticed Lu begin to withdraw. She didn't seem to want to talk anymore about her father or the stories she wrote. Nash's one glance at the notebook had caught sight of a rather lurid title. He wondered if the rumors were true, that the father made no money, only spent or gave it away—and whether the dark circles beneath Lu's eyes, the trip as an invalid's companion, belied who in actuality was supporting the Alcott clan. Sensing she wanted to be alone with her writing again, Nash stood up, mug of tea in hand.

"Miss Alcott, it has truly been a pleasure. I hope we will meet often during our time at sea."

She saluted him again with the cob pipe, a gesture that suddenly smacked of performance, and Nash recalled the gothic title of the story he had glimpsed: *Behind a Mask*. He wondered how far away Louisa traveled in her head when she wrote; how much she tried to leave behind. Nash had known hardship, too, but had surmounted it through brains and education. Where did the smart women go, when they lacked either looks or situation?

Justice Thomas Nash nodded goodbye to Louisa May Alcott, thinking her a most interesting female specimen who didn't quite fit conventional society. He wondered where that left her. *At least she had her writing*, he thought to himself, as Louisa picked notebook and pencil back up. But even strides away, Nash could tell that her hooded eyes—and eagle-like interest—remained firmly fixed on him.

FOUR

✤

A Tale of Two Cities

• —•—• •

FIRST DAY AT SEA
June 16, 1865

Nicholas Nelson sat alone on a deck chair at the stern of the ship facing the wake, a copy of *Emma* resting open on his lap.

It was almost July, the time of year when the strawberries began to ripen and Nick dreamed of being in Highbury again. Hoping to bring back a large shipment, including whatever treasures Admiral Austen might have in store, the Nelson brothers had limited themselves to a handful of books each for the journey. Nicholas had packed all of Austen save for *Northanger Abbey*, which Haz loved but Nick considered rather slight of both heroine and theme. Haz meanwhile had brought along five rollicking tales of heroism and adventure: *The Count of Monte Cristo*, *The House of the Seven Gables*, *Ivanhoe*, *The Last of the Mohicans*, and his new favorite, *A Tale of Two Cities* by Charles Dickens.

Nicholas had long drawn a connection between Austen and Dickens, both in their brilliant sketching of character and understanding of human motivation and weakness. But where Austen used as few words as possible to make her point, Dickens often did the opposite. Nicholas was convinced that Austen had reworked her manuscripts many times over, even though there was little of her original writing, or thoughts on writing, to evince any of that;

this might be one reason for her growing mystique. Dickens, on the other hand, wrote his novels on serial instalment for periodicals and magazines, chapter by chapter, which meant he could not go back and revise; a certain wordiness must be the inevitable result.

But what the two authors shared most in common was devotion to the reader. It was said that Austen had tested early versions of her work with family and friends, reading sections aloud; Dickens had the benefit of witnessing the public reception to his works while writing them, and later re-created condensed versions for the stage in which he played all the parts. Nick wondered if Dickens also acted out loud as he wrote; maybe Jane Austen had done so, too.

"Why, Mr. *Nelson*."

Nicholas looked up from his book to see Miss Gleason standing above him, dressed in blue-and-white stripes with a matching parasol. *How is this happening?* Nick asked himself in desperation, raising one hand to shield his eyes from the sight of Sara-Beth as much as the blinding sun.

"Won't you invite me to take a seat?" She collapsed the parasol and rested it against the small deck table between them.

"Miss Gleason—what a surprise."

"A happy one, I hope." Sara-Beth sat down and rearranged her skirts and crinolines about her. "It was the perfect excuse to avoid Mary-Beth's coming out." She gazed eagerly around the deck. "And where is your steady other?"

"Resting, I believe." Nick felt his mouth go dry.

"Will *he* be happy to see me?"

"I can't speak for him."

"I doubt that." Sara-Beth smiled knowingly. "And who is minding the shop?"

"Our uncle—he is always glad to be of help."

"Unlike my handlers, ha! Nick, are you all right? You look a little peaked."

"Just a touch of seasickness."

"Let me get you some brandy—I insist." She waved to a passing steward. "Now, tell me your itinerary. Haz mentioned making connections?"

"Mm-hmm."

"In London?"

Nick stalled by looking about the deck, hoping to gain time to answer. He knew from experience that a small portion of the truth could sometimes satisfy Miss Gleason's limited attention. "Portsmouth, actually."

"Whoever could live there!" She gave a little yawn, then nodded at the copy of *Emma* still on his lap. "Haven't I caught you reading that before?" Nick shrugged, unwilling to say more. "Nicky, really, how can you stand to read something again? You know the ending." She was the only one in the world to call him Nicky—he had never tried to stop her. There'd be no point.

"I myself always read the last chapter of any book first—to make sure it's worth my while." She stood up with a laugh and popped open her parasol against the sun. "Well, I'm off to inspect the smoking lounge. I understand there is some gambling on board to be had, and I'm as eager to try my luck on water as on solid ground."

Nick watched her leave in utter incomprehension. He did not understand her at all—not one little bit. Her impulsiveness in joining the ship—the unstoppable interest in his brother—such seeming confidence that everything in life would turn out all right. She could have come from the moon. Books had always been the Nelson brothers' way of understanding the human heart, but even Austen failed them both when it came to Sara-Beth.

⚓

FIVE

The Staplehurst Rail Disaster

FIRST DAY AT SEA
June 16, 1865

The ladies' saloon was a surprisingly elegant and well-furnished room, with clusters of sofas and chairs where one could read from the stacks of week-old London newspapers. Henrietta and Charlotte Stevenson settled themselves in a quiet corner where a woman sat alone, her scuffed boots resting on a small stool. A low cap over misshapen tendrils of hair was the only other part of her visible above the newspaper held high in her hands. Suddenly she lowered the paper to stare at the two sisters as if she had known they were there all along.

"It's Dickens."

"I beg your pardon?" asked Henrietta.

The woman pointed down at the news page on her lap. "There was a rail disaster, in Kent."

"Is he—"

She shook her head slowly. "No, thank heavens."

Henrietta, who sat closest, accepted the newspaper from the woman and began to read aloud.

> The train was carrying passengers from Boulogne when some plates, half-loosened by workers, gave way on a bridge at

Staplehurst. The engine fell on its broadside, sparing the first-class carriage, but several other carriages broke off and fell over the bridge into a stream below. Ten persons were killed either from injuries sustained or suffocation in the riverbed, and about twenty others were wounded. The travellers were in many cases returning home after a long absence abroad, some from as far away as India. Mr. Dickens was in the train, but escaped without harm and bravely attended to fellow passengers, several of whom succumbed to their injuries whilst under his care. The foreman is in custody but the carelessness which caused the event extends far beyond the workers. The train was travelling 40 miles an hour, far too fast for such a steep incline, the usual danger signals were not sufficiently activated for that speed, and the lead engine had required frequent repairs of late. As one observer commented, "the jaws of destruction were open awaiting them." The public will demand proportionate punishment of those whose actions, or inactions, have caused this terrible disaster.

"How horrible." Charlotte placed a hand on Henrietta's shoulder. "It's the *Lloyd's List*. Papa is bound to see it." She sighed. "Poor Father. He wasn't even worried about the rails."

"Poor Father? Poor Mr. Dickens!" the woman exclaimed.

"Yes, of course—how right you are." Henrietta passed the newspaper back. "I am sure one does not soon recover from such tragedy."

"It's awful strange, what with my coming all this way to see him." Henrietta and Charlotte both stared at the woman, speechless. "Oh, I have employment, you know, and am fixed on touring the great museums and cathedrals of Europe. But Mr. Dickens—I was meaning to see him lecture in London and visit all the particular places he writes about."

"But how remarkable!" cried Charlotte. "We came all this way to do the same with Jane Austen!"

The woman let out a guffaw. "What is there to see?"

"The village in Hampshire where she wrote her masterpieces, for one."

"And a handful of made-up country villages. Look, pay me no mind, I enjoy the books as much as anyone. But I prefer a little blood and thunder, as they say. *Jane Eyre*: now that's my kind of story." She pushed her cap back, revealing a few premature grey hairs about her brow. "You travel as sisters? I wish I was. I have . . . I *had* . . . three."

"We're so sorry," Henrietta and Charlotte said in unison.

The woman nodded her gratitude. "We're scattered now. My sister Anna will be delivered of her second soon, and May studies in Boston. Painting and art."

"We're from Boston, too." Charlotte sighed again. "But we don't get to study."

"My father is a great proponent of education for everyone."

"Our father is a man of the law," Henrietta explained. "Justice William Stevenson of the Massachusetts supreme court. A moderate."

"But a strict constructionist when it comes to the two of us," Charlotte added.

"Progress is slow, then?"

The two Stevenson sisters turned to each other and laughed. "Glacial," agreed Henrietta. "We're Henrietta and Charlotte Stevenson, by the way."

"Louisa Alcott. But you can call me Lu."

"In that case, you can call us Harry and Charlie."

"That ought to get the men on board a-talking! At least we've none of them in here. I like men, always have, but I mean to get work done."

Charlotte noticed the notepad by the stack of newspapers. "Are you a writer?"

Louisa's plain face lit up. "Not successful—not yet. Girls' stories and gothics, mostly. I tried a grown-up novel, *Moods*, but my publisher made me cut it in half—I think calling it *Mood* would be more precise!"

The sisters laughed together again, charmed by the woman's self-deprecating manner. "Oh, wait," exclaimed Charlotte, "we saw a review of that—in *The Atlantic Monthly*?"

Louisa rolled her eyes. "Yes, it seems everyone read at least *that*. It was by my friend Henry James, although his words were not so amicable." She cleared her throat and dramatically intoned, *"'We are utterly weary of stories about precocious little girls. In the first place, they are in themselves disagreeable and unprofitable objects of study.'"*

"Ouch," Charlotte commiserated.

"James is a writer, too. Keeps it anonymous—for now. But I'll make him eat humble pie if he ever writes a so-called 'precocious little girl' himself. I bet he will, though—he's so tetchy, that one."

"May we know what you are working on next?" asked Henrietta.

"Nothing of substance. I'm all dried up. Besides, it's harder now." She lifted her right hand to display a slight tremble. "I caught typhoid nursing in the war. They tell me the sea air might do me good. And there's nothing like travel for inspiration."

"Or for love." Charlotte nodded in amusement at the roomful of refined-looking mothers chaperoning unmarried daughters. "It would appear we've all of us come up empty in Boston."

Louisa dramatically placed her right hand over her heart. "I want to find a European count for myself—or a poor itinerant musician."

The three women laughed together.

"Our parents' marriage was a most happy one." Henrietta looked at Charlotte. "I suppose Father only wants the same for us."

"And your mother?"

"She died when we were little. Ever since then, our father's been . . ."

"Preoccupied," offered Charlotte.

". . . yes, *preoccupied* with our safety."

"He let you go on ship, did he not?"

The two sisters glanced awkwardly at each other.

"It was our decision." Henrietta hesitated. "*Wholly* our decision."

"You don't mean . . ." Louisa sat up keenly. "Are you stowaways, then?"

Charlotte laughed. "No, we paid full fare."

"But we left him—how do the Germans say it?" asked Henrietta. "*Im Stich lassen*—high and dry."

"Ah, I see now—the *poor father*. But how exciting—I loved nothing more than running away when I was a child." Louisa paused. "Wait—did you say he's on the Massachusetts supreme court? But what coincidence again! I just met someone on board from the state bench. Quite the dashing figure and not that old—at least, no older than me!" Louisa scratched the side of her nose again in thought. "Now then, what was his name. . . ."

As if telepathically, the image of William Stevenson, bereft, waving his hat back at someone on the ship—someone decidedly *not* Henrietta and Charlotte—passed through each of his daughters' heads at exactly the same, sinking moment.

SIX

An Angel at the Table

FIRST DAY AT SEA
June 16, 1865

Nicholas and Haslett Nelson sat across from each other at one of eight long tables in the dining saloon, a wood-paneled room that curved out widely with the beam of the ship. Each table had been set for twelve to accommodate two hundred first-class passengers at two separate seatings.

The Nelson brothers, preferring to eat early as they did at home, were among the first to arrive. The dinner menu before them was also pleasantly familiar: barley broth; beefsteak and oyster pie or roast pork with stuffing (or, in Haz's case, both); boiled cabbage and potatoes; apple tart for dessert. Wine and spirits were available, but neither brother would partake; with Sara-Beth on board, they were determined to hold on to their wits.

"She just showed *up* . . ." Nick's repeat astonishment had by now turned into a statement of unavoidable fact, like Sara-Beth herself. He placed his napkin on his lap. "She claims to have a chaperone."

"I doubt we'll see hide or hair of *them*." Haz raised his eyes to the ceiling. "Every time I consider giving women the vote . . ."

"To be fair, Sara-Beth shows little interest in that cause."

"Only because she has plenty of other ways to get what she wants." Haz stopped talking to stare past the left shoulder of Nick, who had his back to the entrance of the room. Nick turned around in response to his brother's quizzical eye, fearful of Sara-Beth approaching, but saw two other women instead.

"Who is *that*?" Haz asked, his voice rising. The women were different in height and age but shared the same wide-set eyes and crescent-shaped mouth.

"Which one?" asked Nick, turning back to face him.

"Does it matter?"

"You always fault Sara-Beth for treating the two of us like that."

Haz good-naturedly laughed in agreement. The two women sat down at the end of the table directly behind him, and he leaned back from his soup bowl to listen. "They're sisters. They sound upset about someone—a man—their chaperone?"

"But they're dining alone."

"Oh, yes—they're *very* upset. This idea of a chaperone—surely they don't need one," observed Haz. "The taller one looks our age at least. And the younger—what an *angel*."

"Did you know *chaperon* is the hood over a falcon, to stop its desire to fly?"

"You know I didn't." Nick's breadth of knowledge always impressed Haz. As a schoolboy, he had turned to his older brother for answers as much as to books—only sports and stage-acting ever truly captured his attention.

The two women began animatedly muttering as a distinguished man still in his morning coat strode into the room. The dozens of other diners ceased conversation to regard his wavy blond hair and broad-shouldered form. The man looked about, reddened at spotting the two women, then immediately sought the farthest table from them.

"The *chaperone*, I bet," Haz whispered to Nick. "He's not that old and much better-looking than us—which probably defeats the purpose." A second man now entered the room and headed straight for the two women. "That's the reporter they told us about, from London. He knows them, too, it would seem. I wonder why they're not already married."

"I'm sure you'll find out soon, Brother."

The reporter, looking amused by the women's quick dismissal of him, took his seat at a nearby table. Nick watched as the younger sister's face, still frowning from that man's overture, brightened at another new arrival. Turning around again, he witnessed a rather plain-looking woman enter the dining room.

"Lu! Come, do join us!" the younger sister called out, and Nick noticed the chaperone briefly look up with interest before returning to his menu. There was a great rustling sound behind Haz as the woman sat down. She was friendly and buoyant, making the ensuing conversation that much easier for the Nelson brothers to overhear.

"You haven't even said hello to him?" they heard her ask. "Hasn't *he?*"

The angel answered. "He wouldn't dare. He's no fool—just our father's lackey."

"Hush, Charlie," whispered her sister.

Lu? Charlie? Haz mouthed to Nick, and they both shrugged at the surprising use of male names.

"All the more reason to keep to the saloon, then," the woman called Lu declared. "I've loads of ideas for fun."

"Your suggestion of a charity performance, for one," the woman called Charlie enthused, causing Haz to jerk his head up in surprise from his beef-and-oyster pie.

"Such a good use of our free time on board," added her older sister. There was something pleasant about her voice—much calmer than the other women's—that caught Nick's ear.

"We shall condense Dickens!" Lu suddenly cried out. "We did six of his scenes for the Sanitary Fair in Boston two winters back. Raised plenty—twenty-five hundred dollars! Ran short on time and actors, though." She looked about at the other passengers, who appeared either slightly seasick or already bored. "We won't run short on either here—*and we'll have a captive audience.*" Lu winked. "My favorite kind."

The three women laughed freely together, and their ready camaraderie impressed both of the Nelsons. *Women became friends so quickly—why* was *that?* the brothers had to wonder. *Why did men bond most over war and sport, and women over everything else?* Then Nicholas and Haz shared a much more worrisome thought: Were women themselves at war with men today, given the angry clamors for their rights, and in search of reinforcements at every turn?

"But no men!" Lu proclaimed, as if she could read their minds. "We shall do *all* the parts."

The brothers raised their eyebrows at each other. They had a trunk of ten books and week-old newspapers to spare, but only each other for companionship. Suddenly it felt too much like home, and they began to envy the planning taking place at the other table.

The energy in the room, filled to capacity with first-class guests, shifted with one last arrival. Sara-Beth Gleason entered, sans chaperone and wearing the most resplendent dress of all. Although possessing no sense of fashion themselves, Nick and Haz had to admire the uniqueness of her silhouette, the flatter front of her skirt only emphasizing the fuller volume in back. Neither man could begin to guess at the reduced-front crinoline underneath, recently created and shipped to Philadelphia from the French fashion house of Charles Worth.

Sara-Beth made a beeline for the brothers' table.

"Perhaps we should go." Nick stared down at his plate.

"She senses fear," Haz warned.

To their surprise, however, Sara-Beth sailed right past them to join the women instead. Nick watched as Lu jumped up to offer her chair and went to fetch an extra one for herself. How on earth did Sara-Beth Gleason of the City of Brotherly Love already know these three daughters of Boston?

The table of women was full of talk of the charity performance being planned for the final night on ship. Books to adapt were discussed, and the Nelsons grew even more envious as the energetic quartet settled on *A Tale of Two Cities*. They overheard Lu claim that Dickens, the most famous author in the world, had yet to dramatize the novel himself, giving her imagination free rein to do so.

Meanwhile Nicholas and Haslett Nelson would have to settle for ten days of quiet time alone on deck, reading books they had both read before, and staring at the endless horizon, always more empty than clear.

SEVEN

✳

Platitudes

◦————•—————•

THAT SAME NIGHT
Portsdown Lodge, June 16, 1865

The thin white curtains blew back into the study with the breeze. Admiral Sir Francis Austen stood before the open window, peering out at sea through his finest telescope tonight. The four-pull spyglass had been an early gift from his patron, Admiral Lord Gambier, for whom Frank had commanded the *Peterel* and captured forty ships when just a lowly officer himself.

The view of the night sky yielded nothing but a last-quarter moon and summer constellations, and the easterly wind foretold a stormy sea, but Frank could not repress his excitement. He was eager for his visitors from the New World. Had they already met on the *China*? Who might be first to disclose the reason for their trip? Certainly not Henrietta, whose poise and discretion shone through her letters, nor Nicholas Nelson, the very formal and restrained businessman. Frank intuited such similarity between these two eldest siblings, each of them towing a younger, more impetuous one along.

As the sixth of the late Reverend George Austen's eight children, Frank had for a time been indulged and mischievous himself, the boy affectionately called "Fly," until Jane and then Charles had come along and stolen his luster. Perhaps this was one reason why his mood of late kept turning in a more playful direction, after decades of crushing responsibility and deep, abiding faith. There was a change in his bones, a strange new lightness—a buoyancy—to accompany the frailty; he could tell the end was near.

The recent and fortuitous correspondence with two sets of American siblings was also setting Frank's mind to race; he came from a long line of matchmakers, after all. His second wife, Martha, despite being ten years Jane's senior, had proved to be her lifelong friend, and early on Jane had tried but failed to match her with Frank. Jane had even dedicated one of her juvenilia to Martha and given her a place of prominence within the small circle of people aware of her writing. Martha had kept the secret of her authorship for years, until Jane left them all far too early and the question of her legacy had begun. Years later, a widowed Frank had indeed married Martha Lloyd to the satisfaction of almost everyone—Jane's keen eye always won out in the end.

Martha's late-in-life marriage to Frank had not, however, pleased the distant aunt on whose eventual bequest he and his large family had long depended. He had further failed to consider how the date of this second marriage, being the same as his first, might put some relations off. The disapproving aunt had left her nephew ten thousand pounds instead of the hoped-for estate, and a nonplussed Frank had immediately bought Portsdown Lodge, with its fourteen bedrooms, thirty-five acres, and view of his beloved sea. *All's well that ends well*, he had declared at the time, prone to platitudes as he was.

Today Frank resided at Portsdown with six servants and only his youngest daughter, Fanny-Sophia, for company. At age forty-four, Fanny was not married and unlikely to become so. Then again, Martha, nine years Frank's senior, had married him when she was sixty-three (*Hope springs eternal*, he also liked to say). Since Martha's death in 1843, Fanny had run the household for her father, keeping a tight ship but a loose lid on her emotions. Frank found himself increasingly unsure of how she would react next—he only knew that she would, and this shredded his nerves like so much rope.

"Father, the hour." Fanny stood in the doorway to the study in her plain white muslin dressing gown and cap, kerosene lamp in hand, the shadows under her eyes as dark as bruises. "You should have retired long ago."

She always spoke to him as if he was the child. It was not endearing and made him trust her even less. "You must not worry so, my dear. This night owl has lasted long enough."

She bustled over and slammed the window next to him shut. "I wouldn't want you on ship in this wind."

Frank didn't respond. The sea was, in fact, all he wanted. In its place, he would deal with the past before it was too late.

Fanny bent down to give his cheek a dutiful kiss goodnight, and Frank tapped her hand on his shoulder several times in his eagerness to see her go. After she left, he waited for the tell-tale creak of the stairs, the low rumble of breathing through the floorboards above. Only then did he remove an unusual round key from inside his dressing gown collar. The key fit the special Bramah lock to his desk, the greatest security Frank could find for what was hidden inside: most of the little that remained of his famous sister's writing.

Years ago, their sister Cassandra had destroyed nearly all of Jane's correspondence. Of the several thousand letters Jane must have written in the course of her short life, Cassandra had only saved and bequeathed one hundred. She had marked *to be burned* on the rest, as forcefully as if written by Jane herself. But who was now to say? If Jane could have guessed at how much pleasure her books would continue to give, would she have relented? Yes, she at first published anonymously—"by a lady"—in the fashion of her time. But she had also been prodigiously proud of her talent, enjoyed hearing others talk about her books and kept record of it all, and would surely have been gratified by the increasing appreciation for her genius. Other famous authors held on to everything: there were at least ten volumes of Sir Walter Scott's letters alone. Would Jane, discreet as she was, have been able to withstand the world's interest in her as well as in her work?

Bending down on creaky knees, Frank inserted the round key to unlock the bottom drawer to his desk. He pulled out a cast-iron strongbox and placed it on top of the blotter, then used a smaller, different key from his dressing gown pocket to unlock that box as well. Inside were three stacks of paper, each tied with black ribbon. One stack contained dozens of letters from Jane, who had written monthly to each of her sailor brothers while at sea, with almost as many letters to Martha in the second stack. The third had been given to Frank decades ago and under strict instruction; until now, he had kept even the family from its existence.

Cassandra had been visiting Portsdown Lodge in the spring of 1845 when she had pressed it in his hands. Days later, she had collapsed from the strain on her heart and died in this very room. By then, Frank had left Portsmouth, under orders to depart for the Royal Navy's North America and West Indies Station where he was to take command. It was their brother Henry who arranged for Cassandra to be brought home to Chawton and buried next to their mother.

Chawton had been the beloved home of Mrs. Austen and both her daughters, as well as Martha, who lived with them for years before her marriage to Frank. In 1809, all four women had moved into the little steward's cottage on his brother Edward's Chawton estate. Whenever Jane or Martha traveled from the village, they kept in constant touch through letters—letters that Frank now examined by firelight, an unintentionally large fraction of Jane's physical legacy, plunder should it fall in the wrong hands. Like Cassandra, Martha had been a lodestar for Jane; someone to write for; a way home. Martha also helped keep house so that Jane could write, just as Fanny now did for him. But Frank needed no such freeing of time. If anything, he wished—and waited—for activity.

Just nine more days.

EIGHT

Blood and Thunder in the Ladies' Saloon

FIFTH DAY AT SEA
June 20, 1865

For the first four days of the voyage, the SS *China* lurched with every wave from the tropical winds off Cape Verde and lulled with their every break. These powerful gales had curved back into the central Atlantic due to the dip in a high westerly wind off the Massachusetts coast—at least, this was Captain Norris's explanation to the male passengers as they balanced their snifters of brandy on the bar or circuited the deck railing with a white-knuckled grip.

The female passengers, for the most part, were rarely to be seen. Years of being stuck in bedrooms and parlors were suddenly of great use. The ladies' saloon was full of knitting bags, embroidery hoops, sewing, reading and letter-writing, playing cards and dominoes, and the kind of gossip and amateur theatrics with which more fortunate women whiled away their empty hours.

Hours on the *China*, however, were very full as Louisa Alcott mounted her all-woman production of *A Tale of Two Cities*. The Charles Dickens novel was set nearly a century earlier at the time of the French Revolution and rife with great scenes to perform. Having previously dramatized other famous works, Miss Alcott put herself in charge of the script.

"We have five main characters. Lucie Manette—the angel." Louisa gave Charlotte next to her an intimating look. "The book starts when Lucie discovers her father is still alive, after eighteen years of being falsely imprisoned in Paris. Such a scene—look, tears . . ." Fanning her eyes, she took a second to compose herself. "Lucie brings Dr. Manette back to London, and on the boat to Dover they meet Charles Darnay."

Louisa paused. "A little *too* good for my liking, that one. A French aristocrat who has rejected his debauched family and its wealth, and is coming to England for a new life. Two British spies set him up, and he is put on trial at the Old Bailey for treason to the Crown. The courtroom scene is Dickens at his best." She explained how Charles Darnay is acquitted when his strong physical resemblance to someone else in court—lawyer Sydney Carton—confuses the Crown's key witness. "Dickens loves his doppelgängers. I could talk forever about the character of Carton: The picture of loneliness and self-loathing. All passion misspent in drinking and sarcasm. Hates himself. Shrewd as heck."

"By now Darnay is in love with Lucie, the angel"—Lu's head whipped about in Charlotte's direction again—"and in the courtroom Carton, too, falls for her charms. He's such a dog, though—he'll work his way into the Manette household under the guise of friendship." She stopped and gave a mischievous grin. "Justice Nash would be perfect for the role—*if* men were allowed."

Louisa summed up the rest of the scenes to dramatize, culminating in her favorite ending in all of literature: to save his family's servant, Darnay returns to a France roiled by revolution and is promptly arrested and sentenced to the guillotine; Carton, ennobled by his love for Lucie, uses his resemblance to Darnay to ascend the scaffold in his place.

It was when Louisa May Alcott was overheard by the Nelson brothers at dinner, claiming the pivotal roles of both Charles Darnay and Sydney Carton for herself, that the men on board revolted.

Justice Nash was deputized by the male passengers to raise the matter with Miss Alcott, one of the few women braving the storm-tossed deck. She claimed to have been a deer or horse in an earlier life, so greatly did she need to—as she called it—*trot it out*, and took her morning constitutional with the sunrise no matter the weather. She was inspired by the example of her hero, Charles Dickens, who was known to walk ten, even twenty, miles a day. Seven turns about the ship approximated a mile, during which distance Louisa would inevitably run into Justice Thomas Nash completing the same. It had become a daily ritual between them, and they often found themselves the only passengers on deck as the *China* pitched and rolled with the wind.

"Soon we'll be working on the courtroom scene at the Old Bailey—*your* milieu," she told Nash on the fourth morning of the voyage as they discussed the progress of the play. "Charlotte is to play the lovely Miss Manette."

"Of course." He could feel her watching him as they braced against the wind, heads down.

"And I'm playing both Sydney Carton and Charles Darnay, our two doppelgängers."

"Miss Alcott—"

"I prefer Lu, as you know."

"Yes, of course—Lu—but should you be keeping out all the men?"

She began to swing around a nearby post while calling out, "I shall, and I will!"

"But we're starved for activity."

"What's good for the goose . . ."

She smiled at him as she swung back around the post, a wide, lopsided smile that was not remotely coquettish. Nash wondered if Lu possessed any feminine wiles at all. He enjoyed her company and they shared much in common: a love of Dickens, travel, and nature and—if he read her correctly—a tendency toward self-reproof. No one, he was sure, was harder on either of them than themselves. But it was a bond born of likeness, and Nash, with his pride of intellect, was always most intrigued by what he did not understand.

"You could put on your own amusement," she challenged him.

He laughed. "We seem to lack someone with your talent for direction."

"Or perhaps you possess too many. We women, on the other hand, are well acquainted with being on the sideline. This is our only chance to play at lawyers and doctors, villains and cads. You will not deprive us!"

They were strolling together on the inside of the deck, just beyond the ocean spray. He thought of offering his arm, but Louisa boisterously swung hers whenever she walked, making it impossible to get close. "You would be a doctor or lawyer, then, if you could?"

"Oh no, not me. *I* would be an actress."

Nash often noted this swagger with Louisa. She would play all the men's roles—she would write an important novel just like Harriet Beecher Stowe—she would be the first woman one day to cast a vote.

"I speak for the men on board in asking you please to reconsider. The Nelson brothers are particular fans of Dickens's book."

"And of the Stevenson sisters. The *angel*."

Nash turned to her in surprise.

"Don't look so caught out—the table placement at dinner is excellent for eavesdropping."

Nash inwardly sighed at the female sex's proclivity for both talking and listening at the same time, all appearances to the contrary. He would have to warn Nicholas and Haslett to be more discreet at dinner, when he saw them next.

O n the fifth day at sea, when the *China* reached the midpoint of the Atlantic, the winds ceased and rehearsals for the upcoming charity performance could finally begin. The women cleared a corner of the ladies' saloon farthest from the porthole windows, a shadowy space perfect for running on and offstage and lit by a swinging kerosene lamp. White bedsheets hung from a piece of braided rope, framing the area where two women now stood in costume: Charlotte in a dress of light-colored chintz as the fair and angelic Lucie Manette, and Louisa in her own coat and pipe as Sydney Carton, the self-loathing barrister and Manette family friend. They read in turn from the script that Louisa had copied out:

Carton: *I know very well that you can have no tenderness for me—I ask for none—I am even thankful that it cannot be, for I would surely bring you to misery.*

Lucie: *Can I not save you, Mr. Carton—can I not recall you to a better course?*

Carton: *No, Miss Manette—but if you will hear me through a very little more, all you can ever do for me is done. You have been the last dream of my soul. I*

*wish you to know with what sudden mastery you kindled me, heap of ashes that
I am, into fire . . .*

When Louisa and Charlotte finished the scene, there was not a dry eye
in the ladies' saloon.

"'*The last dream of my soul*,'" repeated Louisa, looking triumphantly at the
others. "Find me *that* in Austen, I say."

From her stool facing the makeshift stage, Henrietta immediately
quoted back, "'*You pierce my soul.*'" There was more sighing around the room.

"Captain Wentworth's letter in *Persuasion*," Charlotte explained from the
stage. "After all, isn't everything really about love?"

"Or, at least, knee-buckling desire." Lu flopped down into a nearby
armchair and wiped her brow. "Where's Sara-Beth?"

"Beating the men at cards. She says they ask her no end of questions
about the play."

"Nash pesters me, too, on our walks," Lu replied. "Okay, next up, the
Old Bailey. I'll be the prisoner in the box, Charles Darnay, and Henrietta
can be the Chief Lord Justice, what with law running in the family and all."

"Harry would make a perfect lawyer," boasted Charlotte. "She's aces
at rhetoric. Outtalked the Harvard men when we audited Nash's lecture
there." The two sisters grinned at each other in memory before recalling
their dilemma with Nash on board.

Louisa put down her script. "He says you won't address him."

"We never see him," protested Charlotte. "He even chooses to dine
later."

A hesitant knock sounded on the saloon door, and Louisa marched over
to answer it. A young officer stood nervously on the other side, a pile of
London papers in his hands. That morning, the *China* had passed the RMS
Neptune, a mail steamer halfway from Liverpool to New York, and been momentarily halted while some hardy crew in a rowboat brought over the latest
newspapers and telegrams from England.

"These are just come from the *Neptune*, miss," the officer mumbled in
announcement. "We met 'n the middle."

Louisa urged him for any news of the rail disaster at Staplehurst and
was passed a copy of *The Kentish Mercury*. As the other women circled round
her, Lu read aloud the horrific details: the passengers who had escaped without injury only to be smothered to death in the riverbed mud, the inquest

which learned that the workers on the bridge had not been within reach of telegraphic communication. One eyewitness told a reporter how Mr. Charles Dickens had run hither and thither in his hat, trying to help every "poor creature" he met; another claimed Dickens had saved him from imminent death by suffocation.

Reaching the end of the account, Louisa stood up on a chair and impulsively declared, "We should dedicate our charity performance to Charles Dickens, the hero of Staplehurst, and our proceeds to its victims!"

"Lu"—Henrietta gave a quick look at Charlotte before continuing, none of the women having been eager to raise the matter before now—"might we not sell more tickets if we let the men join the play?"

Louisa whirled about to face her. "What—so they can make love to us onstage, the cowards?"

This was the Louisa that both Henrietta and Charlotte were beginning to know. She wanted to be in charge of everything and had little patience for the foibles of men. But she also had the biggest heart, which the other women sensed would always take precedence if played upon the right way. Eventually Lu gave in to their pleas at the prospect of more donations.

"Fine." The rolled newspaper was waved like a gauntlet in the air. "But they better behave, is all I'll say."

NINE

Sense and Sensibility

The Massachusetts Supreme Judicial Court
June 20, 1865

With William Stevenson in need of distraction and Thomas Nash suddenly gone, the other five justices agreed to expedite their monthly literary circle. When asked to select the book, William, not surprisingly, chose *Sense and Sensibility*. With its portrayal of two very different sisters, one all head, the other all heart, Austen's first published novel had always deeply moved him.

"The plot commences with the loss of a beloved parent," he opened that evening's discussion, voicing his usual preoccupation with death. "The oldest son now inherits the entirety of his father's estate under the British law of primogeniture, leaving the Dashwood women rudderless, homeless, vulnerable."

Justice Conor Langstaff was first to respond. He had missed the group's last two meetings to assist at home with the arrival of twin daughters; when it came to women's rights, he was also the most liberal-minded on the court. "The legal principle of primogeniture is rooted in monarchy—the less divided up the land, the less people who own it, the less threat there is to a king. But that is of no concern in our democracy. Look at our state's recent legislation on married women's property rights: if anyone should be allowed to retain their earnings, make a will and likewise inherit—and keep all of that safe from another—surely it should be women."

"Hear, hear." To everyone's surprise, Justice Philip Mackenzie banged his unlit pipe against the Philadelphia edition of *Sense and Sensibility* in his lap. One never knew where Mackenzie would land on an issue of law, but his antipathy toward their former colonizer often held the greatest sway. "I am reminded of Lord Hardwicke's Act for the Better Preventing of Clandestine Marriage, which was largely motivated by fear of stolen fortune when young lovers run off together. Again, a sheer matter of property and intrusion by the state."

"That legislation also gave the Church of England the right to perform all marriages in the land," Justice Langstaff reminded the others. "Fortunately, this was undone by England's subsequent marriage act of 1823. No nation can ignore the plurality of faiths today—even sea captains can conduct the ceremony."

"Careful, Langstaff, don't add to poor William's concerns over his girls!" Justice Mackenzie warned with a laugh, causing Stevenson to redden from recognition. "Besides, there is some judicial argument against the legitimacy of marriages at sea."

"What I find interesting about the *book*," boomed Justice Roderick Norton, emphasizing this last word in an effort to redirect course, "are the number of uninterrupted, highly rhetorical speeches it contains. Pages and pages of sanctimonious drivel—when I'd be happy to never know the workings of a mind like Willoughby's."

"I think Austen wrote the earliest drafts as a series of letters sent back and forth amongst the characters." At these words, the other men turned to face Justice Langstaff in both surprise and appreciation. They were each expert at locating the one most salient and significant fact in a sea of information. Langstaff could do something more, however: he could make an imaginative leap.

"I call your attention to chapter fifteen as evidence." Langstaff flipped through the book to the scene where Mrs. Dashwood defends not pressing her middle daughter, Marianne, on the nature of her relationship with John Willoughby, an increasingly suspect young man. "The mother's responses to her eldest daughter Elinor's worries demonstrate the uninterrupted musings of someone with a captive audience and weak mind. In real conversation, she would never be allowed to proceed so far, and without interruption, by someone as rational as Elinor."

"I posit, then, that this is Austen's law novel," Chief Justice Adam Fulbright declared, holding up his worn copy of *Sense and Sensibility*.

"How so?" asked Justice Ezekiel Peabody, always intrigued by anything to do with their profession.

"It's about language," the chief justice answered. "How we wield it, suppress it, indulge in it. Marianne relies on language to judge others—the unassuming Edward Ferrars for how poorly he reads poetry, the dastardly Willoughby for how *well*. The mother accepts as truth whatever Marianne is willing to tell her, and whatever Willoughby pleads, regardless of the evidence before her. Language is always at its most powerful when we use it to distort the perceptions of others and anticipate any retort."

Justice Stevenson leaned forward in his seat. "Meanwhile, admirable characters such as Elinor and Colonel Brandon *show* their care and devotion, rather than shout it."

"'*Actions speak louder than words*,'" quoted Ezekiel Peabody, "as the British Parliamentarian John Pym famously said."

The chief justice vigorously nodded. "I'm not sure I trust a man who rallies on so about his own good deeds—or even worse, his lack thereof. I recall that most disturbing scene where Willoughby attempts to visit Marianne on her sick bed. He is not really there to apologize, I think. He is there to argue his case ad nauseam, confident in his right to speak without any checks on him at all. How he excuses to Elinor—rationalizes—demurs! Willoughby's chief aim, surely, is to restore the Dashwood women's good opinion of him—he is using language purely as a tool for power and influence, *not* for understanding."

"That would explain why the scene left such distaste in my mouth." Justice Mackenzie made a sour face. "I wanted a good rinse after."

The other men all laughed.

"And yet..." Everyone turned to face Justice Langstaff again. "Austen indulges, too, in that scene. She gives Willoughby a large forum, far larger than necessary. I wonder if she included the reader in that arena—wanted us also to feel something for him, in the way that Elinor begrudgingly, but eventually, does. He is surely despicable based on the facts of his behavior, and no amount of affection to or from Marianne should change that. And yet."

The room fell silent at this thought, a most disturbing one, that even Jane Austen, once in a while, lost control of her court.

After *Sense and Sensibility* had been discussed to the full satisfaction of the bench, the six justices departed the courthouse for home. Each had a carriage and driver waiting for them except for William Stevenson, who had taken to spending his evenings walking the city streets alone. Samuel and Mrs. Pearson, meanwhile, had taken to waiting up for him out of concern.

William was starting off in the direction of Beacon Hill when a female hand, gloved in black silk and adorned by a large diamond ring, waved to him from a passing brougham.

"Justice Stevenson!" Constance Davenish tapped the roof of her carriage for the driver to stop. "Thank you, Charles—Justice Stevenson?"

William crossed the street toward Constance. "Miss Davenish, have you had a pleasant evening?"

"Yes, most productive—do join me and we can discuss. The Anti-Slavery Society held a celebration of the goings-on in Galveston yesterday, with the last enslaved people finally learning from General Granger that they are free, thank goodness. June nineteenth—now a most important date."

"The official end to such a stain upon this nation."

"If oppression ever truly ends, once it starts." She swung open the carriage door to reveal an interior luxuriously lined from top to bottom with maroon-colored damask silk. William hesitated slightly before climbing in to sit on the foldaway seat opposite her. As the midnight-black mares resumed their clop, Constance began discussing an upcoming women's rights convention while Stevenson's thoughts strayed in a very different direction. Not since the passing of his wife had he been in such a confined space with a woman who was not a relation.

"Justice Stevenson, do I bore you?" Constance pertly asked. "Why don't you tell me about your evening—the court is in recess, is it not?"

"Tonight was our reading circle."

"Ah yes, the discussions on Austen—the girls told me. I wish I could join, but then I would have to read her." Her ice-blue eyes flashed merrily in the light of the coach lamp. "We ladies do keep our own reading groups to ourselves, so at least there is parity between the sexes when it comes to that."

"Miss Davenish, where were you educated?" William had always wanted to ask this of her; she spoke as eloquently and logically as anyone on the bench.

"At my father's knee. Given the impoverished state of women's education earlier in the century—not that our situation today is much improved—I believe that as good a place as any." She slowly pulled away the glove from her left hand, fiddled with the ring, placed it back on her bare index finger. The diamond had all the semblance of an engagement stone: flashy and declarative. William wondered if Constance's unmarried state extended to buying her own jewelry, or if the ring had been a gift from an unknown admirer. There had long been rumors of a clandestine love affair with a lawyer from the South by the name of Graydon Saunders, whom William had yet to meet in court. "William, we talk around what clearly pains you."

He turned away to stare out the window. "Did you know they would leave me?"

"If I had, I would not have said so. It is not my place." Constance hesitated. "It's no longer yours, either."

"What can you mean?" he asked, turning back to her in surprise.

"Your girls are more than fully grown, William—Henrietta yearns for a family of her own." She eyed him carefully. "You do know that no one is worried about the two of them? Yet Charles tells me poor Samuel is at the tavern most nights, drinking over what he did to *you* in taking them to the wharf."

"They're all I have." His face dissembled as he next said aloud what he rarely did. "Alice wanted many children—wanted to give me a son. After Charlotte's delivery, the doctor advised against it. But she persisted."

"I am so sorry, William—how tragic."

"So, you see, they really are my everything."

Constance surprised him with her reply. "It is indeed the saddest loss, from which one would never fully recover. But—and please bear with me, William, as this will sound far harsher than I intend—we are not talking about your choices as a parent, *your* everything. Surely you can see that Henrietta and Charlotte amount to far more than that. I have not had children myself, but I should think parental love was about *their* happiness, not yours. Frankly, I should think that the entire point of bringing them into the world."

William could only stare at her with incomprehension; few outside of court dared speak to him like this. He could almost feel his learned brain both ache and expand in a very new and different direction.

"I mean *love*, William. Should it not ensure liberty, above all else? If we cannot expect it from those closest to us, how can we demand it of our government?"

The notion that love should look different from how he experienced it was entirely foreign to William Stevenson. He had always regarded it as an extension of his rights as the paterfamilias. But that concept did come from ancient Roman times, he reminded himself, when servitude had been the state of many people—even lawyers like him. America, on the other hand, had just rejected slavery, and William's head began to throb at the possibility of further redress ahead when it came to the female populace of the country.

"William, your happiness cannot truly be so, if built on the suffering of your daughters—it is tainted and weakened by their pain. It is a mirage. It is—I'm afraid—exactly why you sit here alone before me, feeling as you do, the opposite of what you intended."

"*'We do not suffer by accident,'*" he quoted.

"Austen, I presume?"

He nodded. "Elizabeth Bennet."

"Ah yes—of course. I do wonder if your suffering today is not the result of trying to twist such forces in your own favor. The harder you twist, the more fragile and vulnerable it all becomes, until it breaks—until it runs away."

"You once mentioned wanting to be a lawyer, Miss Davenish, but I see a philosopher in you."

"They are not the same?"

He laughed. "Men of law apply what already exists—precedent, statute, a formal constitution. We are entirely rule-bound, I am afraid, no matter our guiding principles."

"I have never been one for rules. Neither are Henrietta and Charlotte—where do they get that from, do you think?"

William looked out the window again—all the talk of his late wife was making him feel strangely disloyal—and saw to his surprise that he was already home. The rules of etiquette demanded he wait for his dismissal, yet Constance sat waiting for his answer instead, the silver streak in her hair caught by the gas-lamp glow, the brilliance of the diamond restored to the outside of her glove. There was an air of watchful expectation about her, and William found himself about to say something in response: it was on the tip of his tongue, not yet formulated but almost there. He could feel his heart beating with its new irregular rhythm, as if responding to every peak and valley of every moment in his life. His body, it seemed, was being ruled by his broken heart.

"Sir?"

From the window of the carriage, William made out the stooped figure of Samuel standing on the darkened pavement below, waiting to help him down. Out of the corner of his eye, he saw the curtains flutter in the lit front parlor as well—Mrs. Pearson. His heart straightened itself out in that moment. William's family had abandoned him and reconfigured itself in one fell swoop. What was keeping him from also playing a part in that?

His own voice emerged from the darkness, surprising him. "Miss Davenish—"

"Connie."

"—Connie, I know the hour is late, but would you like—"

"William, I would *love* to."

TEN

✳

The Audition

◆—◆—◆

SIXTH DAY AT SEA
June 21, 1865

Several men showed up in the ladies' saloon to audition for the role of Charles Darnay opposite Charlotte Stevenson as Lucie Manette. This was no surprise to the play's suspicious director, and a potential casting decision that she vowed to repeal if the men onstage failed to behave. Louisa May Alcott, on board ship at least, was proving to be the most effective chaperone of all.

Haslett Nelson had played many roles while at the Jesuit all-boys school St. Joe's Prep, often cast as the comeliest female characters with his slender hips and longish hair, yet he was the last man left in the room to audition. Finally, Louisa called out his name with a resigned air.

Charlotte began the scene by taking his hands in hers according to Lu's script. In an instant, Haz no longer saw her as the angel at the table behind him during meal seatings, or the play as a chance to move closer. Instead, she was Lucie Manette, supplicating her new husband, Charles Darnay, to be kinder to family friend Sydney Carton—the wrinkle being her kindest of character's knowledge of Carton's undying affection for her.

Lucie: *My husband, there is scarcely a hope that Sydney's character or fortunes are reparable now. But I am sure he is capable of good things, gentle things, even magnanimous.*

(Clings to Darnay, laying her head upon his breast, then raises her eyes to his.)

"Now I'll put my head down, like so," Charlotte gamely whispered to him.

Having only ever performed in all-male school productions, Haz was shocked to discover that his heart did not race as "the angel" clung to him, head against his breast. He was not thinking with his own head or heart, but rather his stomach, that center of intuition that had saved him from a stray Confederate bullet in the nick of time. Haz had excelled at school sports for the same reason: He saw things just before they happened. He knew where things were heading right after they flew.

Haz also knew that, for all Louisa did not want him to win the role, she did want more from this scene than mere newlywed bliss. The other men auditioning had simply grabbed Charlotte in their arms and proclaimed their love. But through gesture, tone, and placement, Haz was determined to bring out more: Darnay's intentional blindness to whatever shapeless bond existed between Carton and his wife, along with his natural aristocratic confidence that all was right with his world—the very notion that Dickens in the book was about to entirely upend.

Lucie: *Dearest heart, remember how strong we are in our happiness, and how weak he is in his misery.*

Darnay: *I will always remember it, dear heart—I will remember it for as long as I live.*

Charlotte communicated to Haz throughout the scene with gestures of her own: a slight nod of the head to one side, the raising of a palm, and always with her eyes—an actor's greatest weapon. Haz could tell that she wanted him to succeed, which made him want to work even harder in return. They seemed united in their intuitive approach to acting, their similar choices, their shared ideas for improving the production. What was that Latin phrase, ad idem—a meeting of the minds? It certainly wasn't physical attraction. It was a creative union so instant that it bypassed the signs of attraction altogether. It didn't need the allure of sex to exist—and this rendered the moment entirely sexless. The bachelor bookseller didn't know it yet, but he was about to make his first female friend.

Fortunately, not even Miss Alcott could deny the attractiveness of Haz to everyone else in the women-only room. Lu might fiercely protect her actors, wanting them all to shine, but she also wanted to raise as much money as possible for the victims of the Staplehurst rail disaster. Once auditions were complete, Alcott proclaimed Haslett Nelson in the role of the heroic, fallen French aristocrat Charles Darnay.

Rehearsals were moved from the ladies-only saloon to the dining hall, where a new stage was eagerly assembled by two of the crew at Charlotte Stevenson's request. This wooden platform pitched one step above the floor of curved oak planks, just low enough that stacked tables and chairs could easily be restored there in time for meal seatings, but high enough that more than a few actors would come close to tripping off the stage while caught up in performing.

When Charlotte and Haslett resumed rehearsing together on the makeshift stage, the entire room quieted down. There was something undeniably electric about unattached and handsome young people being permitted to stand close, to embrace, even—should their director permit it—to feign a kiss. All this at a time when the half-inch sight of a woman's naked wrist above her glove could drive a man to distraction.

Louisa ascended the stage alongside Charlotte and Haz to position them like dolls, playing with the blond ringlets that framed Charlie's exquisite face, firmly guiding Haz's hips closer to hers. In fact, Lu ruled over the entire production with a confidence born of dozens of home theatrical productions and an enthusiasm that was zealous almost to a fault.

"By Jupiter, you two make a handsome pair," Louisa proclaimed, proud of her skill at casting, which extended to her own. She had given herself the roles of both Miss Pross, Lucie Manette's governess from childhood—as devoted to her charge as Shakespeare's nurse in *Romeo and Juliet*—and Madame Defarge, the wily and willful French revolutionary who knits the names of traitors in a scarf while watching their heads roll from the guillotine. Until the right man—*if* the right man—could be found, Lu Alcott continued to play Sydney Carton as well. Such was her intensity onstage, Haz looked as disconcerted by their scene together as he had been inspired by his and Charlotte's:

Carton: *Do you remember a certain famous occasion when I was more drunk than usual?*

Darnay: *I remember a certain famous occasion when you forced* me *to confess that you were.*

Carton: *Well, at any rate, you know me as a dissolute dog, who has never done any good and never will. Still, if you could endure to have this worthless fellow come and go in your fine home, as useless and unornamental as a piece of furniture . . .*

Lu broke character to announce to the room, "Sydney Carton, that sly dog indeed—he's asking to be allowed to still sit and visit with Lucie, now that she's Darnay's wife. How rich!"

Near the dining hall entrance, as far from the stage as possible, Justice Thomas Nash observed the theatrics with a detached air. He had no inclination to perform; his current roles—lawyer, chaperone, persona non grata—were plenty enough for him. For six days at sea, he had been avoiding the Stevenson sisters, hoping that the ladies' saloon would keep them fully occupied by their own sex. As he now watched Charlotte intimately rehearsing with Haz, Nash could only wonder at what William Stevenson would say about his trusted substitute's capabilities.

Nash slunk out of the dining room and ascended the narrow stairs to the main deck. He filled his pipe with tobacco from a passing steward before beginning his seven circuits of the ship. Walking at a slower pace than usual, Nash ruminated over the other unique role he had inadvertently found himself in—protector in absentia. He had almost completed his prescribed one mile when, rounding the corner to starboard, he came face-to-face at last with one of his self-appointed charges.

"You're a poor excuse for a chaperone!" Charlotte immediately burst out. "Six days on ship and we haven't had a word from you yet."

Nash had to laugh. As his eyes met hers, he could feel the iciness of those last weeks in Boston finally begin to melt away. Nash had always appreciated how Charlotte, the mercurial one in the Stevenson family, was also very quick to forget a slight. She moved forward in life, never back, just like

Lu, and the propulsive energy of the ship and all its doings appeared to suit her own. With her lips and cheeks brightened by the ocean wind, Charlotte Stevenson had never looked lovelier.

"I'm to exercise the lungs. Director's orders."

Nash turned about and fell in step next to her. "How are rehearsals?"

"Lu's reining in the men." Charlotte tightened the ribbon on her straw bonnet against the mid-Atlantic wind.

"I saw the Nelsons had joined."

"Are you angling to do so as well?"

"My days of amateur theatrics are well behind me."

"That's a shame. Lu thinks you would make a capital Sydney Carton."

"What do you think?"

She stopped walking to look him up and down, pretending to assess him for the first time. "Well, you certainly possess his sacrificial nature, coming on ship as you did."

He chose not to answer her—wasn't even sure how to. Noticing the latest instalment of *Our Mutual Friend* peeking from her reticule, he asked instead, "Will you try to see Dickens perform in London while you are—"

"Justice Nash, let's speak truthfully." Only Charlotte ever interrupted him like this, as if determined to take him to account. "What exactly did you promise my father in coming?"

"There wasn't time. As you can imagine, William was in a most panicked state—I jumped on board without thinking. I knew I could."

"Yes, you are lucky enough for that. Not like Harry and I." She placed her hand over his extended forearm as they rounded the corner to a blast of wind. "Meanwhile Denham Scott travels at the pleasure of Captain Norris himself."

"Would you and Henrietta like to dine at the captain's table? I'd be pleased to arrange it."

"No, we're a merry group at dinner as we are."

"Miss Alcott is certainly full of high spirits."

"We so enjoy her company." Charlotte paused again. "As she so enjoys yours—on your walks."

Nash fell silent at her hinting tone, which inwardly disturbed him. Accustomed to fielding the overtures of Boston society mothers of unmarried daughters, he was usually adept at recognizing the earliest signs of female interest. Louisa Alcott, however, remained surprisingly difficult to read, for all her cheerfulness and open manners. Hardest to decipher was the pain behind her eyes—dark, impenetrable eyes which drooped sadly at the corners, no matter the width of her smile.

When they had completed a full circuit of the deck, Charlotte released his arm and loosened her bonnet, causing it to fall back from her face. "I must return to rehearsals. But we have made up, you and I?"

"I didn't know we were fighting."

"Didn't you?" she teased, tucking a loose golden strand of hair away from her brow. "No wonder I won, then."

"What did you win?"

"I think that remains to be seen."

She left him standing there in a cross sea, the wind hitting him from two very different directions.

ELEVEN

✵

A Secret History

•———•

SEVENTH DAY AT SEA
June 22, 1865

Henrietta Stevenson, with her delicate Grecian features and gentle manner, had been cast as the seamstress whom Sydney Carton consoles on their way to the guillotine in the final scene of the play. Several men had tried to win the role of Carton, Nicholas Nelson coming closest until Lu deemed him too "soft." Charlotte felt for her sister when journalist Denham Scott nonchalantly strutted into the dining room to read against Henrietta for the much-coveted part.

Carton: *Keep your eyes upon me and mind no other object.*

(Takes both of the seamstress's hands in his.)

Seamstress: *I mind nothing while I hold your hand. I shall mind nothing when I let it go, if it should be rapid.*

Carton: *Our executioners will be rapid—fear not.*

Seamstress: *You comfort me so much. I am so ignorant! Am I to kiss you now? Is the moment of our fate come?*

Carton: *Yes.*

Charlotte sat on a bench at the foot of the stage, watching her sister be pulled in by Denham Scott—something *not* in their director's audition notes. A sudden notion hit Charlotte like a thunderclap as Louisa belted out for the scene to stop: the two people alone onstage had stood like this before.

What on earth? Charlotte asked herself in a panic, jumping up as the room erupted into applause and Louisa was forced to acknowledge that Scott made the best Carton so far ("At least all your *negative* qualities are in alignment with his!" she crowed). But Lu seemed as distressed as Charlotte by the sudden, intimate, and all-too-real display onstage. The search for Carton would continue.

Meanwhile, Henrietta's cheeks were flushed, always a tell-tale sign. She might keep from even Charlotte her innermost thoughts, but the one thing she could never hide was her sense of decorum. As Henrietta quickly left the dining saloon, Charlotte followed closely on her heels.

"Harry—what on earth?" Charlotte ran through the cabin door after her. "How dare Scott grab and surprise you like that? Lu's threatening to banish the men for good!"

Henrietta stood by the dresser, fiddling with the handle of a hairbrush. "I wasn't entirely surprised."

"Honestly, Harry, whatever can you mean?" She took so long to answer that Charlotte went over and grabbed the hairbrush away from her. "Well?"

"Do you remember when we first heard back from Admiral Austen? How surprised we were by that?"

"Yes, and then we wrote him again—*you* wrote—and we invited ourselves here."

"We did, yes, but then—well, do you remember at Constance's salon, when Denham mentioned being recalled to London?" Henrietta began to speak unusually fast. "And the *Admiral DuPont* had just sunk, and the head of Cunard made his VIP offer to the *Herald* and its reporters, and then . . ."

"And then *what?*"

". . . and then Denham managed to get on board in time to join us."

Charlotte stared back at her in confusion. "But why would he do that?"

"I should have spoken sooner. It's all happened so fast." Henrietta reached into the high neckline of her check-patterned day dress and pulled out a garnet ring on a simple chain. Charlotte's first thought was how long Harry had secretly been wearing the necklace, as if her brain could not yet absorb what her sister was trying to tell her.

"What in the world is that?"

"He gave this to me."

"Who—Scott? That's impossible—when?"

"Last night."

"Last night here, on ship?" Charlotte's mouth fell open.

"He loves me." Henrietta suddenly beamed. "And I love him."

"Harry, no! That's absurd!"

"I know Denham comes across as cocky and flippant, but I promise you he is the very picture of industry. He supports his brothers and sisters back home with his earnings, leaving so little for himself. He prizes loyalty to family above all. If he was a character in your beloved Dickens, you would think him a hero."

"But you hardly know him!" Stunned, Charlotte sank onto the lower bunk bed as an image flashed through her head: Henrietta's flushed cheeks in Harvard Yard after Nash's lecture, and again on the steps of the Athenaeum over her broken boot. "Oh, wait—oh—Harry, no! All those walks alone back home, on the Common, and here on board, whilst I nap . . . ?" Henrietta silently nodded. "But why such secrecy from me, your own sister?"

"I couldn't bear to add to your worries over leaving Father. And I had to be certain, before I did."

"Yet you are somehow certain now—here, in the middle of the Atlantic? I suppose you'll tell me next how Scott has swept you away. . . ."

"Denham is indeed more romantic than me—he doesn't want to waste a moment."

"A moment? To do what?" stammered Charlotte.

"To marry. To start our family life together."

"But why such a rush?" She watched in horror as Henrietta blushed, and then Charlotte's own cheeks reddened as the unusual nature of their surroundings dawned on her. "Henrietta Alice Stevenson, do *not* tell me you're planning to wed on ship! Oh my God, you are, aren't you!"

"One day you will understand, Charlie, I promise you. I wish it could be now—I am so sorry for the shock of it."

"And then what—you're to live in England?" Henrietta nodded, and Charlotte crossed her arms against the news as if about to throw a childish fit. "I won't be a party to this, I won't. Father would never forgive me for not stopping you."

"Charlie, if you had an offer to go on the London stage, you would leave Boston in a heartbeat and you know it."

Charlotte started at these words; she was not used to such presumption in her sister. "No, I do not know it! Harry, what has happened to you—really? And you will be so poor!"

"I have no doubt that Denham will continue to rise at the paper. He never gives up when he wants something."

"That something, at present, being you, I take it? You and *not* our money, or Father's station in society—you're so sure of that?"

"Charlotte!"

"How often he mentions having to make his way!" she defiantly exclaimed.

"He is *self-made*—just like Nash. It's a fine quality in a man, wouldn't you say?" She sat down on the bunk bed next to Charlotte, who immediately burst into tears. Harry was everything to her—missing mother, wise sister, compassionate friend—and the mere idea of her absence was intolerable.

"Oh, Harry, I know I sound a brat." Charlotte wiped her eyes on her gingham sleeve. "It's just so much to take in...." Henrietta pulled her close and kissed the top of her head like their mother used to do, although Charlotte had no memory of that herself. "...and poor Father," she added through her tears. Harry's calm and attentive presence at home had always sustained William Stevenson—Charlotte could not imagine returning alone to Boston to face him.

"I wish there was something I could do or say, anything to help you understand."

Charlotte sat up straight and grabbed Henrietta's hands in hers. "We sailed together for a reason—can you not wait to marry?" she pleaded, with as much fire in her eyes as when onstage. "Can you not wait before you desert me for good?"

Henrietta sighed from experience and squeezed her sister's hand in hers. Charlotte had always been impossible to say no to.

Eventually Charlotte curled up childlike in the bottom bunk, exhausted from all the emotion of the day, and fell asleep. Henrietta tucked the blanket about her before quietly leaving the cabin. She and Denham often met by the iron stairs leading to the wheelhouse and this was where she now found him, standing with his profile to sea, balancing a notebook against the deck railing as he scribbled. She watched him for a few seconds before speaking—he always looked so happy when at work.

"I'm afraid you were too convincing in your audition for Charlotte." She saw Denham's face break out in a smile at her words as he tucked the notebook away and turned to face her. They hadn't had a moment alone together since becoming engaged the previous night, and Henrietta had been both shocked and strangely thrilled when he had presented himself to her onstage. "You should have told me you would show up like that."

"An irresistible impulse of mine." Denham grinned. "You know them well by now. So, I take it from your expression that you told her? I am glad. Was it difficult? You said she can be volatile."

"No, I said she's very free in her manners. One always knows where one stands with her."

"And where do the two of us stand?" He held out his hand and Henrietta came over to take it. Minutes passed as they stood there quietly, hands clasped together on the railing, watching the roiling water below until a troubled Henrietta was first to speak.

"You can't see anything, down there, the deeper and murkier it gets. Think of all that's hidden—sea creatures, Plato's lost island of Atlantis, icebergs . . . a whole other world. Like the world of this ship."

"Not icebergs," corrected Denham. "We always get the tip of a warning there."

She sighed from regret. "I should have warned Charlie."

"We ran out of time. Too many ships leaving or sinking . . ." He turned to gently kiss her brow. "How do we fix things for you?"

"She wants us to wait to marry—to complete the journey she and I set out on together, at such pain to our father, and meet with the admiral."

"Loyalty is one of your finest qualities, my darling—along with a surprising mastery of British naval history!" She loved how he always spoke so admiringly of her, even when he teased. "But I am determined to step foot on British soil with you as my wife."

Henrietta regretted never having developed any feminine wiles, for all she could do was ask him again to wait. But he shook his head, then tilted it toward her in that wonderful way of his, so full of anticipation and direction. "My love, I didn't get where I am by giving in so easily. . . ."

Her breath caught in her throat as the warmth of his lips met hers. It only now broke through Henrietta's consciousness how much of love was about touch—and how destabilizing. All she wanted was to be with him, and this desire washed away everything else like the sea. The world was now surface landscape, mere background to her want and need: *he* was its gravitational pull, its chemical center. In their few moments of intimacy together, she had never felt less alone—or more at home with herself. This must be the true power of love: the willingness to leave one's world behind for a place that had been hiding deep inside you all along, another lost island. She was stunned to realize she didn't mind the prospect—she, whom Charlotte had often had quite the job of getting out of doors to *do* things.

She finally pulled back as she recalled her promise to Charlotte. "Can we not compromise?"

"When it comes to love?" He smiled. "Never!"

"No, I mean, what if we still marry on ship, but you head back to the paper as required, and Charlotte and I stay on in Portsmouth as planned?"

"But only long enough to visit with the admiral, you promise? And you and I would reunite in London immediately afterward?" He narrowed his eyes in playful resignation. "I suppose it would give me time to find a proper home for my bride."

She put both her hands on his shoulders and bowed her head against his chest, just as she had watched Charlotte do onstage as Lucie Manette. Henrietta's lack of a mother's guidance did nothing to steady her at times like this. "How do you feel about that prospect?"

"I feel I will regret it, letting go of you so easily."

"I promise I will make it up to you the moment we reunite."

"Why, Miss Stevenson, is that the first hint of flirtation from you, only now that my affection is secure?"

"I've done much of this backward," she admitted, looking up at him with a smile.

"Just so long as you catch me up in the end," he replied, giving her nose a little tap in teasing reprimand.

TWELVE

Wandelprobe

EIGHTH DAY AT SEA
June 23, 1865

Only two days were left until the much-anticipated charity performance to be held the final night at sea. Louisa May Alcott remained in the role of Sydney Carton for now, having rejected every one of the men who had bravely shown up to audition for the role.

"I adore Lu," Sara-Beth whispered to Charlotte as they watched Louisa and Haz in rehearsal, "but does she really make the best Sydney of them all?"

Up onstage, Lu suddenly broke from that character and threw down her script.

"It's all wrong!" she declared to the room, then glared at Haslett. "If only you could play both Darnay and Carton, doppelgängers as they are. We need someone else. . . ."

From the middle of the platform, Louisa slowly rotated her head like a hawk. Everyone fell quiet, watching with increasing consternation, until Lu at last settled her penetrating gaze on Justice Thomas Nash. He had stayed behind after luncheon, most of the other men having decamped to the smoking lounge for cards.

"I don't act," Nash offered in his defense. He was used to Miss Alcott's meaningful looks by now.

"Oh, jiminy *cricket*, of course you do!" exclaimed Lu. "I've been in a courtroom—it's all theatrics if you ask me. You judges are the worst of the lot."

"Louisa!" Henrietta hushed her from offstage, but Lu persisted.

"It's for charity!" she called out again, picking her script back up and knocking off the dust. Nash looked warily about the dining room at Louisa and all the other women staring back at him.

"I really don't think . . ."

Louisa gave him another look. It was more than a dare, although it was certainly also that. It was a look that seemed to say, *I know what you are about—I know what you are afraid of.* He worried he was being manipulated into a dangerous situation, but at that fraught moment, resisting Louisa felt most dangerous of all.

"I suppose I could give it a try."

Charlotte and Henrietta glanced at each other in surprise, while Lu threw her script into the air in victory.

It was fortunate for the production that Nash had developed a proficient memory from his years on the bench, because the next day's final re-hearsal would be without any script in hand. After brisk walks on deck at dawn to expand their lungs, the players returned to the dining saloon, scripts were closed, and breakfast tables made way for the makeshift stage.

With Nash agreeing to the part of dissolute London barrister Sydney Carton, casting of the male roles was finally complete. Haslett Nelson was to play Tellson's Bank manager Jarvis Lorry, family friend of the Manettes, in addition to heroic Charles Darnay. Older brother Nicholas Nelson, with his "soft" manner, had been acclaimed by Louisa as docile Dr. Alexandre Manette, who, through the love and care of his daughter, Lucie, slowly returns to life after eighteen years imprisoned in the Bastille. Finally, Denham Scott was cast as the villains: Monsieur Defarge, a revolutionary marginally less bloodthirsty than his wife, and Darnay's uncle, the nefarious Marquis St. Evrémonde.

Haslett Nelson had yet to fully memorize his lines like the others, but his onstage ease and charisma made up for that fact. Nash, on the other hand, was a model of self-restraint, especially in his love scenes with Charlotte (*"I think Lu might have done a better job after all!"* Sara-Beth later said to her with a wicked laugh). *Wooden* was the word that kept coming to everyone's mind. But Justice Thomas Nash cut a dashing romantic figure, to be sure, and ticket sales would at least be improved by that.

Throughout the script-free audition, Lu dashed about with frantic energy. Whenever someone forgot a line, she would wave her pipe in the air and correct them, Haslett Nelson loudest of all. But the entire room was surprised by who forgot their lines next.

Carton: *No, Miss Manette—but if you will hear me through a very little more, all you can ever do for me is done. You have been the last dream of my soul. I wish you to know with what sudden mastery you kindled me, heap of ashes that I am, into fire—a fire, however, inseparable in its nature from myself, quickening nothing, lighting nothing, doing no service, idly burning away.*

Lucie: *It is surely my misfortune, Mr. Carton, to make you—to have made you more unhappy than before—than you were before—*

"Stop!" cried Louisa.

Nash as Carton stood with his left hand on the small table being used as a desk, shielding his eyes from Charlotte as Lucie with his right. He finally looked up to face not the woman whom his character secretly loved, but the real woman whose wrath had been invoked.

"Dash it, Charlie!" exclaimed Louisa. "You've said that line perfectly at least twenty times before—and your expression! Lucie is concerned—even contrite—but by no means confused about her feelings for Carton. Why, the entire plot hinges on that!" Louisa angrily tossed her head in Nash's direction and scoffed, "As if that sly dog stood any chance at love!"

She turned to fully face him next. "And *you*—Dickens's text says Carton approaches Lucie with 'a fixed despair of himself which made the interview unlike any other'—and you're keeping ten strides from her at least!"

Louisa plopped down in frustration on the edge of the stage just as a very imposing man unexpectedly wandered in. He wore a manicured moustache that curled up at the ends and carried a gold-mounted walking stick. Louisa removed the pipe from her mouth. "Yes—are you wanting something?"

The man narrowed his eyes at her in amusement, then tipped his black silk top hat. "Richard Fawcett Robinson," he proclaimed. "The New Adelphi. I've produced many a Dickens adaptation and understand today is your *wandelprobe.*" Lu's frown of confusion was missed by no one in the room. "What we in the theater call a true first rehearsal, hmm? *Sans* script? I heard of it earlier from Miss Gleason in the smoking lounge—we made a little wager on my attendance." He gave a small nod in Sara-Beth's direction and shrugged, as if to indicate he had lost the bet.

The theater impresario took a seat in the dining chair closest to the stage and held the cane between his knees with an air of expectation. Louisa waved Nash off the elevated platform, hiding none of her disappointment in his performance, and motioned Haz forward instead. "Let's return to the scene between Lucie and Darnay in book two. *A Plea.*"

Haz bounced up onto the stage and immediately started reciting his lines: "*We are thoughtful tonight. . . .*" He comfortably drew Charlotte to him with an encouraging smile, and she responded by placing her hands gently against him. Then, in a moment of improvisation, she tapped his chest several times as if to telegraph Lucie's understanding of her womanly power (the very power Lucie unconsciously holds over Carton as well, but would never consciously admit to possessing).

Lucie: *Will you promise not to press one question on me, if I beg you not to ask it?*

Darnay: *Will I promise? What will I not promise to my love?*

(Caresses a lock of golden hair from her cheek.)

"Imagine if you lost her to the stage." Sara-Beth Gleason stood behind Nash, twirling her closed parasol.

"Pardon me?"

"As chaperone. *Imagine.* Coming back to Boston with nothing—or no one—to show for it." Nash felt his back stiffen. The Nelson brothers had clearly not been exaggerating when they had warned him about Miss Gleason. "Charlie's wonderfully talented, don't you think?"

"Yes, very much so."

"And fully aware of her physical prowess onstage." Miss Gleason tilted her head at him. "You, less so—although I suspect you possess greater talent at pretending than you let on."

Nash knew he was no actor, courtroom theatrics or not, but Miss Gleason still hit her mark. How unconvincing he must appear to everyone, as both Sydney Carton and reluctant chaperone. Turning back to watch Charlotte and Haz, Nash felt another bothersome surge of envy, followed by a sudden, panicked thought: *What if he had been chaperoning himself most of all?* He recalled the famous play in *Mansfield Park* and all the trouble it had led to in the plot—the intimacy of acting combined with the communal nature of performing, the thrill of affecting others and the chance to feign at being someone else. What intoxicating enticement for people wishing to escape themselves—or grow closer to another.

Fawcett Robinson also watched the young couple rehearsing, his face giving nothing away, while an overly eager Louisa stood nearby mouthing every word alongside her actors. When the scene was over, she triumphantly turned to Mr. Robinson for his verdict. Robinson kept his hands firmly rested on the top of his cane, tapped it twice, then stood up.

"Very nice. Very nice indeed." He came forward and proffered his card to a startled Charlotte. "If you are in London, young lady, you must come to see me."

"*Nice?*" Lu exclaimed after him, her eyes lit with indignant pride on behalf of her performers. "I'll say it's nice!"

Noticeably recoiling at Louisa's manner, Robinson turned and left, while Nash inwardly winced again on her behalf. He wished she had a sense of how she appeared to others. Her imagination was so robust, Nash had no doubt that at any given moment she was the protagonist in a dizzying array of stories. The captive in a castle, the runaway in the forest, the misbegotten and mistreated pauper who rises to fortune and fame. But the abrupt manner, the drab clothes, did her no favors. Only in her mind was she a star—a constellation without a firmament, a passion in need of a cause.

"We shall break for lunch!" cried Louisa as the doors to the dining room swung closed behind Robinson. The tables were put back in place and the performers soon joined by the one P.M. luncheon seating. On the menu was veal consommé, a buffet of salmon, shrimp, and herring, a main course of liver, lamb, or pigeon with French potatoes and succotash spinach, and vanilla pudding or lemon cream tarts for dessert.

Little of it appealed to Charlotte Stevenson, however, who was too excited by Robinson's invitation to eat. The minute the tables were cleared, she stepped back onstage to resume rehearsing. Closing her eyes, she again became Lucie Manette, this time reuniting in France with her physician father, now a shoemaker in a garret who cannot stand the light, his years in the Bastille having rendered him weak in both mind and spirit.

Alone onstage, Charlotte cried out Lucie's heartbreaking words of realization at her father's continued infirmity, then dropped passionately to her knees as Lu had directed. There was the sound of a snap, then another cry—the high heel of the boot rolled along the stage—Charlotte tumbled down from it.

Haslett and Nash rushed forward from their positions on either side of the stage, but Louisa Alcott quickly bounded by them both. She was first to help Charlotte up, then gently removed the broken boot to examine her right foot.

"There's no break!" Lu loudly proclaimed to everyone's relief, but Charlotte was unable to put any pressure on the limb all the same.

"This is a disaster!" Lu exclaimed next.

There was only one day left to find a new Lucie Manette.

The Nelson brothers had not visited the smoking room during their time on ship, where men gathered for cards as much as for pipes and cigars. Gambling held no appeal for Nick, whose riskiest move since the war had been to write to an aging sea captain without invitation, and Haz was happily preoccupied by the amateur theatrics in which he starred. But following Louisa's panicked declaration, Haz headed directly for the men's lounge, knowing that this was where he would find Sara-Beth.

She sat at a table in the center of the room playing vingt-et-un, her winnings in a little pile before her lithe but quick hands. She was also the standing victor at nines, the less formal shipboard betting over the number of miles covered every twenty-four hours at sea. Sara-Beth's chaperone was said to wait outside the wheelhouse door each morning to collect from the increasingly peevish men.

"Haz—over here!" Sara-Beth patted the seat next to hers. "Take a hand."

Haz came over and removed his hat. "Miss Gleason, may I have a second of your time?"

Sara-Beth stood up and motioned to the elderly woman standing behind her to protect the pile of winnings. Before now, Haz had not seen this paid companion in Sara-Beth's vicinity and wondered if she was actually on board as Sara-Beth's silent shill—the very antithesis of a chaperone.

"Haz, you look worried—what is it?"

"It's the play. Charlotte's injured herself and can't go on, and Lu is desperate for a new Lucie Manette. We wondered if you might—"

"But aren't you playing her husband, Charles Darnay?" Sara-Beth immediately interrupted him, eyes aglow. "How enticing of you to ask—and out of character!" She looked about at the smoking room, the men fearing her return to the casino table, the little pile of winnings that would only grow with time. "Very well, Haz. I will do it, but on one condition."

Haz gritted his teeth.

"You must commit *fully* to your role."

B ut to everyone's surprise, Sara-Beth Gleason—despite her success at cards—was a disaster onstage.

Haz rehearsed his lines opposite her with a sinking heart. When someone got everything that they wanted simply by being themselves, there was clearly no need to ever transcend or alter their manner. Sara-Beth had never spent a second of her life considering her own behavior in relation to others, and so Sara-Beth did not become Lucie Manette onstage, the perfect Victorian wife and mother—Lucie Manette became the unstoppable and voracious Sara-Beth instead. The effect was completely jarring for everyone watching, Haz most of all.

He found he could not meet her eyes onstage. There was none of his usual ease of manner or playing to the audience: she stirred up emotions in him far too large for that small space. Haz might have sailed to get away from Sara-Beth, but was learning—to his utter dismay—that she followed him everywhere he went. He never saw her coming.

His thoughts whirled around onstage like a child's spinning top. He had lost all sense of himself let alone of Darnay, the character he played. Eventually Louisa Alcott stood up, threw down her pipe in disgust at them both, and called everyone to the floor. Haz gritted his teeth again.

"I'm afraid there's only one solution," Lu announced. "*I* must play Miss Lucie Manette."

THIRTEEN

An Impassable Space

NINTH DAY AT SEA
June 24, 1865

Ticket sales slowed when news got out that Charlotte Stevenson was no longer to play Lucie Manette. A beautiful woman in a theatrical lead role was no accident—it was its lifeblood. But the men on board the *China* were also desperate from boredom and looking for sport. When the play's director stepped into the role, the notion of a homely spinster feigning at being an ingenue struck the men—still smarting from Miss Gleason's daily triumph at nines—as a form of entertainment in and of itself. Ticket sales picked back up and soon approached the record set last spring when Captain Norris cajoled an operatic troupe from Drury Lane to perform while on board.

By curtain time, it was a full house in the dining saloon. Charlotte hobbled in on a cane and new boots from the goods store, and Sara-Beth joined her in the front-row seats that Louisa Alcott had reserved. Lu peered out from behind the curtain, relieved to see that Fawcett Robinson was also back. She knew from experience that the final performance of a play was often the best, chalking this up to a peculiar mixture of finality and regret that could stir even the most placid of performers.

Louisa felt for Charlotte's missed opportunity to shine brightest of all tonight, but she was so full of youth, beauty, and charm that there would surely be other chances ahead. By stepping into the younger woman's shoes this one time, Louisa hoped to transcend her usual position on the bottom rung of the ladder in life, always looking up, even in the full blossom of her own, long-expired youth.

She had taken extra time that afternoon to prepare her hair and dress. Stepping onto the stage, she knew she looked nothing like Lucie Manette as described in the book—Dickens's blond, blue-eyed angel. But Lu wasn't worried. She didn't act for the reasons that Charlotte Stevenson did. Charlotte did not act to disappear but to pull everyone into her charmed orbit instead. Like Lu's youngest sister, May, she was one of those lucky people in life to whom others naturally gravitated. Louisa, on the other hand, could put people off—at least, this was what she was sometimes told. She never noticed while it was happening, which was probably why it happened to begin with.

But onstage, Louisa knew she could do no wrong. If a man was supposed to fall in love with her, no degree of sallow skin or darting eyes could repel him—the words magically masked the reality. This made Louisa feel very brave and daring, like that young girl she had once been, so full of life, serenading her beloved Thoreau beneath his window, leaving a posy of violets on Emerson's front step. That woman was gone, and the more she disappeared, the more Alcott wrote to find her.

She wrote in her cabin all night long, in the vortex. She penned tales of sisters, secret engagements, and the lure of Europe for a young and "precocious" American girl. Travel was creatively stimulating Louisa, just as she had always hoped and dreamed it would. She was not booked to return home until the following summer of 1866: what fanciful stories might be stored up by then, what personages encountered, what hearts might she finally have stirred and perhaps even conquered?

With Louisa having cast herself as Lucie Manette, Thomas Nash felt even less enthusiasm for his own role. Just when he feared that his feelings for Charlotte Stevenson ran deeper than those of a chaperone ever should, Nash was forced to acknowledge their limit when it came to Miss Alcott.

How pathetic, to so thoroughly enjoy one's time with someone—to experience a true meeting of the minds—yet fail to overlook their short-comings in appearance. How shallow Nash felt, how feeble, how *male*. Miss Sara-Beth Gleason terrorized the men on board with her bottomless luck and aggressive manner, yet they could not resist such questionable charms in light of her surface ones. And Henrietta Stevenson might not share her sister Charlotte's apple-cheeked perfection, but she possessed a statuesque figure and striking almond-shaped eyes. No wonder William worried for his daughters. They were attractive enough to marry well, and were so well off themselves as to attract less fortunate men.

Nash's own attraction to Charlotte was increasingly hard to deny. On-stage he was pretending to be a man who has spent his life pretending not to care about anyone, only to end up pretending to be someone else so that he can sacrifice himself for all those people he is pretending not to care about. It struck too close to Nash's own heart, and the genius of Dickens was that eerie relatability: had the great author, like Shakespeare, covered all possible ground with his plots?

These were Nash's internal musings as he ascended the stage for his first scene of the night opposite Louisa. She had done something with her hair—he wasn't quite sure what—and there was a large amount of pink powder on her cheeks. Most of all, there was a glint in her eye, a storing up of energy, a sudden luminous demeanor.

Lucie: *Have I no power for good, with you, at all?*

Carton: *The utmost good that I am capable of, I have come here to realize. Let me always remember that I opened my heart to you, last of all the world, and that it lies only in your own bosom, shared by no one—not even the dearest one ever known to you.*

Lucie: *Mr. Carton, the secret is yours, not mine, and I promise to respect it.*

Carton: *Miss Manette, in the hour of my death, I shall hold sacred this one good remembrance—that my last avowal of myself was made to you, and that my name, and faults, and miseries were gently carried in your heart.*

(pauses)

I make one last supplication, and then I will relieve you of a visitor with whom I know you have nothing in unison, and between whom and you there is an impassable space: please know that for you, and anyone dear to you, I would do anything.

(Carton puts her hand to his lips and moves toward the door.)

Nash brought Louisa's warm hand—calloused by writing, browned by the sun—to his lips. The meeting of minds flared between them, the understanding of what was never to be—and of where that left Louisa May Alcott. Thomas Nash was solely responsible for the impassable space between *them*, as much as Sydney Carton was with Lucie Manette, for all his protestations that he did not deserve her.

Standing onstage together, closer than an unmarried man and woman should ever be, Nash felt all the energy and passion contained within the heart of the sad and lonely woman before him. No one had ever felt more real to him than at this moment, and all this while the real world was perversely stripped away. In pretending to be someone else—someone younger, prettier, more innocent, and much more desirable as a result—Louisa could fully relax into herself without fear of being teased or mocked. She could face a man like Nash with the sheer power of her soul: The one part of her that should matter the most. The part that the world ignored—the part that it preferred women like her to hide.

Standing up straight from kissing Louisa's hand onstage, Nash did not immediately let go as he had done in rehearsals. For one brief moment, he believed his own act. He was not tied to a script or bound by any precedent of fact or emotion. How he felt about Lu in the real world ceased to matter. In fact, time itself seemed to slow down before him, molasses-thick yet strangely permeable in his hands. In that moment, he could do as he wanted—he could do as *she* wanted—with absolutely no repercussions.

There was audible sniffling from all corners of the dining hall, men and women alike; Louisa was triumphing tonight in every way. As the audience continued to hold its breath and applause, Nash looked deeply into Lu's eyes and held her gaze far longer than was proper. He would show her all the appreciation and adulation that she was due. With his manifold faults, the opposite of Sydney Carton's yet their equal in disappointment, Thomas Nash could not give Louisa Alcott anything more than that.

He could only hope that she, too, would always carry it gently within her own most real, and tender, heart.

Once the makeshift curtains had fallen on the final standing ovation and the audience had retired for the night, Henrietta Stevenson and Denham Scott stood alone before the captain of the *China* on its moonlit prow. Charlotte had refused Harry's one invitation to the secret ceremony, leaving no witnesses in her stead. This did not concern Captain Val Norris, however, who was an ebullient man always eager to exercise his authority at sea in the service of love.

On the open water, life and law both seemed very far away. Henrietta had gone from her father's house, where her every move was noted, if not by him then by Mrs. Pearson or Samuel or another servant, to a place that almost didn't exist: the high seas, which belonged to no one and everyone. Louisa could become Lucie Manette and win over a room; Charlotte could impress a world-famous theater impresario while on holiday; Henrietta could cast aside caution and pledge herself to a foreigner for life.

"Your sister won't come?" Denham's beaming face fell. "Oh, my darling—should *I* try?"

"She needs time—only I can remedy that." Henrietta breathed in the calming fragrance of her posy of white bachelor buttons. Tied in purple ribbon, the bouquet had been cut from a pot by the ship florist that afternoon and the dirt gently shaken off.

"Let me make amends." Captain Norris reached into his pocket and pulled out a shiny silver sixpence. "A brand-new 'Young Head Victoria' coin. The father of an English bride places it in her left shoe for luck—not that such a handsome, well-suited couple needs any, I must say. May I have the honor?"

Smiling her permission, Henrietta extended her foot toward the captain as Denham lent his left arm for support.

"Well then, if no one else is attending," the captain happily boomed following the good luck gesture, "let us begin."

When they reached the exchange of vows, Henrietta noted the cadence of the lines from the *Book of Common Prayer*, the lulling rhythm, the way the language kept building and building to the inevitable climax of death—the one finality, the only thing that should ever separate a husband and wife. It was a masterpiece of rhetoric and had worked its charms for centuries for a reason.

"'I, Denham, take thee, Henrietta, to be my wedded wife, to have and to hold from this day forward, for better for worse, for richer for poorer, in sickness and in health, to love and to cherish, till death us do part. . . .'"

For better for worse. It was hard to imagine anything but death keeping her and Denham apart. No wonder their father stayed on at Eleven Beacon Street, where the memory of their mother was writ large on almost every wall and surface, his only way to keep it alive. Yet it rendered him, too, a ghost—a lonely, half-spent widower who threw himself into work and the safeguarding of his daughters' lives, such was the longstanding power of these vows.

"I, Henrietta, take thee, Denham, to be my wedded husband, to have and to hold, from this day forward, for better for worse, for richer for poorer, in sickness and in health, to love, cherish, and obey, till death us do part. . . ." She did not stumble at these sentiments, although the word *obey* caught somewhat at her ear. Alone in the moonlight on the deck of a ship, sailing through waters that belonged to no one—even here the difference between the sexes, as enshrined in the law, still reached them.

"You may now kiss the bride."

Denham grabbed her so hard that he crunched the bachelor buttons between them—Captain Norris laughed at the sound—Henrietta felt all the happiness of the moment. Even the word *obey* seemed transformed, no longer a blind promise but a pledge on which to build a family. She had just given over her whole world to Denham out of mutual respect and love; he had as much as pledged the same to her. When looked at in that hopeful light, what could the difference of one word matter?

FOURTEEN

✳

In with the Tide

‹——·——›

NINE O'CLOCK IN THE EVENING
Portsmouth Dockyard, June 25, 1865

Louisa Alcott tightly hugged both Stevenson sisters at the top of the gangplank. There were many tears and promises to write, and eventually Sara-Beth Gleason joined in, one of the last passengers on ship to depart. She was also first in the foursome to pull away, drawing from her reticule a smaller cloth bag and handing it to Louisa.

"Full of paper money," Sara-Beth proudly boasted, "as much of my winnings as you might accept. You earlier refused our charity, as you call it—now you can see London and Paris in style."

Louisa teared up again while a different foursome paced the dock below. These men gave each other knowing looks at the sentimental display above, all the while inwardly writhing with emotion: Thomas Nash over what to do and where to go next, Haslett Nelson having failed to shake off Sara-Beth, Nicholas Nelson wanting to reach Admiral Austen as quickly as possible, and Denham Scott eager to be alone with his bride.

He secured the first hackney cab in line at the shore end of the dock and waved for the Stevenson sisters to join him. Inside the cab, Denham sat across from the sisters and happily grinned; Charlotte narrowed her eyes at her new brother-in-law with open suspicion; Henrietta shyly smiled, the crumpled posy of white bachelor's buttons back in her hands. She had returned to the sisters' cabin after the midnight ceremony as promised, and admittedly nervous of the wedding night to come. The rewards of marriage would have to wait until husband and wife were ensconced in their new home together. For now, the sisters were to stay at the Fountain Hotel in Portsmouth while Denham traveled the one hundred miles to his newspaper's London office.

Denham was first to break the tense silence in the carriage. "The purser says you took in a record amount last night. I should pitch my editor on the story." He scribbled something in his notepad. "Louisa was mesmerizing. Even Nash appeared affected onstage—for once."

While Henrietta gave Denham a look of warning, Charlotte turned away in silent resentment and disgust. It was difficult to be around such a happy couple, and these last words of the groom did not help. No one in last night's audience could have mistaken Nash's attraction to Louisa, which seemed to ignite and flame onstage before everyone's eyes and left Charlotte alone to wonder: *If this was due to the sheer alchemy of performance, why had Nash displayed no such passion for* her *in their few rehearsals together?* Haz had thoroughly embraced the role of Darnay opposite Charlotte as Lucie—Lu had made a most attentive and solicitous Miss Pross—but Nash had stood onstage and given Charlotte nothing. Less than nothing, come to think of it, since the stage was supposed to offer the kind of high drama one never witnessed in real life. All attraction and desire condensed into one brief encounter—*that* was the romance that audiences thrilled to. And that was the opposite of what Nash had given her, and exactly what he had given Lu instead.

Charlotte could never begrudge Louisa herself such a moment. The Stevensons and Miss Gleason were the picture of feminine beauty, and the entire universe reflected this back at them from the moment they entered a room. Theirs was a world grounded in one's desirability in marriage, and Lu perilously stood outside that world on high seas herself. Last night she had been permitted entry just long enough to experience what other women— prettier women—took for granted. Charlotte couldn't help but wonder how differently things might have turned out, if she hadn't fallen from the stage. At least there was still the matter of Richard Fawcett Robinson and the enameled white trade card safely stored in her reticule. If Henrietta was bent on deserting her . . .

"Charlie," Henrietta finally pleaded, "can you ever forgive us?"

Charlotte shook herself out of her reverie. "I suppose you'll tell me it couldn't be helped."

"I know *I* couldn't." Denham smiled at his glowing bride before turning back to her. "Charlotte, you have my word, I will do everything in my power to give your sister all that she deserves."

"You always did want a brother. Please, my darling." Henrietta affectionately squeezed Charlotte's hand next to hers. "Please understand. I could not be happy otherwise."

But Charlotte knew this was not true. Henrietta had entered a state of happiness that did not require her sister's presence, let alone her understanding, and that was becoming hardest to accept of all.

S ara-Beth Gleason had boarded the SS *China* in Boston with a reticule full of English money drawn from her father's banker, only to disembark with even more. This was despite many incidental expenses during the voyage and the generosity toward Louisa. Nicholas Nelson gallantly hailed Miss Gleason the stateliest carriage in line—a Clarence—and turned to her for the direction.

"The George Hotel until further notice," she answered, naming the most prestigious hotel in Portsmouth and clearly in no hurry to get to London. "And where are you boys off to?"

"We have business here to attend to, as you may recall," said Nick as Haz moped about on the pavement behind them. "I must say, you were very kind to share your winnings just now with Miss Alcott."

"Easy enough to do when one is ahead."

Haz shot her a look but still said nothing.

"May I ask," continued Nick, "if the ladies knew of the engagement between Miss Stevenson and Scott?"

"I bet *she* did," Haz finally called over with a nod at Sara-Beth, who charmingly wrinkled her nose back at him.

"You'll be happy to know, I was as surprised as anyone. Even Charlotte had no idea. Louisa was suspicious, of course, but says she never trusts a newspaperman."

"How difficult for Charlotte, losing her sister to so great a distance," Nick said feelingly.

"There is also the injury to her ankle," added Haz. "Such missed opportunity."

Sara-Beth shook her head at both men in mock pity. "Oh yes, so much missed opportunity indeed."

"I hope Scott's deserving of her." Nick sounded so plaintive that Sara-Beth fully turned her attention on him.

"If he isn't, Henrietta will surely make him so. You know, Nick, you quite remind me of Harry. In Italy, they call it simpatico. It's a pity you didn't move faster there." She held out her hand for him to help her into the carriage, followed by her maid and the woman who had collected all of Sara-Beth's winnings.

It must be easy to gamble when one has so much, Nick thought to himself as he closed the carriage door behind the three women. Sara-Beth always landed on her feet, no matter what impulse she followed. He and Haz had acted on an impulse of their own in coming to England, knowing so little about Admiral Austen, even though Nick found making decisions difficult and Haz was usually too indolent to care. And Henrietta Stevenson had cast aside her entire life in America to follow her heart. What was going to transpire next? It was like the steam that propelled the *China* forward: nothing could happen without the coal below first being lit. One had to take chances in life for good luck to happen as well as the bad.

Nash helped the elderly employer of Louisa Alcott into one side of the London-bound carriage, then came around to assist Lu into the other. He kept his gloved hands on the edge of the passenger door in hesitation, the make-believe moment between them onstage having seeped into real life in some odd, undefinable way. Finally, Lu extended her hand through the open window.

"We're in England now and due for a good ol' handshake. None of these fussy continental ways."

"You'll have your day with Dickens yet," he reminded her as they warmly shook hands.

"I can't wait. *A Day with Dickens*—and that's exactly what I'll call it, when I write it."

"You will have a lot to write about, I'm sure. Our motley crew on board, all at cross-purposes with each other."

"Oh, I don't know about that. Mr. and Mrs. Scott were obviously of one mind."

Nash bowed his head. "Don't remind me. Whatever will I tell her father?"

"Not all of it, I am sure." He looked up to catch her smiling knowingly at him. "I haven't properly thanked you for stepping in like that. You made an excellent Sydney Carton, when it mattered most."

"I'm not so sure either is a compliment in the end." He grinned back. "Where do you head after England?"

"We're to follow the Rhine from Germany to the Swiss Alps, then on to Rome."

"Will I not see you again—in London, perhaps?" She shook her head. He didn't understand why—he had assumed she of all people would strive to stay in touch. "But we are friends, no?"

"Yes, we are. Good friends. So, be a friend, Nash, and don't be polite. Not with me."

They were still holding hands. She firmly shook his one more time, then released it to sit back in the dark recess of the carriage. Her face fell as she did, which saddened him in turn. But when the carriage pulled forward, third in line behind the Stevenson and Gleason parties, she began to wave at him out the window. She waved as boisterously as a boy, as hopefully as a girl.

Waved—Nash somehow knew—long after she could see him at all.

BOOK THREE

—∞—

Hampshire

ONE

✦

Meeting Fly

◦————•————◦

Portsdown Lodge, June 26, 1865

Admiral Francis Austen hardly slept a wink all night. By his own nautical calculations, the SS *China* would have docked in the evening with the incoming tide. He hoped to receive word from his double set of guests that morning, not knowing where in Portsmouth they would first stay upon arrival. For now, he had asked the housekeeper to make up four of the fourteen bedrooms, just in case.

After a hasty early breakfast of biscuits and sardines, his favorite shipboard meal, Francis Austen took his wood-and-brass telescope and mug of coffee out to the hill before the house. Still in dressing gown and slippers, he eased himself into the deck chair with its woven rattan back and pointed the telescope at the dockyard below. He looked past the Hilsea Barracks, where two batteries of the Royal Field Artillery had recently been installed, past the house where author Charles Dickens had been born, past Her Majesty's Dockyard where Frank himself had once set off for distant and sunnier climes.

Today, however, even the English sky was without blemish. It possessed all the clarity of midsummer, the fathomless blue of the sea. A perfect day for his new American friends to visit.

✦　✦　✦

A dmiral Austen?" The strange female voice crackled with energy.

"Sir Francis?" a man's voice softly inquired next.

Frank's eyes fluttered open to reveal three young faces—a woman and two men—staring down at him in concern. He must have fallen asleep. He pulled himself up and the telescope rolled from his lap toward the grass, which was kept short for when the grandchildren visited to play croquet and lawn skittles and drink ginger beer. One of the men reached forward with the agility of a fielder to catch the telescope before it landed and passed it back to Frank.

"Is it you?" a bewildered Admiral Austen addressed the woman, still half sitting up. The two young men glanced at each other in confusion while the woman beguilingly smiled. She was wearing a sailor-like outfit of white and navy stripes, playful epaulettes, and brushed gold buttons, as if selected especially for him—and the smell of jasmine and mimosa again came to mind. . . .

"Sara-Beth Gleason—but you can call me Sara. Never much cared for the Beth part."

While one man blankly stared at her as if this was news to him, the other stepped forward and extended his hand down to the ninety-one-year-old. "I am Nicholas Nelson, as I wrote, and this is my brother, Haslett. We hope we haven't caught you unawares."

Gazing up at the angle of the sun, Frank removed a watch from the front pocket of his dressing gown to confirm the surprising lateness of the hour. "Oh, my dears, no, not at all." He shook Nicholas's hand warmly from his chair. "I received your letter from the third of this month and have been greatly anticipating your arrival. You reached us without incident, I hope?"

Sara-Beth glanced at both brothers and gave a pointed laugh. "Oh, just a bruised heart or two. And what do we call *you*, hmm?"

"Fly," he heard himself say before he could stop himself.

"Father!"

Everyone turned at the sound of his daughter, standing on the lawn behind them with her arms crossed. "Father, you haven't been called Fly in fourscore!" she scolded.

Admiral Austen reddened, then reluctantly waved her over. "Fanny-Sophia, do come—allow me to introduce our guests, who have traveled here from the great distance of America."

Fanny looked the three strangers up and down as greetings were exchanged, taking a little longer when she came to the younger Nelson brother. Admiral Austen was reminded of how rarely he and his daughter made any new acquaintance. Fanny might have ended up at home because she had always been plain and lacking admirers, but the difficult personality had only worsened over time. She refused to change her mood or manners for anyone, whereas Frank had just burst out with an eighty-year-old nickname in the presence of Miss Gleason, so affected by others was he.

"Fly—I like that." Sara-Beth gave him another winning smile.

Frank had received no clue that she was coming, in her little nautical outfit so perfectly attuned to this moment—could not have even dreamt up such a thing. In his near century of life, he had never met a woman more different from his Fanny or more instantly disarming. Miss Gleason seemed to make both her male companions nervous as well, and Frank began to worry for the matchmaking he had planned.

J ustice Thomas Nash woke early. He was used to living on little sleep when legal matters were coming to a head. The seven justices of the Massachusetts Supreme Judicial Court could easily take all evening to discuss a Jane Austen novel, let alone establish precedent for the future of their state.

Up with the sun, Nash spent several solitary hours walking the soot-stained streets of Old Portsmouth. Like the Port of Boston, there was no clear division here between land and sea. The ground beneath one's feet might be steadier than on ship, but the sounds and smells were the same: the baritone blast of the mist horn, the salty peat of the ocean marsh, the air fired high with coal. As one of the most defended cities in all of Europe, Portsmouth was full of fascinating history. But no amount of study could have prepared Justice Thomas Nash for arriving a full month ahead of schedule, all the while chasing down one bewildering young woman and a newly eloped bride.

He had spent the night close to harbor at a new hotel called the Claremont. After checking in late, he had immediately sat down by the window with its view of the docked SS *China* and written at length to William Stevenson. If Nash acted fast enough, the letter should reach the ship's mail-sorting rooms in time for the return journey back.

He had written and rewritten long into the night, ending up with several rambling pages that featured none of his usual elegance of phrase. He tried to convey what had happened without raising any undue alarm: William Stevenson would not be the first father to lose a daughter to a far-off marriage, no matter the state of his nerves. Given the shock of the contents, however, Nash felt duty-bound to show the letter to Henrietta before posting. He would simply have to find his own nerve, and present himself unexpectedly to the Stevenson sisters yet again.

Charlotte woke late at the Fountain Hotel and nudged Henrietta slumbering at her side. The sisters were sharing a massive four-poster bed in a spacious room decorated with floral trellis wallpaper. Their inn was located on the High Street, away from the oily, fishy smell of the harbor and the noise of ship horns at all hours.

Charlotte nudged Henrietta again, causing her to stir. "Harry, do wake up, honeymoon or not."

Henrietta sat up on one elbow and smiled as she looked about. "Everything feels like a dream."

Charlotte rolled her eyes—she was not used to seeing her sister so simpering. "Harry, really—you'll be the talk of Boston."

"I will write Father every day if I have to—I already have a letter at the ready—and he shall visit us next summer. You know how he loves all things British."

"Yes, yes, you have it all arranged." Charlotte eased herself down from the high mattress and grabbed the cane resting nearby. "Look at the time. Our new friends must be off to London by now."

"I wonder what Justice Nash will do next." Henrietta reached up to ring the bell by the bed for breakfast, eager to reach Portsdown Lodge as soon as possible.

Charlotte hobbled over to the washstand and poured out the jug of water. "Louisa wasn't so wrong in wanting rid of the men."

Henrietta hesitated. "But you will miss your other leading man?"

Charlotte examined herself in the mirror above the bowl and pitcher. "Haz? Yes, I suppose so—why?"

"I wondered if he liked you—the *angel* and all that."

Charlotte splashed her face with water, then patted it dry with a towel before opening her eyes widely at her sister. "Haz is so natural onstage, it would be easy to confuse him with Darnay. But I'm sure I'm just a decoy for his true affections."

"It is interesting how you use the word 'decoy.'" Henrietta paused again. "Denham wondered the same about several of the performers."

Settling herself in the room's one chair, Charlotte began brushing out the waves of hair from the yarn braids she slept in. "Acting does that—muddles things."

"Or liberates things already there. Look at Louisa and Nash."

Charlotte stopped brushing to stare at her. "What *are* you saying? Honestly, Henrietta—is this how you and Denham speak, when you're alone together?" she asked in a huff. "Because it's nothing like you."

A young chambermaid knocked and entered the room with a tray containing toast, jelly, coffee, and a message from Nash.

"What can *he* want now?" Charlotte said with a sigh.

J ustice Nash was wanting the honor of arranging their carriage to the home of Sir Francis Austen. When the sisters descended the front steps of the Fountain Hotel half an hour later, Nash stood waiting on the pavement below, the brougham behind him, a letter in his hands.

"Mrs. Scott, would you be so kind as to read this?"

Henrietta took the letter from Nash and, seeing her father's name on the direction, read it then and there. "Justice Nash, it's a perfectly reasonable account. And you have nothing to write an apology for—the family should never have involved you. We will post both our letters on the way to the admiral to ensure they arrive at the Custom House together."

"That's most gracious of you." Nash paused. "I hope my words also convey, to you as well as your father, how much I admired the female activity on board. The charity performance was exemplary."

"Not that you men ever begrudge women for putting on a show," Charlotte interjected.

"I sadly can't dispute that. Your ankle is improving, though?" At her nod, Nash glanced up the street. "Then may I show you both something, before we stop in at the postmaster? It's not too out of the way."

A few blocks later, the carriage deposited the three of them in a cobbled street lined by pleasant red-brick terrace houses, each with matching white-trimmed bay windows and high stone steps. Nash pointed to the one closest before announcing, "They say this is the very house in which Charles Dickens was born."

"We didn't know!" exclaimed Charlotte, and Nash was relieved by her sudden enthusiasm. He knew he had to make amends—through literature seemed the wisest and fastest way.

"His father was transferred here from London by the naval pay office," he explained. "They left when Dickens was only three, but the city must have left an impression. You might recall Nicholas Nickleby and Smike taking the road from London to Portsmouth and seeing the Devil's Punch Bowl along the way."

"'Nature gives to every time and season some beauties of its own,'" Charlotte quoted. "My favorite chapter. The English countryside, so invigorating to Nickleby and Smike *because* they experience it together. That's all we want, Harry and I—or wanted," she pointedly added, while Henrietta reached forward guiltily to squeeze her sister's arm.

As for Nash, he remained impressed by their efforts. Nicholas Nickleby and Smike had pushed through their travels "exhilarated by exercise, and stimulated by hope," and Nash had observed this same newfound spirit in the women on board the *China*. He recalled his time at sea with Louisa, their many walks together, the sense that she was truly free for the first time in her life. He wondered what might come of that in the end. How much strength did the larger world sap from women, in asking those who could afford to do so, to stand idly still in one spot, while rendering the poor transient—if not homeless—for life?

TWO

✦

The Design of the Ancient Mariner

Portsdown Lodge, June 26, 1865

The admiral invited his three visitors into the study, which was full of souvenirs from a life spent traveling the globe: clay vessels by the Lucayans, the first New World inhabitants encountered by Christopher Columbus; a two-handled Etruscan wine jar from Italy full of Frank's Blush Noisette roses; the carved Egyptian candlesticks gifted for his time on St. Helena. Nicholas examined everything in the study with a keen collector's eye, Sara-Beth fluttered on like a butterfly with her limited attention, and Haslett was most eager to see the objects that the admiral had promised would be worth the brothers' while.

Fanny came to the doorway and frowned. "Father, you said *four* bedrooms to make up."

Admiral Austen, who had since changed from his dressing gown into his old naval uniform, looked up from the snuffbox of hippopotamus ivory he was showing Miss Gleason. "Yes, four."

"But George informs me three more guests have arrived. Were you aware? Father?"

Austen became noticeably tight-lipped around his daughter, like a child caught with his finger in the jam jar. Meanwhile, Fanny Austen's constant fretting over her father struck his visitors as unnecessary—after all, the admiral

seemed such a genial, lucid, and harmless old man. But at the sound of excited female voices coming from the hall, all three Americans turned to see
what this latest fuss of Fanny's might actually be about.

"I could swear that sounds..." Nick broke off mid-sentence as the
voices grew louder.

"Good God!" exclaimed Haz.

"Charlie—Harry—I do declare!" cried a delighted Sara-Beth.

She ran over to the doorway and into the arms of both Stevenson sisters,
who happily hugged her back. Meanwhile the Nelson brothers turned in
astonishment to face their host, who was sheepishly hanging back from the
surprise reunion.

"Sir Francis..." a shocked Nicholas began.

"Did you plan all this?" Haz burst out as the women broke from their
embrace.

"Why, Fly," Sara-Beth teased him, *"you little scamp."*

Austen looked almost everywhere in the study but at his quintet of
guests. Sheepish though he appeared, he was secretly very happy inside, his
house full again at last. There were more spoils to divvy up, inevitable ex-
planations to give—and a promise to extract. But it was all going according
to plan.

U ntil it wasn't.
      For one thing, waiting by the carriage at the foot of the drive
      was an attractive older man who had accompanied the two sisters
from Boston. There was also a wedding band on Henrietta's left hand that
had not been placed there by Nicholas Nelson. The admiral's plan to make
a match between them was apparently over before it could start. Perhaps
Charlotte... but he had to rearrange his thoughts there, too, as Nicholas
appeared to have eyes only for Henrietta (*at least he had been half right there*, the
admiral consoled himself), while Miss Gleason clearly had her sights set on
Haslett. The admiral sat glumly at the head of the dining table as his six
guests, embroiled in such unexpected alliances and permutations, caught up
with each other.

"But *we* invited ourselves here in a fit of bravery!" Charlotte happily
cried out to the Nelson brothers.

"We first wrote to express our adoration of Austen," Henrietta explained.

"Nick wrote last month to express the same!" Haz replied in delight.

"And to mention the first American edition of *Emma* in our possession," his brother added.

"All that time on ship and it never came up?" marveled Sara-Beth. "Louisa would have a *field* day with this."

Each sibling gave the other a furtive glance before turning back to their host. Finally, Charlotte asked what all four of them were wondering. "What could have been your design, Sir Francis, in inviting us all?"

The admiral gave a nervous rattle of a cough. "Perhaps I should explain."

"Please do," said the American judge facing him from the foot of the dining table. Justice Thomas Nash had joined the meal on the insistence of the group, who were clearly enamored with each other's company. Even across the long table, Admiral Austen could sense this older man's suspicion about what was really going on.

"I trust we can confide in each other." Frank lowered his voice even though Fanny was in the kitchen below, helping cook with dinner given the increased number at the table. "My sister's legacy faces an imminent crossroads of sorts. No one in the family can agree. If only there was a society of some kind—or someone I could trust—to whom I could bequeath all in my possession."

"Why does this suddenly feel like a contest of sorts?" asked Haslett, and Sara-Beth eagerly leaned forward next to him.

"Oh, I do love contests."

"Because you always win."

The admiral watched them banter in secret dismay. "I simply want everything in the right hands. You each wrote with such overarching love for Jane and her works. I believe *that* to be the real criterion for its safeguarding—not mere ties of blood or circumstance."

There was a surprising resolve to the old man's words. His guests could suddenly picture the daring Sir Francis must have displayed at sea, fighting off pirates, slave traders, and the increasingly desperate forces of Napoleon. As for the admiral's urgency of manner, he had confided in his letters the matter of his declining health. A sad thought fell upon both sets of his American correspondents: no sooner were they making Admiral Austen's acquaintance than it might be lost for good.

Sitting to the right of Sir Francis, Henrietta gently placed her hand next to his on the crisp, white tablecloth. "We are all honored to be welcomed by you on any terms," she assured him.

Fanny appeared in the doorway to the dining parlor. Throughout the meal, she had found several excuses to come and go, but her concern for her father's behavior hung over the room like a shroud. From the threshold, her sharp eye immediately went to Henrietta's hand resting alongside that of the admiral.

"Father, may I have a word?"

After Fanny and Sir Francis left, their voices could be heard from the hallway through the closed dining room door—mostly hers, mostly reprimanding.

"We shouldn't listen," whispered Charlotte, but none of them could help themselves.

What has gotten into you, inviting all these people?

Admiral Austen's thin, reedy voice could barely be heard against his daughter's.

You try me so. . . . I have half a mind to call the doctor again. . . .

Henrietta and Nicholas, the admiral's chief correspondents, raised their eyebrows at each other across the table. "I worry I've contributed to this," he said in a low voice, "by writing of our appraisal work." It was the first time he had directly addressed Mrs. Scott, despite days of eavesdropping with his brother on her shipboard meals.

There was the sound of footsteps marching, drawers opening and shutting in a room nearby.

What have you gone and promised them? These are family letters, of no business to anyone. . . .

Eventually the admiral returned alone to the table and quietly took his seat as if nothing untoward had happened. With a look of meaning at the others, Justice Nash stood up.

"Sir Francis, we've surely tired you in the excitement of our arrival. Shall we come back tomorrow, once you've had time to rest and recollect yourself?"

Sir Francis's eyes clouded over with tears. "Fanny is unhappy with me."

It was the type of childlike lament from an aging relative that they had each heard before, usually of little import. Perhaps Fanny's hissed accusations were right—perhaps they had come this far for no hidden treasure in the end, not that any of them minded. Just visiting with Admiral Francis Austen, in Hampshire, in the county that had raised the world's greatest writer, was treasure enough.

"We have inconvenienced you both," Henrietta offered in apology.

The entire party now watched in astonishment as the ancient mariner placed both hands on the table before him as if to steady it in a storm-tossed sea, and whispered with all the warning of a blood-red sky,

"She wants to burn it all."

THREE

Pride and Prejudice

The Massachusetts Supreme Judicial Court
June 26, 1865

L et's commence with the title."

The other five justices groaned in laughter at their chief justice's opening remark, which did not bode well for a quick deliberation.

"*Pride and Prejudice,*" Chief Justice Adam Fulbright continued. "Such perfect alliteration."

"Even better than *A Tale of Two Cities* or *Love's Labour's Lost,*" agreed Justice Philip Mackenzie. "They say it's from Burney, another lady author—'if to pride and prejudice you owe your miseries, so wonderfully is good and evil balanced, that to pride and prejudice you will also owe their termination.'"

"I thought it Thomas Paine." Justice Ezekiel Peabody possessed the finest memory on the bench and could recite many famous sermons by heart. "His urging our colonies to break away in *Common Sense.*"

"I doubt that," Justice Roderick Norton scoffed. "Far more likely Austen borrowed the phrase from a women's novel."

"Not necessarily." The chief justice lit his pipe. "Miss Austen's father was a teacher as well as a man of God, and Paine's writings were well circulated abroad. Remember, England was at war for most of Austen's lifetime, and several of her brothers served in the militia or navy—the house would have been full of talk of revolution."

"What does any of this have to do with *Pride and Prejudice*?" Norton asked in frustration. "That harpy Mrs. Bennet running around like Chicken Little, acting as if the sky is falling down!"

"But it *is*," countered Justice Conor Langstaff. "With the death of Mr. Bennet, his entire estate will pass to a distant male relation—primogeniture again—and the women will be thrust from gentry to poverty in a trice. Look at what happened to Austen herself when her own father died."

"How," asked a bemused Mackenzie, "did this comedy of manners become our most contentious meeting yet? William, what do you say to it all?"

Justice William Stevenson had said little so far, the long walks and conversations with Constance—Connie, as he now called her—having left him confused. He remained convinced of the rightness in saving his daughters from harm, less so of his chosen means of protection. Keeping them at home, Connie argued, was as good as keeping a horse in blinders. There was no effort to fix the world around women and its dangers particular to them—how convenient for the men who ruled and enjoyed its spoils. This was Constance's entire modus operandi: give women a say in the very doings of the world that held such power over them. She would not rest until each and every woman of age had the vote.

"What strikes me," Stevenson finally answered, "is how Georgiana Darcy and Lydia Bennet could be parented so differently, and given such opposite degrees of liberty, yet both fall prey to Wickham. Austen's reproof here is stinging: protect or ignore them all you want, but no young woman is safe from an irresolute cad unless the world around her does its job first."

"Lydia's a twit no matter what," Norton argued.

"But Lizzy isn't, and she, too, falls for Wickham's charms," Langstaff pointed out.

"They've none of them been educated to meet the real world," posited William. "They're like horses with blinders on—everything is fine as long as someone else holds the reins behind them."

The other men in the room all stared at him in surprise.

"Women *need* reining in, man!" exclaimed Norton.

"And we need their civilizing influence in the home, given their natural role as mothers," added Mackenzie. "Such great influence, as all we husbands can attest to"—this provoked laughter among the bench—"that suffrage would be a mere formality in the end."

"Look at Mrs. Bennet," added Peabody. "Her husband *does* give in and welcome Bingley to Longbourn, *does* relent on Lydia visiting Brighton un-chaperoned, and Mrs. B *does* succeed in marrying off three of five daughters in one fell swoop. She rules the roost."

William Stevenson shook his head. "No, she's cleaning up after her husband. They're in this financial predicament because of him—no wonder her nerves are poor. She has no legal rights over their estate to prevent the entail—something her husband neglected to fix when he could. All property is *his*—until he dies and it becomes another man's. The children are his property, too." Stevenson shook his head in self-reproach. "We regard property as a mere extension of ourselves, but each child is an individual, and their own unique needs should light the way. Lydia clearly needed oc-cupation to release all that energy. Even Mary Bennet had her pianoforte."

"Horseback riding, perhaps?" Mackenzie asked with a laugh.

"At least that would be something! But seriously, aren't our own various pursuits how we learn about ourselves and what we desire?"

"Again," Norton said with a sigh, "what does this have to do with the book at hand?"

"Elizabeth Bennet knows what she desires!" Conor Langstaff, the sleep-deprived new father, dreamily exclaimed. He poured himself more coffee from the large silver pot and began to pace about the room, cup in hand. "For that matter, so does her friend Charlotte Lucas, although it's the very marriage of convenience that Lizzy rejects. She turns down two marriage proposals, in fact, something quite unheard of. She would rather be alone and poor than do what society and her family demand. Such authenticity, such awareness and pride in one's self, is to be admired—along with those fine eyes."

"But hers is a strong pride—strong as a man's—which overasserts itself following a bruising. I believe *this* is what makes her susceptible to Wickham's charms," Justice Mackenzie countered. "Think of Darcy's insult upon meeting Lizzy, so unforgivably harsh—'she is tolerable, yes, but not hand-some enough to tempt me.' He even waits until catching her eye to say it, as if unknowingly wanting to vanquish any attraction. The man has no notion of consequences for his actions."

"Until he meets his match in Elizabeth Bennet!" exclaimed Langstaff again. "She will make him pay the consequences—not all women would, in light of his wealth and social standing. What is it he says at the end, *by you I was* properly *humbled?*"

"Darcy and Lizzy must each humble themselves to receive love," announced the chief justice, and his associates prepared themselves for one of his romantic exhortations. "Elizabeth's keen intelligence keeps her at a remove from others, much like her father's—Darcy's situation in life does, too. They both need to develop those qualities in life and marriage so critical to their success, and at which Mr. and Mrs. Bennet have each failed so miserably. Generosity of spirit—trust and respect—engagement and activity. We must all be the romantic hero in our own lives to realize its full potential."

William Stevenson spotted Constance Davenish's gloved hand waving from the waiting carriage, and these last words of the chief justice hit home again.

"I suppose there was a general air of infatuation in the room over Miss Eliza Bennet," Connie greeted him, making room next to her on the plush velvet seat.

"There was much serious discussion on the folly of pride."

She made a gesture of demurral. "Pride is not inherently a failing—little would get done in this world without it. Look at our country's wonderful can-do attitude. But pride engaged wholly in the self—*that's* where the dragons lie. Superiority, smugness, solipsism . . ."

William had to smile. "I knew you would have a few choice words to say on the matter—even without finishing the book."

She gave that wonderful throaty laugh of hers in response and patted his arm. William felt as carefree as he had in years, then immediately guilty for it. His daughters were gone, separated from him by a deadly, storm-tossed sea. How could he possibly be happy?

Connie noticed his expression change—she never missed a thing. "William, what is it?" He slowly pulled the letter out from his waistcoat pocket. "Oh, I see—you've had word, then?"

He passed her Nash's letter dated five days into the journey on the SS *China* as it headed east to England. It had been delivered to Boston's Custom House by the RMS *Neptune*, a mail steamer traveling west from Liverpool that same week. Connie scanned the postmark and contents with impressive speed.

"But how wonderful to have news so soon! And the girls sound quite well and occupied by this Dickens charity production." William missed the interesting look that Connie gave him with her next words. "Nash gives the very account one would expect from him."

"There might still be some danger ahead—he penned it from the middle of the Atlantic, after all."

"You've had the letter since Saturday, though? You should have called on me. You always can, you know." She hesitated, patted his arm again, this time slowly. He had almost forgotten the feeling that swept over him at the warmth of her touch. It had all the excitement of fear, and none of the worry. Intoxication: that was exactly the word for it.

They traveled together in comfortable silence until reaching the double curved entrance to her home. The horses came to a sudden stop, giving the carriage a jolt of arrival. Connie fell against his chest with her easy laugh, then lingered.

"You will come in? You're not as late tonight—I suppose *Pride and Prejudice* the easiest to dispose of the lot?"

"Certainly the most lighthearted," he replied, choosing his words carefully as he always did. "We're not even attending to *Northanger Abbey*—half the court considers it too derivative and derisive for serious study."

He followed her up the stone steps and through the arched front door being held open by her manservant. William had never before entered Connie's house at such a late hour. He was thinking of Samuel and Mrs. Pearson back home, how they would be worrying and waiting up for him, when his attention was caught anew by the grandness of his surroundings.

"Connie, I must say, you live like an empress."

"Why shouldn't I? I have no one else to please." She threw her fan and evening gloves onto the table in the foyer. "The theater was crowded for such a hot night. *La Traviata*—oh, but you don't care for opera, as I recall."

She led him into the rococo white-and-gold drawing room where she held her famous weekly afternoon salon. He had attended the last one and stayed behind long after all the other guests had gone. Constance had remarked on how quiet he had been, and only then did he realize he had not come to talk but to assess his rivals, who appeared to be many. It turned out his horizon was not that clear when it came to her, and the notion had given him a much-needed jolt of his own.

She sat down on a small settee and patted the place next to her. She was always leading him closer to her, he understood at least that—telegraphing her permission, should he be brave enough to take it. He seated himself a slight but purposeful distance from her. "I suppose the opera is too *large* for me."

"You do like your fine delicacy—your Miss Austen."

"I wish you would try to read her again."

"I am happy with my French authors and their healthy dose of realism. You are getting something from Austen, but realism it is not."

William closed his eyes in mock grimace. "Please don't say romance."

"Never! That word is blasphemy around here."

"Justice, then?"

"Why, yes, of course, William—how fitting."

"Connie."

"Yes, William."

"There's something I've been wanting to ask." He turned to face her on the settee next to him, the dozens of rules of courtship etiquette dissipating like a young man's game. "May I kiss you?"

Constance tilted her chin toward him in ready response, as commanding as a queen. "Oh, my boy, remember what the physician said . . ."

She reached forward to stroke his cheek at the edge of his beard and he pulled her hard against him, forgetting where they were, neglecting every last rule.

"What?" he heard himself ask, then just as quickly forgot his own question.

". . . you must confront what terrifies you most."

And then William Stevenson, to his own surprise, forgot it all.

FOUR

✦

The Spoils to Divvy

•——•——•

Portsdown Lodge, June 27, 1865

The spoils to divvy, and the promise to extract, were both rather large.

Admiral Austen and his six American guests convened the next day in deck chairs on the hill, where Fanny was less likely to overhear or interfere. "There are many letters," Sir Francis shared over glasses of lemon squash. "Jane was a most dutiful correspondent, even when I was at sea. My second wife, Martha, was her dearest friend and kept everything from her as well."

"Sir Francis, how many letters do you speak of?" asked Nicholas.

"Several hundred. But Fanny is most adamant that private letters should stay private. She doesn't wonder that my sister Cass destroyed nearly all."

"Remember what Louisa once proclaimed?" Henrietta asked the other women. "That if she ever became famous, she would make everyone burn what they had from her?"

Nash nodded. "Dickens reportedly did the same at his home at Gad's Hill a few years back—made a big bonfire from it all."

Sir Francis twisted the telescope back and forth in his hands, as if in deliberation. "And there is one thing more." They all leaned forward in their deck chairs, even Sara-Beth who—not being a great reader like the rest of them—was enjoying the sheer excitement of the moment. "It is best I show it to you. If only Fanny would leave the house for a while . . ."

The group fell quiet in thought until Sara-Beth said aloud what no one else dared to.

"Justice Nash should invite her to take a turn about the grounds." She gave Admiral Austen a playful wink. "I am sure not even Miss Fanny-Sophia can resist his charms!"

As the tall figures of Nash and Fanny disappeared over the small rise in the hill, Admiral Austen led the other guests back into his study. This time he bypassed the decorated clamshells and rare beetles under glass to head straight for the Davenport captain's desk. The mahogany furnishing stood tall like a military campaign desk in the center of the Persian carpet, its turned cabriole legs cupped in brass caster wheels. The leather writing pad on its surface was surrounded by a finely scrolled baluster, and there were five drawers on the right side of the base to match the handful of faux drawer fronts on the left.

The admiral's visitors watched in surprise as he removed from beneath his cravat an unusual, round-shaped key. "This lock and key are the famous invention of Mr. Joseph Bramah," he explained. "The greatest security known to man." Unlocking the bottom right drawer, Sir Francis pulled out an iron strongbox and raised it onto the blotter with Haz's ready assistance, then used a second, smaller key from his vest pocket to unlock the lid.

The first two stacks inside the iron box were separately secured by black ribbon and of roughly equal size. "The letters," the admiral announced. Momentarily placing these to the side, he lifted a larger stack from underneath. This was a thick gathering of leaves of laid paper, six inches deep and half as wide, covered in brown iron-gall ink in an even, deeply slanted hand. On a strip of paper pasted to the top was a pencilled note in another hand, which had subsequently been inked over: *The contents of this Drawer for Frank.* That recipient now glanced up at the five eager and excited young faces before him. It was the moment he had been waiting for.

"The original manuscript of *Persuasion.*"

There was a gasp from around him: it was a treasure trove after all.

"Like many authors, Jane discarded earlier drafts once her novels were in print," Frank explained as he began delicately turning the pages. "Tragically, she did not live to see *Persuasion* published. Cassandra, as executrix of Jane's estate, asked our brother Henry to arrange for that—you might recall his well-composed note at the front of the printed edition—then before her own death, dispersed any remaining letters, jewelry, and unpublished works amongst the family. This, Cassy bequeathed to me."

Nicholas Nelson stepped forward. "May I?"

Admiral Austen nodded. "I know you will appreciate its value, as there is no other surviving copy of the completed novels that we know of. And it is no fair copy, so the workings of her mind are laid bare for all to see."

"That would make it invaluable," Henrietta suggested, and the admiral smiled at her in satisfaction.

"Yes, my dear. I knew you would understand."

Everyone joined Nicholas at the desk to more closely regard the "certain object" that Sir Francis had quietly owned for more than twenty years. There were no page numbers on the folded papers, which had been assembled in booklet form, no distinct paragraphs or margins, no formal separation of dialogue between speakers; the writing purposefully filled the pages to the very edge as if a matter of exertion as well as economy. There were, however, wonderful signs of constant and active revision, more than would be suspected from the ease and elegance of the final product and the indisputable genius of its author. Entire sections were sometimes crossed out to the point of blackness, at which point a new scrap of paper had been pinned over as if to rescue the words from themselves.

"As you can see, Jane worked through each sentence, each word, at great length—sometimes too much so, we would chide her." He smiled proudly. "To the family, her writing was perfect from the start. Of course, she knew what she was at. Like a great musical composer, she was playing to a tune that no one else could hear."

"And no one else knows of the manuscript?" asked Charlotte.

He nodded. "I thought it best. Fanny would dispute sharing even it, given that Jane herself, in keeping with the past, would surely have destroyed this working copy upon publication. My daughter relies solely on history to argue—and augur—the future."

Henrietta and Charlotte grinned at each other in recognition. "Our father, as we have mentioned, is on the supreme court for our state," Henrietta told the admiral. "Several of his colleagues would argue for that doctrine as well."

"Strict constructionists," replied Haz. "We have our share of those in Pennsylvania, too."

"Well, *I* believe, Fly, in the spirit of the thing," remarked Sara-Beth.

"Quite so, my dear," Frank answered her approvingly.

Over the pages of the manuscript, Nicholas and Haslett gave each other a look honed from years of silently appraising the objects before them together. "Sir Francis," Nick gently asked, "what do *you* want done with it?"

"I want it put in the right hands. I have learned in my ninety-one years how easily things can become lost or destroyed. It is not about money or title—it's about who will take care of it best."

"There is no established value," admitted Nick. "Nothing like this has come up for sale before. It could be a matter of a few hundred pounds upward."

Haz nodded his agreement. "And will take some time and effort to assess."

Admiral Austen sat down at his desk and folded his hands before him. "I'm afraid I don't have much left of either. There is also the pressing matter of Fanny and *her* wishes." He raised his right eyebrow in silent intimation at the group standing about him. "But I am a man of duty above all. Cassandra entrusted the manuscript to me, only to suffer a fit of apoplexy a few days later in this very house." His face dimmed at the memory. "I had just returned to sea—she passed at four in the morning, the exact same hour as Jane—and poor Henry had to arrange everything in my absence."

The admiral's guests grew quiet at the realization of what such a long life entailed: the witnessing of more loss than most endure. Sir Francis had already outlived all of his siblings as well as several children and grandchildren—his ties to Fanny, as frayed as they were, must be of some comfort to him. No wonder he struggled to please all the descendants, when the truth with genius was that there could never be consensus of any kind—not when their art touches everyone in such universal and uniquely individual ways.

Henrietta came over and half knelt before him. "Sir Francis, what else do you want?"

He smiled as if in relief at finally being asked, as well as understood.

"I want to go back to Chawton—before it's too late."

FIVE

A Man in Love

————•————

Tower Hamlets, June 28, 1865

Mrs. Denham Scott, care of *The Fountain Hotel*,
Portsmouth, Hampshire

June 28, 1865

My most cherished wife,

    I opened your first missive to me as husband in both anticipa-
tion and dread—I had hoped our next reunion would be a most
permanent one! Forces greater than us, however, seem to conspire
its delay. I blame myself, firstly, for letting you out of my arms
at all. Next, Charlotte—having seven siblings of my own, they
make an easy and convenient target. But I only tease: please give
her my most sincere brotherly affection. As the eldest myself, I
understand your not wanting to leave her high and dry, as you
say, given all you have endured together to get here.

    My charms also appear to be no match for those of Miss
Austen. You write of such a strange mission before you: I picture
a straggling crew of Americans abroad, struggling with our
different English ways—can one cut, then switch the fork? Is tea

hot or cold?—whilst crammed into a Clarence to take in every square inch of ground where your beloved Austen once tread, only to descend upon the Knight family and Chawton Great House with barely a day's notice. I am surprised that Justice Nash has inexplicably chosen to make the group tomorrow an even odder set, both in number and manner. I wonder if you will end up correct on his intentions regarding my new sister. I shall have to have a word with him, as the head of the family on this side of the ocean.

I would have had you home days ago if I could, but for now, I will draw it for you with words instead. A small but cosy terrace flat on the ground level of Hanbury Street in Tower Hamlets, off Whitechapel, and only a half hour distant from the paper. The landlady assures me that the brand-new water closet is in good working order, and there is a little nook by the front window where you can read, my darling. I have already started a small collection of novels for you from an amusing little bookshop in Bloomsbury, whose owner won it in a game of cards! Imagine what ideas that would give your Miss Gleason!

Across the way from <u>our</u> home is a rather impressive park for this area of London, where I see many pleasant strolls ahead, complete with a pram one day, and perhaps even a dog (whilst I am still the one drawing it all for you!). I have always wanted but could ill afford one (dog, not pram!), with so many other, more pressing, mouths to feed. But you inspire me to be more hopeful for the future than of old. I am only better for your presence and attendance on me, whilst you deserve only the very best.

In endeavouring to hasten your arrival, I shall make plain another, much bolder plan: I have arranged through connections an audition at the New Adelphi for Charlotte this Monday coming, with Fawcett Robinson himself. I am told he is then off as well, to business in Paris. I have no doubt that Charlotte will take the London theatre world by storm, and admit to a selfish interest in securing her companionship for you. And as it would also separate her from "le chaperon," I would be Daedalus himself, killing two birds at once. You may thank me later, in your wonderful way. . . .

When you write the details of your return, do tell me more about the admiral. My editor at the Reynolds's is most intrigued—our readership grows daily and clamours for gossip. Judging by the interest in all things Dickens, I should think any news of Austen would also be of appeal. And the old man sounds quite easy in his dotage, as well as, naturally, entranced by you. The daughter, however, sounds something awful—these women who never express their natural feminine inclination to motherhood and marriage, only to shrink within themselves while suffocating the lives of others.

Do you remember when we first met in private, that day on the Common, you in that lovely red coat—now with your garnet to match, that stone that dangles so temptingly only for me (do I make you blush?)—and Coco nipping about our heels, and you told me you weren't certain you could ever leave America? Thank you for entrusting me with your happiness, my love. We have our entire lives to spend together, so I suppose I can wait a few more days, as difficult as that is proving to be, to prove my devotion to that worthy end.

Your most affectionate husband,

D.

SIX

✳

Tarpaulin Talk

————•————

The Road to London, June 29, 1865

The Americans arrived in two carriages for the journey to Chawton: the three men in one Clarence, the three women in the other. The ladies were dressed in an array of pastel colors to suit the bright summer day—lilac purple, chiffon yellow, and rose pink—with bonnets of straw and taffeta to match, while Sir Francis met them on the hill in full military costume. The blue of his wool coat was a rich navy and the gold buttons newly buffed. He tucked a wood-and-brass telescope under one arm, and his right hand inside the white waistcoat as if posing for a portrait.

"Father, stand still, please," Fanny scolded before he left, having declined to join the expedition. Instead, she circled the admiral in the front foyer, brushing the gold fringe on the epaulettes, pulling at the hem of the requisition waistcoat. Recent navy regulations prohibited the wearing of one's uniform following honorable discharge, but this was the one rule of his profession that Admiral Austen always chose to ignore.

"I am so grateful for this attention," he greeted his female companions in the carriage, slowly settling on the rear-facing seat next to Henrietta. "Mrs. Scott, you must be eager to get to London. I am sincerely sorry for any disruption of plans."

"Denham Scott is surely the most patient man on earth," Sara-Beth chimed in.

Henrietta blushed, silently recalling the word *dangling* in that morning's post from her husband. "How could I give up the chance to walk in the footsteps of our favorite author, and alongside her very kin?" The admiral now blushed himself and patted Henrietta's hand near his. The carriage headed north on the road to London, giving them both an expansive view of the harbor below, the curve of the medieval sea walls, the billowing white sails of the naval vessels that flocked together like gulls.

"Nash showed us the house where they say Dickens was born," Charlotte mentioned as they left Portsmouth behind. "Did Miss Austen spend time here, too?"

Sir Francis shook his white fringe of hair with a poignant air, as if summoning the ghosts. "Only occasionally. We lived as one family for a time—my first wife, my mother, and both my sisters—but west of here, in Southampton. After our father died. Those were unsteady years for us all—I myself was often away. But oh, how my sister Jane loved the sea."

At these last words, Henrietta and Charlotte stole a look at each other—*this* was exactly why they had crossed an ocean.

"My brother Charles greatly distinguished himself in the navy, and Jane was very proud of our service in war. She had a strong sense of the righteous and was gratified by vindication of any sort. One could not easily sway her." He smiled weakly in remembrance. "She was much like our mother that way."

"Did the family ever figure in the books?" Charlotte asked.

"Perhaps you inspired Captain Wentworth in *Persuasion*?" Henrietta suggested with an encouraging smile.

Sir Francis grew cheerier at the interest of the three young women surrounding him. "I believe myself most like Captain Harville of that book in taste and occupation." He held up the telescope. "Carved by my own hand, do you see? Jane did honor Charles and me in *Mansfield Park* with mention of our ships—seeking our permission first, of course. And when doing corrections for the printer, she would consult us on tarpaulin talk, as we sailors call our turns of phrase."

The thirty-mile journey was to take three hours, most of it along the road from Portsmouth to London. It was agreed that they would turn off at Liss, then stop in Selborne for luncheon before continuing on to Chawton. Henrietta expressed her astonishment at how quickly the landscape shifted, from the sharp blueness of the rocks and sea to fields of radiant, sun-kissed green, while Charlotte called out the wooden guideposts at every turnpike.

"Will we pass near the Devil's Punch Bowl?" she asked the admiral.

"That is further north, a stretch of road under the purview of highwaymen not too long ago—but today *I* am at your protection." The three women exchanged quick smiles at these last words. "Admiral Byng traveled this road to face the firing squad on the deck of the *Monarque*—the only British admiral ever to be executed. And the Duke of Wellington, the Tsar, and the King of Prussia marched together here in celebration of Napoleon's capture. I was away on the North Sea at the time, commanding the *Elephant* 74."

"For seventy-four guns."

"Why, Mrs. Scott, yes!"

"But you are too polite," Henrietta added with a smile. "Did not the *Elephant* capture one of *my* country's ships in 1812?"

"Why, my dear, how do you know all this?"

"Harry's been at the Athenaeum in Boston for months, researching your history," Charlotte boasted, and Henrietta turned to her in gratitude. She had heard few kind words from Charlie since the engagement.

Sir Francis beamed at Henrietta and patted her hand again in his gentle, fatherly way.

"I knew you would come to me," he said next, so cryptically that all four passengers rode at some length in pleasant contemplation of both his meaning and the view.

Sir Francis had sent a letter ahead to his nephew, Edward Knight junior, to alert him to their arrival. Edward had inherited the Chawton Great House estate in 1852 upon the death of his father and namesake, who was one of four older brothers to Cassandra, Francis, Jane, and Charles. "My brother Edward lived to eighty-five. So many in our family have been blessed with long life," Sir Francis shared with his companions on the drive. "How tragic to lose the genius in our midst at barely forty years of age."

As impecunious as his female relations eventually found themselves, the elder Edward had landed on top of the wheel of fortune. At age twelve, he had been adopted by the wealthy childless Knights who, in needing an heir of their own, had taken a fancy to Edward. He had ended up with a new name and enough homes to lend one—the old steward's cottage in Chawton—to his mother and sisters for the remainder of their lifetime. Here, from 1809 until her death, Jane Austen had written or revised all six of her major novels, making the cottage hallowed ground for her admirers.

"You will find Chawton much as it was in Jane's time. There is a great debate in the family as to her inspiration for Highbury, the town in *Emma*. Some believe it to be Alton or even Chawton—there is some argument that the Great House itself was the model for Mr. Knightley's Donwell Abbey."

"So, we shall walk in both her *and* her characters' footsteps!" marveled Charlotte.

The carriages approached Chawton from Upper and Lower Farringdon, then along Gosport Road. The journey had given the sisters their first sight of the rolling hills of England that they had read and dreamed about since childhood—"If one can dream about hills!" Sara-Beth chided them.

"'*What are men to rocks and mountains?*'" Henrietta quoted from *Pride and Prejudice*.

"Jane stood fast to that notion, too," Sir Francis said to the sisters' delight. "She was not as romantic as appeared, but rather overarchingly *just*. She measured everything out most precisely herself, and believed that everyone in life should get their exact due. In the world of her imagination, at least, they always did."

As the admiral's female companions mulled over this fascinating glimpse into Jane's character, the carriage turned right onto a long gravel drive leading to Chawton Great House. Justice Nash and the Nelson brothers stood waiting up ahead, their carriage having arrived first. The coachman helped Sir Francis down from the Clarence, followed by the ladies. As the two groups moved toward each other, the large wooden door to the Elizabethan house slowly opened and a small springer spaniel bounded out.

"Sir Francis, welcome," the housekeeper announced from the doorway. "Sir Edward sends his regrets. The family has gone on holiday to the sea and are sorry to miss you. We haven't seen you in some time."

"Thank you, Mrs. Berwick. Allow me to introduce my guests from America."

After greetings were exchanged and refreshment declined for the present, the housekeeper gave the admiral a heavy iron ring of keys. "Sir Edward has done some improvements to the walled garden—this is the key here—but the rest of the house will be much as you remember it."

Sir Francis turned to his collective escort.

"You've come so far—where should we start?"

For the visitors from America, there was only one answer to that.

SEVEN

A Day with Austen

Chawton, June 29, 1865

At the ladies' insistence, the admiral returned to the carriage for the one-mile drive to the cottage. He asked Charlotte and Haslett to join him, having not yet forsaken his plans to make a match. "Miss Stevenson should rest her ankle, and I shall chaperone!" he declared. Everyone else smiled at the irony of the notion and followed behind on foot.

Heading north along Gosport Road, they passed the rectory, the village school, and the cricket pitch where several of Edward Austen Knight's six sons had distinguished themselves in the sport. At the junction with Winchester Road, the carriage pulled to a stop next to a small duck pond, and Justice Nash came forward to help Sir Francis down.

"This is our one publican house," the admiral announced, nodding at the building on his right, "the only commercial activity of any note, I am afraid, and here"—he took off his cocked hat, trimmed in gold to match his buttons, and swung it in a grand arc through the air—"*here* is my sister's."

Henrietta and Charlotte gave each other a look of excitement that the Nelson brothers also shared, then linked arms as everyone crossed the road to take in the simple yet surprisingly large red-brick two-story home. There was a moulded canopy on carved brackets above the front door, hipped clay tiles, and timber window frames. On either side of the entranceway were two twelve-paned windows looking out onto the road from just a few feet away.

"The larger window beyond was the drawing room, which my brother bricked over for privacy," the admiral explained, pointing his hat to their left, "and this—*this* was the dining parlor, where Jane chose to do her writing." They stood in a row behind a low picket fence, its white paint faded and chipping, as the admiral spoke. "I am told there are now three tenements for estate workers inside and we must respect their privacy as such, but you can imagine—I hope—how my sister would sit by this window, so close to the road, and work at a little round table for her desk. From here she could watch the activity of the village, the people and coaches coming and going in all different directions. I understand there will soon be a rail line from the nearby town of Alton to Winchester, but our village remains off the map for that. It has always rather kept to itself."

He led them a few yards along to the wooden gate and matching red-brick wall that marked the southern perimeter to the cottage's lot. "I believe we may enter here with impunity," Sir Francis informed the group, and they eagerly followed behind as he unlatched the gate. On their left was a hedge of hornbeam, a small orchard and an impressive oak ("Planted by Jane herself!"), and a well-tended vegetable-and-herb garden. On their right was the southwest-facing side of the house with another entrance marked by a canopy, and a nearly identical door next to that which fronted the kitchen.

"Here my Martha loved to toil—she kept the most thorough cookbook for the family, which we treasure still. They each had their roles, you see, in keeping house together. Jane's chief duty was not of such seeming importance—presiding over breakfast." He smiled at the memory. "She took it seriously, though, as she did all responsibility. Especially the tea—she made sure there was plenty of supply and placed its regular order with Twinings in London. You know how we British are on the subject."

They were startled by a sudden creaking noise as the side door opened and an elderly man peeked out. "Sir Francis?" The admiral narrowed his eyes as if straining to remember him. "It's Peter Wright, sir? I worked here for Mrs. Austen and Miss Cassandra—*and* Lady Austen," he quickly added, as if only then recalling the late-in-life transformation of spinster Martha Lloyd to knighted admiral's wife.

"Why, Peter, how are you?"

"Still in the cottage, Sir Francis, as you see." The man gave an easy smile. "We don't go far here in Chawton."

"Peter helped Martha with the kitchen garden," explained the admiral to his guests, then turned back to the old man with a nostalgic smile. "I fear she was quite the taskmaster when it came to that."

"She knew what she was about, that one."

The admiral shook his head amusedly. "My Martha entered a house of ten children and had everything shipshape in no time. Peter, these are friends of mine, from America. They are ardent admirers of my sister's writing."

The greatest look of pride lit up the old man's face. "You must step in, then, for a moment, 'n see the downstairs. We none of us tenants mind."

It took several more assurances but soon the group, to its astonishment, was standing in the very rooms where Jane Austen herself once stood. The drawing room had been transformed into a common gathering space, but the dining parlor remained much as Sir Francis remembered it. All four of the Stevenson and Nelson siblings headed straight for the window where Jane Austen had sat and looked out as she wrote.

"She played piano first upon waking each morning," the admiral recounted, "then after breakfast stayed here to write."

"Piano first?" asked Nicholas. "Perhaps that induced creativity."

"A clearing of the deck," Henrietta suggested, catching his eye.

"Quite so," replied the admiral. "Each note played off the other, arising from the prior, leading to the next. She treated each and every word on the paper much the same."

Charlotte turned from the window, tears in her eyes, and gazed about the rest of the room. "Is the little round table not here, Mr. Wright?"

"The walnut table?" Peter shook his head. "Mrs. Austen gave it to William Littlejohn, another of the servants, when he retired. It's still here in Chawton, though. As I said, not much leaves."

"Imagine if everything of hers could be brought back together somehow," Henrietta wondered aloud. "What we would learn—what we would see!"

"Such a collection would be impossible to appraise," Nicholas observed. "That alone would help protect it."

"Yes," agreed Henrietta, "and that alone should tell us something."

There was such an air of contentment in the room, the kind that one can only experience as a group, all of one mind, encountering every new element together and disposed to think happily of whatever they might encounter next. Admiral Austen took pride in having conceived of and created this very moment, if not yet a successful love match. It was more than just a visit for him, however, or even a much-needed goodbye.

He felt the iron ring of keys in his pocket, and recalled the other secret task ahead.

EIGHT

The Walled Garden

Chawton, June 29, 1865

When they returned to the Knight estate, the admiral led his visitors through the lych-gate to the village church of St. Nicholas, where the family regularly worshipped just steps from their house. There were memorials inside the medieval stone building for Sir Francis's brother, Edward, and the several nieces and nephews whom the admiral had also outlived, and an adjoining graveyard reserved for members of the Knight family.

The stones that marked the graves of Cassandra and their mother were around the back of the church, standing stick upright and surrounded by clumps of wild daisies. Jane was buried miles away in the cathedral of Winchester, where she had retreated in her final days for medical care. "Such an honor, of course." Sir Francis again turned melancholy with regret. "And another significant occasion which duty prevented me from attending."

The rest of the group quietly moved away from the two Austen graves, leaving their host standing there with his head bowed in prayer, and passed one by one through the stile at the back of the churchyard. The Great House was now on their left, and on the right was a small wilderness separated by a ha-ha from the farm fields that bordered Gosport Road. When Sir Francis eventually rejoined them, he pointed out the views through the closed space of orchard trees and vegetable patches, all of it symmetrically divided by pea-gravel walkways along which several Dorking chickens tip-toed about. "Edward did not reside here, but at Godmersham Park. He even graciously lent me the Great House for a time. In fact, Herbert, our sixth, was first to be born here in over a hundred years. The children loved to run about inside these walls, and play hide-and-go-seek. . . ."

The group began to disperse and the admiral advised Charlotte and Haslett not to miss the shrubbery nearby, drawing amused looks from the others.

"This was once your home, too, then?" Henrietta asked Sir Francis as they resumed their stroll together. "No wonder you wanted to come back."

"I had many reasons for doing so." His grip tightened on the telescope in his hand. "Whenever Cass visited Portsdown Lodge, we would read the novels together. She brought along the two unfinished manuscripts as well. My daughter Catherine—the writer, Catherine Hubback—read one so of-ten, she was able to finish it from memory and arrange publication when her husband became unable to provide."

"I understand such devotion to her words. My sister and I both know vast passages of *Pride and Prejudice* by heart."

"Jane once teasingly accused Martha of making her read aloud an early draft of *Pride and Prejudice* enough times so as to commit its entirety to mem-ory." His piercing eyes filled with tears. "It's all in our heads—too much of it. The family considers its reputation as much as hers. But what will that matter a hundred years hence? Jane is the one who is immortal."

"All families would contemplate that," Henrietta assured him. Her own father was from this more reserved generation—so much concern for pro-priety, for what others might think, but also respect for those unable to defend or speak for themselves. "But your family has a far greater burden than most."

The admiral looked fatigued by the very notion, and she motioned for him to rest on a nearby bench. He placed his cocked hat and telescope on the seat to his left, then waited for Henrietta to take her place on his right before joining her.

"Mrs. Scott, you *do* understand, don't you?" he plaintively asked.

"I hope so." She had recognized a special kinship with the admiral from the start. "I think we both struggle with being good and moral, yet true to our own needs and wants all the same. My father will be so disheartened by my sudden marriage—I doubt the generations to come will care. Either way, I'd rather *I* be the one to get my life wrong."

"I thought Cassandra was wrong to burn so much. But it was hers to do with as she wished."

"Precisely," insisted Henrietta. "And now it's yours—she wouldn't have given it to you otherwise. That is both the burden of the legacy and the privilege. We should always be completely free to decide whom to foist it upon." She sighed. "In my country, there is much talk about freedom, yet still so many restrictions. Freedom, by its very nature, must be absolute and available to all—one should never fight for less."

"Well said, my dear." The admiral took up the telescope and pointed it about the garden, twisting it into focus, letting the brass joints catch the late afternoon sun.

"It's beautiful."

"I made it myself." Henrietta smiled as she listened; he had mentioned this fact more than once, clearly proud of his handiwork. "I have come to accept, after so much loss, how only the things we make will last. A topaz cross on a necklace—a family recipe written down—my sister's books. She didn't write those letters to last, but they do, and that's the dilemma." Sir Francis sighed. "If only Jane herself had destroyed it all."

W
hat do you really think was the admiral's design in coming here today?" Haz asked Charlotte as they strolled the shrubbery next to the walled garden.

"What do you think is his sudden design when it comes to the two of *us*?" Charlotte replied, causing them both to laugh.

"I do wonder if he invited us to England to marry off more than just his 'certain objects,' as he calls them."

"Why Haz, how astute! But then Harry went and foiled him—remember his face at luncheon that first day, when he learned about the elopement?"

"You call it an elopement, do you—when you yourself knew in advance?"

"The word can also mean desertion."

He grinned at the sour face she made. "We may be too attached to our siblings for our own good. As for this trip to Chawton, perhaps Sir Francis just wanted to be away. That Fanny-Sophia is rather frightening. Reminds me of Lu."

"Oh Haz, surely not!" exclaimed Charlotte. "Lu is constantly thinking of others and how to please them—that she is so forceful in her opinions is the *only* similarity there. It's the same with Sara-Beth."

"Whatever can you mean?"

"Sara-Beth speaks her mind so—I think you and your brother are intimidated by that. How un*fem*inine," remarked Charlotte, stressing the second syllable in that word. "But she, like Lu, is so brave and loyal— something you men claim to value above all."

Haslett pondered these words as they turned at the end of the shrubbery to complete the landscaped walk. "What cause is Miss Gleason so loyal to?"

"What could she be? Look at how we women are educated! But to her friends—oh, how I wish all my acquaintances were as pleasant and easy as her. She has not complained once during our travels—have you not noticed?" Charlotte *tsk*ed him. "She gave Lu most of her winnings. And you call her spoiled."

"She gets everything she wants!"

"She goes after it, is all—I call that brave." Charlotte shook her head at him in dismay. "She has set her cap at you and the world tells you that this is wrong, somehow, this expression of her will. Why shouldn't she pursue whomever she likes? If we women waited for men to act, the world would have ended centuries ago, making all this just so much swamp and jungle."

She jostled playfully against his side, as if prodding him to acknowledge what everyone else could see, and Haslett growled in reluctant response. "I can't give in to her now, Charlie, not after all these years. I can't let a girl win at everything."

"Oh Haz, if you keep considering it in this manner, you will end up the very *pic*ture of loneliness." Charlotte laughed.

Mrs. Berwick had arranged tea for the visitors in the dining room of the Great House. They sat about the same long mahogany table where Jane Austen herself once dined with her widowed brother Edward and his eleven children, and enjoyed food prepared from the same recipes that Martha Lloyd had decades ago copied down: white soup, spare rib, carraway cake, and currant wine. Sir Francis was touched by this gesture from a longtime employee of the family, one of many who resided in the village and helped on the estate. For the estate was the center of Chawton still, the main employer, the caretaker of it all.

Before returning to the carriages for the long drive back to Portsmouth, Sir Francis showed his guests the rest of the house: the stained-glass memorial windows in the upper gallery, the paintings of his brother and other past owners displayed on each floor, the library that Jane had read from during her own visits. The travelers' last stop was the second-floor reading nook off the Ladies' Withdrawing Room. This was a narrow alcove where one could look out and spy any visitors to the house well in advance of arrival. One needed no telescope for *that*, Sir Francis thought to himself.

Once the young women had settled themselves in the carriage, they leaned out the windows to wave goodbye to Mrs. Berwick. The little springer spaniel ran in circles around the two coaches until the housekeeper called it inside, shutting the massive oak front door behind its happily wagging tail. The driver was about to help Sir Francis up next, when he patted his naval waistcoat as if in sudden remembrance.

"I should return the keys," he loudly muttered.

Nash immediately offered to do so in his stead, but the old man was insistent.

"I shan't be a moment."

*H*e does not have long.

These words of the physician were always in his head. They were in his head when he read Mrs. Scott's first letter, and when he answered Mr. Nelson's. And they were in his head now, as he hurried through the Great Hall of the house. He did not have long.

The collection of books in the Knight family library had always been extensive. His brother Edward had kept first editions of their sister's books as well as many others, and Sir Francis wondered at the value of the collection as the years passed. Jane herself had often ventured in here, slipped a favorite volume from the shelf, absconded with it to the reading nook upstairs. She had been a determined scholar in her way, even though her formal schooling—such as it was—had ended by age ten. Reading had then become her sole education: what proof his sister was of its possibility for success.

He stood in the center of the book-lined room, worrying that he would lose his nerve. No one knew of the existence of the letter that he had hidden on himself that day—especially not Fanny, whose own admonishment he now heard: *What have you gone and promised them? These are private, of no business to anyone.* At the thought of his daughter, he began to panic while a wild cacophony of other voices filled his head: *I'd rather I be the one to get my life wrong . . . if only Jane herself had destroyed it all . . . only the things we make will last. . . .*

Martha had discovered the unfinished letter shortly after Jane's death and taken it; to her dying day, she could not explain to her husband why. "Of *course* its words are hurtful to Cassy—I shouldn't wonder that Jane changed her mind in the writing of it, especially so close to the end." But still, Jane had kept it, and kept it hidden from Cassandra—and so, upon finding it, had Martha. Upon *her* death, the unsent letter automatically had become the property of her husband—as a woman, Martha was unable to bequeath it to anyone else. The law gave her no testamentary right, making it now Frank's burden, too.

What if he hid the letter here and it was found too soon—or ended up burned or discarded like the rest? Nothing in life was promised, he knew that well. For all his clandestine efforts, it could all be undone tomorrow by the dusting of a house girl. At least those with the right to care were gone: Jane, Cass, their mother and father, all his siblings, both his wives. If he acted wisely, the letter would one day enlighten the world; he simply preferred not to be present when that day came.

"Sir Francis?"

Mrs. Berwick stood in the doorway of the library, a concerned expression on her face.

He took too long.

Frank gave the housekeeper an apologetic look.

"Have you forgotten something, sir?"

He shook his head. "No, not forgotten. Only remembering."

Then he passed her the ring of keys and left the library just as he had found it.

NINE

✳

Midsummer

◆——————◆

The Road from London, June 29, 1865

The admiral rode back to Portsmouth in the gentlemen's carriage, giving his female companions the privacy to rest. It had been a tiring visit for them all, ending on a sad note as the carriages drove past the graveyard where several of Sir Francis's family lay buried. He would not be joining them there; he would never pay his own respects again.

The men did not watch Sir Francis as solicitously as the women had done. Instead, they spoke of the ship journey they had just made, asked the admiral about the battles off Santo Domingo to interrupt the slave trade, pined over the loss of their beloved president.

"The immensity of the sea is a great tonic for loss," Sir Francis shared with them. "I so yearned for it at times. I was out of service for thirty years, you know."

They did not know. He still wore his uniform, still carried his telescope everywhere he went.

"With America's defeat in the War of 1812 and Napoleon's soon after, I took leave as our brood grew. We lost Mary in childbirth with Cholmeley, our eleventh, only to lose him in infancy as well. Years passed, a fog really, until I remarried and purchased Portsdown Lodge—thirty-five acres—and there I set my efforts in the main. The contentment of family life, although

I was old for it even then. I built the children little paddocks for cricket and archery, netted my Morello cherries, and had no desire to see the sea beyond the view from my hill." He gazed out the carriage window as he spoke. The past swirled before him, a kaleidoscope of images: family picnics on the hill, ice-skating on the meadow, racing chaises down the lane. All that merriment gone—in its place, only memory and pain.

A quiet fell in the carriage, and Justice Nash removed his tobacco pouch and striking match for the men to light their pipes. The sun was still high in the summer sky—it would not set until almost ten, by which time they should be back in Portsmouth.

"Sir Francis, why did you return to sea after so long?" Haz asked.

"I lost my second wife, then two daughters. I sought distraction, and was called to command the North America and West Indies Station on the *Vindictive*." His face brightened at a happier recollection. "This time I took as many of my family as could fit on ship. My sons George and Herbert, a captain himself, and daughters Fanny and Cassandra as hostesses. My eldest boy—my brave Frank—was already away, commandeering boats to suppress slavery off the Isle of Pines in the West Indies. He was injured there—his arm." The admiral looked over at Nick, whose limp he had earlier noticed. "You boys also served that great cause of abolition, I see."

"It was indeed great," agreed Nick. "We held on to that when the unimaginable was asked."

"Brothers killing brothers." Haz stopped as Nick, who sat next to him, laid a hand on his shoulder in comfort. "I once aimed the barrel of my gun in the face of a classmate from St. Joe's, just as our eyes locked. It haunts me still."

The admiral shook his head sadly. "To ask this of men—no matter the justness of the cause—should demand particular attention and salve afterward." He lifted the telescope. "I was spared your unique pain—my enemy was too far for me to see without this."

"May I?" Nicholas asked, and the admiral passed the spyglass to him.

"My brother was one of the first sharpshooters for the Union," explained Haz as Nick ran his hands along the wood. "They fitted a lens to the rifles."

Nick was about to twist the telescope into focus when he noticed the admiral's hands still outstretched toward him. "It's very handsome," he said instead, and quickly passed the spyglass back. "You have a good hand."

"I made toys for the children—little whatnots—keepsake boxes with hidden compartments only they knew about. My family has always been apt to hide things."

Nicholas nodded. "All families do, I think."

"That's what keeps us united," added Haslett with a laugh.

The mood was lightened by the younger brother's words, and the admiral thought of Miss Charlotte's own high spirits—fiery like Fanny but in an altogether more pleasing way. He wondered if his plan to make a match might not succeed after all. It had always amused the family, Jane's own perspicacity when it came to the eventual romance between Martha and himself. Frank's favorite line from *Persuasion* now came to mind—"*she had been forced into prudence in her youth, she learned romance as she grew older: the natural sequel of an unnatural beginning.*" For all his own efforts at love, the admiral had to acknowledge that some things will always out, no matter what you or others do to encourage *or* prevent them.

He did not have long, and he longed to have a hand in something new again, to feel his own efforts mattered. To not yet be a ghost in the room, but a real, magnetic force between others. Jane must have felt that very consolation with her writing. Perhaps that was the source of her pleasure from strangers' compliments on her books—the knowing that you have left a mark far beyond what any eye could see, and everlasting.

An hour north of Portsmouth, they stopped at a coaching inn along the road to take refreshment. Everyone congregated around the outside table, still full of talk from seeing where Jane Austen had lived.

"Meanwhile our friend Louisa's off to find the haunts from Dickens," Charlotte informed the admiral. "He wrote about so many real places, as if standing in that very street or drinking in that very tavern with his imaginary friends."

"Perhaps it is very real to him—perhaps that's why he also acts it out," Nash suggested.

"Acting isn't about real life," Charlotte replied. "It's about making others believe it is."

A strange silence followed this exchange until Henrietta spoke. "Sir Francis, may I ask, why did your sister decline to particularize places in the novels?"

"Some of it was propriety, of course," the admiral replied. "My sister was a woman of her time—that is not where her genius lay, in any rejection of it. She wanted to portray things as they were, but without offense. Certainly, we knew one or two Mr. Collinses in our day—I had my own contretemps with a Lady Catherine de Bourgh of sorts, an admonishing aunt. But that is all forgotten now, as it should be."

"The justices and I—our literary circle—have a theory," Nash spoke again.

The admiral noticed everyone else sit up in keen interest. How he loved these moments: the eternal puzzle that was his brilliant sister.

"She is looking down at us from her position of genius—through that parlor window—like the eye of God that can take everything in," Nash continued. "She is not really part of any of this"—he waved his hand about the tavern yard—"and I mean that, Sir Francis, most favorably." The entire group fell quiet again at this notion, while Nash left to summon more refreshments for the table.

"Will you be seeing Louisa in London?" Haslett asked Charlotte.

"She's at the mercy of her employer now. They are to leave next week for Brussels and Cologne, then down the Rhine. . . ." Charlotte answered Haz with an air of distraction, for her eyes were not on him.

Meanwhile, Nash stood in the tavern's low-timbered entranceway, instructing a serving maid. But his eyes were not on *her*, even though her cheeks shone bright pink in his presence. Instead, as he spoke his order, Nash stared straight above the young woman's head at Charlotte, who continued to watch him from yards away. Suddenly she, too, blushed, just like the serving maid, while the rest of the table fell silent. At that moment, there were only two people in the tavern yard who mattered—two people engaged in a most intriguing struggle—and all eyes and attention were firmly fixed on them.

Charlotte finally turned back to the rest of the group, breaking her own spell. "I do hope to join Lu soon on the Continent."

Nash caught these words as he returned to the table. "You will not be long in London?"

"Only long enough to meet with Mr. Robinson of the Adelphi."

"An audition?" Nash stared at her in surprise. "I didn't know."

"We just heard this morning by post. It is this coming Monday, then I am to let Henrietta and Mr. Scott settle into married life and shift for myself."

"Justice Nash." Miss Gleason turned to him with a mischievous air. "When does your court next convene?"

"The second Monday in September."

"Why, right when Charlie and Lu could be gallivanting about Italy and most in need of a chaperone!"

Nash downed the whisky he had just been brought. "I'll not be doing any more of that," he stated quietly, as if to himself.

"And you two boys—what do you have planned?" Sir Francis asked the Nelsons. "I sincerely hope the group is not entirely disbanding."

"To see Mr. Dickens speak, for one," Haslett answered. "We were only toddlers when he last visited America. Who knows if he will come to our shores again?"

"Then we should attend his next reading together," Nash offered. "Such a remarkable actor—with just a desk and gaslight onstage, he brings all his characters to life."

"I am so eager to know, Sir Francis—did Miss Austen ever do the same?" Henrietta asked the admiral.

"I can say this—no one enjoyed reading aloud their own work more."

"Oh, that is just as it ought to be!" Charlotte happily nodded. "To take such delight in her words—just like her readers do!"

They returned to the carriages and the final leg of their journey. The men settled back, lit their pipes again, and quietly smoked as day turned to night. But it was the night of midsummer, that abundance of sun and time. With it, one could return home, confront the ghosts of the past, and stir the flames of love for at least one young couple—all in a day's work, the admiral thought pleasingly to himself.

TEN

✦

The Crystal Palace

◦——•——◦

THAT SAME NIGHT
Portsdown Lodge, June 29, 1865

S he finally had the house to herself.

Her father wasn't expected back from Chawton until sundown, and the staff were dismissed for the night. Fanny had urged all six servants to attend the traveling fair in town, watching from the bow window as they disappeared over the incline in the hill. The two youngest maids giggled and straggled behind the rest, featherheaded ducklings just like the American girls in bright bonnets who had early that morning whisked her father away. Fanny felt her face tighten. She could keep watching through the window, now as then—although her father's trusty telescope was gone, the four-pull one from Admiral Gambier rested on its nearby stand at the ready. But she did not have long.

Fanny took a first sip of the Madeira from the pantry—she had never before touched a drop—then crouched down beside her father's desk. Removing a hairpin from her bun, she began to fiddle in the keyhole to the famous Bramah lock. She had some idea of what to do: fourteen summers ago, she had watched Boston locksmith Alfred Hobbs demonstrate how to pick the lock at the Great Exhibition of 1851. But even Hobbs, first in the world to break the Bramah, had taken fifty-one hours to do so; she had nowhere near as much time.

It was her father who had wanted to visit the world's first fair being held that summer in London's Hyde Park. He was in desperate need of occupation, having recently retired from the sea and still not recovered from the death of their stepmother Martha. She had always been Martha to the children, some of them already adults when she had literally *stepped* into their late mother's shoes, once *wore* her shoes, for goodness' sake! There had always been a touch of the common about Martha that she had not seemed interested in rising above: the menial household chores better left to servants, the indulgence of dogs as if children themselves, the loud spasms of laughter (*Oh, how* jolly *their Martha liked to be*).

Fanny had agreed to escort her father to the Great Exhibition against her own inclination—rarely did the two of them travel alone together. She could not have known how that day would lead straight to this moment: on her knees, fiddling with the lock in the desk between sips of the Madeira, going over and over Hobbs's demonstration inside the shimmering crystal palace built especially for the fair. The inventor had shown the spectators how to apply the most careful touch and pressure on the bolt, then to insert a steel needle—as thin as a hairpin—through the keyhole of the barrel-shaped lock. Inside the barrel were eighteen steel sliders, thin as wafers and of varying lengths, which allowed for nearly half a billion different permutations and required perfect alignment. Sir Francis had stood next to Fanny in the crowd, exclaiming in delight at Hobbs's display of skill and proclaiming him a genius like his sister.

Father and daughter had silently returned from the Great Exhibition, and one week later something new arrived at Portsdown Lodge: a Davenport captain's desk from cabinetmaker Gillows of Lancaster and London. Her father was as enamored of it as he was of his handmade wooden toys, and from outside his study she could hear him showing George the secret compartments and extra-secure Bramah lock. This was where her father soon moved all his private correspondence, previously stored in an old ship's chest at the foot of his bed.

The desk's turned legs were cupped in brass caster wheels, just one of its many oddities. Sometimes at night, lying in bed pretending to snore, Fanny could hear the Davenport being rolled across the Persian carpet toward the bow window in the study below. She would lie there, still as death, and picture her father standing before the desk as if at the helm of the *Vindictive* and in charge of hundreds of men, or planning military maneuvers on a battle map before him. All the while he wore the special round key to the lock about his neck as if a medal.

Over an hour passed in the empty house and still she fiddled, and still the lock remained as impregnable and mysterious as her father himself. How ironic that of his many children, she was the one left at Portsdown Lodge. He had preferred almost anyone else to her growing up, Cassie Elizabeth most of all. She and their father had picked cherries together, raced the chaise down the lane, painted *en plein air* with their easels side by side. Now the older Stevenson sister was constantly at his side instead—or was her new surname *Scott*? It was all so confusing, the husband of a few days nowhere to be seen, and that Nicholas Nelson mooning over Henrietta what's-her-name as mortifyingly as her father. . . .

On aching knees, Fanny continued to fuss and push and twist with none of Hobbs's success. Part of her was glad for the security of what was locked inside: Aunt Jane's private letters, the very opposite of her published work. The mere gossip and musings of a spinster relation whom Fanny had never met but with whom she felt a kinship nonetheless. It was clear from the books—was it not?—that Aunt Jane also considered duty and decorum to be paramount to society: the glue that held everything together.

When it came to their famous aunt, the family knew its duty—Jane had made her wishes abundantly clear. Even if she hadn't, everyone deserved a sphere of privacy that would outlive them, no matter the value that strangers might one day place on their words. History was only necessary as a moral corrective on others—if one could learn something charitable and instructive from it. What happened inside a single family, of any intimate nature, could be of no importance to anyone else.

The family had held hard to this notion for nearly fifty years, yet her father was clearly at risk of softening on this point: corresponding like a lovesick schoolboy with young women in America, inviting a group of rough-and-tumble Americans into their home, traipsing about Chawton with his collective chaperone. He was the one forcing Fanny to take action. Who knew what might happen if tradesmen like the Nelsons got their hands on what was in the desk? Family history was kept hidden for a reason.

Another hour passed, another sip of Madeira. She banged the side of the desk in frustration and felt the Davenport shift on its caster wheels. Sitting on her heels in thought, she shoved the hairpin back into her tight bun so hard, it hit her skull. But she didn't feel a thing. *So this is why men drink,* she heard herself think.

She stood up and pushed the captain's desk again, this time letting it roll inches forward and backward on the carpet. The sun was beginning to set. Her father would want the carriages home before dark and would have timed the journey with his usual precision; the poster for the traveling fair promised fireworks. She had just enough time.

The desk slid easily through the study doorway and into the corridor—where George did not hover about, for once—then along the oak floorboards to the front foyer with its checkered marble floor. The desk rotated on the smooth tiles as if with a mind of its own, the turned cabriole legs swerving sharply around the pedestal table in the center of the room before rattling toward the front doors.

This was where she struggled. There were three steps descending to the lawn and here the desk refused to behave. She decided to stop pushing and break its path with her own weight instead. She shimmied sideways and backward down the steps, the desk pressing hard against her until she felt the prickle of the dry parched lawn of midsummer beneath her cloth slippers. She stood on the top of the hill and took a deep breath, then pushed the desk one last time until it came to rest in the grave of white sand and red bricks piled there.

D own the hill, then up, then down again, the carriages traveled. It was Frank's favorite view in all of England, coming over the hill one last time from Horndean, that first glimpse of the harbor full of Her Majesty's fleet. Here the old Saxon forests disappeared as the land prepared to meet the sea, and the green of England turned sail-white with the downland's chalk cliffs.

The other men in the carriage dozed about Sir Francis, but he was too happily agitated for sleep. Hearing the admiration of relative strangers for his sister never failed to stir him. The entire family had known they had a genius in their midst. Thank goodness for his Martha who, by joining the Chawton household of women, had helped free Jane to write.

Following the death of their father, each brother offered up their various rented homes to their mother and sisters. During this nomadic time, Jane wrote very little. Not until Chawton, and the cottage, and the little twelve-sided table. It had turned out, most fortuitously, that there was nothing like a settled view of the world for his sister to look deep inside it, her eye cutting through the layers of grime and gloss that mire us all, as if a microscopic lens. The expansive hustle and bustle of Dickens's London could not provide the best view for her.

He stared impatiently out the carriage window, waiting like a child for the curve of the River Solent, the sight of the Spithead, the entrance to the sea. The same view as from his own hill and the dozens of windows of Portsdown Lodge. The letter stayed safely hidden on him for now; he would keep it secret a little while longer. Life revealed most everything in its time—just like the chalk of the cliffs, which no force of wind or violent water could wash away. It was there all along, waiting to be found. So, too, was Jane's legacy.

The adoration for his sister's writing was destined to grow. This hadn't always been the case. After her death, the books had quickly gone out of print. But the radiance of her words somehow persisted, the flame of her intellect lighting one reader to the next, from the servant William Little-john whose descendants still owned the little round table to his daughter Catherine completing the story of the Watsons—from the justices of a state supreme court in the New World to his kindly new friends in the carriage, the poor brothers who struggled still with a very different kind of war. God help this world should there ever be another like it.

He gazed up from the horizon of the harbor, above the line of trees that marked the start to his property. The sun was beginning its descent, setting the summer sky aflame with the colors of the tropics. This was when the admiral could most imagine himself anywhere in the world: from the coral reefs of the Caribbean to the crystalline rocks of the Baltic Shield. The sea connected everyone in this way, gifting the same view of the setting sun no matter where one stood.

He brought the telescope to his eye, twisted the brass joints, heard the clicking noise from inside. Through the spyglass he saw the tangerine sun setting on his right, its low rays bouncing off the water to the west, then on his left, the eastern sky another ball of orange—the entire heavens were on fire tonight. A thin ribbon of smoke cleaved the horizon behind his beloved Portsdown Lodge, winding upward like a snake, melting the tops of his own trees with its haze. Only one word this time resounded in his head.

Fanny.

ELEVEN

Mansfield Park

The Massachusetts Supreme Judicial Court
June 29, 1865

W hat is our opinion on *Mansfield Park?*"

Chief Justice Adam Fulbright raised his right eyebrow momentously. Although on summer recess, the six justices continued to meet at the courthouse, finding their private chambers most conducive to lengthy and spirited debate.

"It is remarkably short on admirable characters compared to the other works." Justice Roderick Norton snorted. "Fanny Price is nothing to a true Austen heroine."

"I must concur with Roderick—for once!" Justice Conor Langstaff conceded with a grin.

"Perhaps we are to regard Fanny Price as more moral construct than character," the chief justice suggested, revealing his hand up front as he always did. "After all, who in the book has less freedom than Fanny? She is treated as property, even by someone as low as Aunt Norris. For Austen's theme here to work, Fanny needs to be fully at the mercy of everyone else in the book—she cannot have Anne Elliot's ease of likability, or Lizzy's intelligence. In this way, I consider *Mansfield Park* to be first and foremost a treatise on power and the harm that comes from ownership, and how to maintain self-respect in the face of it."

Justice William Stevenson looked up, intrigued, from the glass of Madeira in his hands. "How so?" With Connie's assistance, he continued to mull over the ramifications of his own behavior when it came to his daughters. What might have happened if he had respected instead of commanded? Perhaps they would not have run off—perhaps the three of them would have ended up touring England together instead.

"Let us consider how so many in the book, good or bad, urge Fanny to marry Henry Crawford not out of duty to herself but in service to *him*, to civilize *him*," continued the chief justice energetically, warming to his case. "This is the very notion still enshrined in British law, and ours to nearly as great an extent: that regardless of a man's behavior toward *her*, a woman's duty is first to *him*. This view is, I posit, the very antithesis of freedom—and the very reason there is so much increasing discontent among our female populace."

"Exactly!" Langstaff, the doting new father of twin daughters, jumped up in his seat. "Well put, Adam!"

"That word *freedom*," Justice Philip Mackenzie mused aloud as he rhythmically tapped the cover to his copy of the book. "There is something rotten in Sir Bertram's house—a fundamental misunderstanding of freedom which inevitably leads to its abuse. Freedom is not about ensuring you get everything you want, but rather becoming the best self that you can be. Therein lies life's great reward for us *and* for those around us. I always come back to Cicero," he added to the playful groans of the other men. "'When each person loves the other as much as himself, it makes one out of the many.' E pluribus unum: such a motto takes care of it all."

"Our state legislature put those words on Massachusetts coppers for a reason," agreed the chief justice.

"Yet during the fighting, the Union took up 'In God We Trust,'" Norton interjected, "and now Americans can hold that motto, too, in their pocket change."

"Ah, yes, the so-called Sovereignty of God amendment, which sought to add those same four words to the beginning of our constitution." Langstaff sighed. "How interesting, that the strictest constructionist among us"—he nodded pointedly at Norton—"would permit legislative revamping of the very *preamble* to that great document—so much for its ideas being set in stone! Thank goodness this Christian constitutional amendment failed last year to reach Congress. To regard our Civil War as God's punishment for omitting Him from the constitution is to deny our moral responsibility for the scourge that was slavery."

Norton and Peabody, the two most conservative and religious members of the court, both started forward at his words, and the chief justice was next to jump up.

"I am going to refill our glasses, and we shall discuss this matter calmly and judiciously." He poured each justice more Madeira wine from the decanter, a unifying gesture that he often made at such tense moments. "Now, since the matter of religion has been raised, let us ponder: Where is God in *Mansfield Park*?"

There was a long, stunned silence.

"Perhaps there is no God in *Mansfield Park* because Austen is there in his stead," Langstaff suggested to gasps from several of the men.

"Conor—how blasphemous!" exclaimed Peabody.

"Please, this is a novel we discuss," protested Langstaff with a dismissive wave of the hand. "No one has more power over it than the author. Who else can create a world, populate it, then decide how and when to mete out justice?"

"We should only have such power here," moaned Norton, "limited as we are by the whims of our legislature."

The chief justice continued to stand in the center of the room, decanter of Madeira still in hand. "How, then, does Austen rule the world of *Mansfield Park*? Is she a benevolent god who morally guides and inspires, or a god who leaves her creatures to their own devices?"

"Chief Justice." Ezekiel Peabody put his hand to his chest as if struck. "This discussion!"

"No, Adam is onto something," insisted Mackenzie. "In *Mansfield Park*, power is fully unchecked—wealth and other attractions trump all. If a Mary Crawford can viably tempt Edmund Bertram, there is no hope for anyone. Yet we can see Austen's godlike hand in how each character ultimately reaps what they sow. This retributive form of justice is not always the outcome in our own world— much as we here on the bench may try," he wistfully added. "In our world, Fanny might end up forever banished by Sir Bertram to the slums of Portsmouth for refusing to marry Henry Crawford, and Edmund a lovesick dupe."

William Stevenson finally rendered his own opinion on the text. "I would argue that *Mansfield Park* is about more than just power, which both bestows and requires freedom—it is about whether freedom itself requires *property*."

The chief justice turned to him. "Fanny has nothing—hence she can't be free?"

William nodded. "That's what those trying to control her believe to be true. That's the only way Sir Bertram's threat of her banishment can work. But there is always the freedom to aspire within ourselves, no matter how dire the world about us or our poverty in relation to it—to heed duty to the self, no matter one's lack of property or options. Fanny's refusal to accept Henry's proposal is assertion of the self at its purest."

"Ah yes, well said!" the chief justice readily agreed. "Everyone in *Mansfield Park* believes they can manipulate Fanny—they assume lack of opportunity engenders lack of self-respect. People in power too often assume such weakness in those they govern—something both England and France have been made to understand with the blood of revolution." He placed his hands on the worn leatherbound volume of *Mansfield Park* before him. "Powerless as she is, Fanny is very much a true Austen heroine in taking responsibility for her own decisions and the thinking behind them."

"Connie recently shared with me—"

"Connie?" Conor Langstaff teased William, who reddened at his slip.

"Miss Davenish. She is a great proponent of the teachings of John Stuart Mill, who argues that duty to oneself means self-respect or self-development. Not *selfishness*—and certainly not blind adherence to others or to religion or the past. Such development of the individual requires examination and education. And if there is education, there will be less susceptibility to the power of others—and if there is examination, there will be more genuine power in the self." With these concluding words, William could only think of the three remarkable women in his life, who had each found a way to heed their inner spirit no matter their lack of freedom in comparison to men.

The judges fell silent as they contemplated the unprepossessing heroine of the half-century-old book before them. Of all the characters in *Mansfield Park*, Fanny Price somehow remained the most unblemished by the ill will of others, despite possessing the least amount of freedom and opportunity. She achieved this through duty to, and respect of, herself. And in this respect, she appeared to have ended up the freest of them all.

Connie had been the one to introduce William to John Stuart Mill's lesser-known but no less passionate views on the rights of women. These had taken a radical turn following his friendship and marriage with another great thinker, Harriet Taylor. In 1851 they had written an essay together, *The Enfranchisement of Women*, which cited the example of the Unites States of America as a democracy that rested on the constitutional right of everyone to a voice in government:

> *We do not imagine that any American democrat will evade the force of these expressions by the dishonest or ignorant subterfuge that "men" in this memorable document, does not stand for human beings, but for one sex only . . . that "the governed," whose consent is affirmed to be the only source of just power, are meant for that half of mankind only, who in relation to the other, have hitherto assumed the character of governors. The contradiction between principle and practice cannot be explained away. A like dereliction of the fundamental maxims of their political creed has been committed by the Americans in the flagrant instance of the negroes: of this they are learning to recognize the turpitude.*

Connie had taught William much in the course of their nightly conversations. With a philosopher's intellectual dexterity, she could hold contradictory truths simultaneously in her mind. She took the view that nothing in the world should ever be viewed so strictly that it would fail to serve or account for the complexities of a future time (*"What use is history at all, if we can't adapt it to today?"* she once posited to him. *"We will end up back in the jungle, at the mercy of autocrats, with nothing of our own left to inform and inspire"*).

They were sitting together in her rococo parlor, a room that William especially loved, after the judges' discussion of *Mansfield Park* had run late into the night. The parlor was grand and unequivocal, just like Connie herself, and the couple regularly retired here after an evening out. Samuel and Mrs. Pearson knew not to expect William home again until the early morning, and seemed even happy for that fact as they waved him out the door.

"I always know there is something more insidious at play, when there is such a glaring division between principle and practice." Connie sighed. "You men have long urged that women's lack of property eliminates the need for suffrage, yet married women in Massachusetts and other states now enjoy many of the property rights of men. Tell me then, why are we still not allowed to vote, hmm?"

William had no answer for her; Connie always made perfect sense.

"What is worse," she bemoaned, pouring more coffee for them both, "England remains stubbornly behind us. Everything that I might bring into marriage over there"—Constance waved her hands at all the artwork, sculpture, and books that she had acquired over the years—"becomes my husband's the very instant that vows are exchanged. And the fact that an Englishman can presently sue for divorce on the grounds of adultery alone, but Englishwomen must prove additional causes such as desertion or cruelty? It makes my blood boil!"

"The rationale being the difficulty for men in ascertaining the legitimacy of a child?" William pondered his own question with all the attention he would give a legal factum. "Why should that require such difference between the sexes in the right to divorce?"

"Parliament argues there is insufficient harm—insufficient *cruelty*—to the wife from adultery alone. Another way childbearing is turned against us."

"But men and women both suffer from unfaithfulness."

"Exactly! Yet English law is purely punitive of women on that point." Connie smiled and tapped his forearm with the tip of her fan. "Well done, my boy. We shall make a *féministe* out of you yet. Even if you started for less lofty reasons." She gave him a quick peck on the cheek. "Men in power have long argued a sort of rampant risk of illegitimate children in order to suppress women. Meanwhile, they can be unfaithful, sexually violent, or fully absent, and yet we owe them total fealty in return. Could we be more unequal or at their mercy?"

"This goes back to the discussion tonight on *Mansfield Park*—how we must show respect for each other, for there to be self-respect at all. You see, my love, one can always apply Austen."

"So you say."

William hesitated, trying to summon his nerve. "We have noticed a pattern in the books—the number of heroines who turn down marriage." He had never forgotten the extravagant diamond ring Connie had worn during their first carriage ride together, which had inexplicably not made an appearance since.

"A striking of the blow, in its way." She shrugged. "Perhaps the only way for women at that time."

"Have you?"

"Turned down a proposal? Why?" She gave him a playful look. "Hedging your bets, are you?"

"I am no gambler, as you know."

"I do know." She smiled. "Why is that, William?"

"I try to be content with what I have—I will lose it soon enough. We all will."

"To answer your question, yes, I have. A few times."

"A *few*? You have?"

"Don't sound so surprised."

"Do you regret any of them?"

"Not at all. Why—do I seem unhappy?"

"No, but these men . . . you loved them?"

She shrugged again. "Yes and no. They needed marriage—I didn't. In fact, under our state laws at the time, I would have lost all this. I know they look like *things*"—she waved again about the beautiful room—"but they are an extension of me. Here, no matter the constraints of the world about me, I can express myself. I feel inspired—and *much* more productive when I do head out to fight the world."

William stared at her. "But what does this mean for our life together?"

"We go on exactly as we've begun."

"But I would want you with me, in my home . . ."

"No, William, that was your and Alice's home. Besides, I enjoy living by myself." She stroked his hand next to hers. "And these little reunions of ours are quite nice, wouldn't you agree?"

"But you would make such a mother to my girls," he heard himself stammer. "They adore you so already!"

"William, your girls don't need a mother. And neither do you."

"Me?"

"Oh, my love, do you not see how worried everyone is about you? Poor Nash jumping onto that ship, Samuel and Mrs. Pearson keeping vigil for you late into the night. Even the other justices—they accelerated your literary circle this summer for a reason, you know."

"I've been an imposition." His own words surprised him. In fact, it was a moment of such unusual self-awareness that he wondered what else she might help him see, especially when it came to his daughters.

"Yes, but only because you've been loved. You are, my boy, wonderfully easy to love." She took both his hands in hers and bowed to kiss them. "And I do love you."

It was the first time she had said the words, which had already escaped him in a moment of ardor. But as wonderful as it was to hear such sentiment from a woman again, William also worried—as was his wont—whether he could ever be content enough with only that.

TWELVE

✷

The Moon and Sixpence

• — •

Portsdown Lodge, June 30, 1865

The old admiral lay dying in his bed.

The rumor of it hung over all of Portsmouth: he would not recover from the vandalism perpetrated within his house. It was said that the spinster daughter with the dried-up face, the one the local children made up rhymes about, had waited until her father was gone and the servants dismissed for the day, then rolled the desk out onto the lawn and set it afire surrounded by white sand and bricks. The blaze could be seen from the old city, but by the time the local fire brigade arrived, it was spent.

After a sleepless night, the visitors from America congregated at the George Hotel, where Sara-Beth had rooms, to decide how best to split up the party. The most pressing issue was Charlotte's attendance in London for her audition at the New Adelphi in three days. When Denham received word from his bride that their reunion would be further delayed, he immediately telegrammed back to warn that Fawcett Robinson was due soon on the Continent.

"Charlie, you must get to London," Henrietta urged her sister. They were all six of them gathered in the hotel lobby, sitting closely together on matching sofas and footstools, speaking more loudly than they would like over the noise of all the comings and goings.

"But Harry, Sir Francis may not be long for—"

"I shall stay behind. It's fine. I will make Denham understand."

"All that freedom to travel about," Charlotte said with a sigh, "just from uttering words on a deck."

There was a long, uncomfortable pause, which Henrietta did not rush to fill. She was testing someone, something she had learned from Sara-Beth in their short time together. She had watched lawyers in her father's court do it, too. Let people show their hand sometimes. If only they had done that with Fanny Austen, instead of ignoring her altogether.

Nash finally spoke. "I suppose I could accompany Charlotte to London."

"The chaperone will act after all!" Sara-Beth proclaimed, then turned to the Nelson brothers. "And what are you boys to do?"

"They say the admiral refuses all visitors." Haz looked over at Nicholas as if for approval. "And I am eager for London, I must admit."

Henrietta continued to stay quiet, letting the others do the talking. The group was rearranging itself even more neatly than she could have hoped. She just hoped she was doing the right thing when it came to her sister.

Nicholas cleared his throat. "As one who initiated relations with Sir Francis, I feel a compunction to pay my respects alongside Mrs. Scott." He did not say what they were all thinking—that the reason they had traveled so far now lay in ashes on the lawn of Portsdown Lodge.

Henrietta had not foreseen the possibility of Nicholas remaining behind, and her first thought surprised and troubled her. *But that was silly,* she told herself. He could have no romantic intention with regard to her, a married woman. Henrietta found herself grateful again for the freedom that came with the wedding vows: to move about and pay visits, and not have one's womanly virtue called into question by such simple acts.

"Well, I've decided to meet Lu at Dover and start for Bruges," announced Sara-Beth, "and I'll be taking my little coterie with me. I've been to London before and exhausted all its charms, although I've so enjoyed Hampshire *and* seeing the Nelsons here so full of enthusiasm."

Charlotte turned to Haz. "Since Justice Nash is accompanying me to London, there should be nothing untoward in your joining us, too."

Henrietta watched Nash's handsome face harden ever so slightly at these words, Charlotte's impishly light up, Haz's warm with pleasure, and

Sara-Beth's stay as charmingly inscrutable as the gambler she was. As unromantic as Henrietta was, she found the intense jumble of emotions taking place in the lobby to be undeniably thrilling. Perhaps the persistent courtship by Denham and exchange of vows had freed something else. Suddenly she wanted everyone to be as happy as she was—to know of how happy one could actually be! She thought of the admiral alone in his study, watching for their ship with such anticipation in the knowledge that two sets of siblings, equally matched in age and temperament, were on board. From their time together, Henrietta had gleaned the romantic mischief that might have motivated him. How disappointed the admiral must have been at the failure of any coupling to ensue. *Poor Sir Francis*, she thought to herself with the saddest of smiles.

Standing before the Clarence carriage bound for the rail station, Henrietta pressed the newly silver-minted sixpence into her sister's gloved hand. She was happy to now gift the "Young Head Victoria" coin away, not being remotely superstitious herself.

"But you actors are," she reminded Charlotte as they embraced at length.

"Oh Harry, no!" Charlotte stepped back from her to exclaim. "You're to keep this for the marriage, for prosperity!"

"We were only indulging the starry-eyed captain," Henrietta assured her. "You know my feelings when it comes to such notions. Denham says we make our own luck in life."

"How enterprising."

"Charlie, you will love Denham one day as the brother you never had."

"From a few encounters over a lifetime? Hardly."

"Not a few, I promise." Henrietta squeezed her sister's hands, which still held the sixpence, as Charlotte teared up. "And besides, Fawcett Robinson will be bowled over by you—how could he not? We are all in your thrall, my dearest. You have such a gift for performing—I envy you that. I don't have a talent."

"You most certainly do. You have a gift for rhetoric."

"But no forum for it. I can't be a lawyer or politician or philosopher, and I've no interest in the stage like you or the Girl Orator."

Charlotte pulled her hands away to tuck the sixpence in her reticule, then dried her eyes. "There may not be a profession for it, but you inspire the trust of others. You, my dear sister, will always do the right thing. No one who meets you, even for a second, could ever doubt that."

Now they were both crying, and Nash and Haslett, who had been watching from a polite distance, came forward to separate them. "I am so sorry, but we will miss the train," Nash gently said.

With some trouble, Charlotte's large steamer trunk was lifted onto the driver's seat of the Clarence. Henrietta had decided she no longer needed the trunk herself, being only days away from moving into the terrace flat on Hanbury Street and setting up house for her husband. Until then, a small valise from the ship's general store would suit her fine.

The sisters quickly hugged and kissed again, and Nash helped Charlotte into the carriage with Haslett following behind. Henrietta stood in front of the Fountain Hotel, feeling profoundly emotional as she watched her sister leave, as if life was teetering on the edge of a spinning silver coin and it was hard to predict where it would land—but at least it was in motion. The Clarence lurched forward and Henrietta began to wave, but to her relief it was not like the painful vision of retreat from their father as the *China* had pulled away. Charlotte was moving forward, just as Henrietta had in marrying Denham, and in that moment, she felt only the greatest of excitement for them both.

THIRTEEN

The Bequest

Portsdown Lodge, July 2, 1865

Henrietta and Nicholas paced the admiral's study, both too nervous to sit. They circled the square patch of unfaded carpet where the captain's desk once stood, glanced at the other treasures left in the room. But nothing could be as special as what had been destroyed.

"Nicholas . . ."

He looked up from the book in his hands. "Yes, Mrs. Scott?"

"Please—Henrietta."

"But not Harry?" he asked, surprising her with a grin.

"How we must have confused you at first!"

"I fear we were often confused on ship, my brother and I. From that first night at dinner—*Harry, Charlie, Lu . . .*"

Only then did Henrietta realize that she and Nick had not been alone together before. "Dear Louisa, how I miss her—even her formidable direction onstage!"

"And still how weak my performance."

"It seems a lifetime ago." Henrietta came away from the bow window, where she had been looking out to sea. "I suppose that one of the joys of travel, the retreat of everything you know and have suffered, and the chance to quickly forge a new life—a new world—in its place. Although that is not at all why I rushed into marriage."

She stopped herself, confused by her own babbling (*why had she used the word* rushed?), while Nicholas busied himself by returning the book to the shelf and taking down another.

"You're in the book trade, Nick. Tell me—why do you think Charlie and I so desired the signature of Miss Austen? Is it about feeling close to her, as we did on our visit to Chawton?"

"I have wondered the same with our first editions in the shop. I know that for Haz, there's the thrill of the hunt—he will never be deprived of that."

"Ahh!" Henrietta laughed. "Poor Sara-Beth!"

"Oh, I see, how right you are!" His face brightened with sudden understanding.

"And you? Why do you hunt down books?"

"I suppose to be part of something that will last forever, small as my role of caretaker might be." He came over to her and held out the volume in his hands. "That feels even more important to me after the war."

"A dusting of immortality, perhaps?" Henrietta took the book from him to read the spine.

"It's a first edition of *Mansfield Park*—inscribed."

"My least favorite of Austen, although even that I love more than most other books."

"I think one loves *Mansfield Park* with the head rather than the heart."

"Oh, well put, Nick." Returning the book to him, she noticed how pleased he looked by the compliment. "You always speak so eloquently on literature—is its stock-in-trade satisfactory to you?"

Nicholas slipped the volume back in its place on the study's walnut shelves. "I think I should always be happy as long as I am surrounded by books, valuable or not."

There was a cough from the open doorway to the study. Henrietta and Nicholas turned in unison to see George, the admiral's trusty manservant, standing on the threshold with a foot-long wooden box in his hands. "Excuse me, Mrs. Scott, Mr. Nelson. I'm afraid the admiral remains confined to bed."

"Of course, George. Please let Sir Francis know we understand—our every concern is for him alone." Henrietta's voice caught in her throat as she recalled the admiral's words to her in the walled garden: *you do understand, don't you?* It felt like a lifetime ago.

"Sir Francis did instruct me of late to give this expressly to Mrs. Scott, should it come to . . ." He looked down at the box in his hands with red-rimmed eyes full of tears. "I was to send it on to Hanbury Street."

"To me?"

"Yes, madam. It was his most particular wish."

Henrietta came forward in surprise to accept the slender walnut box, which had been meticulously carved in a pattern of lilies surrounding a coat of arms and the initials "F. A."

"He made that box there himself," George proudly announced. "He could make most anything, my master, he could."

Henrietta turned the wooden box about in her hands, hesitant to open it. The kinship she felt with the admiral already came with a burden: the resentment toward Fanny, whose failure that day to attend on Henrietta and Nick hung palpable in the air. The discovery of a special gift from Sir Francis to a young American woman would only make matters worse.

Nicholas noticed her apprehension and came to her side. "Shall I?"

"Yes, Nick, thank you—please do."

She handed him the box and watched as he carefully unlatched it.

"My word," Nick muttered in shock. They all three stared.

It was the telescope.

B ut why would he leave it to me?"
Henrietta held the spyglass to her eye and peered down the lawn of Portsdown Lodge toward the harbor. She and Nicholas sat by the bow window in matching wingback chairs, a tea tray resting untouched on the embroidered footstool between them. "It's such a beautiful instrument, in and of itself. Oh look, you can see the very waves of the sea from here. . . ." Only when the view of the water became blurry did Henrietta realize there were tears in her eyes, and she carefully placed the telescope back down in her lap.

"No wonder he spent so much time alone in this room." Nicholas held out his monogrammed handkerchief to Henrietta and motioned for her to keep it. "Think of all those voyages, each ship a little world unto itself, and he in control of it all."

"In control of everything but Fanny." Henrietta wiped her eyes, then nodded toward the unfaded patch of carpet. "I worry she somehow planned it all. Sir Francis hadn't left the house in so long, and Fanny was always to accompany him if he did. Then the very moment we take him to Chawton, she goes and . . . but no, that's not right, is it? Charlie and I invited ourselves here first—Fanny had no part in that. She could have no idea we were coming. When I think back on our brazenness . . ."

"This bequest is proof enough against that."

"But why not leave it to others in the family?"

Nick hesitated. "Fanny would learn of it."

Henrietta stared at him in surprise. "You don't think she knows?"

"I think George may have presented it to you as he did for a reason."

Henrietta felt such inner turmoil at the thought. To be caught in this way between father and daughter was both unnatural and unnerving. "Poor Fanny. She must have had it in her head for years, how to get at the contents of the desk. I remember when Sir Francis showed us all the Bramah lock—so proud he was, like a child who has a secret on a parent." Henrietta looked about the room. "He *was* the child to Fanny's disapproving parent. Years of taking care of him perhaps took its toll."

"I fear that doesn't explain all of Fanny."

Henrietta eyed him with interest. Their shared reserve was such an unremarked quality in society. It might be appreciated by some, even if selfishly, but it didn't yield the kind of rewards that risk-taking did. Yet all that quiet watching did gain one insight into the behavior of others. Nick was always so temperate and considerate as a result. *Perhaps her younger sister could be diverted after all,* Henrietta thought to herself, until she remembered Charlotte forgetting her lines onstage, and that strange moment in the tavern yard— the blush on her sister's cheeks over nothing. But Henrietta knew it was not nothing: it would in fact be disastrous for home, should something happen abroad between Nash and her sister that could not be undone.

"May I have a look?" Nicholas asked, breaking her reverie.

"Of course."

He took the telescope from Henrietta with both hands as if accepting a mantle, and cradled it for a few seconds. "I was admiring it in the carriage from Chawton," he recalled, raising the telescope to his right eye while rotating its lens. "We men were talking about the telescopic lens fitted to my rifle in the war. A new contraption. A way to—"

He stopped talking as the twisting of the telescope made a little clicking sound, and Henrietta watched his expression inexplicably shift.

"Sir Francis didn't want to let go of it—what did he say at the time?" Nicholas began murmuring to himself. *"Little whatnots for the children? Keepsake boxes,* like this one here . . . *hidden compartments . . ."*

Suddenly Nick stood up like a shot, then separated the brass draw tube of the telescope from its walnut barrel to peer inside. "My word, of course—he as much as said it!"

Henrietta watched in astonishment as Nick began shaking the barrel upside down until the folded piece of paper fell out, tumbling onto the Persian rug between them.

My family has always been apt to hide things.

BOOK FOUR

The Court

ONE

✴

Reunion

•——◦——•

TWO WEEKS LATER
Boston Harbor, July 16, 1865

William had taken to walking Long Wharf at night. At first, he would pace its length alone, staring out at sea while the servants despaired and the judges used Austen to distract him from his plight. *Do you not see how worried everyone is about you?* Connie had asked him once, and the truth was that William had not. His worries never included his own self, his own development—he never worked to clear the horizon in his mind. He behaved instead like Mrs. Bennet in *Pride and Prejudice*, very much a Chicken Little, giving the outside world such power to wield over him.

Connie never doubted her power in the face of the world's, marveled William as he strolled the wharf on a breezy midsummer night, her arm now linked through his. Up ahead was the Custom House in all its revivalist glory, a four-faced Greek temple–like building fronted by three dozen Doric columns yet assigned to the most mundane business of ship registration and cargo inspection. From its new location, one could see all that arrived by sea in Boston, from two-masted schooners to massive ocean liners, from mail packets and merchant clippers to army ships being recommissioned after years of bloody battle.

William gazed forlornly about the crowded harbor, and Connie firmly squeezed his arm in turn. "William, it's been only a month. You must prepare yourself for a lengthy absence from Charlotte as well as Henrietta, I'm afraid."

Two letters had arrived the week before from Portsmouth, announcing Henrietta's marriage to a Mr. Denham Scott of London. Nash had sounded beyond remorseful in his lengthy missive, while Henrietta could not have sounded happier in hers. After a few days of shock and self-indulgence, William had written his congratulations to Henrietta care of the Fountain Hotel. He had never even met this Mr. Scott, although he had noticed him darting about the courthouse often enough, and still didn't know where the newlyweds were to live or how they were to manage. William could not have felt further from his daughter or her new life.

"Henrietta writes of such enthusiastic new friends," Connie continued. "I expect Charlotte will want to join them on the Continent next. I myself was gone for two years at her age."

"Connie! My heart!"

She reached over with her free hand and gently patted the area of that organ. "The doctor says things here are much better regulated of late. Perhaps I have a calming effect on you?"

He had to smile. "From the many hours of political debate?"

"They've proved a distraction at least, like your beloved Austen." She nodded ahead at a large transatlantic steamship that had just docked. "We should think about a trip together, you and I, to keep you occupied."

"But we would have to travel separately," he warned, an unusual edge to his voice.

"I've done so my whole life. Besides, the Continent is much more tolerant when it comes to such things. We would be of little controversy there."

"But not in England. They are behind even us in such matters."

"Oh, the English can be so purposefully obstinate and contrary—I suppose snobbery over even the most trivial of matters promotes class entitlement. Of course, here in the land of opportunity, we have discovered our own pernicious ways to keep others down."

As he listened, William watched the steamship at the end of the dock begin its disembarkation in order of class. He thought of the people in steerage coming to America for something they could not find at home.

He had never, not for a second, wanted or needed to leave his own. How fortunate he was to be able to say that. Life was hard enough—people died in the very rooms where happiness once reigned—and you had to get up the next morning and face the absence, like the mark left on a wall when a painting was suddenly taken down. None of it ever left you, and the home was a crucible in that way, as well as a grave—from all the complex interactions of love and loss that melted hearth-like in its warmth, one never lost the chance to change and grow into someone deserving of such intimacy. Nothing was more important than the anchor of home and the nearness of those one loved. William understood this now in a most profound way that had nothing to do with fear.

"I waved to Thomas Nash—right there—from the phaeton." He pointed at the very spot where the large steamer had just docked, RMS *Neptune* blazoned across its hull. "The girls were somewhere on deck—I never did see them. Never even got the chance to wish them well . . ."

William's voice trailed off as he watched hundreds of first- and second-class passengers leave the steamship and swarm toward the wharf. Connie was recounting that afternoon's lecture at the Horticultural Hall, when his attention was caught by the sight in the crowd of a straw bonnet trimmed with bright yellow ribbon, the very color that so suited his fair Charlotte.

"William . . . ?" he heard Connie ask, and realized he was staring.

"Oh, I'm sorry, Connie—you caught me at it again. How silly I'm being." It was curious, though, how the bonnet next to that one was trimmed in the very shade of lavender that Henrietta preferred. "I must be imagining," he muttered half to himself. He often thought he saw things when faced with a crowd. Certainly, the man accompanying the two bonneted figures was no one William recognized. For a second, he could swear he glimpsed the tall figure of Thomas Nash among the nearest passengers, but this time said nothing to Connie. He was clearly seeing things.

There was a sudden commotion up ahead, an excitement near the very group he had been examining, followed by the crying out of his name by female voices. Not William, not Justice Stevenson, of course, but *Father, Father!* He was a father, a sad voice inside him cried back—he knew this feeling of parting and reunion—he had daughters, too.

And then all of a sudden they were coming straight at him, both at the same time, the two men behind them running to catch up, the bonnets flying back with their bright happy-colored ribbons dancing in the ocean wind, the other passengers making way . . . *Father, Father!* they cried out, over and over again, louder and louder, even louder than a ship horn if such a thing were possible . . . and then there they really were, back in his arms again, both his beloved daughters, and nothing on earth had ever felt more wondrous or welcome.

TWO

✴

The Stomping Suffragists

•———•———•

IN THE MATTER OF *SCOTT* v. *SCOTT*
Lincoln's Inn, July 17, 1865

Sir Cresswell Cresswell sat alone in his private chamber, mulling over the lengthy divorce petition before him. He had been appointed the first judge of the Court for Divorce and Matrimonial Causes upon its creation in 1857. No longer would the ecclesiastical courts decide such cases; no longer would those seeking to remarry require, in addition to the church's decree, a private act debated and passed by Parliament. Since 1700, there had been only three hundred divorces in England as a result, sought mostly by men. With the establishment of this new court, petitions for divorce had rocketed from three to three hundred in one year.

Sir Cresswell was tired; he had been contemplating retirement when the divorce court appointment was urged on him. In the past handful of years, he had rapidly disposed of one thousand divorce cases, only one of which was later reversed on appeal, a record unbroken by any of his contemporaries. Now well into his sixties, Sir Cresswell sat ten months of the year and never missed a day due to ill health or otherwise. But on clear sunny mornings like this one, all he wanted was to be out on his horse.

Scott v. Scott was next on the docket, an admittedly fascinating petition for divorce. It had been initiated so quickly following a marriage at sea that

Sir Cresswell, himself a creature of speed, had agreed to hear the case out of turn. Already the Fleet Street papers had gotten wind of the suit, given the involvement of one of their own. The public court in the Old Hall—made famous by the Dickens novel *Bleak House*—was packed to capacity. It seemed all of London was eager to hear the testimony of the petitioner, a newly married and already jilted husband.

Sir Cresswell believed himself to be part of the draw for today's spectators in court. The papers liked to boast that the five million married women in England were indebted to him—*Blackwood's Magazine* had even recently produced a rhyme: *"There's many a wrong we could redress well / If aided by Sir Cresswell Cresswell."* Another draw was the young barrister Dr. Richard Pankhurst, a gold medalist who had been called to the bar at Lincoln's Inn in 1863 and practiced on the Northern Circuit. He had been brought down especially by the American-born female respondent in that day's hearing, due to his permissive views on the rights of women.

So permissive, in fact, that Pankhurst was helping to form a national female suffrage society in addition to advocating for property rights for women—the very rights which stood at the heart of the case before the court. With so much at stake, several "manhood suffragists"—as the papers had recently begun calling them—were reportedly in the Old Hall today to witness the proceeding. Women confused Sir Cresswell, a lifelong bachelor, and such presence in his courtroom was slightly jarring. But he prided himself on nerves of steel, a peerless intellect, and a knack for timing his statements to ensure the greatest impact on his audience. A few manhood suffragists were no match for him.

It was rumored that authoress Caroline Lamb Norton might also make an appearance that day in his court. The granddaughter of the great Irish playwright Richard Brinsley Sheridan, Mrs. Norton had decades ago been involved in similar scandal when she had left her own husband, causing her to lose custody of their three young sons. English law at the time considered children the legal property of their father and his wife a part of *him*. Largely due to Mrs. Norton's subsequent campaigning, the Custody of Infants Act 1839 was eventually passed, allowing women to sue for custody of their children up to the age of seven. But Mrs. Norton did not stop her boot-stomping there. She fought for the right to speak before Parliament in 1855 as it debated the issue of divorce and women's loss of personhood upon marriage. Her powerful words were now a matter of permanent parliamentary record:

> *An English wife may not leave her husband's house. Not only can he sue her for "restitution of conjugal rights," but he has a right to enter the house of any friend or relation with whom she may take refuge . . . and carry her away by force. . . .*
>
> *If her husband take proceedings for a divorce, she is not, in the first instance, allowed to defend herself. . . . She is not represented by attorney, nor permitted to be considered a party to the suit between him and her supposed lover, for "damages."*
>
> *[If] an English wife be guilty of infidelity, her husband can divorce her so as to marry again; but she cannot divorce the husband, a vinculum, however profligate he may be. . . .*
>
> *[A man once could] take children from the mother at any age, and without any fault or offence on her part. . . . What I suffered . . . under the evil law which suffered any man, for vengeance or for interest, to take baby children from their mother, I shall not even try to explain.*

Not even Sir Cresswell himself could have resisted such a heartfelt plea: although a bachelor through and through, he had a soft spot when it came to the babies. Eventually, Mrs. Norton's tireless campaigning would also help bring about the Matrimonial Causes Act 1857, the very legislation that had birthed his role as judge. Sir Cresswell might partly owe his judicial existence to Caroline Norton, but she would owe him total obedience in his court—which was always as he liked it.

One final person of note would not be present at the proceeding: the very wife in absentia herself. She had reportedly fled to America within days of the shipboard wedding, the petitioner husband the surprising victim of desertion here. If the respondent wife had remained in England, she would have lost most of her individual rights. She could not sue or be sued by others for any harm or even represent herself in court. Her entire legal existence was deemed to be incorporated into that of her husband for the duration of the marriage.

There was only one exception to a wife's loss of personhood, but it was a critical one: the ability under the new laws to sue her husband for separation or divorce. She simply required more reasons than him to do so. Otherwise, her person, children, possessions, and earnings all belonged to him. Sir Cresswell Cresswell was abundantly aware that his decision in *Scott v. Scott* could help turn the tide when it came to legislatively reforming the property rights of women in England. But for now, the law was the law, and, to a point, his hands were firmly tied.

Your name."

"Denham Scott."

"Your profession?"

"Newspaperman."

"For which publication?"

"*Reynolds's Newspaper,* Your Lordship."

Sir Cresswell examined the petitioner before him. A sense of resentment emanated from his entire being, as if he was as surprised by the fact of the proceeding as anyone. He possessed a charming face with strong bones and full lips, locks of brown hair that fell forward across his high but furrowed brow, and the fashionable rounded beard made popular by General Grant in America.

"And your residence?"

The man's face twitched slightly. "Number fourteen, Hanbury Street, Tower Hamlets."

"You have lived there how long?"

A cough. "Three weeks and a day, Your Lordship."

"And a *day,*" Sir Cresswell intoned with mock grandeur, then turned to the mild laughter coming from the gallery. "You are a most precise gentleman—as is your petition before this court, a Hydra-like beast of many heads. We will first address the suit for divorce, which requires proof of adultery under the law, before considering your, ah, many other complaints."

At this, the petitioner's body slumped even further in his chair.

"You have named a co-respondent."

The counsellor for the petitioner whispered in the ear of his client, who mumbled something to the court in response.

"Speak up, Mr. Scott." Sir Cresswell detested this aspect of both the old and new matrimonial laws—the requirement to name the other party to adultery risked the most unsavory revelations before his court. But adultery was the sine qua non for obtaining a divorce, and the standard of proof increasingly low as a result: the mere word of an eavesdropping chambermaid, sharp-eyed coachman, or disgruntled acquaintance was often enough.

"Nicholas Nelson."

There was a loud collective gasp from the gallery.

"You have evidence of criminal conversation taking place between your wife and this Mr. Nelson?"

The petitioner nodded.

"Speak up, I say."

"A letter, Your Lordship."

This document was now passed along until it reached Sir Cresswell. He read silently but quickly as the petitioner's counsel summarized aloud its contents for the court.

"As you can see from the letter, Your Lordship, the respondent Mrs. Henrietta Scott was in the frequent company of this Mr. Nicholas Nelson whilst on holiday, and the two of them were seen entering her hotel room at the Fountain Hotel in Old Portsmouth on the second night in July of this year. A handkerchief stitched in Mr. Nelson's initials was retrieved from that room after the fact."

"But this letter is not signed." Cresswell frowned. "And you have no idea of the sender?"

"No, My Lord, but it is duly postmarked Portsmouth, as you can see."

Cresswell folded the letter back up with a sigh. "Counsel for the respondent, does your client refute such charges?"

Dr. Richard Pankhurst stood up. "As this court has been informed by affidavit, I was only able to consult with my client most briefly before her departure from England, making the proceeding of this matter greatly to her prejudice. That said, she would wholeheartedly refute any and all such accusations."

"If she were here." Cresswell sat back in his throne-like chair. "I must confess, her fleeing in such manner does not reflect well on her already embattled character." A strange stomping of feet could be heard from the gallery above; Cresswell's right eye twitched. "Of course, this entire matter could be swiftly dispensed with by the court, and in your client's favor, Dr. Pankhurst, should the marriage itself be declared invalid."

"I was instructed against my own advice, Your Lordship, not to challenge the validity of the marriage in any respect."

"Notwithstanding the interesting *dis*interest of either party, it would appear, to challenge the marriage itself," Sir Cresswell announced, "I am bound by duty to ensure its validity under the law. There can be no divorce if the marriage is not valid, and if the marriage is not valid, there can be no right in Mr. Scott to any property of the respondent, as she is also then not his.

"Let us proceed. Firstly, we shall set out for this court the statement of facts behind the petition. Mr. Scott, on the evening of the twenty-fifth of June, you exchanged wedding vows with a Miss Henrietta Alice Stevenson of Boston, from the Commonwealth of Massachusetts in America, correct?"

"Yes, My Lord."

"And this marriage was conducted at sea by a Captain Valentine Norris of the SS *China*, a ship built and registered abroad in the coastal state of Maine, in what were international waters at the time?"

An abrupt nod from the petitioner.

"And there were no witnesses? Quite unfortunate, I must say, and sadly illustrative of the rather reckless manner in which this most important of contractual unions was entered into by the respondent and yourself. Captain Norris did log the marriage in the ship's registry, a copy of which your counsel has entered into court. On this ground, you argue that the marriage is valid and thereby entitles you to all the personal non-leasehold property of your new wife." Again the stomping of feet could be heard from the gallery above, growing louder; Sir Cresswell made a swatting motion with his right hand, as if at a fly.

"Yes, My Lord."

"I must first state that such entitlement under English law is not itself in dispute. If the marriage at sea is valid, you are indeed entitled to the object in question."

A look of pride mixed with relief crossed the petitioner's face at this pronouncement, while Sir Cresswell finally looked up to determine the source of the stomping above: the many high-heeled booted feet from the line of manhood suffragists who were seated in the upper gallery, glowering down at him.

"*However,*" Sir Cresswell declared with his exquisite sense of timing, as the entire row of suffragists stopped stomping to lean forward in anticipation, "there is a prior issue of law which must first be decided." A long, dramatic pause. "That is, whether this court has jurisdiction to rule on the validity of the marriage at all."

There was a gasp from the spectators. To the knowledge of the court,

Sir Cresswell Cresswell had never punted a divorce case from his docket on the grounds that another judicial forum elsewhere took priority over his.

"The marriage took place in international waters and as such, under English law, it is subject to the flag and laws of the country where the ship was built and registered—in this case, the coastal shipbuilding state of Maine. The reasoning of Cunard, the ship's British owner, in moving such work abroad is not of concern to us. It is what it is."

Another long, dramatic pause as the boot-stomping stayed stopped.

"I therefore find that the validity of the marriage in the first part, and the ownership of the object in question in the second—an object which, as I understand it, may already be on American soil itself—are subject to the flag and laws of that young nation, to whose jurisdiction I now remit the entirety of this matter."

The petitioner's counsel jumped up. "Your Lordship, such instances of renvoi, where there is a conflict of laws between nations, are exceedingly rare and accordingly fraught with judicial uncertainty!"

"Are you instructing me on the ramifications of my own decision?" Sir Cresswell raised his voice here for the first and only time.

"But if the American courts should find the marriage invalid under *their* laws, my client will lose a valuable right to ownership that he would otherwise enjoy under our own!"

Richard Pankhurst, counsel for the respondent in absentia, stood up again. "I should warn my learned friend that even if the American courts find the petitioner's marriage valid, he would still lose ownership under their much more progressive property laws for married women."

The face of counsel for the petitioner fell amidst all the jubilant stomping. "I beseech you, My Lord," he practically cried, "where is the fairness in *that?*"

Sir Cresswell *tsked* the barrister. "*That* is neither here nor there. The law on forum sits at the heart of justice. Should the petitioner wish to pursue this matter further, he must do so in America. My decision is final and absolute."

The gallery erupted into applause and much happy stomping. The mysterious gift from the dying Admiral Sir Francis Austen, brother of literary genius Jane Austen, to Henrietta Stevenson Scott of Boston, daughter of a judge herself, was safe for now.

THREE

North and South

Beacon Hill, July 21, 1865

As in the days prior to their departure, Henrietta and Charlotte kept to the attic upon their return. William Stevenson was left to despair alone over the litany of facts before him: Henrietta's sudden and unexpected marriage to a stranger and a foreigner, the separation from that very husband after just nine days, the hasty return home in the presence of yet another man and stranger, and her intention to file suit for divorce posthaste upon the recommendation of both her London counsel, Dr. Richard Pankhurst, and her father's own colleague, Justice Thomas Nash.

William's head was spinning.

He would only meet Constance in secret, hesitant to introduce the evolution in their own relationship to his daughters. Connie was very understanding, her predominant concern being for Henrietta. But her feminist ire was also in full flame, lit by the role that chauvinism appeared to have played in the breakdown of the briefest of marriages.

"Does Charlotte still not speak of it to you?" Constance asked during a clandestine walk together through the public botanical garden across from her home.

"Nash is my only other source and almost as tight-lipped about the entire matter. They all three seem quite attached from the catastrophe."

"And this Mr. Nelson of Philadelphia?"

"Nash insists he is only a friend." William bowed his head. "God help us if he ends up a co-respondent in the case."

"But you know for certain there is to be litigation abroad?"

"Nash says it is only a matter of time. Sir Cresswell of the British divorce court reportedly moves with such speed, a decision may already have been rendered to prevent removal of the property—whatever it may be—from the country. That is why Nash advised Henrietta to sail home immediately with the object in dispute, before any such judgment could be enforced against her there."

"And this Mr. Nelson stays in Boston . . . ?"

William turned to her and raised his eyebrows. "As I said, *attached.*"

"I see." Constance did some quick counting in her head. "So . . . they left on the fifth of July, arrived here eleven days later, and it is now ten days on from that. Word from the London courts could arrive any minute of which they would be unaware."

"I'm afraid so."

"Well, William, as you know, I believe in meeting undeterred whatever is to come. We shall fix on the absolute best legal counsel for Henrietta here at home and prevail in court. She simply made a bad bet—we all do. We win in life as much as we lose. I refuse to let this latest hardship of hers become one iota more difficult than it has to be. For goodness' sake, heartbreak is painful enough—what monsters would we be, to add to any of that?"

William frowned. "I'm afraid there's a complication. Only a justice of the supreme judicial court has the authority to decide divorce cases in our state. My colleagues will be considered inherently partial to my family—at least, those whom I consider friends. The chief justice, Conor, Mac, of course Nash . . . even Zeke has attended church alongside me. All except one will need to recuse themselves due to conflict of interest."

Connie stopped walking, did more counting in her head, and placed her right arm over his. "You're not saying . . ."

William grimly nodded. "Norton."

"That woman-hater?" Connie stroked her forehead in misery with her other hand. "I must admit, I did not see *him* coming over the horizon."

"He's the only one with whom I have no personal relationship. If anything, he is predisposed to think ill of me, given our differences in politics."

Connie patted William's arm in solidarity. "Even more reason, then, to secure the best barrister we can. A good lawyer can surmount anything—and I know just the person."

I t didn't take Justice Stevenson long to suspect that the man lounging behind the paper-strewn desk had once had romantic designs on the woman who had referred him.

William and Constance were sitting with Henrietta in the office of Graydon Saunders, a Southerner who had studied law at Harvard ten years after William. Graduating at the top of his class, Saunders had opened his litigation practice in Boston after gallivanting about Europe, where he had met Constance Davenish on her own Grand Tour at the time.

William had yet to meet this rumored romantic adversary in the judicial arena. Graydon Saunders, Esquire, had never lost a case nor had one appealed to its higher courts, so decisively did he trounce any opponents. Raised in the Allegheny Mountains, he was a robust-looking man with the carriage of a lumberjack, all heart and appetite and vigor—William had to close his eyes at the unavoidable image of Constance being lifted in Graydon's arms.

Graydon took a pull on his cigar as Henrietta described the case. "You're telling me this fella of yours let you go over an old man's dying gift? Well, I never..." He took another, longer pull. "Sudden ruptures between lovers can be something fierce"—William flinched as Graydon knocked ash off his cigar end with a flourish—"and you're sure it's not liable to fixin'?"

Henrietta firmly nodded while Connie reached over and patted her hand. Graydon gave Connie an openly admiring look before turning to William, who felt the sudden heat of rivalry under his collar.

"Norton's presiding, you say." The lawyer shook his head. "That man thinks the sun came up just to hear him crow. Well, Justice Stevenson, I'm 'fraid you're best to excuse yourself now, so I can strategize with the ladies unencumbered."

William stood up, hesitated, then decided to say his piece one last time when it came to the matter of *Scott v. Scott*. "Mr. Saunders, so much would be resolved should my daughter pursue an annulment in either country. If we can nullify the marriage, any argument over property becomes moot. But much as I reason with her..."

Graydon held up both hands in assurance and talked around the cigar in his mouth. "Don't you worry, Justice Stevenson. I'm not in the habit of making exertion or trouble for myself, as Miss Connie here well knows." He winked at Constance, causing William to feel sick to his stomach all over again before heading straight to the best jeweller in all of Beacon Hill.

Henrietta and Charlotte sat on their matching sleigh beds, facing each other across the wide-planked floor. The Portsmouth travel tags on Charlotte's steamer trunk were the only sign in the attic of their monthlong absence from home.

"And this Mr. Saunders advises annulment just like Father?" Charlotte stared at her sister in confusion. "Yet still you won't relent?"

Henrietta stood up and began to pace. "I would have to state in court that the marriage was void from the start." Looking down from the nearest dormer window, she noticed that the late lilac tree had lost all its violet blossoms—summer, the fairest season, was passing them by. "I was not tricked or drugged into it. I considered it a union for life and I want it resolved on those same terms. I wouldn't know how to move forward otherwise."

"But here in Massachusetts, the admiral's bequest stays yours, regardless?"

"Yes." Henrietta cast an eye at the shared desk where the telescope was safely locked away. "Valid marriage or not, under our state's new property laws for women, any inheritance stays mine and mine alone, to do with what I will."

"Well, that's a whole other question. What *could* the admiral have been thinking?" Charlie lay back on her bedquilt, hands folded on her chest, and stared up at the ceiling. "How we need news from London right away. Nash told Father they're trying to lay down cable across the Atlantic again. Queen Victoria's congratulatory telegram to President Buchanan went through in half a day before the first line deteriorated."

"It reportedly took sixteen hours to send those two hundred words from the Queen. It will take thousands more to explain whatever happens next between Denham and me." Henrietta sat down at the desk and rested her head on folded arms of her own, then turned onto one side to observe her sister. "Have you seen him?"

"Nash?" Charlotte shook her head.

"Those ten days at sea coming back—what a blur. What would we have done without him?"

"We would have managed, Harry. We always have."

"Or without Nick, for that matter. He is a true gentleman—one who sees things through."

Charlotte sat up in bed on her elbows. "You need to do the same, Harry, if only to go before Father's court."

Henrietta sat up, too, staring at the attic rafters where Charlotte had once hung sheets for her stage; their shared childhood had never felt so far away. "Mr. Saunders says it will be a stretch to prove cruelty—my only grounds here for divorce—without physical injury. After all, *all* Denham really did was assert his legal rights, over there, over me."

"And if you can't convince Justice Norton of cruelty?"

"Then no divorce. Mr. Saunders says we could both go to Mexico, or move to Indiana for a year. But here in Massachusetts, just wanting a divorce is not enough."

Charlie came over and put a hand on her sister's shoulder. "Henrietta, this has been so wearing on you. Must you really act with such haste?"

"Mr. Saunders says I run the risk of Denham filing suit in London first, where I have no rights of property, and successfully obtaining and enforcing any such foreign judgment in his favor here." She patted the desktop. "I can't risk that."

"Well, at least none of Boston knows of it yet." Charlotte kissed the top of her sister's head. "You'll be on the docket only as H. Scott, Justice Norton—that old crab apple—will preside, and this will all be behind us soon enough."

FOUR

Runaway Bride

Boston Harbor, July 31, 1865

*R*unaway Bride Back in Boston!"

Little Bobbie Acheson was the best newsboy on Long Wharf, and the minute he grabbed the stack of papers off the wagon he knew he had a winner. The RMS *Neptune* and the SS *China* arrived twice monthly but five days apart from Liverpool and Portsmouth, respectively, and the race was always on for the two mail steamers to be first to bring the most salient news from across the Atlantic.

"Runaway Bride Back in Boston!"

Bobbie Acheson ran in bare feet as he shouted—his worn and used shoes never lasted long. He had fifty copies of the new London paper *The Pall Mall Gazette* in his dirt-stained hands, and that night he'd have a hundred more from the State Street offices of the *Evening Traveller*. The latter paper could be counted on to pick up any notable headlines from England for the last two of their five daily editions. The *Traveller* was also the first paper in Boston to employ newsboys like Little Bobbie. He made a quarter a day, couldn't return any unsold papers, and had been running the wharf since he was eight.

"Runaway Bride Back in Boston!"

The sound of Bobbie's shrill voice was the moment that Henrietta's shame hit the city streets—the moment that her entire family had been dreading. Since their dockside reunion, the Stevensons had been living in a kind of protective bubble, with only Graydon Saunders aware of the looming marital scandal along with Connie, Nash, and Nicholas Nelson of Philadelphia, who inexplicably remained in Boston for now.

Haslett Nelson had not joined them on the voyage home. The sisters wanted new friends Louisa and Sara-Beth to know what had transpired, and Nash wanted American correspondents available for any London hearings. So Haz had volunteered to sail to Bruges and locate both women. "I'll just head for the nearest roulette table!" he had called out with a wave from the Liverpool dock before returning to London and beyond.

Little Bobbie Acheson flew along the Boston wharf, calling out the headline, over and over again. He ran up and down State Street, replenishing his stack of papers from the distribution wagon, spilling his little tin cup of coins into the larger one kept there under lock. The world might be begging for a transatlantic cable line but for now, in Little Bobbie, Boston had its own most efficient conveyor of information—and salacious news always traveled fastest of all.

Thomas Nash was first to hear the news. To literally hear it, from the wharf down the street. He was taking his morning stroll before heading to the courthouse; the cabin in the Adirondacks remained unoccupied although still his for the season; the July ticket to Portsmouth on the *China* had long since been cashed in.

Nash knew right away to whom the newsboy's shouts were referring and his heart sank. He did not want to be the first to tell Henrietta, who had been coping so admirably with her estrangement from Denham. Nash certainly did not want to be the one to inform William, who looked as if he had aged ten years in as many days. That left Charlotte, whom the bachelor justice was avoiding for other reasons altogether.

Nash turned from Long Wharf and headed back along State Street to the courthouse. Bounding up the steps, he ignored the looks of the young male clerks who stood about smoking and reading the paper. Nash's own copies of a dozen different publications would be waiting for him in his chamber. Bobbie Acheson might be the fastest news hawker on the docks, but the courthouse clerk in charge of the library's periodicals and papers ran a close second. Sure enough, Nash flew into chambers to discover his most trusted London news source, *The Times*, already on his desk.

RESPONDENT IN DIVORCE SUIT FLEES TO AMERICA
July 17, 1865

Testimony was heard this day at Old Hall, Lincoln's Inn, before Judge Ordinary, Sir Cresswell Cresswell, of the Court for Divorce and Matrimonial Causes, in the petition for divorce by Mr. Denham Scott of Tower Hamlets, City of London, employed by *Reynoïds's Newspaper*, against the respondent, Mrs. Henrietta Scott, of that same address, originally of the city of Boston, capital of the Commonwealth of Massachusetts, in the United States of America. Mrs. Scott was not present at the proceeding but was represented by Dr. Richard Pankhurst, a newly admitted member of the Bar at Lincoln's Court and commonly with the Northern Assizes Circuit.

The facts of the case are these: husband and wife first met in Boston in March of this year, and exchanged wedding vows on the night of June 25th on board the SS *China*. The ship was more than ten miles from the coast of England when the ceremony, conducted by the ship's captain, Cpt. Valentine Norris, took place, and accordingly in international waters. Shortly after this ceremony of marriage, on the 2nd of this month, the respondent was bequeathed property of some private but valuable nature. It is to be supposed that this property may be at the very heart of the rupture of relations between Mr. and Mrs. Scott which occurred shortly thereafter. The respondent is reported to have immediately fled the London marital home following such rupture, and is feared to have already sailed for America in possession of the property at issue.

The petitioner sought from the respondent, firstly, the unidentified property to which is his right under matrimonial law; second, a divorce on the grounds of adultery with the named co-respondent, a Mr. Nicholas Nelson of Philadelphia, Pennsylvania, U.S.A.; and third, the provision of such notice of judgement as

shall be enforceable in a foreign court. Sir Cresswell agreed to expedite the hearing, due to the urgency and threat of removal of the
property from England, and notwithstanding its ex parte nature
given the absence of the respondent from the proceeding itself.
In an unprecedented decision of the court, which was established
in 1857 under the Matrimonial Causes Act, Sir Cresswell declined
to render a decision in the matter, and remitted its entirety to the
jurisdiction of any such American court from which the petitioner
may now proceed to seek remedy and redress.

The petitioner was noticeably distraught at the conclusion of
the hearing and declined to provide comment to reporters in the
gallery.

Nash put down the paper, lit his pipe, and contemplated what the English
decision in *Scott v. Scott* could mean for Henrietta. The expedited Massachusetts hearing was due to start that very morning with Justice Roderick Norton
presiding. The chief justice's decision to appoint Norton to the matter had
been both prudent and unavoidable, given the makeup of the court. Nash
and William had immediately recused themselves from the case; Nash had
decided not to attend the Boston hearing altogether. Both men already knew,
however, that there was not a single precedent in American jurisprudence on
the issue of marriages at sea. With the state court's jurisdiction now sanc-
tioned by the British courts as well, Norton had a clear horizon before him
and the chance to leave a mark on U.S. case law in perpetuity. He was also
as likely to want to keep Henrietta in a marriage, however sour, as he was to
delegitimize it.

At least there would be no protracted legal conflict between the two
countries. This was what the lawyer in Nash had been fearing most: the arrival of a foreign court order from England, requiring that Henrietta hand
over the admiral's bequest to her husband. With Sir Cresswell's decision to
defer to an American court, Henrietta would retain all personal property
under Massachusetts law, even if she failed to also qualify for a divorce.

But the family friend in Nash knew that such legal victory could only
come at a very high price: social notoriety and scandal. Nash was dismayed
but not surprised by Mr. Nelson being named a co-respondent in the London case. Nash had been the one to shrewdly order a separate carriage for

the sisters en route to Liverpool, and to advise against any private conversation with the men while on board the *Neptune*. Of course, this meant Nash himself would be safe from Charlotte as well. But despite all his lawyerly efforts, the damage had been done. How supremely he had failed in his role as chaperone when it came to Charlotte and Henrietta both. He could only wonder at the mess he had made of everything, a misbegotten trail now leading all the way to the highest court in the state.

FIVE

✳

The Blue Antelope

•———•———•

IN THE MATTER OF *SCOTT* v. *SCOTT*
The Massachusetts Supreme Judicial Court
August 1, 1865

Justice Norton had conducted the prior day's hearing in the matter of *Scott v. Scott* with all the enthusiasm of a man being asked to judge the needlework competition at a county fair. He appeared almost as enervated the following day when he delivered his oral judgment.

"Before I render my decision, I must first point out the oddity under our state laws, that this, its highest court, should have jurisdiction over marriage and divorce in the first instance, rather than solely as a right of appeal hereto. But the legislature has not yet removed such power to a court of family law, and so I must rule on what is inherently a most personal matter of little public interest to the state. . . ."

Graydon Saunders sat with one arm casually draped about the empty chairback on his left, while the petitioner, Henrietta Scott, sat on his right. He rolled his eyes at her in exaggeration as Norton continued with his litany of warnings, exceptions, and complaints.

". . . that said," Norton droned on, "a court must be convinced of no bias or harm to a respondent as a result of their failure or inability to appear before it. I am satisfied in this case that no such harm to Mr. Scott would arise by my rendering a decision in his absence."

A nervous Henrietta glanced back at Charlotte and her father, who both winked reassuringly from their front-row seats. Charlotte wore a day dress in green, her lucky color, and clutched the sixpence in her hand, while Henrietta on her counsel's advice was dressed entirely in black. It had been nearly a month, in fact, since she had worn any other color, as if in mourning for a marriage already dead.

"I have also found the petitioner to be a credible witness to the events of her marriage, notwithstanding the proclivity of her female sex toward hysteria"—in anticipation of Connie's reaction, William put his hand firmly over hers—"and therefore entitled, pursuant to the Married Women's Property Act of 1855, to sue for divorce on the grounds of cruelty alone." Norton dramatically paused. "First, however, we must determine whether the marriage was valid at all. There is, unfortunately, no existing case law or legislation at the state or federal level to guide me on the validity of marriages at sea. Fortunately, I am absolved from making any such determination with respect to the marriage, and hence its dissolution, on the basis of lack of jurisdiction."

Graydon Saunders sprang to his feet. "But Your Honor, the English court just awarded this court jurisdiction—"

"Mr. Saunders, sit down. You are a rather large man, and the people in back cannot see."

It was a rare joke from Justice Roderick Norton, and was met with particularly appreciative laughter at that moment from the crowd of confused onlookers in the courtroom.

"My reasoning for this decision is manifold, counsellor for the petitioner will be gratified to know. Firstly, based on recent precedent, I find that the petitioner forfeited all rights to American citizenship from the instant of her marriage to a foreigner—in this case, an Englishman. Secondly, the petitioner intended to make England her place of residence, as evidenced by letters submitted to this court in support of her own petition for divorce. Thirdly, ownership of the property at issue arose from a bequest made on British soil during the marriage. Finally, Cunard, the owner of the ship on which the marriage vows were exchanged, is a British company, and American jurisprudence looks to where a ship's owners are incorporated—*not* to where a vessel is registered—in deciding which laws to apply to any events or malfeasance at sea. Hence, in this matter, English law must prevail.

"According to the July seventeenth edition of *The Times* of London, which arrived on our shores only yesterday, Sir Cresswell of the Court for Divorce

and Matrimonial Causes of England and Wales has made a different determination of sovereignty. Judge Ordinary Cresswell has ruled that where a
ship is *registered* determines jurisdiction. I, however, am bound only by the
laws of the Commonwealth of Massachusetts and of our nation as a whole.

"For these reasons, I hereby also decline to render judgment in the case
of *Scott v. Scott* on the grounds of lack of jurisdiction, and remit the entirety
of this matter back to the courts of England, where the petitioner is welcome to return to seek remedy and redress."

Henrietta gripped the edge of the plaintiff's table with both hands while
Graydon Saunders hit his forehead with an audible smack.

"It's a classic renvoi move," he said, stunned.

"My God," an equally shocked William muttered back, "it's unheard of . . ."

"How Roderick must *loathe* remitting a decision to our former colonizer."

"What does that mean, *renvoi?*" asked Charlotte, who had rushed forward
from her seat to throw her arms around Henrietta in consolation.

"It means the case has been shuttlecocked." Graydon Saunders shook
his head in disbelief. "Norton has essentially lobbed the matter back over to
England, despite their stated deference to the laws of *our* land, and Cresswell
will now have to determine in his court whether to apply English law, or
American law, or refuse renvoi and send the matter back to us all over again.
I need some whisky—boy!" He stood and waved to his clerk, then sank back
down into his chair and mopped his brow with a checkered handkerchief.

"Can they do this?" cried Henrietta with increasing desperation.

"I'm afraid so, Mrs. Scott." Graydon Saunders suddenly appeared smaller
to them all, so not used to losing was he. "Such bandying back and forth
between nations is a rarity, I will admit—what we call a 'blue antelope.'"

"And the danger?" Charlotte pressed him.

"Without a higher court in either jurisdiction to stop it?" Saunders
paused not for effect, for once, but from fear, and William reluctantly
stepped in with the answer.

"That the case, I'm afraid, will never end."

SIX

✦

The Door in the Floor

—•—

Beacon Hill, August 1, 1865

Nicholas Nelson waited on the front stoop of Eleven Beacon Street, red-faced with shame. *What had he been thinking, staying behind in Portsmouth with Henrietta?* Now the two of them had been accused of adultery in a British court—he, who hadn't dared address her alone until that final visit at Portsdown Lodge, and she, the most honorable person he knew. The accusation proved the wisdom of Nash's ordering them to stay apart on the rushed voyage home. With that morning's court decision, Nicholas planned to return to Philadelphia as soon as possible—that was, until the unsigned note had been slipped under his hotel room door.

A nervous servant greeted Nicholas as if expecting him, and hurried him to the drawing room through a pleasantly furnished front hall. There was a bust of Socrates on a pedestal (Henrietta had mentioned how Charlotte tapped its skull for luck whenever she bounded by), a Japanese porcelain vase being used for umbrellas, and a vast mural of a pastoral Greek scene along the entirety of one wall. Nicholas noted the many beautiful young goddesses depicted running in fields and bathing in streams—the seven sister-nymphs, perhaps? He wondered who in the family might have painted or commissioned such a sumptuous, painstaking, and permanent work.

"Thank you, Nick, for coming." Henrietta sat upright in the middle of the settee, hands tightly grasped in her lap. She nodded for Nicholas to also take a seat, but he stayed firmly standing at the edge of the maroon Brussels carpet. "You heard today's decision."

"What can Denham be thinking?" Nicholas burst out, feeling quite unlike himself. "He wants the letter so much? To accuse us—to accuse *you* of anything."

"I no longer know what he thinks. I thought I did." She sat up even straighter. "Nick, I must apologize to you for us both. We have dragged you into this, and now I have asked you here at even further risk to your reputation."

"Mrs. Scott, I cannot accept your apology. All the harm felt is yours." It was clear how heartbroken she was; he recognized it painfully himself. So painfully that he would be glad to soon be back home in his little rooms above the shop. "And now you must wait weeks all over again to see what he does. He has all the power of the courts. It's enraging—can nothing be done?"

"Constance is using her salons to rally editorials and public support. But it's not only a matter of women's rights, for once. My father calls it 'the cold hard vise of the law.' We all have to work within it, men and women both, else it all falls apart." They both fell silent at the daunting prospect of another trial and a judgment in Denham's favor, if only due to exhaustion of the courts. "I keep thinking about the poor admiral, losing everything, all those letters. The manuscript of *Persuasion*, for heaven's sake—such opportunity for scholarship there that could have enlightened generations." Henrietta shook her head. "How Sir Francis entrusted me with the one little bit of paper spared from Fanny's wrath. I cannot lose that now, too."

She stood up and removed the letter from her pocket, staring at it for a few seconds in her hand. It had all the power of a lit fuse and was wreaking just as much destruction. "Should Denham bring Sir Cresswell round and obtain judgment against me . . . I cannot risk the bailiff entering my father's house and seizing this." She held out the folded single piece of paper to him.

"Mrs. Scott, are you sure?" Nick knew right away what she was asking. Despite Nash's best efforts, there had been communication between them on board the *Neptune* after all. The first unsigned note, slipped under his cabin door early one morning, had asked him to stay in Boston until things were settled in someone's favor—and if not, to accept for safekeeping an item of the "highest personal importance." The second note had arrived that afternoon within minutes of Norton's decision.

"I know you will keep the letter safe for me."

"But once things are settled . . ."

She gave a dismissive laugh, as if the idea itself was as ludicrous as the circumstances she found herself in.

"You should know that Haz has written from Baden-Baden and located Lu and Sara-Beth both," he tried to assure her.

"They saw the Cresswell hearing in the papers? That hateful unsigned letter?" He nodded, his cheeks burning again from the shame of it all, while she widened her eyes at him in silent accusation. "Only one person would have motive to write such a thing."

"Haz promises they will check *Lloyd's List* regularly for the court listings and attend any hearing in your name."

"I am so grateful for our new friends, the trust and attention of Sir Francis, the time we spent together in Chawton." Henrietta nodded as if to convince herself. "I don't regret any of it—only what pain it might cause others."

He had always admired her quiet but steely determination. She was so different from Charlotte, just as he was from Haz. Everyone was so different from each other; he had learned that most painfully in war, when neighbors, classmates, and even family had fought against one another, leaving over half a million dead. What if a mural on a wall, a book by Dickens, a song in the air, were all that truly bound us, far more than society or religion or law—or even blood? The splitting apart of America over slavery and states' rights had proved how fragile such bonds could be. Poor Sir Francis, that lovely old man by the sea, thinking his visitors were all somehow fated for each other simply because they loved Jane Austen. Then again, people have fallen in love over much less, Nick consoled himself. "I will never speak of it, not as long as I live. You have my word as a gentleman—Haslett's, too."

"We are both so fortunate to have a sibling we can trust the world to."

"Haz is most loyal. Perhaps too much so. I worry he stays in the family business for me."

"And what about you? You said at Portsdown that you would always be happy surrounded by books."

"I did. But that was before."

"Before the war?"

"Yes, in part." Nick hesitated. "One should learn something from battle, if only how to better live—if lucky enough to survive."

"I thought that larger conflict behind us, but there appears to be so much repressed anger in its place. That anger has changed its appearance, I fear—another old snake in new skin. It only *pretends* to offer us greater freedom. Suffrage for everyone now feels even further away. Mr. Saunders claims that Norton's decision screams the power of a nation over its citizens—a way to keep us in our place, especially women."

"Not even the courts have that much power, Henrietta—not over someone as singular as you."

Nicholas came forward to take her hand, gazed at it far longer than he should have, then kissed it with all the gallantry he had read about and left.

T he door in the floor of the attic pulled down.

"Henrietta, my dear? May I visit with you?"

She was surprised at the sound of her father's voice. "Of course, Father. Do you need help with the ladder?"

"No, my dear, I am not quite so infirm as that." She heard him softly chuckling to himself as he hoisted himself up. His kindly, drawn face appeared above the floorboards, and he peered back and forth between the two twin beds that his girls had slept in all their lives. "When I think of the last time that I looked up here, both my beloved children gone . . ."

Henrietta burst into tears.

"Oh, my darling girl, please don't! It is all in the past."

"No, none of it is—look at what I've done! *Runaway Bride* indeed . . ." Covering her face in her hands, she heard him chuckle again and removed her hands to stare at him in surprise. "Father, are you *laughing* at my situation?"

William clumsily got up from the floor and sat down next to Henrietta on the tiny bed, one arm around her shoulder. "Not at you. Never at you, my brave one. Only at the absurdity of this world. Think of the newspaperman at the *Gazette*, reading Sir Cresswell's decision, and *that* is the headline he takes from it all? *That* is no one whose respect you need."

"But he's not here. What do I do about Beacon Hill? And poor Mr. Nelson caught up in it all—he's been practically run off to Philadelphia."

"Only out of concern for you, my dear, I am certain."

"Father, *The Saturday Press* that has started up again in New York—you mentioned knowing the editor there, Mr. Clapp?" Henrietta brushed away tears with her hands. "Might you put in a word for Nick if they seek critical reviewers? He is so insightful when it comes to books, and the family owes him such a debt."

"Of course, Henrietta, although I am certain you are Mr. Nelson's sole concern at present. We men have got you into this mess when it comes to our remedies under the law, and we must help you find your way out of it."

She crumbled in his arms and sobbed. "Oh Father, who will ever want to marry me, should I even end up free again? Not to mention Charlie's own chances."

"You are both such remarkable creatures. You deserve nothing less than a truly exceptional man, and such a man would never be deterred by what has happened."

Henrietta pulled back to stare at her father. What had happened to him in her absence? "I wish I could be as sanguine as you."

"You and Charlotte have been held captive to my moods for far too long. Connie—Constance—made me see how much everyone tiptoes around me. I couldn't see it myself—couldn't see how small a world I was trying to keep everyone in, in order to keep the pain small as well."

"Well, there may be something to your philosophy, given all the injury I have caused in exceeding it." Henrietta wiped her eyes again. "Father, I can't lose in court over there. It's too important."

She still hadn't told him what was inside the telescope. Only Charlotte and Nick knew of its contents—and *him*, of course, and whomever he might have told in his efforts to win it. But Henrietta knew she could trust her father more than anyone else in the world, and that notion calmed her along with his surprising new manner. To have someone who would always put your health and happiness first—who would lay down their life for you—was one of life's greatest and most ennobling gifts. *He* didn't have that—in fact, *he* had had to parent his brood of seven younger siblings when just a boy himself. But Henrietta refused to excuse him. After all, kind and decent Louisa had also suffered from crushing poverty and financial responsibility for her family, made even worse by the presence of an ineffectual father.

If Henrietta and Charlie, and charmed people like Sara-Beth, had better luck in life, it was only because they'd started out with such a good hand. Although a parent's love for a child was more natural than not, it suddenly felt so potent to Henrietta as to be practically magical: the very thing she had been missing while in England, and it had nothing to do with age. She would want it always, this love of her father, no matter how old she grew. She thought of the admiral and how close the two of them had become—and how quickly—and how that must have made Fanny Austen feel in turn. For the first time, Henrietta felt a twinge of sympathy for the woman whose ill-founded actions had changed the destiny of so many.

"Norton's decision throws a wrench into everything, I will admit." William sighed. "But we have a clear month, if not a horizon, before word might reach us again from Cresswell's court, should Mr. Scott renew his application for judgment." He patted her hand in comfort, just like when she was a child. "Saunders says there is some precedent in English law that such marriages at sea are not valid. You may be unwilling to void the marriage yourself, but there is a chance the court there will do it for you. And then the admiral's gift stays yours, even in England, as you will not be considered married or subject to their laws. And then all of life will be available to you again, as you so richly deserve."

He kissed the top of her head and left her sitting on the bed. She waited until the ladder folded up and the door in the floor closed—waited until she heard the sound of his moccasin slippers fade away downstairs, past the many floors below. Then she lay back on the bed and finally let herself remember what had happened—finally let herself remember it *all*.

SEVEN

Honeymoon in Hanbury Street

FOUR WEEKS EARLIER
Tower Hamlets, July 3, 1865

She raced down the steps to the basement flat in Hanbury and into Denham's arms. The carriage from Victoria station, with Nicholas Nelson still inside, was not yet gone and already Denham was carrying her over the threshold.

He carried her straight past the tiny front parlor and into the bedroom, slamming the door behind them. It had been such a long waiting; never more than a quick touch on the arm or brush of the cheek in the many parks and squares of Boston, before anyone else might see. At twenty-five years of age, Henrietta had never been really kissed—dutiful or hesitant pecks from schoolboys only, leaving nothing in their wake. But as Denham kissed her, every part of her felt changed by him and made over—now as much a part of *him* as her own self, and he a part of her.

When it was over, when he had cried out and shivered from the pleasure that she had given him, she felt another wave of ecstasy followed by the most surprising and incredible sense of power. For as much as she felt at his mercy, Denham seemed equally beholden to her. It had been part of their shared silent understanding from the very start of their acquaintance—the way he looked at her, sought her out, caught her eye when no one else was looking. She had felt truly seen and now, in his arms, she felt all the adoration she had always envied other women and more. It was impossible to believe that anyone else in the world had ever experienced such bliss as this.

They lay naked together afterward, collapsed in each other's embrace, truly joined together. He continued to touch her, even spent as she was, and she found herself kissing him to make him stop, then begging him not to. Looking back, she would wonder at this—at his enjoyment of her submission, of what he was able to make her feel and do in return. But at the time it felt like hunger and desire such as she could only dream of, if she had even known it could exist.

There was a scratching noise on the other side of the door, and Denham sat up and boyishly laughed. "I have a surprise. . . ."

She watched his taut, lean back as he disappeared into the hallway, a beautiful man, every muscle so perfectly, intentionally wrought, then returned with a small spaniel in his arms. The puppy left scratch marks on her own, and Denham kissed the red lines on her skin and promised to better train the little creature he had named Biscuit in her absence.

Nearby church bells rang out four o'clock and Denham jumped up again. "I forgot—my brothers and sisters!"

They quickly tidied themselves and soon the small flat—as cozy as his letters had promised—was full of a group of young people bearing an interesting mix of features similar to his own. They ranged in age from ten to twenty, and Denham was devoted to them all. Henrietta was used to a quiet house at Eleven Beacon Street, made even more quiet by the reading that she, Charlie, and their father constantly undertook. Denham's family was much more active, jostling and joking, always speaking out of turn. There was no "Harry on the right, Charlie on the left," no need for politeness, no reserve. Yet they were struggling all the same. Denham's wages were being supplemented by the oldest siblings taking on servant work, two of the brothers toiled in the warehouses of nearby Tobacco Dock, and one sister had fallen on particularly hard times.

They gave her several handmade wedding presents—a quilt, a wooden jewelry box to hold the garnet, an engraved leather collar for Biscuit. But grateful as Henrietta was, when they had all left, it was as if a tumult had passed. She and Denham stood facing each other just as they had on the moonlit deck, another little posy of white bachelor buttons now in a vase on the sideboard, put there by Denham in tribute to that most romantic moment on ship. They returned to the bedroom and made love again, and in the wake of the overwhelming surge of all her feminine power, she finally told him about the bequest. She would have done so sooner—looking back, she would wish she had—but for all the commotion of their lovemaking and the lengthy visit by his family, who were now her family, too.

"You have it here?" he asked. Getting up, naked, she went over to the small valise she had bought on the ship and returned with the admiral's gift in her hands.

Pulling the new wedding quilt around her, Henrietta watched as Denham examined the telescope carefully, rotated the lens, activated the tell-tale click. Without asking for permission, he pulled the draw tube from the barrel, then shook it hard until the paper fell out to land on the bed between them. He read it carefully, twice, then placed it back down on the quilt.

"We know for certain no one else has seen it?"

"No, but the letter breaks off so— Sir Francis's second wife, Martha, found it after Jane's death. It is quite possible that Cassandra never even knew of its existence, despite its being addressed to her."

Denham got that look in his eyes that she remembered from across the gallery at the Music Hall, the day the Girl Orator spoke. He was always on the lookout: it was how he had survived. Oh, how lucky she and Charlotte were, to never have to look out or too far ahead, to have the luxuries of life constantly at the ready. Henrietta felt guilt over that, always had. She wondered at the London slums where Denham's siblings lived and their little flat skirted—they were just separated enough from such a life. Until the babies came—and at this rate, she blushed to herself, there would be many—and Denham rose at the paper, she could perhaps help with social work. Many women of Boston had taken that on; Louisa had told how her own mother, Abigail, herself the daughter of a prominent family, had been one of the first paid social workers in the city.

"You well know how little *I* know the work of Austen," he said, staring back down at the letter. "But it would seem to me that this answers so much. The lifelong grudge against a sister, the desire for love with the so-called seaside gentleman, the alleged machinations by Cassandra that ruined the budding romance and left Jane with nothing but books to write and a boatload of regret—"

She had to stop him there. "The letter does not precisely say that."

He laughed. "Yes, but we can surmise, can we not, that Jane *would* regret never experiencing something akin to what we have felt today?"

She blushed again at the truth of his words.

"You will no longer apologize then, as you once did, for wanting to be a wife and mother? I will hold you to today, you know. I have never seen you happier or more beautiful." He leaned over to kiss her shoulder, then the space between her breasts where the garnet ring still dangled, left there for this moment with him in bed.

"The letter . . ." Denham stopped to think. "Dickens has destroyed everything, you know—quite a good thing, that, in light of the rail crash he only just escaped. Everyone has their chance in life. Austen chose not to take it."

"What are you saying?"

He shrugged. "It explains so much. The world would be very interested—not just here but in America, too. Think of your little judges' literary circle—the Nelsons' lucrative trade—the pirated editions being made. Anyone who prints the story—"

"The story?"

"—would have sellers' rights. There's no copyright in a letter, after all."

She sat up, clasped the garnet against her chest. "It's private, Denham."

"Privacy doesn't last forever—where would your beloved history be, if it did?"

She stared at him, something inside her running cold as ice. "Her brother is still alive!"

"For now."

"Denham!" She pulled the quilt entirely around her. "My word, what are you saying?"

"I'm just saying that the right to privacy is not so absolute or lasting as any of us might wish. We are all free agents—we have plenty of time to burn whatsoever we choose. If we don't, what is that to the next generation, or the one after that? One day—"

"One day is *not* today."

"But it has to start sometime, Henrietta. Maybe your life of privilege allows for such delicacy, but I am a newspaperman with a living to cobble together. I do not have a wealthy father supporting me."

"Neither do I, in marrying you!"

"Exactly! Now we are one and the same, of the same mind. You have pledged to honor and obey me, while my duty is to provide for my family. You must acknowledge my efforts there." He rubbed his jaw in frustration as he assessed her troubled gaze. "Do you know what I make? Do you know what *anyone* makes?"

She could only stare at him as if he were changing before her very eyes.

"For God's sake, Henrietta, I make *fifty* pounds a year—fifty! A box at the Royal Opera costs eight bloody thousand! Even if we sell this letter for just a few hundred pounds, that's still years of work for me. I could discharge all my family's debts—my brother Spencer could stay in school— Ethan could finally start his apprenticeship before it grows too late."

Henrietta's head was throbbing. He was making the smallest possible sense, but at what cost? Sir Francis had kept the letter to himself for decades—how could she bear him seeing it splashed across the pages of *Reynolds's Newspaper* or *The Pall Mall Gazette*? Should Fanny learn of the bequest from the papers, she would surely alert her father no matter how dire his state of health.

"Denham, I can't. Not now. Maybe one day, as you yourself said. If money is such a concern, perhaps I can ask Father—"

"Your father's money is his, as this is ours." He picked up the letter and waved it freely at her, then checked the pocket watch resting on the small camping chair next to the bed. "Don't worry, darling, I'll take it to my editor—he works long into the night—and we shall see what he says." He got up and began to dress while she watched him, speechless.

"Denham, don't be ridiculous. It's past ten." She reached out for the letter but he held it away from her grasp, then sat back down on the bed to pull on his boots. Henrietta's head swirled—she actually feared fainting from exhaustion if she stood up too fast. She and Nick had left Portsmouth at the break of dawn to reach London as quickly as possible. They had thought they were fleeing only Fanny-Sophia, for who knew what Sir Francis might confess as he faced the end, causing her to come for the letter. Henrietta wanted it to survive, to not be fuel on another pyre, yet at the same time— and yes, she heard a voice inside her say, one could want both—she did not want the world to read it. Not now—maybe not ever. But it should be her prerogative to decide—*her* property to deal with.

"Denham . . ." She got out of bed and grabbed her robe from the small case on the floor. Suddenly she did not want him to see her naked and exposed—suddenly everything happening between them was taking on the violence of a power struggle. She wrapped her robe about her like armor, for the struggle was in fact very real—who would determine the rules for their life together? Had the wedding vows truly suspended and merged her personhood into his, as English law declared and Denham appeared to believe? From the start, Denham had thrilled to the similarity in their sense of humor, interests, and intelligence—how could she become something else to him entirely, and somehow even less, simply because of words exchanged in the moonlight?

"Give me the letter, Denham. I mean it."

"You *mean* it? What does *that* mean?"

She stood before him, hesitating. There would be no turning back once she said it. "It means it is my letter—it was given to *me*—and my wishes regarding it are to be respected, just as I would respect yours."

But he was heading for the door. "We'll discuss this when I get back. I'm sure when you hear how much my editor will pay for it . . ."

She lunged for it again, surprising them both, and he laughed as if it were a game—as if he did not take any of it, or her, seriously. The letter stayed held aloft, for as tall as she was, he was still several inches taller. He did not hit her, but it felt like a slap all the same.

And then he left. Just like that. She dropped onto her bare knees and sobbed, felt the rough wood of the floorboards digging into her skin, didn't care. The little dog Biscuit emerged from wherever it had been hiding and nuzzled up against her lap, but she didn't touch it. She refused to. She had to unmake her home of one day.

When Denham returned a few hours later, she pretended to be asleep, tears silently streaming down her face. She could tell he was happy; she had heard him whistling when he came in. She would have to act fast, destroy it all, just like Fanny-Sophia had.

In the morning, when he woke, she—and the letter—were gone.

EIGHT

The Clairvoyant of Cremorne

THAT SAME DAY
The New Adelphi Theatre, July 3, 1865

"Miss Stevenson? Mr. Robinson will see you now."

Nash and Haz sat on either side of Charlotte in the empty theater auditorium, smiling their excitement at her. She stood up and flattened her skirts, Henrietta's silver-minted sixpence clasped in one hand. The walk down the aisle toward the stage seemed to take forever, yet Fawcett Robinson did not turn an inch at Charlotte's approach. He stared straight ahead from the center of the front row instead, both hands resting on top of the gold-mounted cane between his knees.

"And you will be playing a scene from . . . ?" he boomed from the darkness.

"Much Ado About Nothing."

"Ah yes, sweet Hero."

"Beatrice, in fact."

The famed producer lifted one eyebrow but said nothing at such a curious choice. Nash had suggested it on the train. He had not spoken much during the journey to London from Portsmouth. As Charlotte and Haz picked over the various possible roles for her audition—Juliet, Ophelia, Miranda, Cordelia—Nash had waited until almost all of Shakespeare had been exhausted before making his suggestion.

The moment he did, something went off in Charlotte like a shot. The character of Beatrice from *Much Ado About Nothing* was Nash's declared favorite heroine from the plays—her father had offhandedly mentioned this to her once. Whatever could Nash be up to, in wanting to see her perform it?

"That harpy?" Haz had asked Nash.

"The scene where she implores Benedick to avenge Hero," he answered. "This is after Claudio, tricked into thinking Hero unfaithful, shames her at the wedding altar. They have moved too quickly to marry—everything might fall apart with as much haste. What is that *maxime* by La Rochefoucauld—'jealousy is bred in doubt'?"

Haz had good-naturedly shrugged—so much of Nash's conversation being over his head—while Charlotte firmly set her lips.

"Nash, I want to present myself in the best possible light."

"Everyone expects you to play someone sweet and innocent. You want to pick an altogether different target—a different snap to the bow—to stand out as much as possible from the rest. The world is full of young and pretty faces." He paused. "Do the unexpected."

Charlotte and Haz had raised their eyebrows at each other while Nash turned back to the view of the South Downs passing by. But his words stayed with her. He had risen to the top of his profession at such a young age—he must know something about success.

Now standing alone on the stage of the Adelphi, lit by a single gas limelight above, Charlotte spoke to the darkness. She always felt the same rush of power wherever she acted, be it attic bedroom or shipboard saloon. The whole world was now inside her for the choosing: she was in control of it all. The words of text—the lines—were incontrovertible but sterile; the meaning was hers to decide on and bring to life. This was her singular job as an actress: to create something so truthful as to seem real.

She felt mesmerized by the darkness and the silence that was also hers to break—the audience that she alone could cast a spell over. As Charlotte's voice echoed through the theater, she recalled the words of Denham Scott on the Girl Orator: *Do you not think there is something of the mesmerist in her?* And she thought about Nash in the audience and how he had responded to Louisa on the ship's ramshackle stage, his Sydney Carton to her Lucie Manette, and the strange jealousy it had evoked in Charlotte as she watched. It had been a year of looks and teasing from Nash, and she wanted more—wanted at least as much as Louisa had experienced, real life or not. But Charlotte wasn't allowed to ask for it. So, she vowed, she would direct her magic not at Fawcett Robinson, who from his producer's front-row seat would be expecting it, but at Justice Thomas Nash and his always detached, observant, and unsuspecting soul:

Kill Claudio! Is he not approved in the height a villain, that hath slandered, scorned, dishonoured my kinswoman? O! that I were a man. What! bear her in hand until they come to take hands, and then, with public accusation, uncovered slander, unmitigated rancour,—O God, that I were a man! I would eat his heart in the market-place. . . . That I had any friend who would be a man for my sake! But manhood is melted into curtsies, valour into compliment, and men are only turned into tongue, and trim ones too: he is now as valiant as Hercules, that only tells a lie and swears it. I cannot be a man with wishing, therefore I will die a woman with grieving. . . .

When she was done, there was silence again. Somewhere in the darkness Haz and Nash watched, two sentinels keeping guard over her ambition, but Charlotte didn't need them. Up there onstage, she was finally in charge of something: Her own voice and body. Her own ambitions and desires.

A declarative tapping of the cane—once, twice—sounded from the front row. The stage manager had warned her that Fawcett Robinson rarely gave comment afterward. He took the performances into himself and hoarded them there. His role in this world of theater was very different from hers, a very different kind of power. But Charlotte also knew from the manager what two distinct taps meant, and her heart surged.

Mr. Robinson stood up. "You are staying at the Grosvenor? I will send a message within the hour. Thank you, Miss Stevenson."

And that was it. He disappeared into the darkness and Haz was running down the center aisle toward her. "Charlie, you were magnificent! I've never seen anything like it!"

Still in a bit of a trance, her eyes met Nash's as he reached the stage. He, too, was looking up at her differently. It felt electric as they faced each other, her looking down at *him* for once, the power building inside her.

"Whatever will I tell your father, when I return home with neither you nor your sister?"

But he smiled as he said it.

"I did well?" she asked. With her natural confidence, it sounded like a statement, and he continued to smile up at her.

"You know you did."

"Was it the Beatrice you wanted?"

"I think you also know the answer to that."

Charlotte could have grabbed on to something at that point to steady herself onstage—*was Nash actually flirting with her?* Thank goodness Haz wasn't there to witness any of it. He was up onstage now himself, looking around the sets, peering in the wings. Charlotte knew he yearned to perform, and recalled how during rehearsal there had been no real attraction between them, only a pretend one. They were too much of the same mind, which made them ideal friends, each of them most comfortable in a world of high stakes. But both knew that when it came to love, Haz wanted a challenge—a trophy to win, as in sports—while Charlotte needed a man who stood on solid ground.

She took a step closer to the edge of the stage—but there would be no stumbling tonight. She felt freed by the performance and what its success meant for both her and Nash. She would not be returning to Boston; they might never see each other again. Part of her felt safe to ask for what she wanted—part of her remained in a state of reckless abandonment. All she knew was that she didn't want any part of Nash to feel safe tonight when it came to her.

The concierge at the Grosvenor Hotel passed Charlotte a telegram and a message upon their return. The note was from Fawcett Robinson, as promised, offering Miss Stevenson a contract for the coming season as one of the New Adelphi players. The contents of the telegram, however, were a complete surprise:

NICHOLAS AND I HEADING TO LONDON STOP SHALL REUNITE
WITH DENHAM FIRST THEN VISIT ON THE MORROW STOP PRESUME
YOU PICKED THE OPHELIA STOP ALL MY SISTERLY LOVE H.

"What could have happened to set them off so fast?" Charlotte asked Haz, staring down at the telegram in confusion. "Could Sir Francis have passed on already? Wouldn't Harry mention if that were so?"

Haz shrugged. "Perhaps they felt there was nothing more there to be done—and a new bride would have other, more *pressing*, concerns."

Charlotte playfully smacked the side of his forearm resting next to hers on the concierge desk, keenly aware the entire time of Nash standing somewhere behind them.

"Charlie, we must celebrate your triumph today!" Haz excitedly declared. "You won't be seeing Harry for at least another day, by the sound of it—let's go tripping tonight! Somewhere full of fun."

"Excuse me, sir," the concierge politely interrupted, "but might I suggest Cremorne Gardens?" Opening a large map on the gilded marble counter, he pointed to a small green square. "There's a dozen acres right here in Chelsea, on the banks of the Thames."

Charlotte and Haz pored over the map as the concierge described the variety of entertainment to be found in the gardens on a pleasant summer night such as this. Boston and Philadelphia had nothing as impressive: concerts, fireworks, hot-air balloon ascents, galas, and even the occasional tightrope walk across the river—the most recent attempt having resulted in death from sixty feet and a suspension of such activity ever since. There were supper boxes and an American-style bowling saloon in the center of the gardens that served American-style drinks, a circus and theaters, medieval tournaments and marionette shows, a crystal pavilion and a giant pagoda, lit by hundreds of colored lamps, where thousands of couples could dance about the circular open floor. The concierge discreetly advised that the gardens were increasingly a meeting ground for men seeking women of "ill repute," and was glad that Miss Stevenson would be chaperoned by no less than two gentlemen.

They spent the evening strolling about the gardens, Charlotte pretending to take in all that she saw while pretending not to notice Nash, whose irritation with Haz she finally saw through for the jealousy it surely was. After leaving Henrietta in Hanbury Street, Nick had arrived by coach at the Grosvenor in time to join the group for supper and the excursion to the gardens. He told them about the admiral's bequest of the telescope to Henrietta but said nothing more on the matter. Charlotte was intrigued, but so much had happened to her that day, and her mind kept flitting between the audition and Nash, his sudden willingness to hint at his attraction (*for it was clear by now that he would never declare it*, she stewed to herself) and her sudden change in fortune, the life behind in Boston and the life in London ahead.

Charlotte knew she suffered from self-absorption at the best of times; Harry was so much more giving than her, if less outwardly passionate. But neither of them loved in halves—once someone had their heart, they had it forever. Both women were very much like their father that way.

In the center of the gardens was a tent, a sign on its outside flap promising to tell one's fortune for a sixpence. Charlotte thought of the lucky coin still in her reticule and the success of the audition, and decided to try her luck one more time that day.

Nash dismissed the entire endeavor, but Haz was very game. He accompanied Charlotte inside the tent, and they sat down at a round, white-clothed table across from a woman draped in brightly colored scarves. It was impossible to tell her age—she appeared to have outgrown this very world. Resting on the table before her was a crystal globe on a pewter pedestal.

"The lady first." Haz passed a brand-new sixpence across the table.

The woman smiled knowingly as she took the coin and tucked it away, then started rubbing the cloudy globe with both hands. After several seconds of suspense, she began to speak in a halting, ominous tone.

"I see much good fortune ahead . . . there is a crowd, an audience . . . oh, you are very loved—adored, even." She shook her head in amusement at the look on Haz's face. "It is *not* this man. It is another whom you know, but he resists you. Wait—I see water. Water all around. A great sea—yes! A great sea will separate you from those you love."

Charlotte smiled to herself. It did not take a crystal ball to see that they were tourists from abroad—or that another, handsome member of her party paced the lawn outside the tent. She was determined to keep her face and features unreadable, to act the part of someone with no past.

"Yes, you will be forever separated from the one you love most."

Charlotte shifted uneasily in her seat. They had been celebrating all evening and she had thought far too little of her father, about to lose both his daughters to London—no wonder he had always worried so! But her mind quickly turned back to the Adelphi, and Nash always near, and the desire that she was determined to act upon tonight.

"But I will have children and a family of my own?"

The fortune-teller hesitated, placed both hands on either side of the globe again, shook her head. "No, you will have a great love, but it will be all-consuming. It will require great sacrifice." She looked Charlotte straight in the eye. "You are scared—I see that, too. You will have to ask for what you want. It is waiting for you—but you must be the one to act."

When Charlotte and Haslett emerged from the tent, Nash stood waiting on the lawn outside. "Let me guess—you will have great fame and fortune."

He was teasing her again, but she would have none of it. She would have all the advantage of boldness, just like a man. So she waited to catch his eye, then pushed the tip of her parasol hard into the soft lawn with both hands, gloved fingers interlaced. She made sure to expose the skin about her wrist as she did so—the one glimpse of skin on her entire body—then smiled as Nash loosened his cravat in subtle, unknowing response. But *she* knew.

"She said I will have anything I want—I only have to ask."

Nash rubbed his neck at her words, Haz shot Charlotte a curious look, and Nicholas returned with another pitcher of lager for the group. Eventually they resumed their stroll through the gardens, the moonrise almost full, the fortune-teller's words dangling in the air.

It was long past midnight when they returned to the Grosvenor, with its hundreds of rooms spread out over five floors. The men in the party were staying at one end of the first-floor corridor, Charlotte far down at the other. Somehow, silently, Nash ended up the one accompanying her safely to her door. There was that word *safe* again, she thought, as he followed closely behind her down the narrow passageway. The hot July air had left a stickiness to her touch, causing her to fumble with the key in the door. Still, she took her time unlocking it, just long enough to feel sure, then turned around to grasp the hastily tightened cravat and pull him to her.

She felt so much power as Nash let her—no one warned you what power over a man felt like. It was as heady as performing. He was completely at her mercy in that moment, so at her mercy that she could feel every inch of his body responding to hers—*God help her if either of the Nelsons should catch sight*, a far-off voice inside her said, while at the same time not caring one whit—and he made a sound as he kissed her, so low and deep, a sound that pulled her down into him in turn. And then the whole world beneath her fell away, the world that told her man knew best, man was in charge, and instead, in this one blood-rushing moment, she was in charge of him. No wonder men were scared of women.

There was a loud sobbing noise from the direction of the lift at the other end of the hallway, and Charlotte broke away from the intensity of the moment and the embrace.

"My God—Harry?"

Nash took a step back as well—Haz and Nick came bounding out of their rooms—Henrietta was running in tears down the hallway toward her.

NINE

✳

Holding All the Aces

THE PRESENT
The Massachusetts Supreme Judicial Court
August 1, 1865

Charlotte and Nash had not been alone together since.

The five of them had caught the morning train to Liverpool. Arriving in that northern port city, Henrietta and Nash had immediately sought out Dr. Richard Pankhurst, a highly recommended barrister who had chambers there. When the group met up again at the Albert Dock, Henrietta looked as distraught as Charlotte had ever seen her, and no wonder: she had forsaken her entire life for a man in a matter of days, and was now just as quickly forsaking *him*.

In the privacy of Charlotte's room at the Grosvenor, Henrietta had shown her the telescope and the hidden letter, adamant that no one else know of it. *It was* only a piece a paper, Charlotte told herself, a routine marital squabble—not enough cause for Harry to flee for home as covertly as she had left it. Everything would be resolved soon enough, and surely in Harry's favor, once Denham understood how much the admiral's entrustment meant to her: he simply did not know his new wife well enough yet. But an equally loud voice inside Charlotte screamed over the injustice of it all, the idea that Henrietta had lost her personhood and her property to her husband immediately upon marriage.

They boarded the RMS *Neptune* separately from Nash and Nicholas Nelson, while Haz waved goodbye from the Liverpool dock. Over the ship horns he shouted his promise to find Louisa and Sara-Beth—*if I have to search every last casino on the Continent!* Charlotte still wondered at his older brother joining the voyage home, and worried that Henrietta—demure, practical, principled Henrietta—might end up breaking hearts on both sides of the Atlantic. When they were in calmer seas, Charlotte would warn Harry about the Philadelphia bookseller's affections. For now, Nicholas claimed it his gentlemanly duty, as the admiral's other correspondent, to help bring the bequest safely to America and away from the clutches of both Fanny-Sophia and Denham Scott.

Nash, on the other hand, appeared to suffer from no such gentlemanly compunction. He was behaving as if nothing had happened between Charlotte and himself—as if he had merely lost his head after a night of carousing in Cremorne Gardens. If possible, he was acting even more remote toward her sailing west than he had heading east as an unwanted chaperone. *Well, two could play at that,* she vowed.

Back in Boston, Nash no longer came to Eleven Beacon Street to sit by the fire after dinner, and she no longer hoped to bump into him in the Common on his morning walk. She had been particularly relieved by his absence from the courtroom during the hearing of *Scott v. Scott.* But now, with Norton's minutes-old decision still ringing in her ears, Charlotte raced down the hallway of the courthouse to Nash's private chamber. The clerk in the front room barely had time to address her as she ran past.

"Charlotte, my God—the decision?" Nash jumped up from his desk in alarm.

"Norton's sent the case back to England!"

He took a breath. "Renvoi?"

She nodded. Of course he knew of it, rare though it was.

"Mr. Saunders calls it a blue antelope. He and Father are at a complete loss."

"I can't believe Norton—to what godly end? Their laws are in retrograde over there when it comes to women."

"Harry will lose it all." Charlotte flopped down into the chair and watched as Nash paced back and forth, deep in thought. "Isn't there anything that can be done?"

Nash stopped, stared at the shelves of case law before him, grimly shook his head. "There's no right of appeal from this supreme court. Norton's decision is a final one, I'm afraid."

"Poor Harry. Everything we've done, and she's right back where she started."

Nash brought a few volumes from the shelves over to his desk and sat down. "Not entirely. Mr. Scott will first have to renew his lawsuit in England, where the courts did already reject it once."

"Denham will never have a change of heart. Harry swears it."

"There's also a small chance Cresswell will apply American law if the matter comes before him again—although such deference to a former colony is unlikely, I won't pretend there."

The clerk knocked and entered with a more junior clerk's notes from the courtroom, and Charlotte watched impatiently as Nash read the reasoning behind Justice Norton's decision. "The fact that the instance of ownership arose in England is a damning one, I'm afraid—even more than your sister's arguable loss of citizenship here." He pushed the notes back from him on the blotter. "Our only hope, should the matter come before Cresswell again, is that he will rule against the validity of marriages at sea altogether."

"Can someone please explain to me," Charlotte pleaded in anger and desperation, "how my sister is no longer an American citizen?"

"Our case law is at sixes and sevens with respect to that legal issue, and Congress has yet to act to resolve it. With no clear guidance from our legislature, Norton had much judicial discretion to work with."

"So, we women are wanted to settle the *West*, can even get a divorce in Indiana, I hear, as if that's any kind of a lure—you can leave your husband in a thrice, ladies, if you move out here! Just please, *please* come out here and breed—"

"Charlotte!"

"—lots and lots of babies for us, but God help you if you marry a foreigner to do it!" She put her head in her hands and could feel him watching her, struggling over what to say. When he did speak, it wasn't what she expected.

"You and Henrietta both gave up a lot, leaving England as you did."

"I didn't think twice."

"I know."

She jerked her head up at his tone. "If I can secure a role in London, Nash, I can do so here. I have to believe that."

"Still, not everyone as ambitious as you would have walked away from the Adelphi."

"You think me so ambitious?"

"I think you the most ambitious person I've ever met."

"And you think that unseemly."

"Not at all."

She smirked at him. "Oh yes, you do. It was fine when you thought you were leaving me to London and the stage—attractive even—attractive enough to kiss in a hotel corridor and most likely more—"

"Charlotte, my God—that's not—"

"—but it would *never* pass muster in a wife!"

"Charlotte!" he cried again in disbelief.

"You think it of Louisa, too. Poor Lu, who because of her appearance gets nothing—only what she can make for herself. We women are handed either everything or nothing, based on how much we entice *you*. Well, I tell you"—she stood up, her anger over the court's decision now merging with all her other resentments of late—"if ever a woman could make the world bow to her, it will be Louisa!"

"I don't doubt that, Charlotte—I don't doubt it of you, either."

"Don't flatter me." She shook her head as if she didn't believe a word he said—as if he didn't even understand what they were really talking about.

"I would never do that, Charlotte, I—"

"*I* won't ever fit your or any man's notion of what a woman is supposed to be! And neither will Harry—no matter how many laws you men hurl at her!"

Charlotte stormed out, past the confused clerk, past her father approaching his chamber from the other end of the hall. She had played in this hallway as a child, hidden under her father's desk, looked up at him and all the other men in robes. Back then, she had never once wondered why there were no women about. But today each door she passed represented something much less awesome to her, yet full of even more power: the men who made and administered the law, and were holding all the aces.

TEN

Lost Horizon

‹———·———›

Portsdown Lodge, August 10, 1865

Sir Francis lay in bed, fading in and out of sleep, gazing up at the ceiling with weighted-down eyes. There was no need to look out at sea, no need to watch the horizon in anticipation or fear. He would soon join his departed family in a new celestial order. There would be no divisions anymore, no favorites or long-standing grievances—only gratitude for this final communion among them all.

Fanny knelt by the bed. She was always there now, making hers the last face he would see, but he no longer minded her presence. This was how he knew death must be near. Nothing on this earth could ever again be altered by him; nothing would feel his touch. What a strange notion, to know you were already a ghost. And he would be leaving nothing of value behind; Fanny had made sure of that.

It had been over a month since the fire on the lawn that had led to his collapse. He could not know such destruction and remain pure and steadfast in fatherly love. This caused his Christian soul to despair, coming so close to his own moment of reckoning before the Lord. Fanny's act of desecration was permanent and acutely personal—she knew his wishes, had seen his efforts to protect it all. How did one forgive someone for such violation?

George quietly entered with another letter from America. "Shall you read it to the admiral, miss?" He averted his eyes as he asked. But there was no one else to receive the correspondence, the other children having come and gone over the course of the last several weeks, only to now be hurrying back.

Fanny took the letter from George, still on her knees. This was the only way that Sir Francis could tell she was sorry. She never uttered a word of apology but constantly prayed instead—he could not imagine those prayers or their recipient, given what she had done. But she knelt and prayed as if yielding in supplication before him, his bed as altar, his body as sacrifice.

Admiral of the Fleet, Sir Francis Austen, G.C.B.
Portsdown Lodge, Hampshire, England

August 1, 1865

Dear Sir,

We write today with utmost concern, having not yet received reply to our earlier letter. As we wrote you on the 3rd of last month from Liverpool, and again from Boston on the 16th, we are now safely home, to the great relief of our father. Although our departure on the China caused him great distress, he has withstood it well, for which we are both most grateful and not at all—we happily suspect—the chief female presence responsible.

Of most importance to us, in writing, is an assurance of your own health and spirits. We commenced our correspondence with you at such a tumultuous time for our country, and your gracious replies, offers of hospitality, and most amiable companionship so greatly lifted our battered spirits. We can only pray that we have had some effect in kind, no matter how small.

We want to assure you, in turn, that your bequest is safeguarded in our possession with the greatest of diligence and protection. Do not fear, should you be relayed news to the contrary. There is some dispute with Mr. Denham Scott, who, in being recently betrothed to Henrietta, believes himself entitled to ownership of her personal property as well. We hereby seek to anticipate and address any misgivings or concerns of yours that may arise, should you <u>somehow</u> be made aware of a recent decision by Sir Cresswell of the divorce court, as is being reported in several London newspapers and abroad. Sir Cresswell dismissed Mr. Scott's petition for ownership and, as of today, we continue to prevail in the American courts as well. We are confident that the matter rests for now in Henrietta's favor, and will write immediately should we learn otherwise.

We cannot help but wonder what your beloved late sister would say to this admittedly disheartening state of affairs. Where is love, Miss Austen might indeed ask, as do we—how on earth shall one find a happy ending? She might resolve somehow to write into being a better outcome than appears possible at present. For now, we draw hope and comfort from her works that the full measure of justice is always at hand. The Massachusetts Supreme Judicial Court convened regularly during our absence to discuss your sister's great works, and we share the Ciceronian sentiments of Justice Mackenzie on "Mansfield Park" as follows: "Freedom is not about ensuring you get everything you want, but rather becoming the best self that you can be. Therein lies life's great reward for us and those around us."

Despite the actions of <u>others</u>, we do not see their receipt of any great reward. Their state of loneliness continues, as do their true and deepest desires. We question whether self-respect can even exist without respecting others, and only feel pity on <u>their</u> behalf.

We trust that this letter will reach you, and that someone will take exertion to reply on your behalf and alleviate our great concern for you, our dear friend.

Gratefully and respectfully yours,
Henrietta and Charlotte

He made little movement as Fanny read, just the occasional fluttering of his eyes without seeing, a small noise from the back of the throat that was something less than speech. Did she know how alone she soon would be? The grandchildren never yearned to visit her—she did not craft toys for them, make a little dell among the trees to play in, save the tartest cherries to watch their faces scrunch with delight as they ate.

When Fanny finished reading, she put the letter down on the quilt, then her head, and let out one single, strangled sob. It was as if her very being was trying to hold back even this final display of emotion toward him.

He felt himself raise his left hand next to her head, almost beyond his will. It was taking everything he had inside him, and oh, how he regretted the exertion. But he was her father still, the only one she would ever have— that was always the great privilege and burden of the role. No one else could soothe her pain on this matter, or grant her forgiveness: it all rested with him.

With eyes barely open, he slowly brought the hand down to rest near hers. She grabbed it, hard, but not to keep him there with her. She was holding on to him, instead. She knew what world she had left for herself.

It always came too late, such understanding. Only with crisis did we achieve clarity. The pain cut through everything else, cleared the horizon, made us finally see. No telescope was necessary, at the very moment when there was nothing left to discover.

He fully closed his eyes, his hand still in hers. He had done his last fatherly duty to the end.

ELEVEN

✳

One Tired Little Shuttlecock

•———•

IN THE MATTER OF *SCOTT v. SCOTT*
Lincoln's Inn, September 5, 1865

Sir Cresswell took his seat on the raised podium and surveyed the packed gallery. He attributed much of his own early success on the Northern Circuit to the practice of German physicist Lichtenberg's pathognomy. By closely studying a person's facial reactions and gestures, Cresswell believed he could determine their true motivation and character; given the bizarre matter again before him, he would now need to put this skill to its greatest test.

The petitioner sat facing Sir Cresswell, having renewed his application from two months earlier. This time, however, Mr. Denham Scott sought only a writ of seizure with respect to the marital property he claimed. Sir Cresswell had been surprised by this renewal—he had groaned so loud at seeing *Scott v. Scott* back on the docket that both his young clerks had come running. Cresswell was not surprised, however, by the decision to drop the petition for divorce altogether, requiring as it did proof of adultery. For all the petitioner's continuing legal efforts, he now appeared unwilling, or at least unable, to accuse his estranged wife of *that*.

Sitting a short distance from Mr. Scott were three Americans: a striking young woman wearing a black-and-white ensemble that matched the colors of the barristers' robes, an older woman who possessed worn-down features beneath an equally worn traveling cap and held a notepad and pencil at the ready, and a well-built, well-dressed young man with lively brown eyes. They were all three glaring at the back of the petitioner's downcast head, and nobody whom Cresswell himself would want to cross.

"But the respondent is again not here?" Sir Cresswell asked Dr. Richard Pankhurst, who looked as frustrated as him to be back in court.

"Yes, My Lord."

"Yet this matter is again before me." Cresswell sighed. He closely studied the petitioner, whom he called in his head the "three-weeks-and-a-day" man. Such stubbornness of jaw, yet a sadness about the eyes—there was something else going on with him, Cresswell just knew it.

"I have been asked to adjudicate, once again, on the validity of the petitioner's marriage at sea and any consequent right to the property of his wife. My counterpart in the Supreme Judicial Court of Massachusetts, the Honorable Associate Justice Roderick Norton, has seen fit to deny that foreign court any jurisdiction in this matter. We have before us a most rare and unfortunate instance of renvoi."

There was a muttering of incomprehension throughout the court.

"Allow me to explain in less dizzying, more workmanlike terms. I passed the case to America, and they have passed it back to me. They are saying *English* law is to apply. But what is the law of England here, you ask? It is that *American* law should apply. Hence, renvoi, and the very clear danger of its ceaseless repetition should I indeed toss the case back over the ocean again, rendering it one very tired little shuttlecock—as am I of this matter, I assure the court." Cresswell knew his reputation for being impatient and short-tempered—it was impossible to dispense with a divorce case a day otherwise.

"I should therefore like to inquire, before we proceed further, as to the nature of the object that has preoccupied the courts on two different continents. I can only surmise, given the extraordinary persistence of the petitioner, that the object he seeks to recover must be of equally extraordinary value."

The petitioner quickly looked to his counsel, who stood up. "Your Lordship, the value is not at issue—only the court's assignment of ownership."

Sir Cresswell put up his right hand to silence the barrister.

"It is in our society's great interest that marriage, individually and institutionally, be upheld whenever possible. It is in countries' best interests that they be allowed to apply their own laws to the acts of their citizenry. We have here a days-old union threatened by a mere object. I will not make a decision in favor of English law and issue seizure against an American resident so blindly, when the stakes are so high."

"Again, My Lord, the petitioner would prefer to disclose neither the value nor the facts of the object, if at all possible, but can attest to it being most easy to seize and transport."

Sir Cresswell studied the petitioner again with narrowed, assessing eyes. Being a famous insomniac himself, he recognized the lines of fatigue about Scott's eyes—one doesn't dispense with a divorce case a day without it also taking a toll at night. "The petitioner is to approach the bench," he ordered.

Denham Scott stood up and reacted as if to a noise coming from the three Americans sitting behind him. To Sir Cresswell's relief, there was no sound of stomping suffragists as of yet.

"Mr. Scott, you are most persistent in your application. You have lost a wife, and much time and legal fees, to it. Before I allow you to further exhaust this court's time as well, I must know what you are fighting for."

The petitioner looked back at the front row of scornful Americans watching his every move, then to the rear of the gallery. Following his gaze, Sir Cresswell noticed among the crowd a nondescript group of young people, shabbily dressed and similar in feature to Mr. Scott.

"Your Lordship, the property that I seek to recover is of a most private and confidential nature. It is in written form and connected to one of the great literary figures of our time. As such, its disclosure would be newsworthy and, according to the editor of the *Reynolds's*, could fetch upward of several hundred—possibly even a thousand—pounds." For all his worn-down state, Scott held himself impressively tall, a look of pride in his eyes. "This sum may not seem significant to many in the court, but it represents ten years of work to me at least, and would immediately discharge my increasing legal debts and lift my seven much younger brothers and sisters, whom I support, out of poverty."

Sir Cresswell took all of this in with some alarm: the idea of seven hungry little mouths going unfed struck the bachelor judge to his core. But as much as hundreds of pounds might mean to the young man before him, Sir

Cresswell could not believe he was willing to throw over so much for it. Mr. Scott's pained, brokenhearted visage caused Sir Cresswell to wonder: *What if petitioner and respondent need only face each other, for both love and Lady Justice to be served?*

Dr. Richard Pankhurst stood up to address the bench with all the spirit of a beleaguered parent. "This matter is a waste of the court's time, Your Lordship. The petitioner has just allowed that the property in question is of a most private and confidential nature, yet in the same breath promotes its widest dissemination possible, through publication in a weekly news rag? The petitioner appears not to know top from bottom"—there was now loud female tittering from the gallery above—"and so I ask that Your Lordship apply renvoi and send the matter back again to America, where my client, Mrs. Scott, can renew her suit for divorce on the grounds of cruelty and rest assured of her right to the property in dispute. The prolonged and very public nature of these proceedings on both sides of the Atlantic, in and of itself, has caused my client the cruelest of pain and mortification, I can assure the court, and should satisfy any such grounds for dissolution."

Sir Cresswell listened, but most of all, he looked. In fact, he was trying to read the room in so many directions, it made his head spin: the three angry Americans, the stubborn yet sad petitioner, the impoverished relations, and the suffragists in the upper gallery, boots at the ready. As the Judge Ordinary of the Court for Divorce and Matrimonial Causes, Cresswell had full power to decide the matter. Once he did, there would be no going back, a newspaper headline worth shouting along with an historic legal precedent, and at least one heartbroken newlywed still to deal with.

TWELVE

Emma

⸺ • • ⸺

The Massachusetts Supreme Judicial Court
September 14, 1865

The full court was back in session and *Emma* was on the docket.

"How did we debate Austen all summer and not yet speak of love?" asked Chief Justice Adam Fulbright. Several men snorted, the chief justice being by far the most romantic member of the court.

"We've discussed romanticism plenty enough," countered Justice Roderick Norton.

"Yes, but not desire. The kind of desire that makes a man weak in the knees."

Justice Philip Mackenzie frowned. "Austen's characters may seek marriage as a means to happiness, but one does not see in her works the persistent flame of a Dickens or the violent passion of a Brontë."

"I beg to differ," said Justice Conor Langstaff. "I think what Austen so shrewdly—boldly—does is expose how much *hidden* desire drives us all. Look at Mr. Knightley in our text tonight. The man is utterly besotted and has no idea."

Justice Thomas Nash shifted uncomfortably in his chair, while the chief justice replied with a laugh, "Knightley is indeed the worst of the lot. He greatly desires Emma Woodhouse, yet insists on her improvement. He *insists* on her becoming the woman he wants and needs her to be." Fulbright sighed. "I must confess, Emma as she *is* would be enough for *me*."

"She would be enough for most men," Langstaff readily concurred. "She has all of Highbury twisted around her little finger, and it's not only due to wealth and social standing. There is a wonderful confidence in her, a charm and vivacity, that I, too, find most appealing."

The end of the parasol, digging deeper and deeper into the ground, flashed through Nash's head and he shifted again in his seat. *God help him.*

"What is Austen saying, then?" Justice Ezekiel Peabody inquired of the rest. "That there is little rhyme or reason to whom we love?" He firmly shook his head. "That is not love—that is lust."

"Like Zeke here, I must dissent," Justice William Stevenson announced, "but for very different reasons. Mr. Knightley most definitely loves Emma, but as much *for* those qualities he thinks he wants to change as in *spite* of them. The attraction he feels for her is based on anything but an ideal—Darcy's, too, for Elizabeth. These women act exactly as they are and have attracted these men by doing so—it is the men's social expectation of what a woman *should* be that complicates the plot. Yes, Emma now acts more graciously toward her neighbors, she might even one day finish a book—but that is not why Knightley finally declares his love."

"You mention plot." A befuddled Justice Ezekiel Peabody leaned forward in his chair. "Where is one?" The other men laughed at their most literal colleague, who had reams of scripture and essays memorized but no notion of subtext.

"It's all plot," asserted Langstaff, and the group turned to him in surprise. "There is not a single unnecessary happening in *Emma.*"

"Surely you jest!" exclaimed Norton. "Never have I read so many unnecessary happenings in a book! Pages are lost to discussions of Frank Churchill and his haircut, or a letter from Jane Fairfax, or the gift of a piano."

"I posit that everything happening in *Emma* is happening *around* these so-called unnecessary events of the plot," persisted Langstaff. "Every key incident is hidden by the mundane of life, from the characters, even from us. This was my fourth enjoyment of the book, and still I discovered more."

"Do enlighten us." Norton smirked.

"The strawberry-picking scene, for one. Frank Churchill arrives sweaty, foul-tempered."

"He is late." Norton shrugged. "His aunt has imposed on him again, if I recall."

"No. He has run into Jane *Fairfax*, and no one knows of it—not even the reader." Langstaff grinned in victory as Norton narrowed his eyes, then read to himself the relevant section of text which did indeed prove his colleague's point.

"But what are its great lessons, its themes?" Ezekiel persisted. "*Mansfield Park* and *Persuasion* have such relevance and meaning."

Langstaff paused for effect. "I submit, the picnic scene."

"Emma's insult of Miss Bates—so uncomfortable," remarked Peabody.

"Precisely because we've all experienced it," agreed the chief justice. "We've either perpetrated it ourselves—who among us hasn't made an utterance they wish they could expel from their head?—or been the recipient of such. The most careless words often injure the most. That is why we are in this profession, is it not? To ensure that the exact word is always selected, in order to convey the most precise meaning, never anything more or less. To never cause undue harm to a citizen, or prevent its full redress."

"I believe Knightley's reaction in this scene to be Austen's own," replied Langstaff. "He is reminding Emma, in all his anger, that they must use their good fortune in life to keep the Miss Bateses of the world from falling too low—its most noble purpose."

Mackenzie now lit up, having hungered all evening for such philosophical talk. "It's Cicero again!"

Everyone laughed as the chief justice stood up to retrieve the decanter of Madeira and share it among them. "*E pluribus unum* again, indeed. Treat others as we would want to be treated. There is no currency in dominating others—as I myself know, it's a very lonely, unsteady perch at the top."

W illiam sat alone on the phaeton in front of Constance's house. The discussion with the judges had run late, and his daughters would have retired to the attic for the night. He stayed on the high dimpled seat, reins still in his hands, ruing the great unhappiness of both his children as well as his share in its many complex and continuing causes.

The scandal surrounding his oldest daughter continued to consume Boston society, although Constance was helping William not to fixate on that, surrounded as she was by more radical and permissive minds. Connie coped with uncertainty by taking action: the white-and-gold drawing room was now full of large placards and various pamphlets being drawn up in protest. She was garnering the signatures of hundreds of Boston bluestockings in support of Henrietta's plight and rallying all her formidable resources—resources which continued to include Graydon Saunders. Just the thought of that man drove William to distraction. The ice-blue sapphire ring—the exact same color as her eyes, he had ordered the jeweller—now rested in a pocket of his waistcoat, where it waited for him to find his nerve.

"William?"

He was startled by Connie's voice below him in the dark.

"I thought I saw you there. Are you not coming in?"

It felt rude, to stay up there on the seat looking down at her, but he wasn't ready yet to enter the house.

"My boy, are you all right? Is it Henrietta? Has there been news from London?"

He shook his head before patting the seat next to him. "Would you mind joining me for a moment, my darling?"

She smiled and ascended the narrow carriage step as he gently pulled her up next to him. They sat there beneath the plaid wool blanket on his lap, bundled together against the first cool night of autumn. She pointed out Mercury, unusually visible in the dark sky. "It's at its greatest elongation tonight. Twenty-seven degrees east of the sun."

He turned to her, constantly surprised by all she knew. Knowledge acquired instead of babies—that was the draconian decision women everywhere were forced to make. *But the babies grow up and leave you all the same,* he thought to himself, *while knowledge never does.* He loved the operation of Connie's mind as well as its content—her humor and enthusiasm, her intuitive and incisive understanding. Most of all, he loved her passion, which she had also awakened in him—*no small feat,* he said to himself, and only one reason why he desired even more.

"I don't want to enter this house tonight as a guest."

She patted his arm in hers. "Oh William, you know you're not. Is that why I found you out here?"

"Connie, we are not bound by law to each other."

"We are bound to each other all the same."

"But it's not *quite* the same, is it? If it was"—he found himself resorting to his best lawyerly logic—"you would have no objection." He looked up at the lit windows of the front foyer and drawing room and other guest salons, then, two floors above that, the soft candlelight of her rooms upstairs. The bedroom itself was a masterpiece of Baroque design, everything outsized and large enough for two: the elaborately carved four-poster bed, the divan where she read in his arms (and, he blushed, once did something more), the massive stately dresser drawers. Twelve drawers, in fact—plenty to share.

"What we have is so free, my love," she attempted to soothe him. "No ownership—no rules. We make our life together every day."

"I don't want to own you, Connie." He was treading carefully; any whiff of Protestantism or possession, any display of jealousy over the friendship with Saunders, and he knew she would bolt. "I am just so proud that *you* have chosen *me*. What a joy, truly. I want to revel in it, and shout it to the world. I want people to look at us and know what we mean to each other. The respect, the love."

"William, what are you saying?"

He removed the ring from his waistcoat pocket and held it out to her. "Constance, dear, will you be my wife?"

She stared at the ring for several uncomfortable seconds before speaking. "This comes with too many strings, William, too much alteration. I love you, I love your beautiful, brilliant daughters, but I love my life, too—too much to change it."

"I don't want to change your life." He frowned, the unspoken jealousy over Saunders gripping his heart. "Is there . . . something else?"

"William, my sweet boy, I just can't. I can't live in your family home. I feel—well, frankly, it feels disrespectful to poor Alice." To his surprise, tears filled her eyes, their icy blue finally melting. It was his first glimpse of any vulnerability in her. *But surely we all possess that,* he asked himself, *whether we show it or not?* He thought of Nash and the other men on the bench, how their judicial decisions must be informed by a hidden inner landscape of their own, the law sometimes even cut to fit their individual sense of purpose. *We are carried along in life by everything that has come before,* the lawyer in him was forced to admit, *and far more than we can understand.*

"Your poor wife," Connie spoke again, "who knows none of what is happening, who can't comfort her girls in their time of need. She has missed everything. For all we talk, we never speak of *that*. Such unfairness—I can't add to it."

"I'm not asking you to. I'm asking to live here." He nodded up at the lit windows of her house.

She stared at him in shock. "What are you saying? You would live here, in my home—you and the girls?"

"If you would take us."

"If I would take you?" She threw her arms about him. "Into my home—my beautiful home—that I have worked so hard to make mine? To not give it up, and still have you?"

"Oh, Constance," he said teasingly, as he placed the sapphire on her ring finger, "if you tell me all these months of anguish rested on a matter of interior style . . ."

She buried her head in his shoulder and they laughed together, then kissed at length under Mercury. The planet was in its final night of retrograde (*all that she knew!* he marveled again when she told him this—he who rarely looked up at the stars). When William pulled back, his eyes were as tear-filled as hers.

"My daughters . . ."

"They do want to come, though?" He hesitated at her insistent tone. "Oh William, no—I could never ask them to leave their home, especially not now."

"Somehow I don't think that will be necessary."

"They would stay at Eleven Beacon, then? But you are certain they would understand your leaving *them*?"

He had to grin at the irony in light of his past behavior. "I have not set good precedent there. But fortunately, my daughters are much more tolerant of my own wishes. They only want my happiness. Look at all that has transpired, from my not wishing the same for them."

"What a strain on poor Harry, the waiting and not knowing what Mr. Scott will petition the court next. That cursed telegraph line breaking down . . ."

"I pray for a swift resolution, of course. But Henrietta will always redeem whatever ill opinion of her is out there. She is the most honorable person I know." He leaned back in the carriage seat and pulled Connie against his chest. "The trial has taken such a toll."

"She is heartbroken, William. Both your girls are." He gazed curiously down at her head, wondering if she knew what he suspected. "Charlotte had to leave behind a great deal as well—imagine, the London stage, and performing before the greatest personages of our time. . . ."

"I think Charlotte left behind even more than that. I think I set wheels in motion last June that could only crash in the end."

Constance pulled back to examine his face. "What are you saying?"

"It's not for me to say—not yet." He smiled hopefully at her. "But you'll be proud to know I took a gamble tonight, in more ways than one. I can only hope it pays off for us all."

THIRTEEN

Mercury in Retrograde

Beacon Hill, September 15, 1865

Charlotte dreaded the arrival of autumn. *Where had summer gone?* It had been lost to all the anger she was known for in the family, and to tears she thought she hid well. Her father had caught her crying only once, standing before the half-finished painting of George Washington on the top floor of the Athenaeum, wagging her finger at his imperious face as tears streamed down her own. She didn't like how she was starting to feel about men. Maybe it was punishment for the power she had happily exerted over Nash on that hot and feverish July night—whatever it was, the power was gone. She could not move him anymore—worse, she had left him barely even able to look at her.

Nash had not been to Eleven Beacon Street since their return to Boston. The situation with Henrietta complicated things but frankly, things were already complicated enough. To begin with, their father was rarely home to receive Nash and secretly in love, the single happy result of the family's short-lived separation. Charlotte and Henrietta questioned how long he might go on as he was, taking his mysterious walks, slipping back into his bedroom in the early morning hours. As for Constance, they felt as close to her as ever, yet she, too, kept her romantic life to herself. Charlotte wondered if this was out of respect for both her father's wishes and the memory of their late mother. All Charlotte knew was that she really needed a mother right now, and was missing out on two.

Her older sister was understandably of no help. It was bewildering still, all that had happened. Henrietta, a most respectable judge's daughter, a daughter of Boston no less, was being portrayed in newspapers on two different continents as some kind of hysteric who lured men into marriage, then made off with their property. Charlotte had been avoiding the Common on her solitary walks and had taken to pacing Long Wharf instead. She would stand at the edge of the dock and look out at sea, and remember the poor admiral, and Louisa, and all their dear new friends. Every few weeks, Little Bobbie Acheson would stream past, crying out another lurid headline, and the tears for her sister would start all over again.

For a while, Charlotte had wondered if Nicholas Nelson might end up the knight in shining armor to rescue Henrietta from her plight. He did not care a whit about any local scandal—one benefit of his very interior bookshop-bound Philadelphia life. But the admiral's efforts appeared to have failed there as well. What would his famous sister have said about his meddling? Jane Austen the writer had always struck Charlotte as the consummate matchmaker: creating her very characters *for* each other. She could even change her mind as she wrote. Charlotte had a secret when it came to *Mansfield Park*, which she didn't dare utter to Harry: she had wished Henry Crawford for Fanny Price all along. She couldn't help but wonder if Austen had changed her own mind somewhere in the writing of it, so fascinating a couple as they almost became.

Almost, Charlotte sighed to herself.

Perhaps the admiral's matchmaking had also been a form of storytelling, but one with which he only regaled himself. With Fanny-Sophia constantly hovering, Charlotte suspected the letters across the Atlantic had made Sir Francis feel young again, a second childhood as he neared the end, a chance to share his stories. Despite everything that had happened, she and Harry were happy to have obliged him.

Then, just as August turned to September, a letter from Portsdown Lodge had arrived in Beacon Hill. George wrote to notify the Stevenson sisters of the death of his master and enclose back their original letters to him. He had also included a most cryptic message: *"My master wished for Mrs.*

Scott _personally_ to keep his _particular_ gift and share only as _she_ may later judge. My master claimed the greatest of confidence in Mrs. Scott to do what is best when the time is come."

Now they waited on this side of the ocean. Would Denham file suit again in England? Was a divorce decree and writ of seizure already making its way across the Atlantic on a mail steamer? Or would Henrietta have to file again in Massachusetts to end the marriage and argue cruelty, or move to Indiana for a year or as far away as Mexico instead—roping a third country into the legal quagmire?

Charlotte's head hurt: when it came to love and sex and marriage, the law boxed everyone in. And not just women—in Massachusetts, no one could get a divorce without grounds such as adultery, cruelty, or desertion. Graydon Saunders could spin it all he wanted, but according to their father, no court in the history of America had ever established cruelty in a marriage without physical injury—yet no state had rescinded the long-standing legal right of men to beat their wives. Principle versus practice indeed, as Connie would say. Poor Henrietta couldn't even argue abandonment in her marriage, because she had been the one to desert _him_.

Him was how both sisters referred to Denham when alone together. They couldn't pin him down for all their efforts. The posy of bachelor buttons, Biscuit the puppy, the window nook full of books—he had showered Henrietta with all the things he could barely afford, and which she especially would appreciate. Harry had tried to convey to Charlotte the instant understanding she had felt with Denham—how it had made the sudden and startling rupture even more painful. It was so hard to believe that none of it had been real.

Charlotte, for her part, did not speak to Harry about Nash. It was _her_ first secret between the sisters, and it was a big one. She no longer judged Henrietta for losing her head over Denham and not wanting anyone to know: debasing oneself for a man was nothing to share. Charlotte was mortified by what she herself had done for love. She had gotten carried away by so many emotions, but the ones that lingered were the most distressing. How does one grow up a daughter of Boston, a graduate of Miss Pride's Peacock Academy, a talented enough actress to win a role in the West End—and think only, and far too often, of the brass door handle to the hotel room digging into her back as Nash kissed her so hard, so hungrily, she thought her head would explode?

Charlotte took her walks in the Common at dusk now. She would not run into Nash on his morning constitutional. Louisa had said something once, following her own daily circuit of the *China* with Nash. She had claimed the esteemed justice didn't sit alone in the corner of the ship's dining room, or resist the role of Sydney Carton, merely out of respect for the sisters' plight. She thought him one of those men who so badly wanted to do the right thing that he didn't do anything at all. The moral center, like Mr. Knightley in *Emma*. Except Knightley had eventually given in to his feelings for Emma and vowed his love, even with no promise of return.

Only in books. Charlotte sighed again.

She headed home from the Common, passing the red-leather, brass-studded door to the Athenaeum along the way. She tried her best not to think about the broken heel of her boot months earlier, how she had resisted Nash helping her across Beacon Street, his staring up at their house as if he wished it was his own.

She stepped into the foyer and dropped her bonnet and gloves on the front table, tapped Socrates on the skull with little hope for luck. She could hear the fire half-heartedly crackling in the hearth—Samuel must have set it early tonight. Her father would already have left for the opera; Henrietta spent most evenings working in a local soup kitchen, where no one knew of her infamy, or had the luxury to care.

Coco didn't come springing out of the front parlor to welcome her mistress as she usually did. Charlotte frowned as she entered the room, feeling even lonelier. "Oh. Hello."

Nash stood up from where he had been sitting by the fire. There was no glass of whisky in his hand, no pipe. A copy of *Emma* lay closed on a nearby table; the judges had discussed the novel that very week. Her father had claimed it their best discussion yet, although by no means the weightiest. But what *fun*, he had told his daughters over another late breakfast of his. The justices had laughed often—at Emma, at Mr. Woodhouse and Mr. Elton, at themselves. What a gift books could be, William had then reminded both his sullen-faced children, especially during difficult times.

"You've missed Father. *Fidelio.*"

She hadn't seen Nash in weeks, not since Justice Norton had handed down his decision in *Scott v. Scott*, and he looked quite unlike himself tonight. Even nervous, she thought, as she passed him on her way to stir the fire. Like a little boy with his finger in the jam jar—like he had been caught out.

"I'll tell him you were here." She glumly poked about the hearth, trying to revive the embers. "He'll be sorry to have missed you."

"I don't think he'll be coming back. Not tonight, at least."

She whirled around to stare at him. "You know?"

He gulped. "Do you?"

"About Connie? Miss Davenish?"

Nash came closer, slowly, then stopped a few feet from her. "Oh, no—I mean yes—I did know."

"Father told you? Oh, that's rich—he hasn't said a *word* to Harry and me."

Nash looked both nervous and confused now. He reached out to take the poker from Charlotte's hands as if wanting to demobilize her, then gently rested it against the painted ceramic tiles that surrounded the fireplace. Nash had always commented on this hunting scene whenever he used to visit. He seemed to love the little touches in the house, how they marked an intent to stay forever—*for why else would someone decorate something as ordinary as a hearth?* he had once asked, before realizing too late the full import of his words. And the room had grown quiet then as they each thought of Alice Stevenson and her own dreams, and how their leaving the home was simply not a possibility because that would mean leaving her, too.

"You don't know, then, of what your father and I have agreed?" he haltingly began.

"About Connie?" Now she was the one confused.

His face finally relaxed. "Oh, I see." He took a deep breath. "No, about us."

"You told my father about *us*? About London?" And now she did want to grab the poker, and hold it between them, because he was moving toward her, and taking her in his arms . . .

"Nash, have you lost your head?"

"No, I've bought this house with it. All five floors."

"You're evicting me?" She was squirming in his arms now, and he was kissing her neck.

"No," he murmured again, his lips against her skin, "stand still for once, I'm proposing . . ."

Samuel and Mrs. Pearson never came near the drawing room that night. Charlotte had locked the doors (*our doors*, she beamed at Nash on the sofa, where he lay back, his cravat already on the floor and shirt unbuttoned) and they had made love there by the fire, and fallen asleep, then awakened to make love again as long as all etiquette was being lost to passion. Mercury—the planet named after the Roman god of communication—was no longer in retrograde, when confusion reigns and the universe is rife with misunderstanding. All the while, Coco could be heard from the hallway, scratching on the other side of the door. By now even she realized that life inside Eleven Beacon Street had changed forever.

FOURTEEN

A Heartbreaker, Charlatan, and Thief!

Beacon Hill, September 17, 1865

*R*unaway Bride Snared in Court!"

Little Bobbie Acheson skipped along Long Wharf, crying out the latest headline from London's *Pall Mall Gazette*. No sooner had the *Neptune* arrived in Boston Harbor than Little Bobbie clambered atop the distribution truck, waiting for his stack. The front page of the *Gazette* was gleefully reporting the latest decision from Sir Cresswell's court in favor of the petitioner husband in *Scott v. Scott*; a writ of seizure of the respondent wife's property, it was reported, would surely follow.

"*Runaway Bride Snared in Court!*"

Due to a seasonal shift in the Gulf Stream, the RMS *Neptune* had arrived from Liverpool with the news two days early—and the SS *China* from Portsmouth two days late. Due to the winds and a quicker-than-usual turnaround at the Custom House, a letter postmarked London arrived in Boston at the exact same time as Little Bobbie's shouts.

Mrs. Henrietta Stevenson Scott
Beacon Hill, Boston, U.S.A.

September 5, 1865

Dearest Henrietta,

   *Sara-Beth and Haz sit by me as I write from our rooms
at the Langham—we are all three in a state over Cresswell's
decision today. The old man runs a tight ship, and your lawyer
Pankhurst was most impressive, but Denham nonetheless has
prevailed in the matrimonial court.*

   *We are exceedingly sorry to write you of this, but beg you not
to panic just yet. There is still no divorce, which was the one thing
you wanted and, I understand, sought yourself—and the writ is
a piece of paper alone. Its power in the first instance is contained
to England and Wales, which does Denham no good. Pankhurst
assures us that the legal costs of enforcement abroad should dissuade
Denham from further action. Who is paying his legal fees as it is?
We suspect the Reynolds's editor but have no proof. The only people
to attend on him in court are his many brothers and sisters. A very
tight bunch. I should like them, I think, should they not be supporting
a heartbreaker, charlatan, <u>and</u> thief! They tried to approach us after
the proceeding with talk of their brother's confused spirits, but we
would have none of it—although they did seem most eager for news
of you. Pankhurst advises that, should Denham foolishly not relent,
the matter will go back up to our state supreme court, and that a
majority of five justices would be required, should your father and
Nash recuse themselves, which they surely would.*

   *Oh Harry, you should have seen Denham sitting there in Old
Hall, slumped and full of loathing—and to think, I once almost
thought him handsome enough for you!—although it's a mighty
good thing you didn't, as I wanted to box his ears enough for us
both. I never did trust a newspaperman. But you would have
thought Denham had actually <u>lost</u> something of his, for all he
despairs. Cresswell examined him at length on the object in dispute,
but Denham never cracked. Did you know a Royal Opera box costs
eight thousand quid? As someone not unfamiliar with poverty,
I can comprehend what set Denham off in the first place—it
would be like holding a firecracker in one's hand. But it is his*

dang perseverance that is most unsettling. Can he not see that he drives everyone further and further away, most of all you?

At least he dropped those ridiculous charges against poor Nick. Haз tells us that Nick keeps shop in his prolonged absence and has started writing for The Saturday Press. Mr. Twain has something before them, and my father writes that Mr. Whitman has something coming up soon as well, a new poem in tribute to our fallen president called "O Captain! My Captain!" How I love it already on title alone.

We know you, Harry, our own stalwart captain. You will bear this better than anyone. So, on to Charlotte. Haз is convinced Nash is in love with her—can you believe it? He says he witnessed much in London to make him suspect it so. Sara-Beth, never one to miss a bet, wages it was not your <u>father</u> whom Nash jumped on board for. Yet Charlotte in her letter of August 1st, which only reached Sara-Beth and myself two weeks past, writes not a word of him. The silence, in fact, is most deafening, as I had distinctly asked your sister for news of him in my own letter last. I am afraid there may have been a breach of some kind between them. Tell her Louisa says she must be bold in life.

If only Louisa would follow her own advice!

And now, to write of much cheerier news, we are on our way to Scotland to . . . can you guess . . . conjoin Miss Gleason and Mr. Nelson in wedded bliss! No sooner did Haз arrive in Baden-Baden than he proposed! What is it about travel that makes everyone rush so headlong into love? Sara-Beth and I had been enjoying ourselves most daringly before he found us, flirting shamelessly with every itinerant musician or Neapolitan prince that came our way, and Haз was positively overcome by jealousy. Meanwhile, I have never <u>seen</u> Sara-Beth so superstitious. She has stopped gambling altogether—easy enough to do, for the minute she said yes to Haз, she started to lose! She very charmingly claims she has used up all her luck in winning him after all. She now banks everything on life with Haз, and has designs on his entering political life—all that kissing of babies, I must admit, would suit him well. Although I do consider it optimism of the highest kind, to marry abroad, just as two different countries' courts fail to rule on the validity of marriage at sea, loss of citizenship, renvoi, and a host of other issues too complex for the likes of me.

Finally, and most importantly, we were all so saddened to read of the admiral's passing on August 10th at his home in Portsdown. I so wish I had met him—Sara-Beth is full of talk of his fine qualities and mischievous manner, which she attributes less to a penchant for troublemaking than a sad and lonely heart. She calls him the great romantic, but, my dear friend, I save that particular accolade for you. I do not think someone with such a large heart as my dearest Harry could be destined for anything but a life full of love.

Your most admiring and forever friend,

Lu

FIFTEEN

The Trial

IN THE MATTER OF *SCOTT* v. *SCOTT*
The Massachusetts Supreme Judicial Court
October 23, 1865

T he courtroom at State Street was packed with spectators and news-papermen from both sides of the ocean. The matter of *Scott v. Scott* had been expedited at the request of local counsel for the petitioner, Mr. Denham Scott, who had arrived only two days earlier from England to attend—writ of seizure in hand—and would need to sail home before the winter season stranded him on American shores. Although the enforcement of a writ abroad did not require the physical presence of the petitioner, his London counsel had advised that he would need every argument of law and influence of emotion on his side. "The former colonies are rather wild and unpredictable, Mr. Scott," the barrister had almost spat, "and you have an increasingly gutted demeanor that can only act in your favor."

Given the historic issue at law, the chief justice had decided that the case merited the attention of the entire bench. The entire bench, that is, less *two*: Justice William Stevenson and Justice Thomas Nash would both be absent from the proceeding. They had again immediately recused themselves due to their personal relationship with the respondent, Mrs. Henrietta Scott. They were expected to appear in the gallery of the courtroom instead, next to their new wives and behind the respondent and her counsel, the imposing and smooth-drawled Southerner, Graydon Saunders.

Local counsel for the foreign petitioner had argued in a preliminary motion against the right of the state supreme court to even hold the trial ("Not *again*," Justice Roderick Norton had loudly grumbled) due to the respondent's father and new brother-in-law being among its members. However, the chief justice had relied on the legal principle of necessity in allowing the matter to go ahead: "Where else could it be held and still be subject to the legislative and civil laws of this great state? In a fair and just society, if the choice is trial or no trial, there is only ever *one* answer to that."

Meanwhile, the question at law remained: was Henrietta Stevenson Scott, daughter of Boston, through the mere act of a whimsical marriage at sea, destined to be treated as a citizen of England only, and was the secret, private gift of Admiral Sir Francis Austen to Mrs. Scott—a gift somehow connected to literary great Jane Austen—to be seized and returned to England, where it might end up publicly and brazenly consumed as so much penny press?

While legal pundits and news reporters debated the merits of the case, Little Bobbie Acheson sat on the curb farther up State Street, impatiently waiting outside the offices of the *Evening Traveller*. Its late-afternoon edition would feature the trial, and Little Bobbie was determined to be first in line to grab his stack. At ten years of age, he didn't understand any of what he sold, but that summer had taught him one thing: the salacious and seemingly unquenchable appetite of all of Boston when it came to the matter of love. For that was clearly, at least to Little Bobbie if to no one else, what was really at stake in *Scott v. Scott*: a wife had run away, and the husband had come a-calling.

B reakfast at Eleven Beacon Street on the morning of the trial was an intimate yet tense affair. William joined the Nashes and Henrietta at his former home with his bride of one week on his arm, having rushed back from honeymooning in Niagara. Nash and Charlotte had already enjoyed two weeks in the small Adirondacks cabin, having raced to the altar first. They had been most eager to take advantage of the temporary reprieve in poor Henrietta's ongoing trials *and* to fall back into bed together, this time under approval of the law.

William and Constance were happy to oblige the young couple's desire for a quick marriage, given the perceived greater sexual freedom for people of a certain age. All of this made the distinction between practice and principle seem rather suspect. Perhaps "people" were simply less interested in the old and grey, Constance had wondered aloud to her future stepdaughters on the night before her own wedding, beaming with as much excitement as a bride half her age.

Henrietta stayed at Eleven Beacon Street for now, but even the attic was not far enough away from the newly married couple below. Charlotte and Nash were something beyond happy—a state that Henrietta recognized from her own home in Hanbury Street of less than a day. She was ecstatic for Charlotte, who had married a man so besotted with her that he only wanted her happiness. They would raise their own family in the house of her childhood—they would stay close to her father—they would let her sister live with them forever.

Nash was also adamant that Charlotte return to the stage. Boston theaters were enjoying a postwar explosion, and auditions with several acting troupes had been lined up. A telegram had recently arrived on the *Neptune* from Fawcett Robinson as well, urging Charlotte to change her mind and join the New Adelphi players; that season's leading ingenue was not working out. But Charlotte was content to build a life on the Boston stage. She wanted Nash's happiness as much as he wanted hers, so there was no question of her going away.

This was where Henrietta envied Charlotte and Nash the most. They were both fortunate to have fallen in love with someone who needed little beyond the other's happiness to be happy themselves. A form of romantic renvoi, that rarest of antelopes. Good graces and self-sacrificing attentions constantly passed back and forth between the newlyweds in an endless rally of love. Only on occasion—for Charlotte would not give up her high spirits for anyone—could the most adorable contretemps be overheard between them, always resolved with a kiss by the fireplace, Coco jealously nipping at their heels.

The trial started in an hour, and Charlotte was the only one at breakfast with any appetite. She greedily consumed all the popovers, her favorite, which Mrs. Pearson had made expressly for her. Both the cook and Samuel had asked to stay on following William's sale of the house to Justice Nash. This exchange of living quarters between the two men had been conducted with all the logic and equity of a judicial decision. William had even made a tidy profit from the sale, which Nash had insisted be executed at significantly more than market value. William had then divided the funds equally between his daughters to keep as their own, holding Henrietta's share in trust until Denham's claims on her property were judicially resolved.

As the family exchanged news on anything but the trial, Henrietta returned to the letter in her lap. The new Mrs. Nelson wrote from Rome, full of news of her September wedding to Haz in Scotland with Louisa as witness. The three of them planned to stay on the Continent for the winter, then sail back in the spring. By now Louisa had purposefully lost her elderly charge, who had never really needed her services, and continued to live off of Sara-Beth's winnings from the smoking lounge on ship.

Sara-Beth wrote to Henrietta of how Louisa was "in the vortex," as she called it, writing for hours in their pensione before breakfast, preoccupied with the notion of family the farther away she traveled from hers: How the strength of the family comes from caring about others as much as oneself. How our differences buff each other to a diamond-like shine—by forcing us to see ourselves in relation to others, we gain greater knowledge of the self. But although Lu might miss her own sisters terribly, Sara-Beth expressed no such burning desire to return home to hers. This was a sure sign of connubial bliss and one that Henrietta herself knew well, at which point she put down the letter only to notice it stained by her own tears.

SIXTEEN

E Pluribus Unum

IN THE MATTER OF *SCOTT* v. *SCOTT*
The Massachusetts Supreme Judicial Court
October 23, 1865

Henrietta refused to look across the courtroom at Denham. Just the idea of his coming all this way to increase his chances of legal victory, and not to resolve things with *her* (which she didn't even want, she told herself), stirred up far too much emotion. It was most disheartening for Henrietta, usually the most calm and pragmatic member of her family, that her feelings toward Denham only grew stronger and more confused with time. She was beginning to worry that the emotions would never end, which for some people would indicate a most persistent form of affection. But Henrietta was too angry, and too betrayed, to see it that way, and chalked it up to the stress and strain of protracted litigation instead.

Two parties to a marriage, unable to agree on an old man's gift, resorting to five old men on a bench for resolution, might be seen as reaching a new low in love. Henrietta only knew that she was justified in her cause. She had the full support of her family and friends, as well as the presence in court that day of Boston's leading bluestockings, Girl Orator Anna Dickinson, who was back lecturing again, and William Lloyd Garrison of the weekly newspaper *The Liberator,* a publication newly dedicated to advancing the cause of women's rights now that abolition had begun to take effect.

Henrietta marveled at everything that had happened in the six months since she and Charlotte had raced to the Music Hall to see the Girl Orator speak. Denham had watched Henrietta from across the hall, and she had to steel herself against the memory. That had been at the beginning, when she hadn't wanted anyone—not even Charlie—to know. And now the entire world knew of their coupling! She could not have been less discreet if she had tried.

Graydon Saunders had advised Henrietta to let him do all the talking in court. As her counsel, he warned that men were not used to a woman's voice dominating such a hallowed space and were inclined to consider it strident. As a man, however, Graydon was open-minded on matters of sex to an almost libertine degree. He believed women merely lacked the opportunity to fashion their public voice through practice, as the fine instrument it was. Henrietta did not protest his lawyerly advice but kept her hand to herself, ready to turn it face up at the exact right moment.

Denham's American counsel was first to address the bench.

"In the great history of relations between our two nations, there is a natural respect and comity toward the laws of the other. Our laws differ because our countries are different. On the matter of property law, England has centuries of land and estate inheritance behind it, and an overriding need to protect future generations against any reckless or temporal dispersal. Full deference should be given to decisions on English law by its courts, as it should for those of our own fine judiciary."

Denham's lawyer stopped for effect, nodding obsequiously at each of the five men sitting on the elevated podium before him: associate justices Philip Mackenzie and Ezekiel Peabody to the right of Chief Justice Adam Fulbright, and associate justices Conor Langstaff and Roderick Norton to his left.

"Sir Cresswell, the Judge Ordinary of the Court for Divorce and Matrimonial Causes of England, has recently ruled judiciously and most wisely on the issue of law before us today—one that has already come before the Honorable Associate Justice Norton of this very court and was dismissed due to the *very* deference my client again seeks. A deference to British law in relation to the gifting of property by a resident of Britain, to a woman who married on a British-owned ship, before a British captain, to a British man, becoming in the process a citizen of Britain—property which itself originated in Britain, and was bestowed to the respondent during her habitation, albeit of short duration, with the British petitioner *on British soil*."

Graydon Saunders slightly flinched with every repetition of the word *British* in this speech. Still, Henrietta was glad to have such a brilliant litigator on her side for the much larger battle ahead. Thousands had fought and died to abolish slavery, President Lincoln's leadership and guidance had been lost, and there was still a long road ahead to achieve equality for everyone. Henrietta finally had an opportunity to do something about that herself: not just attend lectures and lyceums, not just listen and agree and nod her head at the words of others. She glanced back to see her father and Constance raise their interlocked hands and motion victory to her with comforting smiles.

Denham's counsel had made a strong opening statement, for which he was known, and which he then undid by going on too long—for which he was also unfortunately known. The patience of Justice Roderick Norton, who had already devoted so much of the court's time and attention to this very matter, appeared particularly strained. Graydon Saunders was determined to keep his own comments as brief as possible as he stood up next to address the court.

"Your Honors, the respondent is not British by marriage or otherwise. Congress has not yet addressed the issue of citizenship upon marriage to a foreigner, and the case law on this point is so varied as to be rendered useless. Furthermore, under English common law, foreign-born individuals cannot become citizens *there* through any process or ceremony—nor can those born in England ever be stripped of their citizenship. Until such time as either country might change those laws, my client was, is, and shall always be, a most esteemed daughter of Boston."

"Your Honors," interjected Denham's counsel, "British Parliament is already readying a bill as we speak, one that will strip women who marry foreign men of their citizenship, showing a willingness to change their own laws—"

"That's neither here nor there," Saunders broke in. "Last time I checked, we were in America."

"You raised the matter, counsellor."

"Gentlemen," the chief justice called down from the podium where he and the four associate justices sat, stone-faced.

The hearing proceeded in this manner for nearly two hours until a break was called for luncheon. A clerk immediately ran up to deliver a message to Saunders, who read it quickly before crumpling it in his hand. "Mrs. Scott," he whispered, "opposing counsel wants to meet with me. But if you've any quibble . . ."

Henrietta shook her head, and Charlotte rushed up to join her as Saunders left.

"Denham just scurried out, too. Harry, what are you thinking?" Charlotte asked—Charlotte, who looked so pink and flushed with love. *That is what love should do to you,* Henrietta was thinking as she helplessly shrugged her response. *You shouldn't feel sick with it, or go to court to enforce it—or run away.*

S aunders returned to the courtroom after a lengthy absence, followed by opposing counsel. Henrietta was surprised to see Denham enter a few seconds later. She had resolved not to look over at him, but it was too late. Seeing into his eyes—seeing up close all the confusion and anger and hurt—she felt a weird, sudden pang of worry for him, the aggressor in all this. He looked so worn down by it all—was he eating enough? Sleeping? Henrietta shook her head as if to stop her own mind, then turned to her counsel. "Mr. Saunders, what is your opinion so far?"

Graydon finished writing in the notebook he carried everywhere, just like Denham; for all the lawyer's ease of manner and chaotic desk, he was deceptively diligent. "I think that boy's mighty confused over *you.*" He closed the notebook and laughed. "Now that there's none of my business—my business is as your lawyer. I tell ya, those judges are hell-bent on the notion of comity. Their respect for another judge, no matter his kin or county, is our greatest obstacle."

"Gray," Connie whispered from her seat as he leaned back familiarly to hear her, "my fellow radicals believe a decision in our favor could affect lasting legislative change both here and in England."

Saunders nodded. "We've a real opportunity here today, we do indeed. I aim to persuade the court that the very essence of life, liberty, and freedom for *all* is at stake. The more we can ingrain women in the constitution, the more rights we can get 'em."

Henrietta was paying close attention to what Connie and Saunders were saying. Her father and Nash could not offer her any such guidance or warning, out of respect for the proceedings. Henrietta recalled the words of the Girl Orator—not just the words, but the rhythm and cadence of what she had said those many months ago at the Music Hall, the day it all began:

> *The widows who see the homes they have helped to earn, the lands they have helped to buy, the very house with which they have been served their household work—swept away from them by an unjust decision of a dying husband, and a wicked law . . .*
>   *Are these duly represented and have they all the rights they want already?*

Henrietta finally glanced across the courtroom at Denham, who had just declined to take the stand on the advice of his counsel. He looked unfit to take action of any kind—quite unlike the young, strapping, confident man with whom she had fallen in love. It would be so easy, as a young woman, to decline to testify as well—and completely unexpected if she were to stand up and speak for herself. At this point, Charlotte certainly would do so— she would fight with all her passion of spirit and stubborn optimism. Today she claimed to be the happiest woman in the world as a result.

Henrietta took a breath and stood up. She might be about to speak in court for herself, but she would strike the blow for all women.

"If it please the court, I should like to say something."

The entire room fell silent as the black-robed men on the podium stared back at her in shock. Always happy to swim against the tide, Saunders said nothing, giving her a wink and an encouraging nod instead.

"I was not aware, Your Honors, that in choosing to marry the petitioner"— for she refused to say his name even in such a forum as this—"my own citizenship in the land of my birth could be threatened. In retrospect, and in light of the petitioner's ensuing behavior, I assure you that I would have given my citizenship in this great country far greater precedence over that decision to wed."

At this very pointed barb, Henrietta heard laughter from the crowded courtroom, as well as angry muttering among men who could only sit and listen to her for once. It felt amazing to have the attention of the room, just like that time she had spoken up in Nash's Harvard lecture on Austen and rhetoric.

"As the court, however, is aware, my ability to obtain a divorce from the petitioner rests on the impossibly high bar of proving physical injury or harm. To lose both my citizenship and my freedom seems an equally high price to pay for the mistake of a moment."

Henrietta noticed Justice Norton dismissively avert his head. It was probably a good thing he had not given himself jurisdiction in her own suit for divorce. She gave silent thanks for his punting the entire matter back to England, for all the trouble it had since caused.

"I value marriage as an institution most highly, Your Honors. Highly enough to be willing to make over my entire life to satisfy its exchange of vows—highly enough that I would never seek to void my marriage by claiming that it had never happened. How could I attempt to negate the very genuine and real act of a moment? We cannot change the past—for that very reason, we need a law that can bend to the future. The fine men of Massachusetts who sit in public office did that very thing, in voting on the Married Women's Property Act these ten years past. They voted for change—voted for increased liberty for married women, at least when it comes to property. The kind of liberty that, in making each of us better off, is to the betterment of all.

"We have just endured one war, to realize such freedom for our country's men and women of color. Black men shall have the vote, God willing—but such participation in the lawmaking of our country should be everyone's due. Only then will we have a country that can hold us all within it, and thereby keep us truly united.

"What, you may ask, does this have to do with the issue before the court? What does a tenderhearted gesture by a dying man mean in the grand scheme of things? I can only say, far more than we today can comprehend. That is the challenge for the law—to comprehend all that might happen, now and tomorrow. Our lack of comprehension or foresight today should never be used as a weapon against positive change. Our development, individually and societally, *demands* change. I beseech the justices of this supreme judicial court to consider the plight of the women in this state, at this time in history, and to uphold and affirm the evolution of their rights, and mine, such as our lawmakers have seen fit to issue and without undue regard to the lesser rights of another country. Countries stretch and bend their own laws for their own reasons—that strikes me as the very reason why this court should not neglect the laws of its sovereignty in preference to those of another.

"Finally, I am most grateful for the significant time and attention that has been paid by the courts to this matter, and to such an unprecedented and protracted extent. I earnestly wish to be the best citizen of this state and country that I can, to move forward in a positive direction and not be imprisoned by the past, and to protect the gifts my friends and loved ones have bestowed on me *not* as a wife, *not* as merely a part of my husband, but as *myself*. The Henrietta that they know and care for—the woman who inspired such generosity and trust from them in turn.

"To betray that trust by depriving me of such gifts does not respect the wishes of the great man who bequeathed them to me. To betray that trust also betrays him. It does not lend itself to the positive development of anyone, man or woman. As John Stuart Mill wrote, this development is critical to liberty for all, for those who give, and for those who receive. Thank you."

Such a sudden uproar burst forth from the crowd at these last two words that Henrietta barely heard them. There was much shouting and protestation from some quarters, but, as is often the way with any critical juncture, the voices for change were loudest of all. Chief Justice Fulbright announced the retirement of the court to consider the issues of law that had been raised, then stepped down from the podium alongside his associate justices Mackenzie, Peabody, Langstaff, and Norton. All five men departed the courtroom, one after the other, heads bowed as if to indicate the majesty and significance of the task now before them.

"My dear, you were marvelous." Connie beamed at Henrietta as she sat down, overcome, while Charlotte rushed forward to hug her.

"Peabody and Norton are our blockers," Saunders whispered to Henrietta, his mind always strategizing. She was still being hugged by Charlie as he spoke, still felt flushed from the effect of her words on so many.

"Mackenzie's a slippery fella when it comes to any deciding vote," Saunders continued. "He can lean so literally on the law as to slide through to the opposite end of its intent altogether. Sometimes that can work in one's favor—sometimes not." He looked over and shrugged at her father and Connie, then turned back. "Mrs. Scott, I must say, you would make a fine lawyer—if only our fine state, or any other, would relent and allow for women at its bar. England, too, for that matter, should you end up living there. . . ."

But Henrietta did not hear his last two words, either. She was tired—tired of not being allowed to try for any kind of profession, tired of being forced to stay in a moribund marriage. A most painful distinction between principle and practice indeed, yet one so heartily embraced by the men in power. Meanwhile, life was going on without her, while she sat mired in the business of the courts, the very kind of forum whose participation was denied her. When would her own life finally, and fully, be hers?

SEVENTEEN

All Remedy Exhausted

THE DECISION OF THE
SUPREME JUDICIAL COURT OF MASSACHUSETTS
IN THE MATTER OF SCOTT V. SCOTT

OCTOBER 25, 1865

My fellow justices and I have contemplated at length the arguments put forward by both counsel for the petitioner and the respondent, as well as those of the respondent herself, in seeking to resolve what can only be termed a most unfortunate public affair stemming from a most private and intimate union.

Irrespective of the cogency and power of such arguments, the court adheres to the principle of *comity* wherever possible. Deference to the decision of our counterparts who preside over their own country's laws is crucial to the concept of nationalism. The court must not act in such a way as to threaten the power of another nation to decide the destiny of its own citizens. We hold to this truth most reverently.

Only one other truth might ever prevail in its stead: the destiny of our own citizens, and of our society as a whole. Should a foreign decision not only *not* reflect, but also threaten to revert, the meaningful progress we have made as a society, then this court shall consider the impact on the greater good of our society in deciding whether or not to enforce a foreign judgment or decree of any kind.

We understand from counsel that the petitioner has of late reconsidered his application before the court. But in the interest of establishing precedent, we have unanimously agreed to proceed with rendering judgment and our reasoning therefor.

We hold, as a majority of the Supreme Judicial Court of the Commonwealth of Massachusetts, that the progress we have made as a society in recognizing the right of all women, spinster or bride, mother or daughter, to retain any and all property, real or personal, that they may receive prior to and during any marriage, such right being pursuant both to the Married Women's Property Act of 1855 and, most importantly, to the principle of liberty, freedom, and justice for all as enshrined in the constitution of these United States, prevails over a contrary decision by a foreign court. Accordingly, we hereby decline to issue an order for the enforcement in the Commonwealth of Massachusetts of the writ of seizure obtained by the petitioner in the matrimonial court of England and Wales, and consider this matter judicially resolved, decided, and fully and permanently exhausted of any and all remedy under law, now and forever.

Signed by the following Justices of the Supreme Judicial Court of Massachusetts:

Adam Fulbright, Chief Justice
Conor Langstaff, Associate Justice
Philip Mackenzie, Associate Justice

Writing for the Dissent:

Roderick Norton, Associate Justice
With Ezekiel Peabody, Associate Justice, joining

The concept of *comity* between nations in respect of the enforcement of laws, should parties elect to enter into contracts outside the borders of their own country, shall prevail over all other concerns, political, social, or economic. This is a long-standing principle of both international private law and our own common law, which must take precedence over the legislative winds that too often blow hither and thither, bestowing rights here, limiting rights there. We therefore dissent from the decision of the majority and would order the recognition by our great state of the writ of seizure issued by the English court in favor of the petitioner.

EPILOGUE

✻

Chawton Revisited

Chawton, July 1880

O CAPTAIN! my Captain! our fearful trip is done,
The ship has weathered every rack, the prize we sought is won,
The port is near, the bells I hear, the people all exulting,
While follow eyes the steady keel, the vessel grim and daring;
*   But O heart! heart! heart!*
*   O the bleeding drops of red,*
*   Where on the deck my Captain lies,*
*   Fallen cold and dead.*

*   —Walt Whitman*

Charlotte and Nash ascended the incline to the walled garden, where the playful shouts of children could be heard coming from inside. Husband and wife held hands tightly as they walked—it was an emotional return to Chawton for them both.

Fifteen years had passed since their last visit to the village, and Charlotte Stevenson was now one of America's premier actresses. All the major roles had been performed in theaters across that country: the Duchess of Malfi, Marguerite from *Faust*, Beatrice, Ophelia, Lady Macbeth. Charlotte was soon to make a much-heralded return of sorts to the London stage—the long-ago audition before Richard Fawcett Robinson would finally reach its fruition in her West End debut at the Adelphi as Lucie Manette in *A Tale of Two Cities*. Few other roles could have enticed her more.

It was July, the crowning time of summer in England. The midpoint of the year and a month of endless days when much could happen—when much *did* happen, fifteen years ago. It was strange to think of what the day at hand owed to the happenings of that earlier July, when Charlotte had enjoyed her first taste of womanly power over Nash and Henrietta had begun and ended a marriage in a matter of days, leaving behind a young man in Hanbury Street with much growing up to do and a heart so broken, he had resorted to the law to restore it.

Reaching the top of the incline and the gates to the walled garden, Charlotte put her hand over her husband's arm in a motion to stop.

"You must be tired, my love."

"No, I only mean to look out." She breathed in the fragrance of nearby roses. "Such storybook beauty here."

"As only an author could dream up." He nodded down the lawn toward the Great House, which after three centuries was showing its Elizabethan age. "Denham was wise to sell his interest in the *Reynolds's* when he did, and at such profit. One never knows what the future holds—look at how much even a house can change."

"Not Eleven Beacon Street, though—thank you for that." She squeezed his arm, then let go as he went to open the garden gates. A handful of children ran about on the other side, descending in age from thirteen to five and calling out each other's nicknames—Lu, Billy, Nicky, Ally, Gray—until Charlotte heard her own.

"Charlie!" Henrietta cried as she ran down the pebbled path toward her, the long narrow skirt to her white cotton day dress scooped up in her hands. They collapsed in each other's arms, sobbing, and Charlotte felt the shocking frailty to Henrietta's bones, a literal wearing down from grief. She couldn't help but remember the last time that Harry had run into her arms like this, at the end of a very long London hotel corridor, although from a very different kind of loss.

Nash held back from the reunion until Henrietta lifted her head to motion him forward. "Brother, I am so glad you could come."

"A much longer visit this time," Charlotte promised as Nash and her sister hugged. "The new chief justice can accompany me until September—not that I ever needed a chaperone."

The three adults smiled in allusion to that long-ago voyage, before descending back into melancholy as the children, all of them possessing the high cheekbones and almond-shaped eyes of their parents, continued to run about.

"They've grown so in the past two years," marveled Charlotte. "Look at Louisa, corralling them all."

"She would do anything for her younger brothers and sister. Just like her father." Henrietta's eyes filled with tears and Charlotte pulled her close.

"Harry, I'm afraid now Louisa's not well."

"You saw her?"

"Just before we left. She doesn't always take visitors, being the most famous person in the world." Charlotte sighed at the memory. "Her spirit was as indomitable as ever, though I worry it's a brave act."

Nash nodded. "Lu was never one to put anyone out." He took his wife's other arm to gently pull her back as the littlest of the children ran between them.

"Gray, *stop.*" Henrietta scooped up her five-year-old son, and they pressed their foreheads together in a familiar manner. "Mummy wants you to meet someone. Graydon, this is your Aunt Charlotte's husband, Chief Justice Thomas Nash. He heads up an entire court in America. He makes the law."

"Well, we interpret the law . . ." the youngest chief justice in the history of Massachusetts was quick to correct.

"Oh, Nash," teased Charlotte, exchanging a knowing look with her sister. After all, they had both witnessed the Supreme Judicial Court of Massachusetts, in a complete legislative and judicial vacuum, rule that Henrietta had a right to retain both British property *and* her American citizenship. The 1865 decision in *Scott v. Scott* had since become a staple of legal education across the States, where a handful of law schools had even recently begun to admit women.

Henrietta capably lowered her youngest to the ground, and Charlotte bent to give Graydon an affectionate hug hello. She would always feel for his plight as the baby in the family who would end up with no memory of a parent. Not being born a boy had led her own mother to persist in childbearing against everyone's advice and wishes; the putrid fever that Graydon had recovered from last winter had killed Denham, who had nursed his wife and family for weeks, instead.

"Billy is interested in the law," Henrietta said as the older four children now straggled over. "His namesake has written from Egypt—he and Justice Mackenzie leave for Constantinople next, but promise to be back with us in the spring."

"I am so glad Father travels again. He was not enjoying retirement as a widower."

"Neither was Mac," added Nash. "Their friendship is a real blessing, for all they sometimes disagreed on the law."

"Thank God I have the children to occupy me." Henrietta pulled all five close to her, kissing the tops of the girls' heads, rustling the cowlicked locks on the boys'.

"And there is your suffrage work with Dr. Pankhurst and his new wife, Emmeline," Nash pointed out. "Connie would be so proud of you both. What is it Richard often says—life is nothing without enthusiasms?"

"I remember the admiral telling me on this very spot how he returned to sea on the *Vindictive* after Lady Austen's death." Henrietta's drawn face softened, just for a second. "His taking as many of his own children as he could fit on board."

"And how lovingly he, too, spoke of both his wives." Charlotte bit her lip. "So much good fortune perhaps brings more than one's fair share of pain."

Nash patted his wife's arm in consolation at these words. Despite all the roles and efforts and tears, there were no children running about their own home. Charlotte remembered too well the other fortune told her in the heart of Cremorne Gardens—another reason why she rubbed Henrietta's silver sixpence in her hands before leaving the wings of any stage to perform.

A silence fell on the small group, and little six-year-old Ally—named Alice after a beloved maternal grandmother—pulled on her mother's sleeve to whisper something in her ear.

"Always hungry—like someone else I know." Henrietta smiled at Charlotte before tapping Ally's nose. "Mrs. Berwick has been most accommodating. We agreed on four o'clock for a picnic tea."

Henrietta led everyone out of the red-brick walled garden where so many family and friends, lovers and strangers, had gathered over the century. A very different group of visitors from fifteen years ago now descended the sloping lawn, the littlest members running ahead and occasionally tumbling down. The children of Sir Francis had also played here once, and Henrietta mentioned what the housekeeper, Mrs. Berwick, had earlier shared: the tobogganing on this very hill by generations of Knights and Austens, the summer fêtes thrown for the village, the Christmas Eve gatherings held here after church.

Mrs. Berwick stood waiting for them near the eastern wall of Chawton Great House, where yew hedges shaped like salt-and-pepper cellars towered before the ivy-covered red brick. A handful of wool blankets had been laid out nearby on the freshly mown lawn, and the children were already digging into the wicker picnic baskets, but Mrs. Berwick didn't mind. "We haven't as many little ones here as of old. A house needs a family, I think, to keep it young."

They dined on cold chicken and salad from the estate's kitchen garden, followed by Martha Lloyd's famous pound cake. Then the children ran off in the direction of the man-made Wilderness, carrying sugar buns brought warm from the kitchen in their dirt-stained hands. Eventually they disappeared inside the red-painted shepherd's hut that stood among the oak, beech, elm, and many other trees that had been planted a century ago.

The three adults lay back on the blankets, grateful for the sudden calm, and looked up at the bright blue sky in quiet contemplation and mourning. They had visited together so many times over the years that there was never any awkward silence between them, nor any need for words.

Despite the ocean that separated the sisters—just as the fortune-teller in Cremorne Gardens had foretold—hardly a summer went by without one of them undertaking the ten-day crossing. The arrival of the telegraph in 1866 further fostered their closeness, conveying frequent good tidings of yet another child for the Scotts and Charlotte's latest triumph onstage, as well as the tragic news of Constance Stevenson's death from cancer only five years after she and William were wed.

Both sisters had often wondered at how differently life might have turned out if the telegraph had been invented sooner—if Justice Thomas Nash had not managed to jump on ship in time and Denham Scott had not failed to—if Graydon Saunders hadn't breached his ethical duty to his client in the pursuit of love. For it was Saunders who had told Henrietta that Denham Scott was at Long Wharf and aiming to leave on the last steamer of the season.

Denham had written daily to Henrietta since the court's verdict—letters that she showed only to Charlotte—while repeatedly delaying his departure. He quoted John Stuart Mill, owning up to his need to *develop* as a husband and to not just financially provide. He praised Henrietta's composure and effectiveness in court, claiming no such talent for himself and desperately wanting back his wife with so many talents of her own: "I once wrote you, in my arrogance, that I am only better for your presence and attendance on me, whilst you only deserve the very best. I see now that in those pretty words, there was an ugly ignorance regarding your own development." He even begged Henrietta for the honor of paying his respects to her father and stepmother. This brave willingness to face a family so hardened against him threatened to soften Henrietta's heart—and succeeded in melting Charlotte's. She inched closer and closer to the legal and marital tinderbox, treading carefully with her own words, until one night by the painted parlor fireplace she finally blurted out, *"Oh Harry, are you really so sure?"*

But it was the threat of Denham's permanent removal to England, news of which arrived courtesy of Henrietta's lawyer, that had cleared the horizon and granted clarity at last. Henrietta found herself racing in a phaeton next to Charlotte as they had once done at the break of dawn, Samuel again at the reins. The sisters arrived to discover Denham exiting the Custom House, unable to procure a ticket home ahead of winter and stranded on their shores after all. Graydon Saunders would later claim his own share of credit for the marital reunion, telling anyone who would listen that he had once let a remarkable woman board a ship home without him and knew too well the hindrance to romance that can come from distance. "And besides," Saunders loved to opine, "the courtroom's no place for courtin'."

As for his commitment to Henrietta's development, Denham had ended up as good as his words, having learned from his wife their true power and import for all his practice of journalism. His was a profession of economy—Graydon and Nash's of exactness. It was Henrietta, with no profession to call her own, who had shown how words can sting as much as actions, false accusations can upset the world, and the genuine expression of remorse and understanding can—with a loving and superior partner—breach almost any divide. In the many years since their newsworthy rupture, Denham had proved to be a most doting father, the very brother that Charlotte had always wished for, and the attentive and supportive husband that her sister today so greatly mourned.

M ummy, may I look?"

Henrietta opened her eyes; she hadn't meant to fall asleep. She sat up with a start and gazed about. Charlotte and Nash lay closely together on one blanket, quietly talking and pointing up at the rain clouds that loomed on the horizon, while Nicholas stood before his mother, tiny hands outstretched. One end of the walnut box could be seen poking out from her bag. "Would you like a look, Nicky? Come, sweetheart, sit with me."

He was her most solitary child, much like his own namesake Nicholas Nelson—the one to whom a heartbroken Henrietta had entrusted so much. Nick remained a bachelor, filling his days by writing critical reviews for *The Atlantic Monthly* and other periodicals while continuing to run the shop. Recently he had asked Graydon Saunders to help him establish a trust to which he would bequeath the entire contents of Nelson Brothers and Co. upon his death, with the hearty permission of his politician brother. Nicholas planned to establish a museum in Philadelphia to house the various literary collections that he had amassed and kept safe from customers' prying eyes in the private rooms above the shop: collected first editions of Jane Austen and Charles Dickens, Mary Shelley's astonishing *Frankenstein*, the personally inscribed copies of Louisa May Alcott's books. Lu always sent these to Nicholas from the first printing, as he was her most fervent devotee. Senator Haslett Nelson also often sought refuge above the shop, the happy but fatigued husband and father of three daughters who each took after their mother to various and alarming degrees.

"Here, see?" Henrietta said to her middle son, removing the telescope from its carved box. She had never shown it to the children before. For all the admiral's delight in his handcrafted toys, the telescope represented a most painful chapter in Henrietta's life.

"You pull apart, then twist! Perfect for spying pirates up ahead." Nicky fumbled with the telescope, which gave its tell-tale click. The unsent letter was back inside, returned to Henrietta by special messenger from Philadelphia immediately following the groundbreaking decision in *Scott v. Scott*. The admiral's deathbed instructions for its safekeeping had been both generous and vague: *My master claimed the greatest of confidence in Mrs. Scott to do what is best when the time is come.* Henrietta was still unsure. She now knew that she always would be. But that was never a reason not to act.

Henrietta guided Nicky into her lap and helped him bring into focus the new flint-walled church at the bottom of the sloping lawn—rebuilt in 1871 after its medieval predecessor was destroyed by fire—then the graveyard, then past the old stone wall to the farm fields and beyond. Meeting Charlotte at the Great House had been no coincidence—nor had waiting until the Knight family's annual July stay by the sea to invite themselves here.

"A lovely old man made this, the sea captain—Mummy told you? He gave it to me before he went to heaven, just like Daddy." She kissed his head. "And one day, *I* will give it to you." Nicky looked back up at her so excitedly that for a second she forgot the pain—the early loss of her mother and the recent one of Connie, the strangely lasting trauma of the first separation from Denham and this most permanent and much more painful one. Then it all came flooding back. The past always would—she knew that now, too. But finally she felt ready to cast the most contentious part of it to the winds of chance—the ultimate mark of both freedom and forgiveness.

Mrs. Berwick opened the large Elizabethan oak door; a new springer spaniel nipped about her feet. The Stevenson sisters stood together on the front stone step, a slender walnut box in Charlotte's hands.

"You've been so kind," Henrietta was first to speak, "and we don't mean to impose on the family in their absence, but may we see the house again one last time?"

"Of course, Mrs. Scott—Mrs. Nash—do come in."

Mrs. Berwick closed the door behind the two sisters and led them into the Great Hall, the scene of so many Knight family and Chawton village celebrations. It was a large square space, with high dark wainscotting made from the estate's fallen oaks and family portraits proudly displayed about the walls. Charlotte looked for and found the series of carved witches' marks by the mantel that the admiral had once shown her and Haslett in his matchmaking zeal.

"When I think of Sir Francis, his final visit here . . ." Mrs. Berwick stopped to collect herself. "I don't dare speak of it to the family, of course. But with you ladies . . . so tragic, all of it. The fire—the needless ruination. We've none of us quite recovered from the loss. Mr. Austen-Leigh's book is such a godsend that way."

The memoir by Jane Austen's nephew James Edward Austen-Leigh had been published on Jane Austen's birthday in 1869, four years after the admiral's passing. Ironically, it was the death of Sir Francis—hastened by the destruction of the legacy—that had motivated the writing of the book. For the first time since Jane's brother Henry had composed the notice to the posthumous publication of *Persuasion*, the family had shared with the world all that they were willing to.

For several years and with the assistance of his large extended family, Austen-Leigh had gathered what letters he could, most of them having been scattered over time or otherwise destroyed, the various drawings and sketches—scant as they were—of his aunt and certain family homes, and the recollections of those in the family who could speak to Jane Austen's manner and looks. They wanted to help the world understand how to birth, nurture, and grow such genius in its midst, while still respecting the private life of its greatest novelist. It was this continuing discretion that had long haunted the Stevenson sisters as they grappled with Henrietta's unique burden: not only a private letter, but one never sent or even finished.

The sisters had watched with shared pride and interest as the Austen-Leigh memoir created a sea change in Jane Austen's popularity, moving discourse on her books from judicial reading circles and the educated elite to people of all backgrounds around the globe. Finally, readers could glimpse the ordinary woman behind the books—making her genius all the more extraordinary and accessible—and the interior worlds she ruled over with the infinite wisdom and unblinking justice of a god.

"Oh, we have them now, you know." Mrs. Berwick stood with her back to the sisters, staring out the large mullioned front window of the Great Hall. "They wander down the drive, take a peek over the gate. Little pilgrims, I call them. More and more they come, walking in her footsteps, trying to find what was in the books. George Knight is only twenty and not yet master, but already he fumes about it all."

Mrs. Berwick turned around to see the walnut box ajar in Charlotte's hands and a telescope now tightly gripped in Henrietta's. The housekeeper looked curiously back and forth between the two women.

"You know, Mrs. Scott, it's most strange. I saw Sir Francis once stand just as you are, on his last visit here. I came upon him unawares in the library. He was looking about the books, quite dazed-like if you ask me. Almost as if searching for something. Rather suspicious—but then again, that was his way."

And right away, both sisters knew. They knew exactly what to do. They could picture the sweet and confused old admiral hoping to slip the unsent letter inside some random book, where no one would find it too soon, but one day someone might. Wanting the world to know more about his own sister—only not on his captainly watch.

Everything eventually reveals itself, if we don't destroy it first.

At this silent thought, Henrietta looked over at Charlotte: there was no need to repeat the words aloud. The sisters' eyes met in instant understanding, the gift of their birth and childhood, the great fortune of their own story's beginning. They turned back in unison to the housekeeper, their faces brightened with all the emotion, enthusiasm, and adventure of life.

"Mrs. Berwick," Henrietta announced as Charlotte nodded her agreement, "we would love to see the library."

A Note from the Author

I began writing this book the day before I learned I had cancer; I finished it exactly six months later, the week of my first follow-up in which I was declared cancer-free.

During this time, writing was my greatest distraction, entertainment, and consolation. I was able to write solely due to the tremendous efforts of Dr. Lindsay Shirreff, her assistant Janny Cho, and my entire surgical team at Mount Sinai Cancer Centre; Dr. Natasha Leighl and Dr. Marcus Bernardini of Princess Margaret Hospital; my first readers, agent Mitchell Waters, author Molly Greeley, and my mother, Patricia Jenner; and my most loving husband and daughter.

Two real-life stories inspired this work: an 1852 correspondence between Sir Francis Austen and two Boston sisters, whose Harvard president father had been introduced to the works of Jane Austen by members of the United States Supreme Court; and the life and work of Abraham and Philip Rosenbach, Philadelphia book collectors and founders of the present-day Rosenbach Museum & Library. Two books that aided me greatly in my research, and which I would press into your hands if I could, are *Jane Austen's Best Friend: The Life and Influence of Martha Lloyd* by Zöe Wheddon and *Reading Austen in America* by Professor Juliette Wells.

This book is entirely a work of fiction. Some of the characters are inspired by real people (notably Sir Francis Austen, Fanny-Sophia Austen, Louisa May Alcott, Dr. Richard Pankhurst, and Sir Cresswell Cresswell, whose death in office occurred two years before the action of my plot); mostly they are not. Every word is my own unless indicated otherwise in the text, with one exception: the third paragraph of the first letter from Sir Francis Austen. This has been copied in its near entirety from a real-life letter sent long ago to two women in Boston, whose bold-for-any-era gesture of writing to a sibling of their favorite author both gladdens and inspires me in infinite writerly and human ways.

And of course, I must thank Jane Austen most of all, for never failing me, even when life sometimes does.

About the Author

Sarah Sims

NATALIE JENNER is the internationally bestselling author of *The Jane Austen Society, Bloomsbury Girls,* and *Every Time We Say Goodbye,* which have been translated into more than twenty languages around the world. Formerly a lawyer, career coach, and independent bookstore owner, she lives in Oakville, Ontario, with her family and two rescue dogs.